# Also by Roger Alan Bonner

## Novels

*A Thing of Dark Imaginings*

## The Belt Stories

*Milky Way Tango, volume one*
*Milky Way Boogie, volume two*
*Milky Way Waltz, volume three*
*Milky Way Gala, volume four*

## Novellas

*Sentinel*
*The Trader*

**In eBook and paperback from Amazon.**

# A THING OF DARK IMAGININGS

*A novel by*

**Roger Alan Bonner**

*Copyright, disclaimer, and keywords*

© 2018 Roger Boner. All rights reserved. Except for brief quotations embodied in critical articles or reviews, no part of this book may be reproduced in any manner without written permission from the author.

ISBN 978-1-948988-02-5.

Graphical image produced by Betibup33 Design Studio, on Twitter @Betibup33. All rights reserved. Published by Roger Boner. Produced and distributed by Kindle Direct Publishing and Amazon Digital Services.

My thanks to the Durham Writers Group and the Raleign Critique Group for comments and critique.

This is a work of fiction, a toy, not a tool. It has been created primarily for the entertainment of the reader. All legal or natural persons, places, events, and institutions mentioned herein either are products of the author's imagination, or are used as fictional elements of a story. Any resemblance to a real person, place, event, or institution is coincidental and unintended.

Keywords: Attorney General, big data, campus shooting, depression, forgiveness, grief, guns, hallucinations, homicide, mass murder, National Rifle Association, police, possession, psychosis, revenge, second amendment, serial killer, sniper.

# *Come in and get warm*

There was in him a vital score of all...
As if the worst had fallen which could befall
He stood a stranger in this breathing world
An erring spirit from another hurled
A thing of dark imaginings …
*Lara,* Lord Byron


I've got a little list, I've got a little list,
Of society offenders who might well be underground,
And who never would be missed - who never would be missed.
*The Mikado,* W. S. Gilbert.


No trait is more justified than revenge in the right time and place.
Meir Kahane.


Violence is good for those who have nothing to lose.
Jean Paul Sartre.

## Table of Contents

*Prologue*   *1*

*Cleaning Up a Kill Party*   *3*

*Loss and Grief*   *20*

*The AG*   *35*

*Running in Circles*   *42*

*The Funeral*   *52*

*Unexpected Visitors*   *70*

*The Deal*   *83*

*Making Plans*   *97*

*Tracking the Game*   *114*

*Visiting Lelah*   *127*

*A Bullet Salutes No Flag*   *144*

*Tidying Up*   *162*

*Reading Tea Leaves*   *177*

Dreams of Mayhem     190

This Animal Schemes     204

A Near Miss     222

Circling the Wagons     239

Fire Drill     259

Fall Back and Reload     278

Metamorphoses     302

Head Fake     321

Cul de Sac     339

Cat and Mouse     354

The Cobra Strikes     372

Settling an Account     392

Resolution     402

Epilogue     410

Acknowledgments     415

About Roger Alan Bonner     416

# *Prologue*

It was Tuesday, the grass silver with morning dew. He parked the big white cruiser near a classroom building, killed the engine and got out. He looked around - where is everyone? Chief said to be careful, and now, where is everyone? This place should be busy. He took a deep breath.

I don't like this, not at all.

Two blue and whites with Damascus markings pulled up, their rotaries flashing. Two young patrolmen got out and drew their weapons. One looked at Roundtree and said, "Who are you?"

Roundtree flipped out his lapel, showing his badge. "Dan Roundtree, Abingdon." He looked at them. The tall one was calm, but that blond patrolman was scared, his eyes open too wide. Roundtree thought, this guy will bust in and draw fire, then blast anything that moves. Screw that. "Holster your weapons, guys. I want you to tape the building, keep everybody away from here. But stay outside. Is that clear?"

"You need backup, Inspector?" the blond patrolman asked.

"No. Just tape the building. And kill the damn lights."

The two moved to comply. Roundtree reached into the Ford's glove box, pushed a revolver to the side and pulled out a tactical flashlight, a light with LEDs, a red laser in the center, a blinding light. He took another breath. Come on, Dan boy. Get moving.

He scanned the windows but saw no one. He moved to the front of Schaefer Hall and stopped near the bank of doors. He listened. Moans and cries came from inside. Suddenly one of the doors swung out hard and banged against the wall. A young girl came through, crying, moaning, running. She hurled herself down the front steps and fell and bounced on the concrete. Then she jumped up bleeding and ran. Roundtree waited for a shot. None came.

He crouched low and got ready to roll, to evade. He opened one of the doors slowly. He peeked inside.

The smells were strong ... cordite ... urine ... blood ... fear.

## *Cleaning Up a Kill Party*

Roundtree stood for a moment. He found himself clenching his jaw, and he stopped that. He gently opened a door and entered. He switched on the flashlight and cast a circle of bright light around the foyer, looking for a weapon pointed at him. There was no weapon. He took a deep breath and exhaled. He switched off the light.

Any other day, the foyer would be a welcoming place. Today, a dozen students were there, dressed in jeans, t-shirts, jackets. Most were alive so far. They were on the floor, surrounded by books, laptop computers, cellphones, notebooks … and blood, in small and large pools, in smears, in streaks, splattered on the floor, on the walls, on the chairs. To one side, the large glass window fronting an office had a bullet hole. Around it, blood spray decorated a spider web of cracks. A body lay outside, at the base of the window. A pool of blood oozed out from under a mass of long brown hair. A bust of the college founder was in the center of the foyer, several bodies at its base. A couple of students were weeping, staring at the wall. Several others were staring at nothing, their eyes blank, unfocused, unresponsive.

He knelt down next to a young girl. Roundtree looked around the foyer, then he looked at her. "Hey, are you okay? Are you shot?"

She looked at him through tears and shook her head. "I … I don't think so."

Roundtree nodded. "Can you stand up? Can you walk?"

The girl nodded.

"You want to help?" Roundtree said.

The girl stared at him.

"Leave this place. Get out of here." He pointed a thumb behind him. "Right through that door. Get away from here."

"Okay." The girl struggled to her feet, turned away, and approached one of the other students. Roundtree watched the two of them stumble towards the front doors.

He stood up, spotted a stairway to the upper floor and headed towards that. Leading with his flashlight, he climbed to a landing midway up the stairs. The landing was a slaughterhouse. Eight bodies were there, with blood spray on two walls. A red pool dripped down three steps onto the landing. Roundtree glanced at each student. Two were barely conscious. Six others were not moving.

He looked up to the second floor. He stood on the landing for a long moment with his eyes and mouth open wide, listening. He could hear sirens from outside, but he heard nothing from inside the building. Stepping around the blood, he moved up the stairs and then to the side of a hallway. He stopped again, alert, barely breathing. Then he moved down the left side of the hallway, checking rooms as he went. In minutes he finished. There were no other bodies and no shooter on the second floor.

"Huh," he muttered. "What's all this?"

Leading with his flashlight, he went back down the stairs, into the front hall. A door led to a hallway towards the back of the building. Roundtree went in that direction.

He found the back door. Several people had tried to escape out the back, then found themselves trapped, a dead end, the back doors locked. The mistake was fatal. They died within a few feet of escape.

Roundtree returned to the front hall and exited through the front doors. Yellow crime scene tape encircled the building. An ambulance had parked nearby, and a few people gathered around it, just beyond the tape, twenty yards from the front of the building. A reporter stood outside the tape, yelling questions at policemen.

Roundtree waved at the paramedics, got their attention, held up two fingers. "Hey guys, the building is clear. You two, go in. There are wounded in the front hall."

"Anywhere else?" one of the paramedics asked.

"Halfway up the stairs, on the landing. Maybe."

Two of the paramedics exchanged a look - *Uh oh* - and then headed for the front doors.

Roundtree pulled out a cellphone and hit the speed dial for the Chief. The line picked up. "Chief, this is Roundtree. I looked over the shooting at Schaefer Hall."

"What happened up there?"

"Later for that. I need several items, and I need them now. Are you listening?"

"Go ahead."

"I did not find a shooter. He might be on the loose, so close the roads around the college ASAP. Three cars ought to do it. I have to guess, but I think you're looking for a young male carrying a semi-auto pistol. He'll have blood on him. Bring dogs for checkpoints and also to hunt the campus."

"Okay."

"Ambulances. There are a couple dozen casualties. As many ambulances as you can get here fast."

"Okay."

"I need patrolmen for crowd control and first aid."

"Anything else?"

"Uh, yeah, a coke," Roundtree said. "No … a six-pack."

"Okay. See you soon." The connection went dead.

Roundtree walked to his car, pulled a first aid kit out of the trunk, and headed back into the building.


Late in the afternoon, Roundtree left the campus for his apartment in Abingdon. He drove the big cruiser slowly, under the speed limit.

As he drove, he aimed his car down the road and focused on staying between the lines. He was exhausted. His face sagged. He had left

Schaefer Hall with blood on his pants and his jacket. Now that blood was on the front seat, steering wheel, and turn signal.

The morning had been for survivors, the afternoon for the dead and the dying. Ambulances, forensic teams, and policemen from several jurisdictions arrived at the college. Before help arrived, Roundtree saved two young people, staunching their bleeding until the med techs could take over. That took time. Later another student, a young girl, stared up into his eyes while blood flowed from her nose, her mouth, and from an upper chest wound. She coughed up blood for a while. As he held her, her eyes began to wander and lose focus. Then they went blank and she ran out of time.

He drove slowly through Abingdon's streets, past the post office, past the civil war museum, past a couple of dozen tourists. Someone waved at Roundtree. He did not wave back. A woman, a blond in a late model convertible, honked at him for going too slowly, for being in her way. Roundtree did not react, even after she yelled and gave him the finger. He thought, you know, dearie, it's unwise to flip off anyone who's wearing as much blood as I am.

Lucky for you, I am tired.

His clothes were glued to his body, coated in a vile mix of sweat, dirt, and blood and other bodily fluids. He shook his head - I should know better than to wear a suit to work. They say people respect a man in a suit. Maybe it's true on TV. And maybe it's true before the shift.

But after a day like today?

He arrived home and parked behind an old two story building done in butterscotch brick. It held four apartments. He trudged up the stairs to the second floor, unlocked a door, and entered his apartment. He peeled off his jacket, then he went to the kitchen and dropped the jacket into a trash can.

Even Goodwill will not want this one. Maybe I could put it on eBay.

Two people died on it. If that's a selling point, I'd rather not know.

He stripped off the rest of his clothes. He threw his shirt, pants, and socks into the garbage. He went to the bedroom and tossed his underwear into a laundry hamper.

Being naked did not make him feel better. He went to the bathroom and turned on the shower. He stepped in and stood there for several long minutes as needles of hot water strafed his body. It was blessed relief. Then he reached a hand up, leaned against a wall, bowed his head and vomited onto the floor of the shower. He stood up, took a deep breath, then bent over and vomited again and again. Several times he turned his face up to take in hot water, rinse his mouth, and spit the water out. Finally, he stopped retching and stood there in the hot stream, bent over, his head bowed, waiting for the retch to wash down the drain.

When he emerged from the shower, he was breathing hard as if he had run a race. He stood in front of the mirror and toweled himself dry. When he finished, he stopped and spoke to his reflection, "You look like shit, old man."

He went to the kitchen, poured a glass of milk, took the glass to an easy chair in the living room, and sat down. He took a long drink and placed the glass on a small end table.

Roundtree looked around the room - at walls in need of paint, at an old coffee table he meant to refinish, at an Indian print rug whose once bright reds had turned dark. He looked at a not-quite-full bottle of seventeen-year scotch sitting on the mantle over the fireplace. He bought it two years ago, just before he quit drinking. The bottle was a memento. With each year, Roundtree and the scotch would age together, the scotch becoming more valuable; Roundtree, less.

He closed his eyes and began to whisper a single word. It was a meditation, a mantra, a nonsense word, meaningless. He repeated it to occupy his mind and relax his body. After ten minutes, Roundtree did begin to relax. He fell asleep in the easy chair.

Roundtree returned to the college the next day. He parked the cruiser next to a blue van marked 'FORENSICS'. He picked up a manila folder from the bench seat, got out of the car, and held up a piece of paper - a campus map of Whitetop Mountain College.

A three-story building was in front of him, reminding him of his elementary school, decades ago. The building was cheap construction, melamine on steel. The billionaire who founded the college knew how to squeeze a nickel. Solar panels on the roof, facing south. Roundtree glanced at the map again, looked back up at the building. This one has to be Holten Hall. To the west, out of sight, is Schaefer Hall.

He looked out at the valley below, rolling away to the south, gray peaks repeating to a jagged horizon. Stunning, though when you lived in the mountains you came to take the views for granted. Turning back, he looked up at the big mountain looming over the college. Then he chided himself - staring at the view is an excuse to delay. He turned back to face the buildings and the rest of his day.

He walked up to one building, then around it. Schaefer Hall was on the other side. Roundtree scanned the campus. A few bystanders watched from behind the building. A larger crowd gathered in front of it, outside the yellow police tape. They were students, friends of the victims, or friends of friends, many of them crying, embracing each other, others staring at the building in stunned disbelief.

Roundtree stared at them and snorted. Yeah, right. The young think they will live forever.

Time to wake up, kiddies.

Naturally, they had already begun the informal memorial, the pile of flowers, balloons, stuffed animals, photographs, and other sentimental shit that people piled up to celebrate the latest mass shooting. An offering to the patron saint of psychotic homicide.

Roundtree stood still for a moment and pulled the prelim report from the folder. A campus shooter, a white male in his twenties, a ne'er do well, showed up yesterday morning with a semi-automatic pistol and several clips of ammunition. He entered Schaefer Hall and started shooting. In all, he killed seventeen students and a teacher. No one knew why, but it was early. The department shrinks would figure out something to tell the public.

Sometimes, motive could help you catch a killer. With the killer dead, motive was less interesting. Knowing motive would not revive the dead.

"Huh." Did the shooter stop himself? Or was he stopped?

Did he act alone? The report did not say.

Roundtree took a step towards the bank of front doors facing the quad. Then he stopped himself and stared at the building. I'm not ready to go in there, not quite yet.

He looked down at his sport coat. I can't believe I wore a sport coat for this; I should know better.

He walked slowly around the building, looking at everything, registering everything, trying to picture it all, trying to make it fit what the patrolmen thought might have happened.

You walked around the building, just like this, didn't you, my man? You scoped out the college before your Big Visit. Roundtree looked up at the eaves. This one has good passive security. Did you notice that? Double camera coverage on each side of the building. Not an easy target, not if you want to escape.

Did you want to escape, my man?

The windows are double pane. They don't open, do they? No fresh air here, nothing but AC. No escape, either. He looked away, across the

*11*

quad. Schaefer was in a circle of classroom buildings. Further out, there were dormitories, a library, a student union.

Why did you choose Schaefer?

Open lawns were in front and in back of Schaefer, no buildings, no trees. Roundtree wondered if the shooter had approached along the circle of classroom buildings. No reason to do that, unless campus security was alert and fast.

Something else to look for in the video feeds.

Try to relax. He stopped again and took a breath.

His mind wandered. Our gear keeps getting better. But the people? Not so much. We used to rely on witnesses. Now we have security cameras, genetic testing, chemical analysis, most of which tells us that eyewitness reports are crap. People see what they want to see, hear what they want to hear. We used to have revolvers, now we have Glocks. We have Tasers.

We have psychiatrists now; he smirked, they're as full of shit as ever. While we're complaining, let's not forget - crazy people have Glocks too. He stopped and winced. Damn it, stop bitching. Get on with it.

Roundtree came around to the front and climbed a broad set of stairs towards the bank of doors. As he approached, a young policewoman came outside and took off a surgical mask.

She looked up and smiled at Roundtree. "Hey Inspector. I was wondering when you'd get here."

Roundtree looked at her. How had she known he would work this case? Jenna - Jenna Riser, that was her name. She was young, blond, slender. Attractive. Worth remembering. Roundtree liked her, in a helpless, harmless, fatherly way. He recited the Old Man's Mantra - nothing beats being young. She was a couple of years out of college. Roundtree, like most old policemen, was ex-military. Jenna was ex-biotech lab.

"Good morning, Madam Technician," Roundtree said as he walked up. "Anything I need to know?"

"It smells like a slaughterhouse in there." She grinned at him. "You want a mask?" She reached a gloved hand into her pocket, pulled out a white surgical mask.

Roundtree shook his head. I use my nose. I use everything.

She continued, "We ID'd the shooter. He saved the last shot for himself."

"How do you know?"

"Eyewitness. One of the students, a guy, took a head shot. It bled all over, so he played dead. He gave us the shooter."

"The kid survive?"

"So far."

Roundtree nodded. Good. I hope he makes it. "Do we have the video feeds?"

"Not that I've heard," she said.

"Okay. Thanks Jenna."

"Hey, I saw your Tides won last night. Again. Your crystal ball is staying shiny. How do you do it?"

Roundtree shrugged. "Simple. The parent club's in first place, so the good players stay in the minors."

"Ah. Shrewd."

Roundtree nodded. That's right, babe, age and guile.

He put Jenna out of his mind and took what would be his last clean breath for a while. Then he walked up to a door, opened it, and stepped inside.

He stopped and waited for his eyes to adjust. He was in a broad foyer, corridors running away and to the right. To the left, an office was behind a glass wall. The action started here as classes were changing and students were moving. Several 911 calls arrived between 9:03 and 9:04.

In the center of the foyer, blood spray covered half of the billionaire's bust. A blue lab tag fluttered from a clean spot on the right cheek.

A complicated outline in white marker was on the floor next to the base of the stand holding the bust.

Roundtree took a long, slow breath through his nose. The front hall still smelled of blood and urine. And gunfire.

There were several pools of blood on the floor, and blood spray on a wall to the right. Each had a blue lab tag next to it, with an accompanying outline in white marker on the floor. Blood spray and blue lab tags decorated the glass in front of the office.

Roundtree stepped around a pool of blood in front of the door and entered the office. A piece of duct tape held the door open. There was a counter to the left and a wide desk to the right. A chair behind the desk had a patch of blood and a hole in the middle of its back. There were two blood smears, now dark and dry, on top of the desk.

Roundtree walked back to the front hall and opened the manila folder. The building schematics showed the bodies on each floor. Seven bodies had been in the front hall where Roundtree now stood. At the back of the building, another six kids died inside a locked back door.

Roundtree headed down a hall towards the back of the building. It was an unexpected relief. For a while, there was no blood on the walls. The smell of death was weaker. The hallway smelled of magic marker. Everything was clean, scholastic, normal.

Then Roundtree came to the back door and everything changed. The smells of slaughter returned. There was an explosion of blood on the floor, the walls, and the doors. Chalked outlines, smearing the blood on the floor, showed where the victims lay themselves down for the last time.

Roundtree stared at the outlines, gritting his teeth against a gag reflex. He stopped, looked away from the carnage, then he looked at the back doors.

You were systematic, my man. You already figured out, there are no other exits. Nobody had time to panic, bust through a door, or smash through a window. You moved fast. You had the gun up, sighted down the barrel. When you saw a person, you pulled the trigger. It felt like a video game, an arcade game. They weren't people, they were targets. BANG.

You hit the foyer, shot for less than a minute. Pandemonium ensued. The scared survivors fled to the back of the building, but you let them go. First things first, you took your time, cleaned out the foyer. Then you went to the back, shot everyone there.

It happened fast.

Next you reload and head upstairs to get the people trapped up there. You would have made a good terrorist.

How could you be so clever? Did you pick Schaefer because you knew the back doors were locked? When did you learn that? How far back did you go?

Roundtree returned to the front hall and stopped at a staircase rising to the second floor. He looked up. *The sooner I go up there, the sooner I can leave.*

He climbed to the landing and stopped, confused. Several chalked outlines were halfway up the stairs. Stranger yet, there were numerous evidence tags stuck all over the landing and the stairs above it. Roundtree glanced at the tags. They had marked a pile of notebooks, laptops, backpacks, furniture, chalk erasers, and other flotsam on the landing. Even a few folding chairs. One lab tag read, 'Football'. All of it was confiscated as evidence.

*What the hell? What happened here?*

Roundtree continued up to the second floor. There were two chalk outlines past the stairs, and bullet holes in the walls.

Roundtree turned back and looked down at the landing below. Son of a bitch, they used the high ground; they bull rushed you, didn't they, my man? You got off a couple of shots, then they threw everything they had at you. They were desperate. They ran over you on the stairs. You shot a couple of them, but most of them went right by.

There will be no other bodies on the second floor. At least, I think so.

He completed his sweep of the second floor but learned nothing more. Nothing happened beyond the stairwell. He returned to the first floor. Jenna was down there, supervising the work of a print team. Roundtree walked past them without saying anything.

He went outside and sat down on the steps in front of the building. God, I would love a smoke. My ex-wife convinced me to quit. How's that for ironic? She nags me, so I improve, I quit. Hardest thing I ever did. Then she leaves me.

What's with that? Does that seem right? Maybe it was. I guess I wasn't fast enough.

Out beyond the police tape, the crowd was larger than before. The pile of balloons, stuffed animals, and candles was larger too.

Roundtree sat there and savored the clean air outside the slaughter hall. For a moment, he stopped thinking about how and why these people were murdered.

His cellphone rang, and he pulled it from his pocket. "Roundtree."

"Good morning, Inspector. This is Rick Harris, from the ME's office."

"What can I do for you, Mr. Harris?"

"We started the autopsy on the shooter, and I wanted to give you prelim results."

"Okay."

"Well, the shooter shot himself in the temple, but that's not what killed him. His larynx was crushed. Somebody got their teeth on his throat and bit through his windpipe. He choked to death."

"Jesus." They crushed his windpipe. So while he's choking, he tries to shoot himself in the head. He misses. No, amigo, no last bullet for you, you get to die the hard way. "Where did you find him?"

"Halfway up a stairwell leading to the second floor."

Roundtree nodded. You find courage in the oddest places. "Okay, thanks. How long until you're done?"

"Six, seven days. The blood work takes a while."

"Okay, thanks," Roundtree said. He broke the connection.

Roundtree sat there, his good feeling having evaporated. Jesus Christ almighty. The shooter trapped everyone on the second floor, so they rushed him. Brave kids. Somebody took him down like an animal, fangs to the throat. Jesus Christ.

The nightmares ought to be interesting.

## *Loss and Grief*

Amir Hawari drove his wife Serena to the police station in Abingdon. The police would brief families and friends of the shooting victims. She sat in the front seat, weeping in the quiet, dignified manner that was her way.

Amir drove on, taking care. He neither spoke nor cried. His family in Lebanon was Arab, French, and Greek; his stoicism was Greek. He occasionally glanced at Serena. He thought, she will cry it out and then she will bounce back. She will get through this. His gaze returned to the road and he thought about her. An odd combination - soft, emotional, feminine, but tough as nails when needed.

Finding her was the luckiest day of my life. We should have had more children, but God gives, or not.

A kid who loses his parents is an orphan. He gets a word. We need another word for parents who lose kids. 'Childless' does not begin to cover it. We need a new word.

Is it sinful to complain about misfortune? I should know the answer to that, but I do not. Another of my many failures.

He tried to focus on driving. That was difficult. Amir found himself gripping the steering wheel hard. It was an effort for him to register and obey street signs, traffic lights, speed limits. At one point, passing through a small town, he looked over at the sidewalk and thought he saw

Lelah. He gasped and stared, but it could not be. The vision showed her as she was years ago, at ten or eleven. He was mesmerized until he ran the car up over the curb. That jarred him back to reality. He stopped short of hitting anything else.

Serena stared at him. He felt foolish and then alarmed when a police car pulled up behind him, its lights flashing blue and white. A young officer walked up to Amir's window and asked if everything was okay. Amir thanked him and said, yes, he was okay. He noticed the officer's eyes scanning Amir, and Serena, and the car. Amir explained, they had received bad news, a death in the family. The officer asked, can I escort you somewhere? Amir replied, no thank you, that is not necessary. Amir promised to try to stay safe. He thanked the officer again. The young man nodded, walked back to his patrol car, and turned off the lights.

When Amir started driving again, the policeman followed him for two blocks and then turned off.

As he drove, his mind returned to Lelah's death. I cannot cry for her. Why is that? I adored Lelah. I would have done anything for her. Yet now she is gone - gone forever - and I cannot cry. Everyone says that crying is healthy, it lets you release your anguish, it lets you begin to heal.

I wonder if they've got it backward. You cry when you're ready to let go. Maybe that's why I cannot cry. When I think about it, the truth is, I don't want to let go.

I want Lelah back. That's all I want. I don't want to be healthy. I want my daughter. The smart move would be, don't want that.

I cannot do it. I guess that means I am not very smart.

Amir guided the car through the countryside and the hills. If a man were God-like, if he knew the past and the future, if he knew how life would proceed, and when it would end, then this would all be natural. Dust to dust. We are not owed tomorrow. Your last day will arrive on its own. You can count on that.

That man would not feel grief. He would be a rock, weathered against the to-and-fro of life, riding the rhythm of fortune and misfortune, of win and loss, to a doom he neither relishes nor fears. Amir imagined men of faith living in that fashion.

Oh Lord, thank you for my victories, and for my defeats. Come get me, I am ready.

Amir shook his head, I am not that man.

I cannot visualize the adult Lelah. Why is that? I can picture my only daughter, at three, at ten, at fourteen. I remember when she began to develop breasts and stopped sitting on my lap. I can see her glee at jumping over a rail for the first time. I can watch her learning to walk, motoring around the apartment, pushing a milk crate along for support. I can see her leaving the house on her first date with a boy. But I cannot see her as an adult, as she was on the day she was killed.

When the police called with the bad news, Serena took the call. Amir was not home. He arrived later to find her sitting with several friends. Serena said, please do not make me do this. Of course not, he replied, I will take care of it. He drove out to Abingdon, to their morgue. They rolled out a body on a gurney under a sheet. When they pulled back the sheet, Amir looked and saw a piece of surgical tape over the right eye. He almost fainted. He wobbled and said, yes, that is my daughter. Then they put the sheet back and rolled her away. They thanked him.

Amir put his hand against the wall and stood there in the morgue for a long time before he could walk out. That was that.

Since that day, Amir could not remember his daughter as an adult.

He tried and failed to smile. God, hear me. Hear my testimony. I speak to you today as a humble man, an unbeliever who needs help. I ask only because we are all God's children. Even me.

Or so I am told.

He listened for a moment, but there was no reply. There never was and he stopped expecting any a long time ago. Amir shrugged. There … see? I am not too proud. I asked for help, but You did not answer. Little wonder my faith has lapsed.

He pulled into the parking lot next to the police station and thought, maybe this is denial. Maybe, rather than feeling awful, my body is protecting me, feeling nothing, nothing at all.

Numb.

He killed the motor and looked at Serena. She was still weeping. Should I wait for her to get control? No. No point to it. There will be plenty of tears at this meeting. Amir got out of the car, walked around to the passenger door, and opened it. "Come on, sweetie, let's go see what the police can tell us."

She did not look at him. "Do you want to know?"

Amir nodded. "Sure I want to know. You shall know the truth and the truth shall set you free." He looked sideways at her. "So it is said. I feel a need to be free."

She stared at him for a moment. "Are you getting religion?"

"I don't know. Was that a religious quote?"

"I think so."

"Well. How 'bout that?"

They walked across the parking lot and into the police station. They came to a long counter with a uniformed officer behind it. Amir approached the officer. "We're here about the shooting at Whitetop Mountain College."

The officer was a young man, slightly older than Lelah would have been, with close cropped hair and blue eyes above a weight lifter's body. He looked up at Amir and nodded. "That was a bad one. I'm sorry. They're meeting at the Baptist church."

"And where …?"

"Out the door, turn right, down the block, it'll be on your right," the officer said. He pointed with a pencil.

"Thanks," Amir said. He turned to Serena. "Okay, let's go join the rest of the miserables."

She winced.

They found the First Baptist Church. They walked down concrete stairs to the basement, to a large room tiled in pale green linoleum that glowed under fluorescent lights. The church held fundraisers, pancake breakfasts, and bingo there. A grid of folding chairs, most of them occupied, faced a lectern.

The size of the crowd surprised Amir. There were friends and families of the victims, easily identified - many were crying or leaking tears. On one side of the hall, attorneys had set up two tables under a paper banner proclaiming *Legal Services*. Several young people in suits were handing out literature.

A sign read, *Retain your rights, you might be entitled to compensation.*

Amir said, "Look at that. We cannot get our daughter back, but these nice people will help us sue somebody - for a small fee."

She stared at the table. "Bloody parasites."

They sat down and a young woman stopped and handed them a piece of literature entitled, *Campus Security at Whitetop*.

Amir looked to the other side of the room. Over another table a banner read, *Whitetop Mountain College*.

"So the lawyers are on this side; defendants, on that side," he said.

Next to the college table, a simple sign sat on a second table, *Police Department, Victim Counseling*.

Amir said, "I'm surprised they're not selling pistols, strictly for defensive purposes, of course."

"The church won't allow it," Serena said.

"No?"

"We passed a sign on the way in - no guns allowed," she said.

"The NRA lets them get away with that?"

Serena looked at him. "The gun people?"

Amir nodded. He looked around. Several uniformed policemen were in the hall. None carried a sidearm. A couple of the policemen were much larger than average. Amir stared at one and thought, that guy does not need a firearm.

At that moment, a middle-aged black man in tan slacks and a rumpled gray sport coat walked to the lectern.

"Okay, please everyone, take a seat," he said. Several people sat down, and the noise level fell slightly.

The man took off his jacket and draped it over a chair, then turned to the lectern. "My name is Dan Roundtree. I'm an Inspector here and I'll be the lead investigator of this incident.

"This meeting is just for planning purposes. We've just started investigating, so I don't have much to tell you yet. A couple of patrolmen are going around, passing out an information package. Please read it. It gives you contact numbers if you want to receive information or, even better, report something. It also tells you of the services we provide to victims. I encourage you to use these, particularly counseling. We will do what we can to bring whatever justice is available. However, what may be more important is that you get back to your lives. We can help you do that."

Someone spoke, loud enough to be heard, "Easy for you to say."

Roundtree scanned the crowd. His eyes found the speaker. "Actually, no … it's not easy for me, not at all. I spend my time investigating homicides. This was murder, pure and simple. But let's be honest. You'd like to get your loved ones back. We cannot do that for you. What we can do is help you help yourselves, help you get back to living. That's all you can do. Your loved ones were victimized. Don't you be a victim too."

The buzz of conversation rose, but no one challenged Roundtree directly. Amir believed him. Maybe others did too.

Roundtree looked down for a moment and then looked up at the crowd. "Let me add - you'll see in this hall lawyers from the college, and other lawyers too. You can talk to them if you want to sue somebody, but the police department is not involved in that at all."

Roundtree paused. "That's all I have to say. Thank you for listening. Let me now introduce you to our chief psychiatrist, Dr. Melany Templeton." A thin blond woman walked to the lectern and greeted the crowd. She dressed like a professional - modest dress, heels, styled hair, mechanical smile. Gold rimmed glasses hung on a chain around her neck. Roundtree left the hall through a side door.

Were it up to him, Amir would have left too. Maybe this Doctor Templeton could help him feel better. He grimaced. He wanted Lelah back, alive. Dr. Templeton could not provide that. No one could. Not ever.

Serena made no motion to leave, so Amir stayed in his seat and tried to listen to the psychiatrist.


Roundtree returned to the 'bullpen', the open area of desks used by Abingdon's four inspectors. His computer was already on, so he switched to the department's email and messaging programs and stared at the new entries on the screen.

The department had downloaded security feeds from the college. Roundtree looked forward to examining them. The IT people had asked, how far back should the tapes go? He smiled. "Two months. I want everything back to the first day that students came to the campus."

The IT people complained - they might not have enough room on their storage drives. Roundtree listened and experienced his usual reaction: I don't care, okay? I do ... not ... care. He held onto a curse and instead mentioned that a young man just killed nineteen people, including himself. Maybe if we try hard we can find enough storage for the security feeds. That was the end of the complaints.

He also planned to go back to the college and talk to the campus security people. He was thinking about his day when a voice intruded, "Roundtree." He looked up. His Chief was looming over his desk.

"Good morning, Sir. What can I do for you?"

"Certification, Roundtree," the Chief said.

"Sir?"

"We keep having the same conversation, Inspector. I'm getting deja vus of my deja vus." He spoke with a slight angry undertone, not quite concealed. "So, this morning, right now in fact, I want you to take your sidearm, get in your car ..." The Chief pointed with a finger, "... and drive out to the range. Then, I want you to pass the certification requirement for the use of a firearm."

Roundtree kept a blank expression. "I'm sorry, sir. I keep meaning to do that, but being your best investigator occupies my full attention."

The Chief's face was frozen: he did not laugh, or smile, or react in any way. He stood there and stared at Roundtree. Nothing moved but his mouth. "Here's the big picture, Roundtree. Unless you certify and soon - like today - I will have no choice but to take your badge and your firearm and place you on administrative leave. If I have to do that, we will revisit this issue in your annual review, and further actions will follow. Now, it is entirely up to you, but I think you would prefer I not do any of that." The Chief's eyebrows rose. "Okay?"

Roundtree's first thought was, well, shit. He said, "Yes sir, I'll get right on it. I will do it today. The mass murder can wait."

As he turned away, the Chief spoke over his shoulder. "Editorials give me a hard-on, Roundtree." He headed back to his office.

Roundtree was wearing a side holster which he kept empty in the office. The Chief had started that practice so the more impulsive members of the public would not be tempted to grab a sidearm and start shooting bystanders.

The Chief understood the urge - after all, who doesn't want to shoot a few strangers from time to time?

The Chief did not know that Roundtree usually went on his rounds without a firearm. Strictly speaking, that was against department policy, but Roundtree had thought it over. He believed that a firearm made an officer a target. So he usually relied on caution, judgment, and persuasion to get an armed suspect to calm down, put down the weapon rather than use it, and let a situation defuse. He carried a tactical flashlight and a small Taser, just in case persuasion failed.

When persuasion failed, Roundtree would evade, take cover, and call SWAT.

Months ago, a desperate and dim young man had taken a few hostages while trying to rob a bank. In several minutes, the police surrounded the bank and snipers took up positions. Roundtree arrived and stripped to his underwear. He picked up a portable radio and walked into the bank, hands held high. When he got to the door and opened it, the robber was waiting and pointing a pistol at him.

The robber said, "You look silly."

Roundtree nodded. "I get that a lot. I'm not armed, as you can see. In fact, I'm here to save your life. There are a couple of snipers out there. As long as we're talking, they won't shoot. But what you're doing is dangerous, and some of these guys can be a bit trigger happy. So … do you want to live, or not?"

"I've got hostages."

Roundtree said, "I know. That won't make any difference. For you to pull the trigger, your skull needs to be intact."

"I'm not afraid of you."

"I believe you. I know you've got guts. But still, the question is, do you want to die today? Because that's what's about to happen."

The young man thought it over, then handed his pistol to Roundtree. As he was handcuffing the young man, Roundtree said, "You want some career advice?"

The young man shrugged. "Yeah, sure."

"You want to steal? Learn to write code."

"Do they teach code in prison?" the young man asked.

"Hell no."

Roundtree made the "all clear" call over his radio, led the man out of the bank and walked him over to a patrol car. A news photographer took a photo of Roundtree leading the robber across the street in front of several policemen. He was unarmed, in his underwear; they were wearing helmets and combat armor, automatic weapons raised. The photo was published with a simple caption: 'Courage'. It won a prize for journalism.

Roundtree sat at his desk, thinking, I am a rebellious SOB. It hampers me. Fine, I have to do this. He took a deep breath, opened a side drawer, pulled out a six-shot revolver, and slid it into his holster.

An hour later, he entered the police range, a large, single story building decorated in Warehouse Chic. The range master was typical: a skinny white guy, a calm, laconic fellow with a buttermilk accent, a worshiper of the one-inch spread, a 'gun person', ex-military, ex-sniper, a combat vet. He worked hard to make sure the police did not lose the arms race to the Bad Guys. His name was Lewis Becker.

"Hey there, Lewis," Roundtree said. "How are things?"

Lewis Becker nodded and grunted.

"I'm here to certify. I need a box of 357 mags."

"What brand?"

"Whatever."

"Czech it is," Lewis said. He leaned to one side so he could see into Roundtree's holster. "Inspector, when you going to replace that butt picker with a Glock? Better gun, more accurate, more firepower, more capacity."

"Never. I'm not looking for firepower, and I don't trust automatics."

"So what do you do when the Bad Guy has an automatic?" Lewis said.

"Run away and call for backup."

Lewis shook his head.

"You know me, Lewis. I'm a talker, not a shooter."

"Yeah." Lewis handed over a box of cartridges in 357 magnum and a target sheet showing the outline of a Bad Guy. "I need you to put four shots into a six-inch circle in the upper torso at twenty-five feet."

"No you don't. I've read the regs, Lewis. I need to exhibit 'substantial competence' to discharge a firearm accurately and safely." Roundtree waggled his fingers to indicate quotation marks.

"Just hit the paper, okay?" Lewis turned away.

"Sure." Roundtree thought, why so picky? Most cops can't shoot worth shit. I should keep that to myself.

The pistol range was indoors, a long poorly lit room with thick concrete walls and a maximum depth of 50 feet. The back wall slanted so that bullets ricocheted down to a dirt surface. Empty cartridges littered the floor and the air held the permanent sharp, metallic tang of cordite. Roundtree walked to a station, a little open-ended booth with a counter and an overhead line to hold a target sheet. He attached the sheet to the line and ran it out to twenty-five feet. A set of ear protectors were on the counter. Roundtree nestled them over his ears and loaded the revolver.

He stood there for a moment, thinking. Then he turned and waved to get Lewis's attention. Lewis turned to watch. Roundtree faced the sheet, raised the pistol, and put one shot between the eyes, two other shots on the nipples, and the remaining three in a straight line extending up from the crotch.

He pointed the pistol skyward and dumped the hot empty brass on the floor. Then he collected the target sheet and returned to the counter.

He offered it to Lewis, "Here you go. I made this just for you. Let's see, what should I call it? How 'bout *Bad Guy with a Big Dick?*"

Lewis stared at the sheet. "Roundtree, you are weird."

"Do I pass?"

"Yes, you pass." Lewis held up the target sheet. "And Roundtree ... thanks. Really. I will cherish this."

Roundtree grinned at him and turned away, thinking, the son of a bitch will probably put it on his bathroom wall.

He went to his car and sat there. The range visit had consumed most of his morning. Let's put off the visit to campus security. Let's go look at some video.

## *The AG*

When Roundtree returned to the police station, a patrolman stopped him in the hall and gave him a manila folder.

"What's this?"

"Your shooter," the patrolman said. "The late Larry Bright. Twenty-seven years old, lived with his mother in a double-wide outside Lynchburg. Has a short psychiatric history, nothing spectacular. He drove a cab, part-time, before he blew."

"Okay. Thanks."

Roundtree opened the folder as the patrolman continued down the hall. He looked down at the first item, an 8" x 11" paper copy in black and white of a photograph out of a high school yearbook. A thin young man with dark hair, in need of a haircut. Serious expression, not friendly, but not unfriendly either.

Roundtree stared at the photograph and mumbled, "This could be anyone."

He went to the bullpen, sat down at his desk, and read through the file. There was not much. School reports. A few tax returns. A report of mediocre credit, seldom used. A criminal history reporting no prior arrests. A few letters from teachers, one from a guidance counselor, another from a speech therapist.

Roundtree stopped and read the report from the speech therapist. Larry had a ferocious stutter in middle school. Roundtree thought, Jesus, a stutter in middle school? That must have been brutal.

One of the guys Googled the mother. Ivana Hanson had lived in the same trailer park for the past thirty-five years. She ran a register at a Stop-N-Shop in Lynchburg. All that time, she had one address, one bank, two cars.

Roundtree read the report and grunted. Two cars in thirty-five years? She must know a good mechanic.

In all that time, she voted in one election. Roundtree muttered, "Good God." The report described a modest life of little hope in raising a black sheep.

Where was the father? What's his name? Ah, here, Michael Bright. Michael and Ivana divorced in 2001, when Larry was thirteen. Roundtree looked back at the grade reports. The kid had straight A's in grade school. By high school, the As had become Cs and Ds. Dad left and Larry fell apart.

Roundtree looked back through the file for a psychiatric evaluation, but there was none. He looked again at the criminal history report. No notations, or complaints, or any mention of the kid in any police report. Zippo.

The kid went from zero to nineteen kills in about twenty minutes.

Roundtree put the report into a drawer and locked the drawer. He sat there for a long time, thinking. This is another waste of time. The time to pay attention was when the father left. A stutter in middle school? Were people asleep?

Roundtree sat there and fought sadness. He would do his job, complete the investigation. Curious minds will want to know, why did he do it? Cause he was empty inside, except for a ton of anger. It consumed him. So, how did he do it? Roundtree snorted. That was no mystery. He cased the school and decided to waste a bunch of students, their crime being their happiness, their progress, their achievements, their expectations. He picked a vulnerable target and then dished out a little payback.

He wasn't avenging himself against them. He was avenging himself against Everyone. If he could have shot Everyone, he would have.

Did he hope to survive? Roundtree paused for a moment. Probably not. He probably planned a suicide by cop. It did not work. The students got to him before that could happen.

A crushed larynx.

Hell with this, Roundtree thought. Forget about it. Let's go watch a little video. He stood up, went to the video room, and got the technician to run the college security feeds through one of the monitors.

He started with the video from Schaefer Hall on the day of the shooting. The technician gave Roundtree a remote control which allowed him to move from one frame to the next, to crop or enlarge or reduce the image.

Roundtree sat down with a 2 liter bottle of generic diet root beer and a huge bag of potato chips. He started clicking on images with one hand, eating chips with the other. He began with images from 7 a.m., two hours before the shooting started.

The end of the workday came and went with no sign of Larry Bright on the last road to mayhem. Eventually, Roundtree pulled his gaze from the computer monitor and scanned his surroundings. The night shift was reporting for duty.

Larry Bright died wearing a pair of blue jeans and a dark jacket, so Roundtree looked for that in the images. Unfortunately, that was almost a uniform on this campus. Finally, after finding a hundred guys who resembled Larry Bright, Roundtree came to an image whose time mark read '9:25 a.m.'

No point in going further. Larry Bright would not be seen alive again. Roundtree logged out of the session and turned off the video monitor.

He stood up, stretched, turned the lights out, and left the video room.


Skip Taylor was standing in his office in front of the TV, watching the morning news. He wore an unbuttoned white dress shirt over a pair of underwear, no socks yet. There had been a mass shooting in some dinky little college out towards the Blue Ridge, out where God-fearing folks bitched if they could not buy their ammo at the 7-11.

Taylor was a politician, the attorney general for the Commonwealth of Virginia. He had to look good for TV cameras. That was part of the job, so he tried to watch his weight. Virginia's DOJ building had a gym in the basement. He would stop there on the way to work, rip off a quick and sweaty thirty minutes on an exercise bike, then shower and put on a suit in his office. Then his day would begin.

Except that today, he was not ready for this. He briefly watched the local morning news channel. Their very attractive reporters stood around the crime scene, speculating furiously about what might have happened. They talked about what it all might mean, if they ever found anything to report.

Taylor stared and clenched his teeth. He yelled at the TV, "Christ on a crutch, you people are useless." He aimed the remote at the TV and pushed a button as if delivering a punch. "I need information, not cleavage."

The screen switched to a national news show. Two anchors were listening to audio feeds from a large staff of people who were working the phones, calling the AG's office and the FBI as well as the NRA, local politicians, and various gun violence celebrities.

Taylor calmed down. A morning shooting at Whitetop Mountain College. There were multiple casualties, the single shooter among them. No report on possible motive.

For the thousandth time, Taylor wondered absently, why are we so hung up on motive? What's the point? If someone is wacko enough to kill a dozen people, who cares what the psychotic motive might have been? If you spot them in advance, just give them a pill. Or two.

But we cannot spot them in advance. They look like everyone else, as a hand grenade resembles a rock. Most rocks do not explode. He sighed.

His interest in the shooting dropped significantly when he learned the shooter was dead. He could not prosecute a dead man, so the incident offered no political benefit.

Then he reconsidered. Not so fast, Skipperoni. What about a conspiracy? What about terrorism? Maybe the guy was a terrorist. Oh, oh ... maybe he was a *Muslim*. Or a Buddhist. That would be weird. A Buddhist serial killer? Has that ever happened? Don't Buddhists tend to be a bit spaced out? Sedated from hyperventilating, or whatever it is that they do?

Taylor became excited. He had to slow himself down. Calm down, Skip. Think it through. You've got time.

While we're at it, he thought, why would terrorists hit Whitetop Mountain College? After all, there are many other colleges that are ... how should I put this? ... better known.

Normally, the cutting edge of law enforcement would not be part of the AG's duties. Strange but true. His job was to make sure that law enforcement in Virginia, broadly defined, had the resources to do the job the voters demanded. He had people to handle the allocation of resources across various law enforcement organizations. Those people had people too - the edge of the sword - who had to enforce the law, hand out speeding tickets, tackle robbers, and shoot at muggers and child molesters.

His secretary's voice came from the intercom on his desk, "Sir, your nine thirty just arrived."

Taylor took two long steps, leaned over and spoke into the intercom, "Abigail, cancel my appointments for the morning. We have a situation here."

"Yes sir. Does that include Marcus Long?"

"God, no. Him, I'll see. Postpone everyone else. Apologize for me. Try to reschedule them for later in the week."

"Yes sir."

Taylor thought, I will meet with the president of the National Rifle Association. I need him. When the Lieutenant Governor calls, I take the call. Or my wife, or Mom. Or Mr. Long, who makes it the Gang of Four. Yes, I will meet with Mr. Long. That should be an interesting conversation.

## *Running in Circles*

Amir was lying in bed, sleeping the sleep of the dead. The house was dark. He lay next to Serena. She was on her side, snoring softly. He had learned to listen to her snore rather than try to block it out. Eventually, it would melt into the background and disappear.

Interesting how the mind filtered out background noise.

In the middle of the night, Amir heard a key turn the front door lock. He woke up a bit. Seconds later, he heard, "Hello, I'm home."

His head left the pillow. What the hell? He paused to listen and heard someone downstairs, moving across the floor. He heard another noise, like a backpack hitting the floor.

Amir sat up and thought, Lelah?

He got out of bed and stood still, listening. No other sound came from downstairs. He thought, well, now I'm up, may as well check it out. He stealthily moved across the floor and down the stairs to stand before the front door.

He looked around the first floor but saw no one else. There was no backpack on the floor. He reached out and tried the front door. It was locked.

Then he stopped. Okay, I'm on autopilot. I need to stop doing that. Lelah is dead. I saw her body with my own eyes. He stood there for a moment. I guess I heard nothing, nothing at all. I imagined it.

He trudged back upstairs and returned to the bed. It took a long time to go back to sleep.


Roundtree sat in front of the video monitor. I am such an idiot. I wasted a day looking for a thin young man in a dark jacket, as if he would be walking across campus with the other students.

But he drives a cab.

So he takes his cab to the campus. If he survives the shooting, that's his getaway car. If he doesn't, it doesn't matter.

Could he catch a cab? Leave the driving to someone else? No, Roundtree answered himself. A Lynchburg cab might not take him to the college. It would be an expensive ride, and the driver would probably turn him down.

Could he catch a cab from Abingdon? Possible, admitted Roundtree. Complicated.

But why mess with all that? *He's got a cab.*

Roundtree went to the bullpen, grabbed the campus map, and returned to the video room. He asked the technician to reload the tapes from the shooting day.

"Again?"

"Yes, again, wise ass. I missed something," he said.

"Missed something?" The technician seemed to savor every syllable.

"It happens. Just load the tapes, before I arrest you for being ugly."

"Alright, alright, don't get your pecker up." The tech said. He turned his attention back to a control board to load the video.

Roundtree spread the map out over the workstation. The main classroom buildings were in a big circle, serviced by two roads, Lee Avenue on one side, Washington Avenue on the other. On the map, Lee Avenue was marked 'commercial traffic only', but Washington Avenue was open to the public and served several faculty parking areas.

Roundtree leaned back in his seat. That's why you hit Schaefer, isn't it, my man? Better access. You could drive right up to it, park, go inside and raise hell. If you were injured, you'd only have to make it a few feet to the car to escape.

So ... you didn't plan on someone biting through your windpipe, did you?

Blue Bird Taxi. That's what we're looking for. Roundtree picked up the remote and activated the feed from the rear camera behind Schaefer Hall. He started clicking through images. From 7 a.m. to 8:43 a.m., there was nothing. Three cars parked there and did not move. Then, like a gift, an image suddenly showed a car, an old Chevrolet, with a light on top that said TAXI.

Roundtree muttered, "Bingo." He enlarged the image in small increments until the portion showing the cab filled the screen. A mailbox blocked part of the cab, but on the left rear door, Roundtree could see, in bold letters, BIRD, above the numbers 509. He took out his cellphone and ran a quick search. 5 and 0 and 9 were the last three digits of Blue Bird Taxi, in Lynchburg, Virginia, the employer of record of the late Larry Bright.

Roundtree pocketed the phone, looked at the cab captured on the monitor and said, "Hello, my man."

Skip Taylor sat at his desk, thinking about the meeting in ten minutes with Marcus Long. Next year, I run for the Senate. The U.S. Senate. He smiled. He thought about it again.

The United States Senate. Senator Taylor. Ohhhh, that feels good. That feels real good.

To get elected, I need the NRA. Nothing more, nothing less.

I'll oppose Stennis Gardner, most likely. A good man, a black man from Richmond's central ghetto. His Daddy, a minister, gave him a fine mind, a bass voice, and a gift for oration. And no shortage of guts, either.

Head to head, in a straight up fight, I don't think I can beat Gardner. He's a better man, for what that's worth. Taylor chuckled to himself. However, he's liberal by Virginia standards. He is unable to overlook the knee-buckling homicide rate among urban blacks, or that Virginia exports guns up the east coast. Cops from Maine to Baltimore routinely find our pistols at their crime scenes. Courtesy of Mr. Long and the NRA.

Gardner is a combat vet - two tours in Iraq, one in Afghanistan. A smart man, a fine man, but not an NRA man.

So I have a chance. That is why the time is now. For a moment, I have leverage - what will the NRA do to keep Gardner out of the Senate? Lots, I bet. They'll tell me they like me, but the truth is, they hate Gardner more than they like me. Yes. This is the time to strike.

He smiled. It doesn't need to be pretty; it only needs to work.

At the top of the list - line up money, line up votes. Contrary to what everyone believes, the NRA is not a wealthy organization. In fact, their political contributions are usually modest. But they are hell on wheels when it comes to getting out the vote. They get out the vote better than anyone else. They are amazing - better than any labor union, better than the veterans, better even than the Catholic Church. Taylor grinned and shook his head in wonder. Many people are not Catholic. They might be atheists, or worse, Methodists, or even Baptists. Guns are different - in Virginia even atheists worship at the Altar of Firepower.

The intercom buzzed, *"Mr. Attorney General, Mr. Long has arrived."*

Skip Taylor got out of his chair and went out to the front office. He spotted Long and held out his hand. "Mr. Long, hello. Thanks for stopping by. I appreciate it, especially under the circumstances."

Marcus Long stood up and shook hands. "Think nothing of it. I was already in town on other business."

Taylor nodded and thought, yeah, I'll bet you spend a lot of time in Richmond.

The two men went to Taylor's office. Long sat down in front of the desk. Taylor closed the door, then moved behind his desk and sat down.

Taylor studied Long. The man looked as if he had just left a plantation in a silk carriage - soft hands, soft features. He was fussy - trimmed mustache, yacht club blazer, prep school tie and diamond cufflinks. Old money, comfortably sloshing around in tax free and off-ledger locations.

Taylor hid a smirk. He did not own cufflinks. "I would imagine you're quite busy at the moment, given the news."

Long tilted his head. "Oh? What news might that be? Did I miss something?"

"The college shooting this morning," Taylor said. "I understand it was bad. Seventeen students and the shooter."

"Ah yes. That." Long's last word dismissed the subject. "Terrible. However, it is not the first collective shooting we have had. Nor will it be the last. In any event, that does not affect me at all."

"You don't get protesters at your headquarters?"

"Of course we do. I think it's fine, first amendment and all that. As long as they're peaceful and I can park my car in front, I have no problem with protesters."

Taylor stared at him. Homicides don't get your attention? Really? And you're successful?

Long noticed the look. "Mr. Taylor, as an attorney, you can understand the situation. Over the years, the NRA has devoted enormous effort and resource to developing favorable judicial interpretations of the second amendment. Once in place, those rulings are durable."

Long looked down and idly picked at a manicured fingernail. "So we don't get excited at shootings, or at protests."

Long clapped his hands once and sat up straight. "But enough of that. Down to business - we do a lot of thinking about politics at the state and local level, and you, Mr. AG, have come to our attention. We think you would make a fine candidate for the Senate race next year.

"Senator Jellison is retiring, and the only real opponent you might face is this negro fellow, Gardner. Now, it will come as no surprise that we like you more than Gardner. But there is something we would want in return for our support. We would want you to help us establish campus carry and concealed carry throughout the state of Virginia."

Taylor turned away towards the wall. He did not want to be caught staring like a rube. So ... *if I don't comply, the NRA will not support Gardner. That's good. I may have a little leeway here.* "Would you be satisfied with more lenient treatment of carry in rural communities?" Taylor said. "Police departments in Virginia advise against open carry in urban environments."

Long shook his head. "No. That would fragment our lobbying efforts. It would cost a fortune. No, we want to push a legislative agenda at the state level, nothing below the state level. We're taking that approach across the entire country, by the way."

Taylor kept his mouth from dropping open. *More lenient carry laws in the inner cities? In the ghettos? In Roanoke, Portsmouth, Suffolk, and* right here in Richmond? We'll be arming drug gangs. It'll be a bloodbath. Hell, what am I talking about? It's already a bloodbath. The bloodbath will get worse.

Surely, one of these days, the voters will wake up. The AG's mouth twisted into a half smile - call me a dreamer.

Taylor looked out the window. I have to say yes. My route to the Senate goes right through the NRA. I have to say yes. Otherwise, Gardner beats me.

"Mr. Taylor?"

Taylor looked at Long. "A moment, please. I need to think about this."

"Of course. Take your time." Mr. Long leaned back in the chair and clasped his hands together in his lap.

Taylor sat there for dramatic purposes, but he had made up his mind. He stood up, reached his hand across the desk. "Mr. Long, I believe I can help you establish more lenient carry laws in Virginia."

Long grinned hugely. He stood up, shook Taylor's hand, and said, "You know, I think this may be the beginning of a beautiful friendship."

Taylor was surprised. The meeting was over. No wrangling, no negotiation. Just, here's what we want, can you do this for us, yes or no? Is this how the truly rich behave? Here's what's for sale, here is what we can give you. We are offering, do you accept? Take it or leave it. Taylor tried to cover his surprise. "Can I walk you out, Mr. Long?"

Long shook his head briskly. "Not necessary. I know the way. We will be in touch when the time comes."

"Excellent. Well, I'm looking forward to working with you. Again, thank you for stopping by."

Just like that, the deal was made.

Taylor returned to his office and stood in front of the window. He looked at the city park outside. No, this is not the start of a friendship, Mr. Long. I know something you don't, my gilded and cocky friend.

Virginia is urbanizing faster than most states. It's the feds, of course, all that fed money around Washington, Norfolk, and Newport News. And Langley. And a few other places. Hell, if it weren't for the feds, this state would be Arkansas with nicer beaches.

Now, a Senate term is six years. In six years, Virginia's population will be almost 95 percent urban. The jobs are in the cities. The lion's share of the money will be urban. Even now, if not for the Navy around Norfolk and Newport News, the DC suburbs could buy the rest of the state.

In six years, with an urban population, after all those funerals, there will be huge anti-gun sentiment in Virginia. Since voters have some memory, well before the next election - two years before, I should think - I will need to switch sides. I'll need to address the violence and suppress guns. If I don't, I'll get voted out. I'll get beat by Gardner or someone else of that ilk.

When that day arrives, Mr. Long, you may feel that you have been used, deceived, manipulated.

I feel bad about that. But you know what? It couldn't happen to a nicer guy.

## *The Funeral*

Amir and Serena drove through the mountains of southern Virginia. At any other time, the fall foliage would have been colorful and wonderful. Yet Amir could not enjoy it. The college was no longer an adult rite of passage, a place of learning, maturation, and seasoning, an idyllic garden of the mind, where healthy young people studied hard and learned to manage a budget, have sex, and smoke pot. No. It was a murder scene. It was where his only child was killed just as she was beginning to explore the joys and agonies of adulthood.

Serena seemed to enjoy the drive. The scenery was a kaleidoscopic explosion splashed across the sunny side of mountains and valleys. Every so often, she would point out a particularly spectacular sight.

For his part, Amir concentrated on driving. He tried to hide his sadness. As he steered the car along what felt like a tunnel through the trees, he wondered if he would ever be happy again, if he would ever be anything but miserable. He did not know and at the moment did not care. The best he could manage was numbness. He knew that Serena worried about him, so he tried to wear a happy face for her sake. Yet he did not have a happy face to share.

Amir had considered going to a therapist. He attended one meeting with Serena. That ended abruptly when the therapist seemed to suggest that his daughter was not worth all the anger and depression that he was feeling. He must let go, forget the daughter, save himself, and continue to live his life as best he could. Amir thought about what she said. Then he stood up and walked out of the meeting.

Serena finished the session, then came out to find him. Amir told her, you may see that person if she helps you. But I find her indifference intolerable. I do not need to pay an hourly rate for indifference. It is freely available everywhere.

Amir thought he was being calm, quiet, reasonable. Serena saw, though he could not, that as he spoke his eyes had turned yellow, a danger signal. She stayed out of his way and tip-toed around the house the rest of the day.

They arrived at the college. Serena, studying a campus map, directed Amir to a parking lot downslope from the main campus. They parked and got out of the car.

To the south the Smokies were gray and blue and massive. She turned to marvel at the view. "Good heavens. It always amazes me. It's so beautiful here."

Amir glanced at the mountains and nodded. He waited. Finally, she turned to walk up the hill along a concrete footpath. He followed her.

Near the top, they spotted Schaefer Hall. It still looked like a crime scene. Two police cars were parked nearby on the grass. Yellow police tape encircled the building and the parking lot.

For a long minute, Amir and Serena stood staring at the back of Schaefer Hall. Then they walked around it and came out onto the central quad. Serena saw the memorial in front of Schaefer Hall and approached it. Amir followed her.

The memorial was massive, a huge pile of balloons, signs, cards, candles, stuffed toys, and ribbon. There was even a menorah, a single candle lit. Serena walked up to the memorial and looked at the memorabilia. She turned and called out, "Amir, come see. It's beautiful."

Amir approached it reluctantly and looked at all the items students, families, and friends had left in front of Schaefer Hall in memory of the victims. He felt a surge of anger and gritted his teeth. It feels like they are celebrating the murders. I should not react. I know that's not it.

I should not have come here.

He saw a number of photographs, propped up, facing the quad. He stared at one, then another, and suddenly there was Lelah's photograph. Someone had taken the shot from the college 'pigbook' and expanded it into a glossy but grainy 8" x 11" photo. A rush of recent memories surged into his head: an excited Lelah in a peach gown, waiting for her date to arrive and take her to her first formal dance. A quiet Lelah, sitting at the kitchen table, studying for a test. A tearful Lelah, with equally tearful friends, leaving a high school football game, a loss. An exuberant Lelah, holding the letter of admission from Whitetop Mountain College. Finally, a somber Lelah, hanging up the phone after breaking up with her high school boyfriend.

Suddenly, Amir's heart skipped a beat and he could not take the next breath. He was suffocating. He dropped to his knees, his hand on his chest. He looked back at the photo. It suddenly burst into flames, which quickly spread to the rest of the memorial. His mind screamed, what is happening? What is going on here? Are we under attack? Is it another attack? Then he looked up and Schaefer Hall burst into flame as if hit by a bomb. Amir looked around. Bodies and splashes of blood surrounded the memorial.

He put his hands to his head, smelled blood on them. Then he moaned and fell sideways onto the grass.

Serena, who had been admiring the memorial, turned to see Amir on the ground. She quickly came to him and knelt next to him, "Amir? Are you okay? Darling, what's wrong?"

Amir was conscious but he could do nothing except lie there gasping. After a long minute, he found he could breathe again. He looked up at Serena, "I think I'm okay." He turned his head to look at the memorial. The candles continued to burn, but Schaefer Hall was not burning, it was intact. There were neither bodies nor blood on the grass.

Amir's eyes were wide in shock and fear. He looked at the memorial, then he looked up at Serena, who was still kneeling next to him, staring anxiously at him.

I imagined it, he thought. God in Heaven, I imagined all of it.

Serena called campus security on her cellphone. She reached into her purse, extracted a small pill, and held it out for Amir. "Here, chew this."

He took the pill and wondered, what is this? He popped it into his mouth, started chewing, and made a face. It was an aspirin. He looked up at her. "Thanks, but I'm not having a heart attack."

Amir made as if to get up, but Serena pushed him back down. "Stay here. Help is on the way."

Five minutes and a dozen onlookers later, a golf cart pulled up and a medical technician with a small suitcase got out and knelt next to Amir on the grass. He asked Amir questions, moved him to a sitting position, opened the suitcase, and pulled out a stethoscope. He listened to Amir's heart, then his lungs. He checked Amir's pupils, then his pulse. Then he began attaching electrical leads. Ten minutes later, the technician glanced at the display. He hung the stethoscope around his neck and said, "Well, the good news is, you are not having a heart attack. Nor are you having a stroke. This looks like a panic attack. I don't think you should drive for a while. You should see your doctor as soon as you can."

He looked at Serena. "Can you drive him home?"

She nodded.

The technician offered use of the college's medical facilities, but Amir chose to see his own doctor, and later that day he met the doctor.

His doctor gave him pills for anxiety.


The next day, the police were offering a briefing to the friends and families of the shooting victims. Serena and Amir were at the kitchen table, having coffee. Serena wanted to attend the briefing but was nervous about Amir's attending.

He insisted. "Of course I want to go to the briefing. I want to know why Lelah's dead."

She leaned back in her chair and held her hands out, as if begging. "What if you have a relapse? What if you have another anxiety attack?"

Amir shrugged. "I don't know. Call 911, I guess."

She drove them to the police station in Abingdon. This time they met in a large meeting room inside the station. It was half as crowded as the first meeting - there were no attorneys, no psychiatrists. A lectern was at one end of a long conference table. When Amir and Serena arrived, the chairs at the table were occupied, so they sat down further out, in two chairs backed against a wall.

A young woman, one of the youngest in the room, was sitting next to Serena. They chatted briefly, then Serena said, "Who did you lose?"

The woman turned teary eyes to Serena. "My brother. Nineteen." She shook her head. "Nineteen. I still can't believe it."

Serena put an arm around her shoulders.

At a minute after 10 a.m., Inspector Roundtree entered the room, stopped, and looked across the crowd. He moved to the head of the table. "Hi everyone. For those who missed our first meeting, I'm Inspector Roundtree and I'm here to tell you what we've found about the recent shooting at Whitetop. If you're here for some other reason, you're in the wrong room."

He looked at the crowd; no one left the room. He took a remote from the lectern and fingered it. While a white screen slowly unrolled from the ceiling, Roundtree walked to the door, dimmed the lights, and returned to the lectern.

"I have a slideshow. At least, I hope I do." Someone laughed. Roundtree clicked a button, and a blank square of light appeared on the screen. He pushed another, and an abstract pattern appeared. Then a photograph from a high school yearbook appeared. "Can everyone see clearly?"

Amir stared at the young man in the photograph. You are dead. That is too bad. That is a shame. I would enjoy arranging your demise. If we were in Beirut, I could do it. But not here. Forgive me if I do not grieve for you.

Roundtree looked around, then continued, "Before I begin, what I'm about to show you might be relevant in a lawsuit. With that in mind, I have placed this presentation on the police website. Your attorney can download it if they wish. We also gave it to the college and to several law firms."

He turned towards the screen. "This was Larry Bright. He was the shooter at Whitetop. A twenty-seven year old Caucasian, he graduated from high school up in Lynchburg, where he grew up and lived with his mother."

Someone from the crowd exclaimed, "Great. One of those." Someone else shushed them.

Roundtree turned towards the voice. "You're not wrong, you know. Larry Bright was a troubled young man. When he was twelve, his parents divorced, his father moved out of state. My opinion is, he did not adjust well to that. By middle school he had a serious stutter and his grades dropped. He was twenty years old when he graduated from high school."

"Here's what he looked like in the fifth grade," Roundtree said. He touched the remote and a different photo appeared, a young boy under an oversize Little League cap and a shock of dark hair, laughing, a huge grin on his face, lively dark eyes. Amir stared. It was strange - the happy boy in the photo would turn into a mass murderer.

"And here he is ten years later," another photo appeared. Larry Bright was an adult, but the expression on his face was one of distrust, anxiety, suspicion. The eyes staring into the camera were narrow; the mouth a straight, flat line.

"Larry made a modest living as an adult. A speech therapist in his high school helped with the stutter. Nonetheless, Larry never thrived. He bounced through a series of low level jobs - clerk in a grocery store, stock boy in a supermarket. For the last three years, he drove a Blue Bird taxi here in Abingdon and up in Lynchburg. He had a checking account and a credit card. He never applied for a bank loan. He drove a twelve year old Nissan Sentra, paid for in cash. Clean driving record, no arrests.

"None of this was cause for alarm. I suspect that each of us knows young adults like Larry, people who haven't quite found their place in adult society."

Someone laughed. Amir looked across the crowd. What was funny about that?

Roundtree turned away from the screen. "Any questions or comments?"

He paused, then continued, "One item stood out. Larry was a loner, in a way that few people are. I spoke with several acquaintances: his mother, his doctor, several teachers, his supervisor at Blue Bird, several co-workers. They knew of no friends, no girlfriend, not even casual friends. No one could tell me much about him on a personal level. No one knew that he had no friends. Larry made no impression on anyone."

Roundtree looked out at the crowd. "I guess that's something not easily detected these days."

He turned back to the screen. "Let's look at the day of the shooting. The evidence suggests that Larry acted alone. There is no evidence that he knew any of the victims. Why he decided to kill a collection of strangers is something we'll never know. In my view, he probably hit Schaefer because he could drive his cab right up to it, as if he were making a pickup. Of course, that is true of many other buildings on campus.

"Once he decided to kill, the rest was easy. He already had the perfect cover, a taxi cab that was familiar to everyone on campus. Campus security would have no reason to notice him. He would blend in with the students, right up to the moment he began shooting."

Roundtree fingered the remote, and an airborne photo of Schaefer Hall appeared on the screen. "That morning he drove his cab to the campus. He parked behind Schaefer by 8:45. Around nine a.m., things started happening. The first 911 report of an active shooter arrived at 9:03 a.m. He had a Glock with several spare magazines. We found one in a jacket pocket, unused. Three others he used and discarded.

"He circled the building, entered through the front door. He immediately started shooting. He killed five people in the front hall and two more in a first floor office, one of them a faculty member. He moved to the back of the building. The back door was locked. He trapped and killed six more people back there.

"He then returned to the front hall and took the stairs to the second floor. Here is where his plan went off the rails. Students on the second floor heard the shooting. A dozen students rushed him when he came up the stairs. They threw everything they had at him, computers, chairs, books, everything. He managed to kill three more people before a male student got to him and bit through his windpipe." A sudden rise in conversation swept through the crowd.

Amir glanced at Serena, who wore a look of revulsion.

"You okay?" he whispered.

She nodded.

Roundtree stood there quietly, waiting for the noise to die down. He continued, "Larry Bright shot that young man at close range, and the man later died. It is likely that by 9:15, Larry Bright himself was dead of asphyxiation. Campus security arrived at 9:25."

Roundtree paused. "It took less than fifteen minutes for him to kill seventeen students, a faculty member, and himself."

Again, the crowd grew restive. Someone exclaimed in a strained, excited voice, "Son of a bitch."

Roundtree continued, "That is just about everything I've learned so far." Roundtree turned away from the screen and faced the crowd. "Questions?"

A man raised his hand. Roundtree smiled at that and pointed to him.

"Where did he get the gun?" the man said.

"We don't know," Roundtree said. "I'm still working on that. We have the weapon, of course, and the serial number. The gun shipped last year to a gun shop in Knoxville, Tennessee. We do not know how Larry Bright obtained that weapon. We do not have a sales receipt. I should mention, the gun shop in Knoxville has not been cooperative so far."

Amir thought about that. He shrugged. In this country, if you can't find a gun, you must be deaf, dumb, and blind.

"Are you working with any other agencies on this investigation?" a woman asked.

"We're talking to the FBI. But you have to understand, they get many requests for help. All we can do is ask and then stand in line."

The next day was Lelah's funeral, at a funeral home in the neighborhood, near Monument Avenue. Amir woke up, remembered what day it was, and immediately became grim. He had taken part in numerous funerals back in Beirut, back in the bad old days.

Those funerals had brought back no dead, corrected no injustice, and given him no feelings of warmth or healing or remembrance. They offered a display of love for the departed, for the benefit of family, neighbors, and other people, most of whom Amir did not count as friends.

He liked the idea of an Irish funeral, a drunken celebration. That made sense. He had never been to one. Getting drunk at a funeral appealed to his sense of loyalty. Your friend died? Yes? That is a good time to misbehave. If you are not angry enough, not sad enough to do that, you must not have cared much.

It was useless. A lapsed Muslim, Amir did not drink. He had to take his grief and his anger straight, undiluted.

His best friend in the neighborhood was Sam. Amir thought Sam was a typical American, a broad, solid fellow, a business partner of long standing. Sam was a combat vet with bad combat experiences. God might forgive and forget. Sam could not. After his discharge from the army, he left the Church and got on with his life, determined to enjoy it until the day when it would end.

He would joke about it. "Ah, yes, it's a merry life, followed by flames."

Sam offered to come to Lelah's funeral, but Amir declined. So Sam skipped it, with Amir's blessings.

In spite of his misgivings, Amir could see that the funeral helped Serena. She enjoyed the party and the support of her friends.

The funeral home itself was dark, quiet, calming, a place of reflection, the darkness tastefully broken by the occasional candle or fresh flower sitting in a circle of light. Amir's resolve lasted until he took his seat next to Serena in the front row of the funeral home. A woman, a close friend, sat on her other side, her arm around Serena, extra tissues in hand. Serena sat there weeping.

The casket, in front of the assembled chairs, was closed. A large black and white photograph of Lelah was in front of it. A lectern stood next to the casket.

Amir looked at the photograph. Joy and life and humor shone from it like light from a white sun in a blue morning sky. The face in the photograph was that of a beautiful and lively young woman just beginning to enjoy being who she was.

Judging from the photo, being Lelah was fun.

The thought crossed Amir's mind, that is not what Lelah looks like now. He felt a surge of anger so strong that his breath caught and stopped for a moment. Then he saw again the unwelcome memory - she was shot in the face at close range. Amir winced and wished he did not know that. The Undertaker had been unable to repair the damage to his satisfaction.

The surge of anger grew into a torrent. He briefly had a fantasy of standing in Schaefer Hall, chucking a Molotov cocktail at Larry Bright, setting him afire and watching him scream, then watching him burn. Then Amir remembered to breathe and to stop grinding his teeth.

He was trembling. He looked sideways, at Serena. She had not noticed.

A woman approached Amir, stood over him and patted him on the shoulder. Amir looked up at her and thought, who the hell are you? Then he chided himself, there's no point in anger, it serves no purpose. It is too late. What could be lost has been lost.

Don't hide in anger. Don't beat yourself up. Miss her, remember her, honor her. She would want you to live your life. Try to honor that desire. Try to live.

After a long, torturous moment, he found some relief in closing his eyes and shutting out the view. He did not want to see anything of the funeral. He had already seen more than he wished, more than he needed. He wanted no further encounters with strangers who wished him well.

He wanted his daughter back, smiling, shining, breathing ... alive.

An imam approached the lectern and presented a sermon. Amir sat there, nursing his torment. He heard none of the imam's words. Eventually, mercifully, the man finished.

Amir sat up straight and opened his eyes. He looked around the crowd. Everyone was standing still, watching them, and waiting to follow Amir and Serena out of the funeral home.

He said to Serena, "You want to leave? We can stay as long as you want to." She looked at him and nodded. He offered her his hand, and she stood up, took the hand of her friend and headed to the aisle and towards the front door. Stone-faced, Amir let go of her hand and walked behind them.

After the wake, the party left the funeral home and slowly returned to their cars, stopping often for conversation and consolation. In their cars they lit their headlights, lined up behind a black hearse, and ventured out onto the roads, a convoy heading for the country cemetery where they would bury Lelah. At the cemetery, the funeral party converged on the rectangular hole waiting to receive Lelah's pine coffin.

The cemetery was new, atop a hill whose young trees provided little shade. Amir looked around and thought, they have ample room for expansion. It will happen, that much is certain.

Death and taxes.

The imam said a few words over the coffin. Amir stared as workmen lowered the coffin into the earth. He thought, over time the coffin and then Lelah herself will feed the worms. The worms will make soil. The soil will feed the trees and the grass. The trees will grow and provide fruit and shade. There will be flowers. Long after that, Lelah will be here, in bits and pieces, scattered among the trees and feeding the grass and the flowers.

She would have approved. One life ends, another begins. That is the sole item in this stupid charade that makes sense. I understand that we are mortal. As Tolkien put it, mortal man, doomed to die.

I do not understand why we are so murderous, so cleverly homicidal, without cause or reason. I miss Lelah. I suspect I will miss her for a long time. God, I feel lousy. I never thought I would be burying her. That is so wrong. I am her father, I was supposed to die first. That was to be the way of things. That should be the way of things.

This whole thing is wrong.

Several dozen people made their way back to the house. Serena's friends had prepared a vast and varied collection of Middle Eastern and Mediterranean entrees, hummus, spicy pumpkin, lamb, cakes, pies, flaked pastries, coffee, fruit juice, and sparkling water. The house, indeed the neighborhood, smelled of food.

When Amir emerged from his car, he saw Sam sitting in a rocking chair on the front porch. Amir walked up and said, "Hey there. Where's your better half?"

Sam pointed with a thumb. "Inside with the hens." He was wearing a brown corduroy jacket and a red tie that strained to encircle his neck. He stood up. "You look like a guy watching a short fuse burn."

"I believe I am managing to behave myself," Amir said.

Sam nodded. "Yeah, maybe." He looked at the crowd approaching the house and dropped his voice, "Anything I can do? You want to get drunk? Grab a machine gun and go squirrel hunting? Hire a couple of hookers? Throw rocks at greenhouses?" Sam paused and looked around again, "Or, if it's your thing, we could go back and pee on the funeral home."

Amir chuckled. "None of that. But …" He thought, harming Larry Bright's friends and family will not bring back Lelah. Hell, they might be as puzzled as anyone.

"But?"

Amir shook his head. "Never mind. Something stupid. I'll keep it to myself."

Sam looked at him for a moment. "Oh, well. Yeah, we wouldn't want to be stupid."

Amir chuckled.

"Alright. Well, if you won't change your mind, I think we should at least eat … dessert first," Sam said.

Amir followed Sam into the living room. Sam approached Serena and told her a joke. She smiled.

Amir looked around and could see no reason to stay in the crowd. He went outside and sat down in an old swing on the porch. He greeted the occasional visitor as they climbed the front steps. Many of them stopped and said a few words, but Amir did not encourage conversation. After a polite interval, the visitors went inside.

He sat by himself, relaxing, looking out across the front yard. Then he noticed someone in his car. He leaned forward to get a better look. It was Lelah, sitting behind the wheel, smiling at him, just as she had sat when he drove her out to Whitetop Mountain College. The last time he would see her alive.

Amir reacted with a start, as if someone had slapped him across the face. His good feeling evaporated. A hot flash of anger. The choked feeling in his chest and throat returned in full force. He looked back into the house and was immediately cautious.

Amir touched his forehead. He was sweating. He thought, I need to stay out of there. If I am hallucinating, I need to keep that to myself. I need to be alone and deal with this.

Control. I need control.

A walk. That's it. I'll go for a walk. He went into the house, moved next to Serena and said, "Listen, Serene, I'm going to take a short walk, maybe burn off a few calories."

She smiled, but looked puzzled. "A walk? To burn off calories? With all this food? You're not having an affair, are you?"

"Just trying to stay cute for you."

She looked at Amir. He wasn't smiling. She said, "Well … okay then. That's different. Get to it."

Amir turned and headed for the front door. Serena watched him leave. A worried expression crossed her face.

## *Unexpected Visitors*

Amir went back to the porch and strode across the front yard. Lelah was still in the car, smiling at him. Amir looked at her but did not smile back. He thought, you are dead. I saw your body. I touched it. It was cold. I am not going to talk to a hallucination, not in front of my wife's friends.

He headed down the sidewalk at a brisk pace. After several blocks, Amir was perspiring and breathing deeply. He took off his tie and unbuttoned the top button of his shirt. He rolled up the tie and stuffed it into a pocket.

Suddenly he heard a car horn blare loud and close by. He stopped himself just as a car jerked to a halt in front of him.

The driver, a bald man in a dirty t-shirt, half a well-chewed cigar clamped in yellow teeth, yelled, "Hey, buddy, you trying to be an angel? Pay attention, will you?"

Amir waved at him, apologizing. "Sorry."

The man shook his head and drove on.

Amir thought, if I'm hallucinating, this is risky as hell. Can I trust my own eyes? He looked both ways, up and down the street, then looked again. He continued walking. Passing one of the houses, he saw a young girl walking up steps to the front door. It was Lelah, at the age of twelve. He stared at her. She turned and looked at him, then faded away.

A block later, Amir passed the high school football stadium, where a soft composite track encircled the football field. He turned and entered the track and began circling it, walking fast. He wiped perspiration from his face.

On one lap, he looked over into the visitor bleachers. The teenage Lelah was sitting there, leaning back, watching him, her legs crossed.

Amir ignored her and kept walking.

On the next lap, she was not there, but after he passed the bleachers, Amir looked behind him. There, thirty yards back, was Lelah, following him. Amir laughed as he wondered, what is this? Am I being rude to my hallucination? Is she looking to speak with me?

He walked for another hundred yards and then glanced behind him. She was still back there. Amir thought, this is silly. He stopped walking and stood there thinking and waiting for her. She walked towards him and then, as she came close, faded into nothingness.

Amir turned and continued walking. It is official - I am losing my mind. I am hallucinating. What is going to become of me? How can I even begin to have a life if my senses will not tell me what is going on in the world? How can I live?

How can I live with Serena? I have lost my daughter. Am I going to lose my wife and everything else too?

Amir began to cry. He continued to walk around the track, tears streaming down his face. After a few minutes he settled down to quiet sobbing, but he continued to walk.

A minute later, a young man who was jogging on the track, a worried look on his face, approached Amir. "Hey, mister. You okay? You need help?"

Amir tried to compose himself and nodded. "Yeah, I'm okay. Thanks for asking."

"Okay."

"We had a death in the family."

"Okay."

"Thanks for asking."

"Sure. Okay then." The young man nodded and went back to jogging.

Amir continued to walk. Suddenly, with no warning, his head jerked up. He began to hear someone, a woman, screaming. The screams sounded nearby, no more than a few feet away. Amir looked around. There was no one near him.

The screams continued. Amir wondered, what is happening? Who is screaming? They became screams of fear, agony, and bodily harm, as if a predator tore flesh from a weaker prey. Then the screams changed, now coming from a male voice, a voice shouting out in rage, fear, and anger. Amir froze for a moment - where is all this noise coming from? Who is screaming? Am I screaming? He covered his mouth with his hands, but the screams continued. His hands went to his head, and he bent over in pain, wishing the screams would stop.

The screams changed yet again, into the voice of a beast, a predator with teeth, claws, and a huge chest, a loud rumbling that grew into a roar of anger and dominance and aggression. It was an animal voice that said, I own all of this. I own you.

Amir stopped walking. He bent over in pain and distress, crying quietly. "Please. Please stop. I cannot take this. I can't take anymore."

As suddenly as they had begun, the screams and the roars stopped.

Amir was trembling. Sweat covered his body. He walked drunkenly over to a set of bleachers and fell to a sitting position. Stunned and terrified, he tried to think. What am I to do?

For a long time, he sat on the bleachers, his head in his hands. Then he felt the presence of someone else. He looked up and saw Sam approaching. Sam did not say anything. He came up, sat down next to Amir, and put a hand on Amir's shoulder.

"Looks like you're having a tough time, my friend," Sam said.

Amir nodded. "Maybe."

"Anything I can do?"

Amir smiled weakly. "I'll let you know."

Sam nodded.

"Thanks, Sam."

"De nada."

Amir sat there, waiting for a joke, but none came. He looked at Sam, who was sitting there, a serious expression on his face.

Sam said, "Listen, Amir. I want to tell you a little story. I hope it will help. I've been watching you lately. Truth is, I've been worrying about you. The last couple of days, you remind me of some of the guys I served with."

Sam clasped his hands and looked down at them for a moment. "We were in combat, which is scary. Nothing's happening most of the time, then all hell breaks loose, with shooting and explosions. A minute later, that all calms down. Then you look around and count heads, starting with your own."

Amir nodded.

"After the shitstorm, you check your body for blood. Am I shot? Then you check the other guys."

Amir nodded.

Sam continued, "And you do that day in, day out, and you learn to protect yourself. A lot of guys, once they've seen enough, they stop caring about the new guys. Why invest the emotion, right? That's a bad first step. Then they stop caring about their buddies. They get numb and that's worse. They stop performing. Then they stop caring about themselves, and that's still worse. They get dangerous, maybe suicidal. Bugger it, why worry? That manner of thinking."

Amir nodded.

"Before you know it, an argument over a card game ends in gunfire."

Amir nodded.

"If you find yourself sliding in that direction, it's time to talk to somebody," Sam said. "Don't just suffer in silence. Okay?"

"Sure. Okay."

"And keep in touch."

"I will … and Sam?"

Sam looked at Amir. "No problem."

The day after the funeral, Amir and Serena sat in their living room after a light dinner, watching the evening news. The anchor was a dignified middle-aged man. Serena enjoyed the news because it was, well, new. Something new for each day.

In Argentina, the government was investigating yet another ex-president. With a national election a year away, a voting rights group was suing the state of Florida for manipulating its voting regulations. Again. Willowy Jennifer Willow - she insisted that was her real name, but no one believed that - was marrying for the fourth time. Oddly, she had invited her ex-husbands to the wedding and, oddly, they planned to attend.

For the first time since the birth of Christ, the Beirut football club defeated Naples.

"What!?" Amir exclaimed.

As a hurricane approached the Florida panhandle, Texas prayed for rain. Amir muttered, "To which God?"

"What?" Serena said.

"Nothing."

Forests in California burned.

Then the news turned to the mass shooting at the little college in the mountains of southwestern Virginia. Amir and Serena looked up from what they were doing and listened.

The anchor talked about the victims, what they were doing at the time, what they might have done had they not been murdered. Grief settled onto Amir's face. He teared up and Serena's face became sad. Then two screens showed photographs of the victims, one at a time. When Lelah's photograph appeared on the screen, Serena buried her face in her hands.

The story turned to gun control, as described in interviews with several liberal and conservative politicians. Amir watched the interviews and began to get angry, but he remained silent.

The anchor expressed wonder at the long-established pattern: each mass shooting preceded cries and protests for stricter control of firearms, with no action, no follow-up, no results.

Then the anchor said, "And this from the National Rifle Association ..." The video showed a slender, well-dressed, middle-aged man speaking into a cluster of hand-held microphones. The caption at the bottom of the screen read, '*Marcus Long, President, NRA*'. "I do not understand the hue and cry in these cases. Honestly, don't people have better things to do?"

Mr. Long glanced down and picked at a fingernail. Then he looked up at the reporters. "Allow me to offer two points that even the simple-minded might follow. First, if a few students had been armed, they might have been able to defend themselves against this shooter, this Larry fellow. Second, if someone out there wants to change the Constitution, that can be done. Until then, the Constitution establishes the rights of citizens to own weapons. Complaints, protest marches, and letters to the editor accomplish nothing. It is theater. Phony news, nothing more.

"We at the NRA do not object. We support freedom of speech. We just think some of it is a waste of time."

Amir stared at the screen and thought, well, that is putting it plainly. Different day, same tune.

Serena sat on the couch shaking her head. "I can hardly believe it." She sat there, shaking her head. "I used to think this place could do anything, but we cannot fix this."

Then Amir clearly heard a deep, resonant male voice, a bass voice, a voice coming from the large chest of a large man, *There stands a man who desperately needs to die.*

Amir's eyes bugged out in surprise. What the hell? He looked around the room. but no one else was there.

Amir thought, oh no, no, not again.

*Yes again, Amir. I was with you at the track. I am always with you. I am your drunken uncle, the little devil on your shoulder. Your evil twin Skippy. You and I need to talk.*

This isn't happening, Amir thought. This cannot be happening. He felt his heart rate increase. He began to sweat. He thought, please go away, leave me alone.

*Don't pretend I'm a stranger, Amir. We're not different. No, we are the same, you and I. You can think of me as the little corner of your mind that you've come to ignore on your path to becoming such a goddamn coupon clipping pussy.*

"I need some air," Amir said.

Serena looked at him. "You okay?"

"Yeah, sure," he said. "I'm going out to the porch."

*That is a good idea, Amir. You don't need Serena thinking that you've got this little voice in your head. That was my mistake. I should not have spoken up in her presence. I apologize.*

Great, Amir thought, this is just what I need. A well-mannered psychopath in my head.

The voice chuckled, a rumbling, *Ha, ha, that's a good one, Amir. But you and I have work to do.*

What work?

*As I said, that fellow needs to die. You and I are going to arrange it.*

What? No. Absolutely not. I am not killing anyone. If you're a part of me, you must be the insane part. Or the stupid part. No way. Forget it.

*Insane, eh? That's debatable. Hear me out. Remember Beirut? They gave you a gun, but you did not take a side. You hedged, you kept your head down, you shot a few people. Mainly you survived. You abandoned your family and your people because you were afraid.*

Amir thought, that was a good move. I would do that again.

*So you say. You fled to the U.S., the Golden Mountain. You thought you would be safe. But there's something you did not know - the biggest killer of Americans is - Americans. They practice.*

*Murder is part of their culture.*

*You built a good life here - a wife, a beautiful daughter, a nice house in a nice city, a good car. Yes, well done. Congratulations. However, now the bloody bastards have taken your only child.*

*You dare sit there and call me insane? Grow a fucking backbone. And wake up to the world in which you live.*

So now you will sell me the old values? Amir thought. Seriously? Look at Beirut. It used to be a garden. Now it's a city of ghosts. When I think of Beirut, I think of bullet holes and corpses.

*Muddy it up all you want, Amir. What Beirut or America turns into is not your concern. No. That will happen without your help. What counts are your own reasons. And don't try to tell me you don't have reasons. I know better. I read you more easily than a book.*

I would not know the first thing about killing someone, Amir thought.

*Sure you do. You were a soldier of sorts. You've done it any number of times.*

That was combat. I am not a murderer. I'm too old. I know better now.

*No you're not and no you don't. That's why I'm here. Admit it, Amir. You want to kill somebody.*

You know what? You should become a Baptist. Yeah, that's it. A southern Baptist. You'd fit right in, Amir thought.

*I expected you to writhe like a snake to try to get out of this. That is so you. So let me come to the point. You think you have a choice? Trust me, you do not. You and I are going to do this, Amir. We will kill that pathetic little man, or I will kill you.*

Yeah? I don't think you can make me do this.

The basso voice laughed, a rumbling, low, booming echo.

Suddenly, Amir felt flush, his temperature rose by half a degree, and his pulse rate sped up. Soon his heart was hammering in his chest and sweat was running down his face, dripping into his eyes. Terrified, he lay back in the chair, his mind screaming with alarm. Half a terrible minute later, the symptoms suddenly disappeared. His pulse slowed. He felt normal again. Bathed in sweat, smelling his own fear, he sat there trembling.

*You see? I can hurt you. I can end you. I am that little micro-bomb in your brain. You cannot run away, and you cannot lie to me.*

They execute people in Virginia, Amir thought. I don't want to die.

*That makes sense. We won't die. Not yet and not soon. We're going to thread that needle. We're going to kill without being caught.*

Crime doesn't pay.

*You should put that on a tee shirt. Or a bumper sticker, if you have the nerve.*

You just want revenge.

*You say that like it's a bad thing. Think of it as civil disobedience. That's an American tradition, right? Rebellion against oppression. These fellow Americans of yours, some more than others, murdered your Lelah. They need a lesson in the Golden Rule. We're going to see that they get it. If we have to live in a goddamn bloodbath, the gun people, starting with that dickhead on TV, should contribute their fair share of blood.*

I don't even own a gun.

*This is America, remember? They'll give you one.*

But I don't know how to shoot.

*Oh brother. Stop making excuses.*

And if I refuse?

*Then you'll die before your time. If you want a life, you're going to have to earn it.*

# *The Deal*

Amir sat on the couch on his porch. The neighborhood was quiet. It was past rush hour. The light was failing, gray dusk going to dark. With few exceptions his neighbors were indoors, having dinner, supervising homework, watching the news. Too late to be active, too early for bed.

He sat there and stared at his neighborhood. Suddenly, the view before his eyes changed. He saw it as it would appear after a decade of combat. The houses were marked with bullet holes, the streets littered with debris, the cars burned or blown up, the tires long since stolen or burned up, the trees shredded, the lawns destroyed. The scars of shooting, shelling, and panic. Starvation. There would be tribal revenge. Gang rape. There would be death, spontaneous public executions, more than anyone ever wanted to see.

Surprise gripped him. Beirut, he thought. This scene reminds me of Beirut.

He sat there, eyes open, seeing what was in his mind. He did not see what was real, what was in front of his eyes, all around him.

When I was a child, my neighborhood was downtown. Though I did not realize it at the time, it was fashionable. It had shops, boulevards, parks, restaurants. The neighbors were prosperous and attractive. I liked it. I was happy.

The more vivid picture, which came later, was different. By then the green was gone. Most other lively colors were gone too. Except red. When people died they lay in the sun in pools of red. The pools turned brown in sunlight, black in moonlight. The shops and restaurants became shells. Yes, the lively colors were gone, replaced by shades of brown, tan, and gray. Except for the bombers and the gunships, the sky was still blue.

We could not spoil the sky, no matter how hard we tried.

It was a sniper war. I was thirteen. No one said, you're a soldier now. No. They just said, here, here is a rifle. Go and shoot the enemy.

Who are they? I asked.

Jews. Iranians. Sunnis. Christians. Anyone you don't recognize. If you don't know them, they don't belong here.

So shoot them?

Yes. Shoot them, they said.

My best friend was Salih. I remember him well. He was tall, brainy, funny, and skinny. We made jokes then - he was a natural sniper, a difficult target, too skinny to hit. They gave Salih a rifle too. But our rifles didn't shoot worth a damn. Salih said, hell with it, we may as well throw rocks.

After that, we went into the city to look for soldiers, live soldiers. We would make them dead if we could.

I remember my first kill like it was yesterday. I was inside a building with three walls, looking through a gun sight, through a hole in the wall out onto an open plaza. A young soldier, a fool, was walking down what had once been a sidewalk. I spotted the man. I thought it was a trap, so I took my time, scanned the neighborhood, looking for a trap or a trick.

I didn't find one. I remember sliding the crosshairs to the middle of the man's chest and pulling the trigger. The bullet went through him as if he were pudding. It ricocheted off the wall behind him, causing a small explosion of dust. The man jerked, and fell, and lay there without moving. I watched him for a while, but he was dead. So I forgot about him.

That first kill was a surprise. I was expecting a big event. I thought I'd feel something. But it was no big deal. I found the target and shot it. Bang. Goodbye, fool.

Next.

As days became weeks, we began to lose friends in the fighting. The war became more vicious, the bombing worse. The shooting spread and became more deadly. The fighting was not between armies, it was between men, one on one.

Friends disappeared one by one.

Then I noticed, I no longer cried when I lost a friend, even a good friend. It happened all the time, so why cry? You know it's going to happen and keep happening. It's not going to stop. Besides, I was too busy to cry. I was busy staying alive.

I began to dream of my death. I accepted that I would die soon. I expected that.

One evening, Salih did not return to the basement. I remember being tired and dusty and thirsty, but I went out to look for him. I found him in a pile of rubble, in the remains of a bombed-out house. He was lying on his stomach in front of a large hole in the wall, his rifle in his hands, his head hanging down over a pool of blood. He could have been sleeping but for the blood.

I approached him and saw the hole in his forehead and the blood on the back of his head. I pulled his rifle away from him. I remember wondering, should I say a prayer? But what's the point? God takes you or He does not. Salih prayed every day. That didn't seem to help him very much. I stood up, slung his rifle over my shoulder, and made that long walk back to the basement.

Two weeks later, my family introduced me to Serena. They shipped us both away from the fighting, to the United States. An uncle lived in Mobile. We moved to Richmond much later.


Amir returned to the living room. He was alone, Serena had left the room. He sat on the couch thinking, I have a voice in my head, a Beast, not a man. Strange that he can speak, that he can do more than growl.

In his head, he heard the rumble of the bass voice. *That is not very flattering.*

Do you care?

*Fuck no.*

I need to think, please leave me alone for a while.

*You do that. Think.*

Amir sat in the easy chair, in the quiet of his living room. He tried to imagine himself as an assassin. That was what the Beast was talking about - assassination. Of gun people, whoever they were. This is not someone else doing this, this is me, or my mind, or a corner of it. I cannot believe what I am feeling, and hearing, and seeing. But it is real. It is hard to believe it controls me, but it does. I watched it. I am convinced.

Do I have a choice? If I throw myself on the mercy of a psychiatrist, they will dope me to the eyeballs and pronounce me not quite cured. I will be in 'treatment' forever, a zombie. My life with Serena will be over. Having lost Lelah, I will lose her. Then I will lose everything else.

Is therapy the answer? Even if I have my head shrunk, I cannot hide from the Beast. Unless I obey, the Beast will kill me. Or actually, I will kill myself somehow. I will have a heart attack or a stroke. Or maybe I will cross a double yellow line at high speed, knock the rear wheels off a tractor-trailer. Or I will walk onto a busy street, or jump from a cliff. There are many ways to die. The Beast will choose mine.

I never thought my life would end like this. I thought someday I would get sick and die, quietly, in a hospital like everyone else.

Am I imagining all this? Amir took a deep breath and shook his head - no, that is a dead end. I have to trust myself. I have to trust what I hear, what I see. Let's focus - how can I survive?

Can I survive?

Late in the evening, Serena returned home. Amir had not moved. She sat down next to him on the couch. She looked at him, brushed a hand through his hair, gave him a sad smile. "These are hard days."

"I wish it had never happened," Amir said.

"Me too."

Serena sat for a long minute. "I'm going to be seeing a therapist for a while. Once a week, on Wednesdays."

Amir nodded. "Good luck with it."

"I wish you would do that too, Amir. I know how unhappy you are right now. Maybe it would help."

The bass voice spoke. *Be careful, Amir. Do not tell Serena or anyone else what's going through your head. If she somehow manages to figure it out, we will have to do something to keep her quiet.*

Amir thought, I am not going to harm Serena. Forget it. I will kill myself before I'll do that. And I'll take you with me.

Gun people, okay. But no innocents.

*Then you just be careful.*

"Amir?" she said. "What do you think?"

"That therapist we talked to was an idiot," Amir said. "Telling me my only daughter is not worth all the angst. That was not helpful."

"It was an unfortunate choice of words," she said.

"What does a therapist have, except words?"

She looked at him. "I hope you can find someone to talk to."

"I've been talking to Sam," Amir said. "I think that helps. And I'm talking to you right now."

Serena looked at him and nodded. "Okay. It's a start, I guess."

Serena walked into the house, carrying a bag of groceries. She passed the living room and noticed Amir. She stopped and looked twice - he was sitting upright in an armchair, eyes closed. She thought he might be asleep, so she said nothing.

She went to the kitchen and unloaded the groceries. Good grief, he looks miserable. I need to distract him, get him away from his thoughts, get him back on his feet, get him busy with something. I know my man … he will sit there and try to figure this out. But there's nothing to figure out. It's death. We live, we die. We take up space and resources for a while. We are happy, active. Then we become sick and sad. We die. We expire, and make room for the next generation.

It is easy to feel guilty when someone dies. But there is no need. Your time will come. All of us will walk that path eventually.

Serena shook her head as if to shake loose her thoughts.

Amir opened his eyes.

"Hi there. Everything okay? You okay?" she said.

"Yes, I'm fine." He looked up. His mouth smiled at her. "I was meditating. I used to do it when I was younger. Then I got busy at the store, and Lelah came along, so I stopped. I thought this would be a good time to start again."

"Aaaaaoooommmm," she said.

"Not exactly."

"Maybe I should try it."

"Wouldn't hurt."

*You just stepped in it, Amir. Meditating is a good excuse to leave the house. You're going to need excuses. You do not want her joining you. She would not approve of what you will be doing.*

Relax, Amir thought. I'm being normal. That exchange was normal. I need to exude normalcy around here.

*Unless it is abnormal to exude normalcy.*

Oh please. Just stop.

Serena nodded. "I'll think about it."

See? Amir thought. That was a 'no'.

*I didn't hear a 'no'.*

Trust me, she just said, no.

"Listen," she said. "I've got a counseling session with Dr. Templeton. You don't want to come?"

He looked up at her. In a voice long on politeness and short on sincerity, he said, "No thank you."

She hesitated. "Anything I should pick up while I'm out?"

Amir shook his head. "Nothing comes to mind."

"Okay, see you later." She leaned over to kiss him, then headed for the door.

"Have fun," he said.

"Oh yeah."

Serena drove the old sedan onto the interstate towards Abingdon. This stretch of road had speed traps, so she set the cruise control below the speed limit. Normally, she would play a game, try to spot the speed traps early. But today she had other things on her mind.

She stayed in the right lane. Everybody passed her.

Dr. Templeton had encouraged her to contact her friends more often. That did not work. Her few closest friends - those she would have talked to in any event - were helpful. Others, more distant, would steer the conversation to the shooting. They would revel in the excitement and misfortune. It was news and different. It was entertainment.

Spectators, not friends. Oooohhhh, they would say. They would salivate and ask, then what happened?

Goddamn Jerks.

Her mouth twisted to one side. The truth is, one good friend is better than a hundred acquaintances. Perhaps that is why Amir is so reserved.

He never engages in small talk. I should ask him about that. He will probably say it is a waste of time.

Serena arrived at the police station and signed in at the front desk. She passed the large room where the police had posted information about the shooting. When she looked inside, the photos, press clippings, patrol entries, and interview reports were gone, packed away.

That surprised her, then she realized, what is there to do at this point? The victims are dead, the shooter is dead. There is no one to chase, no one to capture, no one to prosecute. The police are done here.

They will just have to wait for the next one.

She shivered briefly, then continued to the elevator and took it to the third floor. She found the small conference room and entered. The room had a small table and two comfortable chairs.

A minute later, Dr. Templeton came in. "Hello. Have a seat." She sat down and looked at Serena. "So. How've you been?"

"Okay, I guess."

"What have you been doing lately?"

Serena thought for a moment. "I've been trying to take your advice - look for opportunities to talk to people, try to look to the future, not the past."

"And how's that going?"

"Fifty-fifty. It's good to get out, distract myself with other matters." Serena briefly teared up. She wiped a hand across her face. "I'm doing it because I feel I should do it, not because I want to. You know? I'm just going through the motions."

"I hear that a lot," Dr. Templeton said. "But did you know, going through the motions works. It sounds unlikely, but it works. If you can't do it the way you want to, then fake it. Eventually, you'll find you can do it."

Serena said, "I believe you. I think it does work, some. Remember, you told me to contact everyone I knew, go out of my way, connect with people? Remember that?"

Dr. Templeton nodded.

"That's been good, mostly. I have several close friends. We do a lot together. They have been great. They sit with me, cry with me if I want that, and laugh if I want that. My best friends have helped."

"Women?"

"Yes, of course." Serena laughed. "But then there are these other friends, or just acquaintances, I guess. We get together, they express their regrets, offer their condolences. Then they want to know all about the shooting, like I'm a substitute for a reality show."

Serena's face wore a crooked smile. She glanced at the doctor. "I think there's a reason I'm not closer to these people."

"Sure. Everyone has acquaintances," Dr. Templeton said. "You shouldn't expect too much."

"I don't." Serena paused for a moment. "Then there's Amir. He is reserved, an introvert. He doesn't try to talk to most people."

"Men are often less interactive than the average woman," Dr. Templeton said.

"Amir is less interactive than most men," Serena said. "But he is smart. He has a knack for getting right to the heart of the matter. He sees what others do not. Sometimes, I think he sees the future."

Serena hesitated, then she stared into space. "He is scary at times. He is often a couple of steps ahead of everyone else, and he gets impatient. He stops listening once he's made up his mind. Often, it takes me a while to figure out what he is thinking."

Dr. Templeton gave Serena a blank look, thinking about what Serena had just said. "Interesting. How is he doing?"

"He worried me at first," Serena said. "Lelah's death hit him hard. He adored her."

"And now?"

Serena threw up her hands. "I don't know. I think he is doing better. I hope he is. Before I left for this appointment, he was in the living room, meditating. That's good. He has a close friend - one close friend - a guy named Sam. A good, strong, reliable man." Serena grinned. "Amir calls him his 'foxhole buddy'."

Serena hesitated, then said, "It is odd how events play out. Amir was an arranged husband. I was just a teenager. I thought he was a quiet Lebanese businessman, older than me, a bit dumpy, nothing special. But you know what? He is thoughtful and considerate. He's gentle. He knows how to talk to me and how not to. He knows when to be quiet. He was a wonderful father. We tried to have more kids, but it did not happen."

"So he was a good choice."

"Yes, he was."

"Tell me more about Sam."

Serena blew out her cheeks. "Oh, man, big … I mean, football player big. A teddy bear. Easy going, funny at times. Smarter than he acts, smarter than he looks."

Dr. Templeton smiled at that.

Serena continued, "He's one of Amir's business contacts. He was in the Army, tells funny stories about that. He makes combat sound like a camping trip, stories about hand grenades and toilets, that sort of thing. Rock of the earth, a good man." She thought for a moment. "They are Mutt and Jeff."

"You know about Mutt and Jeff?"

Serena looked calmly at Dr. Templeton. "We actually had TV in Lebanon."

"Sorry, I didn't know they would get American TV."

"Everyone gets American TV."

"Huh. Interesting," Dr. Templeton said. "Is Sam married? Kids?"

"Yes to both. I know his wife," Serena said. "Lydia. She adores him. Together, they're hilarious. I sometimes get a vivid picture of the two of them - he's twice her size …"

Dr. Templeton said, "I see."

Serena and Dr. Templeton talked for another twenty minutes, about Amir, about Lelah, about children, the past, the future.

Then, a minute short of an hour, without checking her watch, Dr. Templeton said, "Well, Serena, I think you're making progress. I feel good about what you've told me today. So … we'll talk again next week?"

"Yes, I would like that," Serena said.

"Oh … and Serena, I have one request. Keep an eye on Amir, would you? Tragedy and the quiet man can be a combustible mix."

Serena looked up at Dr. Templeton.

"It is true," the psychiatrist said. "They make movies about it, but it is true. Talking to people, especially when your emotions are high, is useful. It is therapeutic. The different point of view helps. Even acquaintances, whose motives you might doubt, can help. There you are, all wrapped up in your thoughts, spinning round and round. Someone else with a different perspective can distract you, show you a different road, help you stop spinning. They can show you that not everything is great, not everything is terrible. Amir will improve faster if he finds someone to talk to."

Serena frowned. "He's an introvert."

"Then that can be your job. Distract him. Get him out and run him."

"Okay. I'll see what I can do."

Dr. Templeton nodded and stood up, ending the session. "Until next time, Serena. Enjoy the rest of your day."

## *Making Plans*

I'll just tell her I went for a walk, Amir thought.

*Yes, that's a good cover. You were out walking, to get in shape. Now, where were we? Oh, yes, it is agreed ... gun people only.*

Yes, gun people only. Who are they?

*Anyone with a hand in Lelah's death.*

Anyone who could have, but did not, take action to prevent her death.

*You would have made a fine lawyer.*

No need to be insulting. So it is ... gun shop owners, politicians friendly to the NRA, NRA execs, some judges. People pushing guns.

*Yeah. People pushing guns. Leading men in action films?*

Amir thought, how could they have prevented Lelah's death?

*Never mind. Just a thought. Soldiers? Police?*

They're just doing a job.

*Yeah, but they're shooting black men in the back. Kids too. The police are, anyway. It's a black thing. I just thought I would check.*

Gun people. People who have blood on their hands, who make a living promoting guns. In America. Okay. He was walking through the neighborhood, towards downtown, the VCU campus on his left. He had no reason to be there. He was just out walking, finding a space for a quiet conversation with the Beast.

The university neighborhood was quiet, with moderate traffic, distant noise from two freeways, and a few people outside, walking, or working, or sitting. Amir looked at them. He envied them. They seemed calm. Most seemed happy. Many of them were not yet out of their twenties, in school with minimal responsibilities. Just like Lelah. Except, of course, they were not being shot at.

*Of course they're fucking happy. Lelah was happy too ... until she got shot.*

Amir winced and thought, we're drifting. What else?

*You need to learn to shoot again.*

What will I be shooting?

*A rifle.*

AK-47?

*No. Single shot, bolt action. A hunting gun.*

Amir thought, I know a bit about this, you know. A single-shot weapon is not good in a firefight.

*You won't be in a firefight. You'll take one shot. Only one. Then we turn around and leave - immediately and fast.*

Just like Beirut.

*Yes. Except that if you hit something, it'll be on the news.*

And have you picked out the caliber, honey?

*Twenty five oh six.*

Twenty five caliber? What are we shooting, rabbits?

*Have no fear. It will be more than enough.*

The AK was a 9 mm. So ... 25 caliber. Are you sure?

*While you were staring at the librarian's tits, I was reading.*

And if I get into a firefight?

*Then it's surrender or suicide. So don't.*

Shoot and sneak?

*Yes. Discretion is the better part of ...*

... Valor?

*Yes.*

You think I lack valor? Amir thought. You do think that, don't you? You think I lack valor.

*Yes. Face it, you're a rabbit, Amir.*

You might be right.

*We shall see.*

Roundtree walked into the police station and automatically headed towards the bullpen. He passed half a dozen cops, said his hellos, sat down at his desk. Now what?

He had nothing to do, no next three steps that he needed to take. He knew everything that anyone could know about Larry Bright. He knew his likes and dislikes, his political leaning (none), friends (none), and hobbies: NASCAR, weight lifting, and western style shooting. Larry was a revolver expert. The rest of his existence was the emotional equivalent of bagging groceries at the Stop N Shop.

Roundtree smiled at the irony. Like Roundtree, Larry was a revolver guy. But when it came time to kill multiple people, he left the revolver at home and reached for the Glock, a more modern, more lethal weapon, designed to kill people fast.

Roundtree wondered, is that progress?

Western shooters were fond of saying, when a man with a rifle confronts a man with a pistol, the man with the pistol dies. Yet in crowds - in shopping malls, churches, airports, elementary schools, train stations, colleges - dangerous people did not usually pack rifles. No. They packed pistols. They traded firepower for concealment, for surprise. In that world, within fifty feet, Glock was king.

Just as Roundtree was chiding himself for bouncing around in his own head, the Chief approached him.

"Roundtree."

"Sir."

"Are you ready to close the Whitetop case?"

Roundtree nodded. "I was just thinking about that." He paused, then he noticed that the Chief immediately became irritated at not having his question answered. Roundtree suppressed a smile. "The shrinks are still busy with people. But my stuff is done. The shooter's six feet under, as are most of the victims. So … what's the point?"

The Chief gave a single nod. "Good. I'm detaching you for a while."

Roundtree thought, that sounds painful, but I'm probably just imagining that.

The Chief continued, "You'll be joining a youth gang task force over in Richmond. They've got a growing drug problem there, and it's been getting violent. More violent. Our teenagers are graduating from video games to the real thing. So … you have two jobs. First, be as helpful as you can. Second, learn as much as you can. You'll be the department expert when that crap lands here. Seminars and street cops. Okay?"

Roundtree passed a hand over his jaw. "Yes sir. It sounds interesting."

"For myself, I hope it stays dull … at least here in Abingdon. Any questions?" the Chief said.

"Can I get per diem in Richmond? It's a long commute."

The Chief nodded. "You'll move to Richmond for the assignment."

"For how long?"

"If you do your usual outstanding job, they'll probably keep you as long as they can."

"Chief, level with me. Are you just shipping me out of here?"

The Chief looked straight at Roundtree. "I'm sorry, Roundtree, have I not told you lately I loved you? You need a hug?" Roundtree grinned, and the Chief continued, "I wouldn't normally lend any of my guys, but it's been quiet around here since Whitetop. I don't have an argument to keep you here, and in truth, it may prove useful for us."

"I love it when you get mushy."

"I'm here for you, Roundtree. Be in Richmond day after tomorrow, okay?"

"You got it."

"Alright, thanks." The Chief turned and walked back to his office.

Amir drove to a gun shop - *Bob's Guns* - outside Lynchburg. It was a ramshackle single-story building, with a shallow parking lot just off the highway.

The Beast chimed in, *Parking is risky here. That's one way to thin the gun nut population.*

You are so funny, Amir thought. He got out of his car, stepped into a wall of noise, and winced. *Bob's* had a deep shooting range in the back. At the moment it was loud with the boom of shotguns, the pop of pistols, the blast of rifles. Some pistols were loud, some rifles were loud. Shotguns - all shotguns - were deafening.

Amir walked into the store. It was poorly lit with racks holding rifles, air rifles and pistols, bows and arrows, camping gear, and a dizzying assortment of gun accessories. It was also quiet. A thirty-foot glass case ran along the far wall and held pistols under bright lights. A man stood behind the case. A cash register sat on top. The wall behind the case held rifles and shotguns, with a few hunting bows at one end.

Amir approached.

*You're looking for Chas.*

The man behind the case, middle-aged with thinning blond hair, looked up and noticed Amir. "Hi there. Welcome to *Bob's*. What can I do for you?"

"I'm looking for Chas," Amir said. "I talked to him on the phone about buying a used rifle."

"I'm Chas. Are you Amir?"

"Yes. Pleased to meet you." Amir held out his hand; he had learned to shake hands firmly, an American custom. It was not that you squeezed the other man's hand. Instead, you made your hand into a rock and let the other man squeeze the rock.

They shook hands, and Chas reached behind him, touched several weapons, then pulled a rifle off the rack. Next to the semi-automatics and the shotguns, this rifle looked like a toy - slender, simple, with a black plastic stock and a long thick barrel of black stainless steel.

Chas handed Amir the rifle, "Here she is. A used twenty-five ought six. Single shot. Are you planning to do some hunting?"

Amir took the rifle and held it up with one hand, trying to find the center of gravity. He shook his head. "No. Just some recreational shooting. I'm looking for a hobby, something to get me out of the house. I plan to terrorize paper."

Chas nodded. "I hear that. My old lady keeps nagging me to retire. Screw that, she just wants someone around to run errands. I like it here in the shop just fine. Except for the range noise, it's quieter than home."

"Yeah. And there's just something fun about things that go boom," Amir said. He moved the bolt and slid it back. Well oiled, it moved smoothly.

"There is that." Chas watched him handle the rifle, then said, "No offense, but have you ever fired a rifle?"

"A little bit, as a teenager, a long time ago," Amir said.

*You should keep your AK-47 exploits to yourself.*

Thank you, but I'm not an idiot, Amir thought.

Chas said, "Alright. I need to mention, our range master is a hard ass, so you need to obey several rules. First, you don't walk around the range with the breech closed. It's closed only at a station, when you're sighted on a target. Second, you keep your trigger finger straight, like this." Chas reached out to demonstrate. "You don't touch the trigger unless you're sighted on a target. And third, don't ever point the rifle at anything you're not about to shoot. Not ever. Break any of those, and the range master will ride your ass, and he may ride you right off the range. Fair warning. I own it, but he runs it."

"Bolt, finger, point," Amir said. "Bolt, finger, point. Got it. Thanks."

"Also, we have overhead lights to show when the range is live, when everyone can shoot. Green, the range is live. Red, the range is closed. That's when you put down your weapon.

"We close the range so folks can go out, take down old targets, and put up new ones. When the lights go red, you open the breech, set your rifle on your station. You'll have several minutes to do whatever you need to do to get back to shooting."

"Bolt, finger, point. Green light, red light," Amir said. "Okay. Got it."

Chas checked Amir's equipment and set him up with paper targets, a heavily packed pillow that would support the rifle, and a box of ammunition. Amir held the rifle upright, opened the bolt, gathered the accessories, paused for a moment, then walked out to the range.

Even with ear protectors, the noise was oppressive. On the far left, several men and a woman were shooting skeet, their shotguns loud enough to shake the windows, or your back teeth. Next to them, half a dozen men and women crowded into a thirty-foot section, shooting pistols at targets at close range. To the right, eight men were at stations, shooting rifles across a flat range backed by a hill three hundred yards away.

Amir carried his rifle out to the right. He walked up to the range master, who turned and glared at him. "You need something?"

The bass voice growled, *It's not obvious?*

Amir ignored the remark. "An open station?"

The range master grunted and pointed to a station in front of him. "That one."

"Thank you." Amir moved to the station, which was a modular chair with a level surface, once found in middle schools. It was solidly built, like a picnic table. His accessories were in a bag. He laid the rifle down, sat down, reached in and pulled out the box of shells. He opened the box and slid out a plastic frame holding sixty cartridges.

He picked one up and examined it closely. There was a small copper-colored bullet on top of a much larger cartridge. The shell looked beautiful and lethal.

*It's a little rocket, isn't it?*

It is, Amir thought, a lot of hell in a tiny package. He put the box and the shell on the surface of the station and put the pillow in place. Then he picked up the rifle, laid the barrel on the pillow, and sighted downrange.

Amir heard from behind him, "Hey, pal. I know your breech is open. Nonetheless, keep your finger off the trigger until you're ready to shoot."

Amir turned his head and nodded. "Sorry. I knew that. Rookie mistake."

"We don't like mistakes."

After a few minutes, Amir was comfortable with the rifle. It was heavier than the AK and would take some getting used to. Suddenly the overhead lights turned red, and the shooting and the noise stopped.

*Can you smell anything?*

Gunpowder? Amir thought, my nose is reeling at this point.

Amir took a target sheet and walked onto the range, following the other shooters. The range had a series of wooden fences at intervals out to two hundred and seventy-five yards. Amir selected a spot at one hundred yards, stapled his target sheet to the fence, and returned to his station.

The lights turned green.

He began shooting, a shot every two minutes or so, taking his time, trying to learn how to quiet his body, to hold everything still, and hit the center of the target.

At one point, Amir heard behind him, "Take your time, mister. You've got time, no hurry."

It was the range master again. Amir turned and thanked him, then turned his attention to his rifle.

*Slower, slower.*

Yeah, thanks, Amir thought. Now be quiet.

*I'll be quiet when you do it right.*

It felt like a few minutes later when the voice spoke again, "You've taken a dozen shots. Maybe with the next red light, you might clean that barrel."

"I have to clean it after a few shots?" Amir asked.

"Every half dozen or so. If you don't, you'll lose accuracy. Soon, you'll foul the barrel."

Amir turned. "I have a lot to learn."

The man shrugged. "So learn."

Amir remembered, bolt, finger, point. He waited. When the range lights turned red, he entered the range, pulled his target down, collected his gear, and went back inside the gun shop.

He went to the glass case and held up the paper target, which was rectangular with a series of concentric circles in the middle. The paper was a sandwich, two dark layers on both sides of a fluorescent sheet. Bullet strikes stood out in bright green against a black background.

Amir's target had a few hits within the circles and several outside of them. Chas looked at it, frowned and said, "Well, I see you hit the paper at least. That's good."

"It's a start," Amir said. "I'll take the rifle." Chas then offered to set him up with the maintenance products he would need - cleaning fluids, cleaning patches, cleaning rod, several types of oil. After he had loaded the bag, Chas paused. "You want a silencer?"

"What for?"

"Squirrel hunting in the suburbs?"

Amir laughed. "No thanks."

*He's testing to see if you're felonious.*

I think he was just being funny.

Chas reached down and pulled out a little paperback book. "Here, this is our rookie special. A little book on guns and shooting. Do read it. It'll help." He dropped the book into the bag.

"Thanks." Amir handed Chas three hundred dollars in cash and took the shopping bag with the gun accessories.

The Beast spoke up, *This little rebellion will not work unless your shooting improves.*

That's true, Amir thought.

*That was surprisingly easy, don't you think? We just walked in and got a gun. No credit card, no ID, no background check.*

I'm obviously 21, and a responsible adult.

*Like Larry Bright?*

Yeah, like Larry Bright. Better than Larry Bright.

*They didn't take your little single shot rifle seriously.*

I got that impression too.

*That's a mistake.*

We shall see.

Amir returned home from the range and put the rifle and other gear in the garage. The next morning, after breakfast, he took everything into the kitchen, pulled out the rifle and the patches, the oil and the boresight laser and the little book. He sat there reading and polishing and cleaning and oiling.

Late in the morning, Serena returned from a counseling session. She came into the kitchen, saw Amir, stopped and said, "What the hell? Is that a rifle?"

Amir looked up, smiled, and said, "Hi there. Yeah. I thought I'd pick up a hobby, do some shooting, just paper targets, nothing serious. So I went to a range and bought this from a guy. Two hundred dollars and change. It's a single shot target rifle. I shot it a little bit. It was fun." He held up the target sheet and laughed. "See?" He waved the sheet, "Admittedly, I could do this better."

Serena looked at the sheet and laughed. "Well, at least you hit the sheet."

"We'll never know," Amir said. He returned to rubbing oil on the bolt. "I could count how many shells I used, but I don't want to know."

*This is brilliant, Amir. Hide it in plain sight. Absolutely brilliant. These people watch too much TV. They think, if it doesn't have a big magazine, it can't be a gun. How weird is that? And if she's going to make a stink, it's better we know now.*

I have my moments, Amir thought.

He looked up at Serena. "If this bothers you, I can take it out to the garage."

"No, it's okay. I hope you'll finish soon," she said.

He peered at the bolt, rubbed it, and nodded. "Almost done now."

She looked at the rifle and said, "You know, I don't think Lelah would want you getting into shooting."

Amir stopped and looked at his wife. "Well now, there's something you need to know, oh wife of mine. Before she went to school, she was bugging me to take her shooting."

Serena stared at him. She looked surprised. "I don't believe it."

"Believe it," Amir said. "Cross my heart and hope to … whatever. I told her a story about one of my uncles taking me to shoot back in Beirut when I was twelve. She figured, she wanted me to take her shooting." His mouth contorted and he grew thoughtful, "We never got around to it. We ran out of time."

"Did you talk about the fighting?"

Amir said, "No. She didn't need to hear that. She knows about it already. It's in books."

Serena looked down. "I see."

A look of sadness crossed Amir's face, then suddenly disappeared. "How was Dr. Templeton?"

Serena nodded. "Good."

"So … she's helping you?"

"Yes. I think so," Serena said.

"Good. That's good."

Serena grew still, nervous that he might ask for details, but he did not. They sat at the table for a minute, Serena thoughtful, Amir busy. Then she said, "There's a craft fair downtown this afternoon. Would you like to go with me?"

A can of lubricant in one hand, Amir put on reading glasses and peered closely at a part. "I'd like to, but I scheduled that time for a walk."

"All afternoon? Must be a long walk."

"Two, three hours. I've been reading about grief and depression. Some doctors treat depression with exercise. I thought I'd give that a shot. In any event, I could use a little exercise."

Serena stared at him. Amir? Is that you?

"Tell you what," he said. "Go to your fair. I'll take my walk downtown, find the fair, and then I'll find you. How's that sound?"

"Okay. Maybe we can have lunch."

Amir grinned. "I'll be sweaty and stinky."

"A pizza counter maybe."

"Yeah, okay. I'll need about an hour head start," he said. "When were you going to arrive?"

"I don't know."

"Let's pick a time. Maybe meet at the fair at two?"

"Yeah, okay. Two," she said.

"Okay." He leaned back, looked at the assortment of gun gear, grabbed a trigger lock, pressed it into the trigger, and locked it in place. "I'm done ... until the next time."

*We need to get back out there, Amir, check the sights, maybe get better sights installed.*

Yes, we need to do that, Amir thought.

## *Tracking the Game*

Amir was walking and sweating profusely in the middle of a warm afternoon under a blue sky. I don't know how much longer I can go, he thought.

*Just a bit more, then we'll head back to the car.*

Why did we need to drive way up here for a walk, anyway?

*Your first target is here.*

Here?

*Yes, here. See that big office building down there on the right?*

They're all big.

*The biggest one.*

Yes, I see it.

*That, my reluctant hero, is the headquarters of the National Rifle Association.*

No kidding?

*No kidding, Amir.*

And that smug little bastard on TV? Mr. Teflon? Remember him?

*Works in there. In that big building. Right there.*

Amir stopped on the sidewalk, his mind suddenly a black, blasted landscape. He looked up at the building, a steel and glass box like thousands of others. You're up there, aren't you, my friend? No doubt on the top floor, in a leather chair. You're sitting in a corner office, AC keeping it cool. Meanwhile, Lelah's in the ground, feeding the worms.

Maybe you will join her soon.

The basso voice rumbled, a low, guttural, animal sound.

Amir thought, hot and cold running secretaries to service your every whim. Have you broken in your desk yet? Hot cocked one of those secretaries on it? Or maybe you're in a corporate jet, going somewhere nice to vacation and dine on the corporate nickel. All deductible. A guy who's got his society thoroughly figured out.

A blue chipper, swimming in cream.

No matter. You think people ought not to complain when someone is shot? You think that?

You don't understand why people would waste their time being sad about losing a loved one?

Fine.

When I drill you, when I punch a bullet through the third button down, hopefully your family won't mourn. Hopefully no one will. I know I won't.

Don't think of it as revenge. Think of it as speech. Nothing says 'fuck you' more clearly than high-speed lead.

The bass voice rumbled. *I like your thinking.*

You would, Amir thought. He glanced at the NRA building. Three hundred yards or so. The building faced the street, with parking lots on the sides and behind it. Across the street was another office building - at two hundred and eighty yards - equally undistinguished, a glass and steel box, with its own set of parking lots. Amir continued to walk towards the two buildings. He looked around. The neighborhood had many security cameras trained on the buildings and on the parking lots.

*That is expected.*

Of course, Amir thought. He did not - in fact, could not - avoid the cameras. No problem, he was camouflaged for the prosperous suburbs of Fairfax County: t-shirt and shorts, fluorescent running shoes, baseball cap - the Yankees of course - huge sunglasses, headphones the size of coffee mugs.

He walked past the buildings and was soon on a bridge crossing I-66, an interstate that hosted traffic jams twice a day, into Washington, then out.

*The police will be in cars. We'll come in on foot, shoot during rush hour, leave on foot.*

A grove of trees and light brush lined the interstate. On the far side of I-66, Amir came to a four-lane road with a stoplight. He turned right and continued walking. Soon there were no more cameras. He stopped for a moment, pulled out a phone, and tapped into a map utility.

Amir looked at the map. Okay. We are here. This road in front of us is route 29. It goes under the Beltway. Further east it becomes Lee Highway and goes into DC.

*The police will be all over the place, but especially on the main roads.*

Reversing himself, Amir turned and walked back toward the two buildings. In the building opposite the NRA headquarters, he saw a ground-level maintenance room. The door was open. He was tempted to walk over and examine the room, but under the gaze of the cameras, he did not dare. Inside, he could see lawn and gardening equipment, for the groundskeepers. Across the street, he saw a sign announcing the six reserved parking spaces in front of the NRA building. There were a couple of handicap spots.

A smaller sign marked a space reserved for the president.

*He parks his car right there.*

Yes, I see it, Amir thought. He stopped for a moment and looked back across the street. He could see the door to the maintenance room in the other building. He looked to the executive parking lot - two hundred and fifty yards, tops. He looked at the trees lining I-66 - two hundred and eighty yards from the parking lot, three fifty from where Amir stood.

*Looks like we'll need a disguise. At closing time, the groundskeepers will be gone. That room will lock up after five or six.*

Open space and cameras. We'll need to hide in plain sight.

*You scared?*

Sure I'm scared, aren't you?

*Nothing scares the Beast.*

Oh, so now you're a brand, eh? What's next, your face on a cereal box? Amir continued to stare at the building. I'll need to shoot out to two hundred and fifty yards. I'd like to quiet the rifle.

*It's quiet already. The twenty-six inch barrel does that.*

Quieter, Amir thought.

*A silencer will mess up the accuracy of the shot.*

So get off your ass and figure it out.


Two days later, Amir was in the living room, in the easy chair. He had a laptop in his lap and was studying a map of the area around Fairfax City, a couple of miles from NRA headquarters.

Serena came home and walked in through the front door. She entered the living room and said, "Hi, sweetie." She walked over for a kiss. Amir quickly expanded the map view to include all of Virginia.

She looked at the laptop. "What are you doing?"

"Looking at walking routes. I got a bit lost on a walk the other day," he said.

"You are walking in Richmond?"

"Yes. And a few other places."

"The walking is having an effect," she said. "You look like you've lost some weight. You look good."

"Thanks. You want to go for it?"

She smiled at him. "Maybe later." She straightened up, "What would you like for dinner?"

"Your company and something to eat," he said.

"I think I can manage that." She turned and went to the kitchen, humming a tune.

*You know, Amir, I cannot help but wonder if she might figure us out. First, he takes up shooting. Then he takes up walking. Hmmmm.*

Maybe I can distract her with sex, Amir thought. Keep her dizzy and cross-eyed.

*Shrewd. And if she divines our little plan?*

Amir thought, we've already had this conversation. If you know me as well as you say you do, then you know we're done with this subject.

*Alright, alright.*

Besides, everyone grieves in their own way.

*Yeah. Some talk to therapists, others eat chocolate and donuts, and others shoot strangers.*

Exactly. Something for everyone, Amir thought.

Amir turned his attention back to the map. He expanded it to show more detail. Okay, you're chief of police. Suddenly, you get a call, there's an active shooter at NRA headquarters.

*First, you seal off the neighborhood.*

That's right, but how?

*As the search area expands, the odds of capture decline.*

Agreed.

*The chief doesn't want that to happen. He's disciplined. Time is his enemy. He closes the fastest roads. He does not want the quarry to go far. He wants the quarry taking the slowest roads.*

I-66 closes ASAP, Amir thought. It's right there.

*That's right. I-66, route 50, route 29. They all close fast.*

The Beltway maybe?

*That would be one hell of a mess. But yeah, that too.*

We need to vanish. The more time passes without capture, the larger the search area. Time is our friend. We need to delay capture. We need to get out of sight, stay out of sight. We need the police to scatter their resources.

*Yes, that follows.*

Amir continued to look at the map. There's a park about a mile from the NRA. We could walk there in twenty, twenty-five minutes.

*Too long. Choppers will be overhead in five minutes. Maybe ten. Squad cars in what, fifteen?*

Amir switched to the satellite view. Wait a minute, look at the terrain to the north. It's all wooded. Miles of woods.

*We need to explore that. See if there are any trails.*

Yes, we need a trail.

*Or a parking lot?*

There are none close enough, Amir thought. No, it has to be a trail. Once we cross Oakton Rd., our odds get much better.

Serena approached the living room. "Hey, Amir, dinner's ready. Didn't you hear me call?"

"Sorry, I was distracted."

"Let's eat. Then you can distract me," she said.

Amir got up.

*Fuck her dizzy, Amir.*

Thanks, Romeo. I'll try.

As the sun began to peek over the horizon, the man lay in an alley between two buildings, a blue plastic tarp for a blanket. Some indirect light fell on his face, just enough to elicit a slight reaction, a wrinkling of the nose, not enough to bring him out of a troubled sleep.

He was dreaming of sand, yellow, tan, and golden, and of hot winds, brown and gray shadows, the muffled thump of artillery, and the rapid popcorn cacophony of many rifles firing. Then, in his dream, the sun went down and the desert sky turned blue and purple, heralding the beginning of the fighting hours.

That woke him up. Time to kill.

He reached for his rifle, the *Merchant of Death*, but it was not there. It would never be there. He shook his head and chuckled to himself as he often did - just as well it not be there. Now that he was awake, now that he was home, he did not need a rifle. Certainly not that rifle. The *Merchant of Death*. He laughed out loud. A silly name, carved into the stock.

No, no more of that.

He threw the tarp aside and inhaled the clean, crisp morning air. In a couple of hours the air would be foul with heat, yellow sun, and auto exhaust. But now? Now it felt clean and uplifting and sharp and pure. It felt like a dream of youth, like the heady aroma of glory days, endless summers, long past. Virgin air, never breathed.

He stood up and squinted at the cityscape out beyond the far end of the alley. The shadows said it was between 6:30 and 7 a.m. Today would be busy. It was Sunday. He would check that, of course, but he thought it was Sunday. He was nearly certain. The farmers' market three blocks away would open at 11 a.m. The shops would begin to open at 10. The Lord's Day, a good day to interact with tourists and suburbanistas.

The man reached into a duffle bag and pulled out his prize possession, an army field jacket, in bleached-out desert camouflage, with STANTON M. over the left breast pocket. Stanton, Michael J, Recon, sniper, citizen of the world, extraordinaire. At least, he had been, once upon a time, in a world far, far away.

Now he had an easier career and easier work. At 10 o'clock he would take his broom and check with the shops, see if they needed their piece of sidewalk swept. That would yield enough cash to get something at the farmers' market. Maybe an apple and a piece of homemade cheese.

That would get him to the afternoon. The sun would beat down, it would warm up. He would find a shady spot, catch up on his beauty sleep.

After two or three hours of siesta, he would go to the Methodist church and dip his clothes in their boiling tub. Put them on a line to dry. Later he would return to the sidewalk for a bit of money from the dinner crowd. He would wear the field jacket, create a little sympathy, maybe run into another vet, maybe a vet with money to lend. Wouldn't that be great? A vet with money. Then off to the coffee shops to see if they needed help disposing of today's paper - his chance to catch up on the news.

He kept an eye on the fighting in southern Afghanistan. Despite his coming home, the Army was hanging in there, punching back around Kandahar, continuing the good fight.

He had been through bad times, but now?

He was feeling good. Though it was a bit early, he headed over to the first-to-open coffee house. Sweeping their sidewalk took fifteen minutes and earned him ten dollars.

When he finished, the girl behind the counter said, "Hey buddy, you want a coffee?"

He shook his head. "Not at these prices. I'm still short of my first million; the market keeps reversing on me."

She grinned. "This one's on the house."

"Then yes, thank you." He accepted the tall hot paper cup, dumped milk and sugar into the coffee and took it to the low brick wall in front of the courthouse. He sat down on the hard brick and took a careful sip of the steaming brew, heavy with calories and aroma.

He watched people walk by on the sidewalk. Two policemen passed by on foot patrol. He nodded at them, said good morning. They tipped their hats and walked on. He thought, only in a place like Fairfax was there enough money for Sunday morning foot patrols. He saw a taxi drive by. He waved at the driver. He noticed the lady who ran the consignment shop, cute, pert, a go-getter. He did not wave. Why bother? She never waved back.

No problem, free country and all that. I fought for it, now I get to tolerate it.

He reflected on his life, his change in fortune. This is my town. I live here, I own it, these are my people. I know them, they know me. Whatever my failings, and they are many, these are my blessings.

He saw a man walking down the sidewalk, a stranger. So early in the morning, wasn't that odd? He watched the man approach - a middle-aged man, not dressed up but well dressed, in clothes of quality that were not new. A prosperous man who walked like an athlete, someone who took care of himself, good balance, a long stride.

He looked like an Arab. Brown skin, prominent nose. Arab, right? Or Jewish, or American Indian. Or maybe a curry Indian, for that matter. Or Italian. Stanton M laughed.

The man approached. Stanton M said, "Hey there. Good morning."

The man noticed him, slowed but did not smile. "Good morning."

"Say, you look familiar. Have we met somewhere?"

The man stopped and looked at him. "I don't think so."

"Now isn't that something. I could swear we've met."

"Where?"

"Afghanistan, southern part of the country, around Kandahar, maybe."

The man laughed out loud. "Wow. I didn't expect that one. No, I've never been there, not within a thousand miles. Thank heavens."

"You look middle eastern," Stanton M said.

The man nodded. "Father's side, but in Lebanon, not Afghanistan."

"Ah," Stanton M said. "The Mediterranean. A lovely part of the world."

"Maybe," the man nodded. "Some of it, some of the time, yes."

"Do you miss it?"

The man shook his head.

"No?" Stanton M said.

The man waved his hands around at the city. "This is peaceful."

"That's true, I guess," Stanton M said.

The man stood for a moment, thinking, then said, "Well, good day. I need to get moving."

"Have a good day," Stanton M said.

## *Visiting Lelah*

Amir was in a city, in a neighborhood he did not recognize. The neighborhood was friendly, with restaurants, clubs, and a lively crowd on the sidewalks. An open public square surrounded a large fountain, a rope of water arching through the air. Several large pieces of metal sculpture gave it a fashionable, civilized feel.

He set up a firing site in an alley between two buildings. The alley looked out on a concert hall over two hundred yards away, where a politician would give a speech. Amir squatted behind a box that would support the rifle. He peered through the gun sight, which magnified the front doors of the concert hall and made everything seem brighter.

Then Amir realized, the Beast was quiet. That was strange. When had the Beast ever been quiet?

The doors to the concert hall opened and a wave of people in expensive suits and evening dresses emerged onto the plaza outside the hall. He watched them through the sight. They had enjoyed themselves. As they emerged they chattered with each other, smiling, happy and excited.

There was a slight breeze from left to right. He reached up and touched a knob on the scope, clicked it once.

It was difficult to focus on a single individual, but Amir had learned to be patient. I can thread that needle, he thought. I can do it. He patiently sat there, peering through the sight. Then he spotted a lectern, a cluster of microphones mounted on it.

Ah, Amir thought, that is where Mr. Gun Rights will meet the press after his speech, make a statement, rally his fans.

He'll be among friends when he dies.

Perfect.

Amir adjusted the focus, looked briefly at the microphones, brought them into high detail, then looked at a gauge within the sight, a rangefinder. Two hundred and sixty-six yards. At that distance, his bullet would drop less than two inches.

He looked up to rest his eye for a moment, then saw a man emerge, surrounded by a crowd. The star of the evening. Amir let him take a position at the lectern. The man began speaking.

Amir put the crosshairs of the sight over the third button on the man's white dress shirt. He gently squeezed the rifle and the trigger. The seconds ticked by. As he was beginning to wonder if it would ever fire, the rifle bucked against his shoulder.

Two seconds later, all hell broke loose. A woman screamed. A man in the crowd pointed and yelled, "The alley. He's in the alley. There's a shooter in the alley."

As Amir lowered the rifle, he thought, how could they spot me so fast at this distance?

The crowd broke apart and exploded into motion, just like a flock of birds fleeing from a fox. Amir slipped the rifle into a guitar case - his camouflage for the evening. Suddenly, he heard multiple gunshots. Bullets began ricocheting down the alley, gouging dust and stone from the walls.

A bullet hit the guitar case and kicked it a couple of feet away. Then he felt a tug at his ear. He raised a hand to touch his ear; he was bleeding.

"Mother of God," Amir swore. How can I get away if I leave a trail of blood? He grabbed the guitar case and hurried to the back of the alley, exiting onto a dark street. He crossed the street and walked rapidly down another alley. Before taking a turn, he paused to look behind him. I could use an AK right now. Damn.

Don't get into a firefight. But I'm in a damn firefight. Now what?

Run.

Several people burst into the other end of the alley. One pointed and yelled, "There he is! Get him!"

Amir took off, ran down the street and into another dark alley. Surely, he thought, they will not follow me through this alley. It's dark and narrow. It has the kiss of death written all over it.

I sure could use an AK right about now.

He hurried to the end of the alley and paused to look back. Suddenly the crowd appeared at the other end of the alley, turned, and flew towards him.

"Fuck this!" Amir exclaimed. He dropped the guitar case and began to run. Now he was feeling the full effects of adrenaline, panic, and fear.

He kept running and wondered how long he could go before his body gave him his first - and maybe only - heart attack. Suddenly, Amir felt a tug at his hip - a bullet had hit him. He fell to the ground, rolling as he landed. He lay there for a second, stunned, then rolled over to look up. He tried to get up, to keep running, but he was injured and slow. Half a dozen people swarmed in front of him, like a wave crashing against a rock. Time froze. Amir saw a man skid to a stop, raise a pistol.

Then he saw the sudden bright flash and wondered, is it all over? Already? He held up his hands and screamed, "Noooooooooooooo!"

… then his face hit the carpeted floor of his bedroom. What the hell?

He felt hands grab him and turn him over. It was Serena. "Amir, Amir," she said. "Are you alright? What happened?"

Amir pushed himself up onto his knees and hands. His pulse was galloping. He looked at her, then he looked around the bedroom. "Jesus. Good God." He looked up at Serena again. "A nightmare. Whoa, that was nasty. I dreamed that someone shot me … good grief." He turned over and lay down on the floor.

"Should I call a doctor or an ambulance?"

"I don't think so," he said. "It was just a nightmare. Give me a minute, and I'll get up. I don't think I hurt myself. At least, I hope not."

"You want to talk about it?"

The Beast chimed in, *That's a bad idea, Amir. Tell her you don't remember all of it. Then make something up, something innocuous. Better yet, say nothing.*

"I don't remember everything," Amir said. "It was dark, and people were chasing me. I ran but I couldn't get away. They came closer and closer. Then one of them shot me. That's when I woke up."

He lay there for a moment, then looked up at Serena, "That was a hell of a nightmare. It was so vivid."

"Can you get up?"

"I think so." He pushed himself up off the floor and stood up. "Okay, that's better. No damage, I think." He looked at Serena. "I'm sorry I woke you."

"That's okay," she said. "I'll go and make a glass of warm milk."

"Don't bother, I can do that," he said.

"No, it's okay." She turned and left.

Amir watched her leave. He bent over, his hands on his knees.


Amir sat in the kitchen, sipping his glass of warm milk. Serena had gone back to bed.

That dream was incredibly scary, he thought.

The Beast chimed in, *You getting cold feet?*

If I am, what does that make me?

*A coward.*

That's harsh.

*No it's not. When a coward encounters fear, he quits.*

Maybe.

*If you let Lelah go unavenged, then you could look forward to seeing her in the afterlife. You could tell her that you were too afraid to avenge her.*

I do not believe in the afterlife.

*Then you might ask yourself, why bother? After all, you cannot bring her back. She is gone, never to return.*

I know.

*So? What's the point?*

What's the point? I was harmed. My family was harmed. My only daughter was murdered. I cannot let that pass unanswered. That, I cannot tolerate.

No one gets a free shot at destroying my family and friends. There is a price. Those responsible must pay. It must hurt, so they notice it, so they remember it, so they don't do it again.

Even if it solves nothing, I cannot let it pass.

*Old Testament thinking. And I thought you were so modern and civilized.*

Sorry to disappoint you, Amir thought.

Amir parked the car and killed the engine. He checked the time on the dashboard, 8:10 a.m., a sunny weekday morning near Fairfax. He got out of the car, extended both arms and stretched. He walked to the front of the car, put a foot on the bumper, and tightened the laces on his running shoes.

He was wearing a sun hat with a wide bill and a flap extending down over his neck, t-shirt and shorts, running shoes, headphones over the hat. He fit the headphones over his ears, turned on the music player, and slipped it into a pocket. Then he started walking.

The music played in his ears, and it was natural to let the tune call the tempo. The NRA headquarters, with its museum and firing range, was on the right. No security guards were visible. Amir smiled, they are there, you can count on it. These guys will have good security.

He could see twelve cameras on the two buildings.

He had bought a compact laser rangefinder. Looking at the two large office buildings, he stopped, pointed the rangefinder at the far building, then again at a car in the front parking lot. Slightly more than two hundred yards between the car and the building.

He passed the NRA building and continued to walk north. Two blocks later, he crossed over I-66. Traffic was bumper to bumper, moving slowly. Amir came to Valley Road, and turned onto it and soon found himself on a quiet, wooded suburban street lined with large houses. He checked the time - 8:27.

He kept walking, turned on Maple Hill, and continued to Maple Glen.

The bass voice spoke, *Who came up with these street names, Dr. Seuss?*

Yeah, they are poetic, aren't they? Amir thought. Prosperity Drive indeed. Amir snickered. No doubt a neighborhood of advertising executives.

Then he stopped and stared. The road in front of him looked like a construction site, covered in dirt, the houses half finished, many shrouded in blue protective sheeting. Weeds and wildflowers had sprouted in what would someday be manicured lawns. Work trucks parked on the street in both directions.

He continued. He stepped around several trucks and open utility ditches. He passed by all of that and turned onto state road 664, a busy road. A short walk on that, and then on to History Drive, an older, more settled neighborhood.

Amir walked for what felt like a long time. He pulled out his cellphone and brought up the map. He continued to Cobb Hill Lane, to St. Helena, and then past Vale. He checked the map again. He was miles from the NRA. He listened carefully. He could hear the distant noise of rush hour traffic, the sound of radial tires on concrete, car horns, even an ambulance siren. After crossing I-66, he did not see any traffic.

The bass voice rumbled. *That is enough. I think we know all we need to know.*

Amir walked up to the counter at *Bob's Guns*. He was carrying a gym bag with gun accessories. Chas looked up. "Hey, Amir. How you?"

"No complaints. Yourself?"

"I'm good."

"Do you have something for me?" Amir said.

Chas turned and pulled the rifle off the rack. The rear sights were gone, replaced by a short scope.

Chas turned and held up the rifle for Amir's inspection. "This little baby now has a three X sight," he said. "The mount allows you to adjust its position. This knob is windage, and this one is range."

"It's so simple," Amir said.

"Part of its appeal. Russian design. Serious hunters, especially old guys, are fond of these. They're rugged and reliable, and they give a good sight picture out to three hundred yards or so, especially in dim light."

Amir nodded.

Chas handed Amir the rifle, then held out a little book. "This is the product manual, on the care, feeding, geometry, and use of the sight. Do read it, eh?"

"I will, thanks," Amir said.

"Anything else?"

"I need a box of twenty-five ought sixes."

"Chevy or Cadillac?"

"Oh," Amir said. "Better make it Cadillac."

"The good stuff then," Chas reached down and pulled up a box of ammo. "You been shooting a lot?"

"I'll probably run out soon," Amir said.

"Any progress?"

"I reliably hit somewhere on the paper," Amir said.

"That qualifies you for house hunting." Chas snorted at his own joke.

"You made that one up?"

Chas nodded.

"Alright then."

Amir put in earplugs, picked up the rifle, and left the shop for the firing range in back. At the range, the range master saw him and nodded. Amir nodded back and thought, God, that guy is a grim little bastard. Then, instead of going to a station, he sat down on a bench, leaned the rifle against the wall, opened the product manual, and began to read.

The range was quiet. There were no shotgunners, no teeth rattling twelve gauge blasts. Two people were popping away at targets, a woman shooting a small pistol, and a man shooting a rimfire twenty two caliber rifle, a pop gun.

After half an hour, Amir moved to a station and looked downrange through the sight. He could see the targets and the fences clearly. After a short wait, the red lights came on. The shooting stopped. Amir took out a target sheet, walked to the 250 yard line and stapled the sheet to a fence rail. He returned to his station, the lights turned green, and the shooting resumed.

He looked downrange through the sight. There was little wind. The telltales - plastic strips hung throughout the range - were limp.

Amir began shooting, one shot at a time. He shot six times, then stopped, pulled out a cleaning rod, and ran a cleaning patch through the barrel. He glanced at the range master, who smiled at him and nodded. Amir smiled back and thought, that guy is obsessed.

He looked through the scope at the target sheet, where six little fluorescent marks stood out. They were two inches low of the bullseye, three inches to the left.

Amir bent over the sight. One click on this knob in that direction, he thought, and a click on that knob in … this direction.

The Beast spoke up, *You sure about that?*

Uh, this knob … in the other direction?

*That should be better.*

Amir clicked the knob twice. Then he shot twice and looked at the sheet through his rangefinder. You were right, he thought.

*That's me, always helpful.*

Amir returned to his shooting. He shot several groups, six at a time, cleaning the barrel between groups. Finally satisfied, he cleaned the barrel one last time and zipped the rifle into a soft cover. When the red lights came back on, he walked downrange, collected his target sheet, and returned to the store.

Amir approached the counter. When Chas saw him, Amir held up the target sheet. It had a large irregular hole in the middle where the bullseye had been.

Chas laughed. "I believe that sheet's dead, Amir. You have killed it."

"Yes it is," Amir said. "That's a good sight. Thank you."

"How far were you shooting?"

"Two fifty."

Chas looked impressed. "Wow. I'd say you're ready to do some hunting."

"Nah." Amir looked down, shook his head. "I don't hunt, long as there's a grocery store. Once I'm fed, it's live and let live."

"For me it's fast food joints," Chas said. "Cheeseburgers. Yeah. You know the worst aspect of hunting?"

"What's that?"

"Hitting something, then having to collect it and do something with the carcass. You can't just leave it out there. That would be wasteful, right? Eat what you kill, and all that." He paused. "I lost a friend that way."

"You're kidding."

"No. He shot a deer and then tried to haul it back to his truck. Those suckers are heavy, several hundred pounds, sometimes more. He had a heart attack. They found his body, right next to the deer. He moved it about a dozen yards, then keeled over," Chas said.

"Well, there you go," Amir said. "He should have stuck to grocery stores."

"Or cheeseburgers."

Amir stood at the gate to the cemetery and took a deep breath. He was in the foothills of the Shenandoah Valley, on a hill overlooking a state highway. It was a beautiful location, verdant and quiet, overlooking the valley, washed by warm sun and a cool breeze.

A spot from which the dead could watch the sunrise.

The Beast spoke up, *Or they would, if they weren't rotting in the dark under six feet of earth.*

Amir thought, you're funny. You should tour. Now be quiet.

*Touchy, touchy.*

Amir scanned the cemetery grounds but saw no one else there. He found himself indulging a new habit - estimating yardages to various objects. It was one hundred and fifty yards to that large old oak tree. He squinted - three hundred and fifty yards to a line of naked bushes, two hundred and fifty yards to a huge crypt made of deeply stained stone.

One hundred and eighty yards to a fresh mound of dirt, prominent, naked, and brown. He began walking in that direction. He walked up to the mound of dirt, then moved to the side to get a better look at the gravestone. It was a simple slab of white marble with three lines of script:

*Lelah Hawari*
*b. 11 October 1997*
*d. 12 September 2015*

Amir stood there staring at the gravestone. Then he said softly, "Hey, Scooter. It's me, Dad. Do you like the spot we chose for you? Your mother picked it out. I like it too. It's got a view and some trees. It's in the country. We thought about getting you a spot in the city, closer to home. But this place was so nice that …"

Amir's voice caught, and he stood up straight, looked at the sky, and took a deep breath. He felt weepy. He waited for the feeling to pass. It did not.

"Actually, Lelah, the truth is, I feel like a bit of an idiot, standing here, talking to a mound of dirt. Yeah, I know what you'd say. I should be used to that by now. Wise ass." He chuckled and shook his head. He felt tears on his cheek. He reached up to wipe them away. "Anyway, your mother said I should come out here and have a chat with you. She said it might help. I'm not sure what that's supposed to do. She says I'm still in denial, but I don't think I am."

Tears began streaming down Amir's face. It became difficult to speak. "She's a smart lady, and I don't mean to judge, but frankly, it sounds idiotic to me. Hang on ... I need a moment here." He began to sob in great gasps of air, an agonized animal keening escaping his lips. Trying to speak, he doubled over, wrapping his arms around his midsection. He clenched his teeth and grunted with the effort it took to speak, ripping each word from inside, "I know ... what's happening. I'm standing here ... talking to ... a pile of dirt. You're under ... under the dirt and you're not ... coming back ... ever." Amir was shaking with the sobs. "And ... I understand ... that."

Amir collapsed face-down onto the mound, wracked by great, shuddering, agonized sobs.

After several minutes, he stopped crying. He moved upright onto his knees and looked at the gravestone. "So anyway, I don't think I'm in denial. I know what's going on." He looked down at his shirt, now covered in front with streaks of mud, the dirt mixed with tears. He tried to brush it off. He tried to wipe the tears away but managed only to smear dirt across his face.

Amir looked down at himself again. "Jesus. I'm a mess." He sat there in the grass. Then he stood up. "The truth is, Lelah, I'm not doing so well. I think about you a lot. Little scenes play in my head all the time, from when you were a kid. I remember one time, we were at a park in West Virginia. They put an old railroad car in the park, on a section of track. Remember? You must have been - what? - three maybe. You ran over to the track, jumped high over a rail, and landed with both feet on a wooden tie. Then you looked up at me, with a huge grin on your face.

Hey, Dad, look what I can do. Showing off. Everything was new then, everything was fun. For some reason, that scene stuck in my head. I see it over and over. I see your grin ... over and over. It hurts every time. I used to love remembering that, but now I just wish it would go away. I hate that feeling. I never thought I'd be burying you. Never."

He paused to take a deep breath. "Your mother wants me ... to get more involved in the mosque." Amir looked up at the sky, as if begging, and rolled his eyes. "What's the point? I want to know what kind of God takes my daughter from me ... what kind of God does that, eh?" His voice wavered for a moment. "Why would I worship a God who would do that? That's a good question but forget about it. I don't even bother to ask, not anymore. Most people would just mumble something they memorized, then stare at their shoes."

He stood there thinking, then began pacing back and forth in front of the gravestone. "I understand combat death. I've been through that." He was gesturing as he spoke. "I lost plenty of friends in Beirut. Every soldier knows he's hunter and prey. Every grunt understands that last letter to next of kin. But this? No. No way. This, I can't make sense of. Religion is no help at all."

He paused, then continued, "I cry a lot these days, for no reason. Something in my head sets me off. For a while, after you died, I didn't cry at all. I couldn't do it. That was weird.

"I'm angry a lot. At everybody. It doesn't make sense." He looked up at the sky for a moment and ran a hand through his hair. "I struggle to be polite to people who have done me no harm. Sometimes I think I'm losing my mind."

He stopped moving and took several deep breaths, then he shook his head. "My dreams scare me. In some - most - blood is splashed all over the place. And this voice in my head just wants to kill people. Gun people. You know, people who make a living promoting guns."

Amir laughed out loud, then suddenly stopped. "I can't talk about that … to anyone. The therapist would go straight to the police, and I think it'd scare your mother. I'm not even sure I should discuss it with you, Lelah. I would hate to lose your good opinion. Of course I know what you'd say. You'd tell me I was full of shit. Okay, fair enough, maybe I am." A pained expression crossed his face. "But I just put you under this pile of dirt … and left you out here. That changes everything."

He stopped moving and looked down at the gravestone. "You have the easy part … you died. Someone else made all the rest of your decisions for you. I have to live with that. I think I'm making a mess of it."

He stood there for a long time, staring at the gravestone.

"Well, that's it. I'm just about done here, I guess," Amir said.

The bass voice broke the silence in his head. *Alright Amir, you've had your little cry. Nothing's changed. Nothing can change. So let's go. We have work to do.*

Amir leaned over and put his hand on the mound of dirt, leaving an imprint.

"See you later, Scooter, maybe sooner than you think."

His head down, Amir turned and walked away.

# *A Bullet Salutes No Flag*

Three weeks later, Amir's heart was pounding.

The bass voice spoke, *Easy does it. Just waltz in like you own the place. Piece of cake. Easy, breezy, lemon squeezy. Painters can go anywhere. Painters and white vans.*

Amir felt a tingle as the hair on the back of his neck stood up. He was wearing an Oakland A's baseball cap, white coveralls, coarse work gloves, and work boots. He had bought them at Goodwill. Splotches of white paint covered the boots. He carried a five-foot piece of white 10" plastic conduit on one shoulder, an orange plastic bucket, and a flattened piece of cardboard that could form a small box.

It was mid-afternoon. Amir had been keeping track of two trucks parked in the rear parking lot. One, a big Ford crew cab, just drove off with four men aboard - the grounds crew. The other, a white van from *Kenny's Plumbing Pros*, was right behind it, with three men.

*Okay, Amir. Showtime.*

Amir entered the main lobby of the building. It was a standard layout - tile floors, with stone in high traffic areas. Steel and chrome decorated the surfaces. Large pieces of meaningless, mediocre art adorned the walls.

Inside the door, Amir stood the conduit upright and stopped. He looked around. It was not a high-security building. There were two guards, at opposite ends of the lobby, but no x-ray or chemical scanner. Amir felt one of the guards staring at him.

The bass voice whispered. *He's checking us out. You need to move. Nobody just stands around in this place.*

Relax, Amir thought. I'm a painter, remember? We take our time.

*What do we do if we're challenged?*

Stand still and answer. We cannot run.

*That guard is giving you the once over.*

For effect, Amir felt in two pockets and pulled a piece of paper out of the second one. The guard did not react.

He did not mind my going through my pockets. He looked down at the piece of scrap paper.

*Oh yeah? Here he comes.*

The guard approached Amir.

*Now would be a good time to have a pistol. An automatic. With a spare clip.*

Just stop it. Try hard not to be stupid. Amir watched the guard approach. He stood there thinking, stay cool, stay cool, please stay cool.

"Uh, sir, could you move to the side with that ... stuff. You're blocking a door," the guard said.

"Oh." Amir looked behind him, then smiled as if embarrassed. "I am, aren't I? Sorry." He picked up the conduit and moved to the side, away from the traffic.

"Thank you," the guard said. He turned and walked back to his post.

*Whew. Impressive. Your luck is holding.*

A desk with two people was at the center of the lobby, two banks of elevators beyond it. Amir picked up the conduit and approached the desk. A young man looked up. "Can I help you?"

"Yeah. I'm with Kenny's Plumbing. We sent people here earlier to do a repair. I'm here with something they need."

One of the men looked at a computer screen. "B2. Second basement," he said. He pointed a pen to his right. "You can take the stairs over there or the elevators." He pointed the pen behind him.

"Do I need to sign in?"

"Yes. And I need some ID."

"ID?" Amir said.

"Yeah. You know - a driver's license?" the man said.

Amir looked embarrassed. He felt in a pocket. "Uh … I don't have ID. I must have left it in my other pants."

The man stared at Amir. "You don't have a driver's license?"

*Amir, get away from this asshole or I'm ripping his fucking throat out.*

Now who's scared? Amir thought.

"Yes, I have one, but not with me," Amir said.

"How did you get here?"

Amir motioned with a thumb. "With one of the other guys." He stood there trying to look helpless, but not too helpless. "Look. I'm just here to help my guys fix a couple of toilets. If I need ID, I guess we can come back later," Amir said.

The man leaned back and stared at Amir. Then, deciding, he motioned to a visitor register. "Sign here. Next time, bring your ID. You need it to get into some places."

"Sorry, my mistake. Thanks," Amir said. He signed the register, *Salih Nefti,* and noted the time. Then he hoisted the conduit and walked across the lobby toward the stairs. One of the guards took two steps and opened the door for him.

"Thanks pal," Amir said.

The guard nodded.

*I can't believe this. I can't believe we got in.*

Amir moved down a corridor. This isn't the NRA. This place isn't exceptional at all. No need for them to be paranoid.

*Yeah, we're not shooting them, we're just shooting one of their neighbors.*

Exactly. Someone else's problem.

Amir went down to the second level of the basement and waited. Electrical equipment for heating and cooling lined the walls; pipes and conduit crisscrossed the ceiling. It was a good place to hide. No one was down there. There were no cameras in either the basement or the stairs. Amir found the bathroom. He put blue tape, in an 'X' design, in several locations.

*What's with the tape? Secret code for painters? Does it mean, cut here first?*

Something like that. A diversion, in case someone checks the work.

Just before close of business, he hoisted the conduit, went upstairs, exited the building, and approached the outside door to the maintenance room. It was locked. He looked around, then put the conduit down and took a small pry bar out of the bucket. He shoved it between the door and the door jam and pushed. The lock sprang open.

The bass voice spoke. *The tools and lawn mowers weren't worth a deadbolt?*

Yeah, Amir thought, this building is second rate. Smaller trade associations and non-profits with lousy security. That's just economics. Some folks can't afford it.

*Let's face it. Some places - most places - aren't worth terrorizing.*

Amir pocketed the work gloves, pulled on a pair of surgical gloves, entered the room, and closed the door. He worked the cardboard into a 12" box, with small slits in opposite sides, just large enough to admit the barrel and the scope's line of sight. He moved a folding chair next to a larger box, on top of which he placed the 12" box. He looked around, picked up a brick, and placed it on top of the box.

He peeled back a piece of duct tape that covered one end of the conduit and extracted a rifle topped with a sight mount. He clicked the sight into place, tightened a small fastener, and leaned the rifle against the wall. Then he unlocked the door, went outside, and closed the door behind him. He lit a cigarette and took an occasional puff, blowing smoke slowly through his lips. Amir stood there, hoping he looked like a contract painter, enjoying a cigarette at the end of a workday. Then he went back inside the room, leaving the door ajar.

*You remember what this guy looks like?*

An Italian movie star? Slightly pretty? Yes, I remember what he looks like.

*You need to be calm when you shoot. Otherwise, the scope picture will be jumping all over the place.*

I know, Amir thought.

*Maybe he's not in his office. He might be on travel. He might have a meeting that runs late. He might be blowing his secretary.*

Or she him.

*What then?*

Amir shrugged. We go home. Better luck next time.

*You're centered for two hundred yards. We're close to that now. You can just lay the crosshairs on the guy. No need to adjust anything. Just center the crosshairs and pull.*

I know.

Suddenly, Amir saw his target emerge from the front doors. He stubbed out the cigarette on the side of the building and put the butt into a pocket. He turned and re-entered the maintenance room, leaving the door open. He sat down in the chair, picked up the rifle, placed the muzzle into a slot in the box, and peered through the sight. In the crosshairs of the scope, a man wearing a dark suit and brown shoes had just exited through the front door of the NRA building. Seen through the scope, the man was walking straight towards Amir.

*You sure that's the guy?*

He matches the photograph, Amir thought. I'll wait until he turns towards that Lexus.

*That won't give you much time.*

I really do need you to be quiet here.

The man in the crosshairs pulled a key fob from his pocket and pointed it at the Lexus. The parking lights flashed.

Before the man pocketed the fob and reached for the door handle, the rifle bucked back hard against Amir's shoulder. It sounded like someone hitting a carpet with a tennis racket. He lost the scope picture as the rifle recoiled against his shoulder.

*Get moving. Close the door, quietly. Flatten out the box. Put the rifle back in the conduit and tape it in.*

Amir slid the rifle back into the conduit and taped it. Then he attended to the door and the box. He took his time and looked around the room - have I forgotten anything? After a moment, after seconds that seemed like minutes, he was satisfied.

*Go, go, go. Go now.*

He picked up the bucket, put the conduit over one shoulder, and went from the room into an interior corridor, closing the door behind him. Amir took a deep breath and headed for the rear of the building. In a minute he was outside.

He walked - nice and slow, nice and easy, a tired working man on his way home. As he walked he made sure the conduit rested between his face and the cameras. He walked out to the street and turned. Two minutes later he was crossing over I-66, carpeted in rush hour traffic in both directions.

So far he heard no sirens. Amir thought, my butt is twitching.

*Worry about your undies later. Keep moving. Don't stop. Hurry, but don't look like you're hurrying.*

He turned left at Valley Road. A minute later he heard a helicopter flying overhead, then he heard a couple of sirens in the distance. Police sirens. Without looking up, he kept walking - long strides, slow gait. The helicopter hovered over the NRA building. He heard an ambulance siren; it was approaching. A second helicopter arrived and began flying a slow circle over the neighborhood. Then a third helicopter arrived. A fourth helicopter landed near the NRA building.

Moving through a wooded area, Amir heard another police siren. This one was close and approaching fast. He took several quick steps to back up off the road and into the trees. He stopped. A police car sped by, its siren blaring, blue lights flashing. Amir stood there, frozen.

*You can breathe now.*

Shut up, he thought.

Amir turned onto a pedestrian/bike path - a nice one, wide, done in concrete. He continued walking and was soon under a green, leafy canopy, in dark shadow. He could hear sirens in the distance, first three, then two more. Twenty minutes later, Amir could still hear multiple sirens, but they stayed far away.

*Sounds like all hell is breaking loose back there. You think you got him?*

We'll know soon enough, Amir thought. I didn't try to look.

*Too bad. That picture would be worth having.*

You'll be able to find plenty of pictures on the internet.

*Not the view through the scope, you won't. The internet won't have that one.*


Roundtree sat in a lecture hall with a couple of hundred cops. The subject was youth gangs in and around Richmond, Washington,

Petersburg, and Portsmouth - the poorest and most dangerous neighborhoods in Virginia. There are people in those places who'll kill you for fifty bucks. You might think, fifty bucks? That's all it costs?

Roundtree smirked. It's fifty bucks because anybody can do it. Many people have guns. Many are dumb enough to use them. Some of those know how to use them.

Welcome to supply-side economics, white boy. Now, give me your wallet. Okay, thanks, and one more thing ... BOOM. You can do your testifying in heaven.

The seminar, at the University of Richmond, had many flavors of law enforcement personnel. There were urban and rural policemen, detectives, forensic investigators, anti-drug and anti-corruption cops, financial investigators, a couple of hundred men and women trying to contain the energy and enterprise of young hoodlums. Gangs were everywhere trying to make a dollar by stealing it or breaking a law or even a person if necessary.

Roundtree felt old. In this crowd he was old. The anti-drug guys, young and fashionable in their death-wish manner, spoke a language he did not recognize. That more than anything else made him think, maybe he had been in this job too long.

Two young men sporting short beards, long hair, t-shirts, belt badges, and Glocks were talking, one telling a story. Roundtree heard, "He shows lookin' to cop a dime, thinkin' he's all that, thinkin' maybe he'll jack us, so's we bum rushed him. Nuff o dat shit."

His friend grinned and giggled. Roundtree stared. What the hell was that all about?

Then Roundtree heard the familiar little jingle, his phone announcing a text message. He looked at it, a single line from his Chief,

*Call me now. Right fckg now. Chf.*

Roundtree stood and began to excuse himself as he moved down the aisle, squeezing past men who were, more often than not, large. As he moved, cellphones began to go off around him.

It almost sounded like a concert. Half of the cops there were fumbling for cell phones. Something just happened.

He finally fought his way out of the lecture hall, found a quiet spot in a corridor, and called his boss, "Chief, this is Roundtree. What's up?"

"Roundtree, thanks for getting back," the Chief said. "All hell is breaking loose. Someone just shot the president …"

Roundtree's mouth dropped open.

"… of the NRA."

Oh. Roundtree relaxed. "Where?"

"NRA headquarters, up in Fairfax. So drop whatever you're doing, get up to Fairfax City, introduce yourself to Max Pressler. He's the …"

"I know Max," Roundtree said. "We're friends, known him twenty years."

"Good. They're forming a multi-agency task force, local cops, some city PD's, even the FBI has a piece of it. Max is coordinating the task force and recruiting investigators. He asked us to contribute, so you're it. Your detachment just moved from Richmond to Fairfax. Try not to screw up."

"You can count on me, Chief."

"Actually, I know I can, Roundtree. Thanks. And good luck," the Chief said. The phone beeped again, and the line went dead.

Jesus. The president of the NRA. Who would want to shoot the president of the NRA?

Then Roundtree laughed. Duh. Many people. Some people don't like guns. Moreover, the NRA got a large fraction of Congress elected. Some people don't like Congress.

And many people have guns. How many of them might be pissed off enough to do something about it?

Maybe one? 'cause that's all it takes.

Roundtree stood in the corridor, thinking. The president of the NRA. There are not many people whose murder would shock everybody. The President of the United States, of course. The Pope. The CEO of Apple, definitely. Academy Award winners. The Fed Chair. And maybe, arguably, the president of the NRA. He might be in that class. Yeah, he would have country rock star status.

Jesus Christ Almighty.

Amir came in through the front door. "Hello. I'm home."

He looked into the living room, did not see Serena, then moved into the kitchen and found her at the kitchen table.

"You just missed dinner," she said. "Where were you?"

"I went for a walk up around Gainesville. I was looking at their civil war park. Well, one of them, anyway. I managed to get myself lost."

"Use your map," she said.

"Yes, thank you. I did. I'm not dim, you know. The map on my phone was wrong. I found places that weren't on my map," he said.

The bass voice rumbled. *You mean, they weren't on the map of Gainesville.*

Shut up, asshole; you can be funny later. Amir leaned over and looked at what she had just finished. "You want to keep me company while I eat?"

"Sure."

Amir opened the fridge and pulled out a big bowl containing a spicy mixture of rice and pumpkin. It was still warm. He smelled it and a look of lust crossed his face. He turned and noticed Serena's coffee cup.

"You need a refill?" he said.

She shook her head.

He dished out a pile of rice and pumpkin and put it in the microwave. Two minutes later, he pulled it out, and the smell filled the kitchen.

Amir sat down, took a bite, and then looked up in happy satisfaction. "So ... what did you do all day?"

"I saw Mimi and Sarah for lunch, and we did a little shopping in the afternoon," she said. "Didn't buy anything."

"I've noticed that," he said. "You go shopping with a friend, you never buy anything. You go alone when you're actually buying stuff."

"Shopping is all about the company."

Amir nodded. "Like American football for men. The game lasts long enough to go through a six-pack and a couple of pizzas. Actually, maybe a couple of six-packs."

"I suppose. But you never watch American football, not even with Sam."

"I didn't play as a kid," he said. "I like soccer, once in a while."

"While I'm out, you want me to pick up anything?" she said.

"Nothing comes to mind."

The Beast chimed in, *You need more practice ammo. You probably ought not to mention that. Not that it matters, I doubt Macy's carries ammo. But if they did, it would be the best.*

Yeah, blessed by John Wayne, Amir thought.

*Who?*

Never mind. Damn, I feel buzzed. You know what I feel like? I feel like having sex. Is that normal?

*Who cares? It's sex. If you're nice to her, maybe she'll let you fuck her. You should go for some horizontal calisthenics, a little rock and roll. You earned it today.*

"So tell me," Serena said. "What's Gainesville like?"

Amir looked up from his meal. After a brief pause, he swallowed heavily and said, "Have you ever been somewhere that you looked around, at the buildings, at the city, at whatever they built, and wondered, why'd they bother? Why'd they stop here? Why didn't they just keep going to some other place, some better place? Ever been in a place like that?"

"Sure. Syria."

"Yeah, well, that's Gainesville. It's a truck stop. Their best attraction is a big civil war park."

Serena stared at a wall for a moment. "Let's see … the north won their civil war. Wasn't that a long time ago?"

"Yeah. The south won the battle at this park, though," he said. "Two battles, in fact. South won both."

"Huh. That's unusual."

He talked around a mouthful of food. "I guess the first beating didn't convince."

Serena nodded. She watched him chug through the plate of food. "Would you like to watch the news?"

"National, yes. Not the local," he said.

"I know," she said. "There is no news …"

"… on the local news," he finished her sentence. "But they've got the best news babes."

Serena shook her head in dismay.

"You don't agree?" Amir said.

"The men aren't much to look at," she said.

"Yeah, makes you wonder if women watch the news. Now I think about it, men don't watch the local news either. Just the babes."

"You're speaking for yourself?"

Amir nodded. "Sure." He turned and looked at the clock in the kitchen. "Twenty minutes. I can squeeze in a shower." He stuffed the last of the food into his mouth and stood up. Serena laughed at him. He left the kitchen. Soon she heard the shower running.

Ten minutes later, Amir returned to the kitchen. He hovered over Serena. "You may now kiss me."

She did that. Then they moved into the living room, turned on the TV, and sat down side-by-side on the couch.

The picture formed of a news anchor with a grim expression,

"Assassination rocked the political landscape today. A gunman shot and killed Marcus Long, the president of the National Rifle Association. Cheryl Bradley is reporting from the crime scene at NRA headquarters in Fairfax, Virginia. Cheryl, what have you found out?"

The picture changed to show a young woman reporting on the shooting. So far, no one mentioned seeing a gunman or hearing shots. No information on a suspect or a possible motive. Amir stopped listening and stared at Ms. Bradley's breasts. She began to speculate about what might have happened. Amir tried to picture her as a redhead. He shook his head - she didn't know anything.

The bass voice gloated. *Well, well, well. We got him. Nice work, Amir. So far, no mistakes. Nobody knows nothing.*

Next to him, Serena was staring at the screen in shock, "My God." She turned to Amir. "What is the world coming to?"

Amir looked at the screen, which showed the NRA headquarters, the Lexus, and the parking lot, all encircled in yellow police tape. Several policemen were standing near the Lexus, talking.

Looks like we finally got on the scoreboard, Amir thought.

*You know what they say.*

No, what do they say?

*Only a good guy with a gun can stop a bad guy with a gun.*

Does anyone really believe that?

*People - some people - believe all sorts of crazy things. The police will be looking for you.*

How?

*Let's see ... the forensic guys might pull off a miracle. And there are the cameras; no telling how good they are. So far, it seems you got away clean. The game's just starting. You just butt-fucked the NRA. One thing, though - that rifle just became a major liability.*

Amir suddenly heard the TV announcer again: "Mr. Long leaves behind a wife and five children."

Amir thought, I'll bet they're having a rough night.

*You should know.*

I'll bet Serena doesn't want to have sex.

*You don't know that. She might. Sex and violence are like carrots and peas. It's evolution, baby. Women go for the biggest, roughest dick. It makes them feel safe. It tells them their children might be safe.*

Amir thought, How exactly would you know that?

*Either books or the Discovery channel. I forget which.*

## *Tidying Up*

Roundtree parked his cruiser in the parking lot behind the NRA headquarters building, killed the engine, and got out. He looked up at the building. It was a big bastard, a big box of glass and steel. A hive for worker bees. He grunted. Making sure Americans had enough guns paid well.

He ran his hand over his holster. It was empty. He wondered, do I need a weapon? Not likely. In this neighborhood, if I need it, I can borrow it.

He began walking towards the front of the NRA building. Yellow police tape encircled it and the building across the street. A policeman stood between the buildings, in the middle of the road, directing what little traffic there was. Beyond, in both directions, the road was closed to the public.

He had phoned Max Pressler. The police had nothing at the moment. It was a clean crime scene. Thanks for your help. There will be a briefing later in the day.

Roundtree came to the tape and ducked under it. He looked around; a dozen patrolmen were keeping people outside the tape. He walked across the ground, surprised that no one challenged him. Do I look that much like a cop? That's depressing.

Is it time to buy a new suit? Can I get a wash and wear version? Do they make that? Or maybe I should shop at Goodwill, with the immigrants and the junkies.

He approached a patrolman and peered at his badge. "Hello there, officer ... Buxton. I'm Dan Roundtree, from Abingdon."

The man nodded. "You're expected."

"Can you tell me anything?"

The patrolman waved a hand at the neighborhood. "Numerous cameras here. The victim was hit on the walkway in front, right over there." Roundtree's gaze followed the officer's gesture. An evidence team had already left their markers all over that spot.

"Did the victim say anything?"

"No reports."

"Too bad," Roundtree said. "Where was the shooter?"

"That building across the street. Forensics is looking at a maintenance and storage room. You can see the door, there, on the right." He pointed.

Roundtree looked at the building. Two hundred yards, too far for a pistol, so it's a rifle. Great. That's just great. Who are you, my man? Are you a real sniper, a combat vet, or just somebody who watches too much TV?

"Okay, thanks. I'll mosey on over there."

The patrolman nodded.

Roundtree thought, Christ, I hope you're not a combat vet. A lot of soldiers discharge with PTSD, but only a few get treated. All of them can shoot. He winced, then he crossed the street and walked across the grass, stepping carefully and looking down to see if anything small might be lying in the grass. Nothing.

He came to an outside door, then stopped. He reached into his pocket, extracted a pair of blue latex surgical gloves, and put them on. He looked closely. An evidence team had already dusted and marked the door, so Roundtree used two fingers gently to turn the knob, opened the door, and entered the room.

He found the light switch, looked for an evidence tag, and turned on the lights. He closed the door and stood there. He smelled cordite. The room stank from it. He looked around the room but saw no other evidence tags.

He opened the door, by a foot. Then he stood in the middle of the room and looked out … and found himself looking right at the executive parking lot in front of the NRA building.

"Huh." That was easy.

Roundtree opened the door, turned off the lights, and exited, closing the door behind him. He found a technician and told him to have a chem team and a print team cover the room, starting with the inside of the door and the door frame.

The technician said, "Our guy probably shot from there."

Roundtree nodded. "Smells like it."

"I missed it. My allergies are acting up. Anything else?"

"Scour these grassy areas. The parking lot in back, too. The guy might have dropped a cartridge, or his driver's license," Roundtree said.

"That'd be nice."

Roundtree smiled. Nice. Yeah. You never know. We might get lucky. Don't underestimate the power of stupid.

He returned to the door and stood there, facing away from it. Okay, my man, you like to shoot from a bit of a distance. Too close for a military sniper, but you might be ex-military. Most of the shooting in urban combat is less than two hundred and fifty yards.

You like to have a plan. You see all these cameras. How can you avoid them?

He kept looking and thought, not in front. Too many cameras. You don't want to be in front anyway. That's where all the commotion is. No. You want to leave by the back.

Roundtree walked around the back of the building, to the parking lot. He counted six security cameras aimed at various parts of the parking lot. Well, the back of the building is not so good.

Then he walked around to the side of the building, stopped, and looked around. At the top of the building, way up high, was a single camera.

Uh huh, Roundtree thought, one camera, just one. Well now, that's a bit more promising, isn't it?

That afternoon, Roundtree went to the police station in Fairfax City, to a meeting room on the sixth floor. He walked in, saw a long conference table, and sat down in the middle of it. Max Pressler entered the room, saw Roundtree, and nodded to him.

Within a minute, three men and two women entered the room. Pressler straightened up in his chair. "Welcome everyone. Welcome to the task force. Our job is to catch the guy who shot the NRA president. Also to make sure the shooting stops."

There was a collective groan from the participants.

Pressler nodded and handed out single sheets of paper. "The Commonwealth of Virginia appreciates your help. I'm giving each of you an info sheet for the task force. It has names, emails, phones, and assignments of everyone in this group.

"Let me start by talking you through the members and the assignments."

He gestured towards a middle-aged woman who looked like a school teacher, bookish, polite, a bit round. "This is Kelly Nelson. She's a criminal psychiatrist, out of Fairfax." Ms. Nelson looked around the table, nodded to a couple of acquaintances.

"Next to her is Rick Summers, out of Portsmouth."

A bald, heavyset white man said, "Hi guys."

"He'll be our tactical officer," Pressler said.

"Next to Rick is Heywood Miles, out of Richmond." A thin black man with a mustache nodded to others at the table. "He'll be handling your data requests. He'll also be our liaison with the FBI."

"Next to him is Dan Roundtree, out of Abingdon. He'll be handling field work and forensics."

"Hi everyone," Dan said.

"Next to Dan is Ed Shapiro, out of Roanoke. He'll be handling field work. He's also a sharpshooter." A tall, thin man nodded to everyone.

"And this is Elaine Wisler, out of Newport News. She'll be handling fieldwork and interviews." A young woman looked around the room, nodding at people. Roundtree thought, she looks about thirteen, fourteen tops. Unthreatening, good material for an interviewer.

"Okay," Pressler said. "Dan, Ed, and Elaine have been at the building. I'd like you three to tell us what you know."

Roundtree looked around. "I'll kick off. The shooter had some skill. He shot Mr. Long from a maintenance room. A rifle shot, a bit over two hundred yards. Probably not military. So far, he left behind no evidence - no shells, no prints, nothing to show he had been there. Except the smell of cordite. That lingers. I told the lab guys to go over a couple of items, but I suspect the site is clean. I'm looking forward to seeing the security tapes." He leaned back in his chair.

Ed Shapiro said, "I explored the neighborhood. So far, no one saw our guy. He exited the scene quickly. Fairfax PD reacted fast but saw nothing, and there was no pursuit. If it were me, I'd have a pre-planned route, most likely to the north. That neighborhood is miles of heavily wooded suburbs, with big houses, big yards, parks, and walking paths."

He turned to Elaine Wisler, who said, "We're waiting for the medical examiner's findings. I spent a day talking to security people at the NRA and across the street. There are several retail establishments, so I talked to a few of their employees. This guy was a ghost. No one saw anyone out of the ordinary. One thing is strange - no one heard a gunshot. The first people to get to Mr. Long thought he had had a heart attack. Only after they saw blood did they figure out he'd been shot."

Pressler said, "Nobody heard a shot? A silenced rifle, maybe?"

Shapiro shook his head. "A silencer screws up the aim. A two hundred yard shot might be workable, but it would be easy to miss."

Everyone sat there, thinking for a long moment.

Miles said, "We need to know exactly how fast the PD closed down the roads."

Pressler said, "Like Ed said, they were fast. Twelve minutes to the first chopper, thirteen to the first car."

Summers interrupted, "C'mon guys, you're spinning. We need to know what to look for. Why did somebody want to kill Mr. Long? Was it personal or business? Was it a contract kill? Was it political? I mean, let's face it, there is a long list of folks don't like the NRA much."

Ed Shapiro said, "Yeah, that's my main question. Was this guy a pro? Because so far, he looks like he might be."

Roundtree said, "If it's political, why shoot the president? They'll just replace him."

Elaine said, "Send a message?"

Kelly Nelson said, "If someone shoots the new president, that'll answer that."

The group suddenly became quiet, as if the air had left the room.

Roundtree said, "It might be personal. It might be a shooting victim, or family, or a friend."

Rick Summers said, "So what do you think? Maybe a hundred thousand family and friends of shooting victims."

Roundtree nodded. "A lot more than that, I would think."

Pressler said, "Yeah, but most shooters have a history of bad behavior. We can spot them."

Several people laughed out loud. Roundtree glanced sideways at Pressler and said, "Did a new study just come out?"

There was more laughter.

Pressler said. "I just wanted to see if everyone was awake." He stood up. "Okay. I knew you guys were the best before you walked in here. Nonetheless, you have managed to scare the shit out of me. I don't know that we'll catch this guy, but you have your assignments. Let's run the drill and find out as much as we can. If this guy can be caught, then let's get him."

Pressler turned as if to go, then changed his mind, and faced them again. "Oh, one more item. I might want to seed stories into the press. So don't talk to reporters. I will handle that, and I'd like our group to speak to the public with a single voice ... that being mine." Pressler raised his eyebrows and looked around the table.

Several nodded.

"Meeting adjourned. Thanks for coming."


Skip Taylor stopped himself from punching the wall. God damn Marcus Long.

Taylor sat in his office, trying to figure out what he should do next. *The Senate, the Senate, I have to get into the Senate. If I just stay calm, think it through, and focus, I can do this.*

He sat down, head down, hands folded and resting on the desk. He looked like he was praying; he was not. *I can get past this, I'm sure I can, but it is difficult. Why does everything have to be difficult? I hate feeling sorry for myself, but it's hard not to.*

*I was all set. Everything was ready to go. I did my job with no major screw ups. I got the NRA to agree to provide the votes. Okay, admittedly my big advantage was the color of my skin. Still ... a wise man recognizes his strengths. People were beginning to talk about me. I was getting good press. Average to good, anyway. Then someone shoots my primary sponsor, and the man dies. He fucking dies. What's with that?*

Crap.

So now what? Now what do I do?

Of course I feel bad about Marcus Long's death. I would not wish that on anyone. Nonetheless, I cannot afford to sit here paralyzed, wallowing in tears. I need to think. This is important. My career is at stake.

His intercom came to life, "Mr. Attorney General, I have Chief Pressler on one."

Taylor hit a button and spoke forcefully, his voice conveying a manly vigor, "Chief, this is Skip Taylor. Thanks for getting back to me."

A man's voice came through the intercom, "No problem, Mr. Attorney General. What can I do for you?"

"I know how busy you must be, what with the Long shooting, so I'll be brief. I want to relay the Governor's view that it is critical to catch those involved in the shooting. It is equally critical to make sure that such blatant assassination does not become part of the landscape here in Virginia.

"This hurts Virginia, Chief. Mr. Long was an important part of the political and business community. He will be missed. So I hope you understand, the Governor and I would like to see an all-hands-on-deck effort made here. We'd like to see the shooter caught and the matter resolved. Quickly."

Pressler said, "Yes sir, I think that's how everyone feels. I've put together a task force of experts, the best in Virginia. The FBI will assist. Nonetheless, I have to caution you. We think we're looking at a sniper. It's happened before. We learned the first time that catching a sniper can be difficult to impossible. It can be incredibly dangerous. This could take a while."

"Exert yourself, Chief. The good people of Virginia are counting on you," Taylor said. His tone said, *Get off your ass.*

"We'll do our best, sir."

"That's what I want to hear. If you need anything, just give my office a call," Taylor said.

"Thank you, sir. I will do that."

"Thanks, Max. Good luck with it." Taylor punched a button, broke the connection.

Goddamn Marcus Long. Why couldn't he hang in there? If he had to get shot, next year would have been so much better, so much more ... convenient.

Ah well. Bugger him. I'll just have to work with his successor. Hopefully, they'll pick someone soon. I can wait a bit, but not too long. Hopefully the new guy will be less of a twit, not that that matters much.

Taylor leaned back in his chair and rubbed his eyes. It was not yet noon, and he was tired. I am in favor of Virginia. I am on her side, most of the time. Yet we seem to breed Marcus Longs ... guys that are frilly, inbred, dim-witted, snooty, and rich. Old money. A guy who pays a servant five dollars to wipe his ass and pretend it doesn't stink.

Suddenly, he recovered from the funk. The Attorney General sat up straight in his chair and straightened his tie. Hell with it. I'm a better man than this. I'll work with whoever takes over at the NRA. If Long offered me a deal, maybe the other guy will too.

It still makes sense. It's still politics.

Like Abingdon, the Fairfax police department had an audio/video center, three in fact. Roundtree sat at a video station, a thick software manual lying on the desk.

The screen was blank. He stared at it and muttered, "Shit." Then he found a button on the monitor with a little sunburst on it. He pushed the button, and the monitor gave a whirring sound, and suddenly a directory window appeared on the screen.

Roundtree wondered, why can't they label it 'on/off'? He answered himself, because it is a global product. So no language. You're lucky they have a manual in English.

People wonder why twelve-year-old Chinese kids run rings around us. Why is that, do you suppose?

On the screen, there was one directory for every one of the thirty-six security cameras on the NRA building and its neighbor. Roundtree saw a little icon that looked like a tic tac toe board. He pushed that and a six-by-six grid of little windows appeared on the screen, each showing the initial frame of a specific camera. He clicked on one of the little windows, and the scene enlarged to fill the entire screen. He looked around the screen and sure enough, there was the little game icon. He clicked on it and the six-by-six grid reappeared.

He thought, okay, I can drive this rig. He paused for a moment, then clicked on one of the little screens, the feed from a side camera. Roundtree looked at the manual, then keyed in a command. The date listed on the image advanced to 12:01 a.m. on Shooting Day.

Roundtree stared at that. Might as well call it what it was. The image showed a wide expanse of grass with parking lot lights to the right. At that time of night, there were no people in the image, and few lights. The shooting was later, in the afternoon. He keyed in another command, and the screen began to present a slideshow, each image showing for ten seconds.

Roundtree sat in his chair, put his elbows on the desk, and propped up his head as he watched the images march past. It was too slow, so he shortened each image to three seconds. Then he hunched over in his chair and stared at the images.

By six a.m., the images showed the sun rising. The neighborhood was in low light. Half an hour later, the shadows were sharp. He began to see more people, each frozen in a slice of time as they went about their business in front of the stutter-shot camera. There were office workers, delivery service workers, construction contractors, executives, and security guards.

Roundtree pulled out his cellphone to make notes:

*Deliveries - to whom, by whom?*

*Contract work - where, for whom, by whom?*

*Security shifts?*

He sent the note to Elaine Wisler, who was interviewing office workers at the NRA's neighbor.

Roundtree thought, I could be staring at the shooter and not know it. Can we identify people who could be carrying a rifle? He typed out a message to Heywood Miles.

*Heywood, do we have image recognition software? Can it scan images and select people who might be carrying a concealed rifle? People carrying oblong packages, for instance? Dan.*

He looked back at the screen. Could our shooter disguise himself as an executive? Then a thought occurred - not just any executive, but a guy lugging a golf bag. Slide the rifle in next to the five wood.

After lunch, Roundtree got an answer:

*The software can recognize a face. Once you specify a person, we can spot that person in a collection of images. However, the software cannot identify, say, 'everyone wearing a baseball cap' or 'everyone wearing a suit'. Sorry. H.*

Well, better than nothing. Roundtree continued looking at images, three seconds at a time. After a while, he programmed an alarm in his phone, reminding him to get out of the chair every half hour. It was dull work.

Day turned to evening. Roundtree was again looking at the afternoon images from Shooting Day. He went through the images once, then did it again, looking for packages long enough to hold a rifle. Of course, a pro might well have a rifle that would break down and fit into a small suitcase or a backpack.

Even so, you had to start somewhere.

He grew tired and his eyes were burning, then he saw a man wearing painter's overalls and a baseball cap. The man was walking around the back of the office building at 4:17 p.m. Balanced on his right shoulder was a long piece of white plastic tubing, a plumbing product. He carried an orange bucket in his left hand.

Roundtree stared and thought, my, my, what a fat piece of conduit. Who carries a piece of mainline conduit around an office building? Around a construction site, sure, okay, but construction at the building finished long ago. Who needs to be redoing their plumbing? Who needs conduit? Who needs *mainline* conduit?

What, did someone flush a cat down the toilet?

Before he left the video station, he sent Heywood a text: *There's a guy I want to track through all the images. Teach me, okay?*

He also sent a message to Elaine: *In building B, find out who had plumbing work done on Shooting Day. I got a guy carrying a big piece of mainline conduit in a building that should not need conduit.*

On his way back to his hotel room, Roundtree thought, it's probably nothing. It lets me collect my per diem without blushing. When he got back to his room, he had a coke, showered, and flipped through the cable channels, looking for a football game.

## *Reading Tea Leaves*

The bass voice spoke in Amir's head. *Have you been paying attention to the news?*

Yes, Amir thought. The investigation is up and running.

*They have put together a task force.*

Yes, they have.

*We know one of them, this Roundtree fellow. They might discover your identity.*

I doubt it. I could hardly recognize myself in that costume.

*Contractors are everywhere.*

That's right.

*Contractors and white vans.*

A bit of a cliche, don't you think?

*Maybe. We should lay low for a while.*

For a while.

*Be careful what you say, especially over the phone or the internet.*

I'm not an idiot, Amir thought.

"Terrible, terrible," Serena said. She was staring at the TV, shaking her head in dismay. She turned to Amir. "Can you believe this? ... Amir, are you watching this?"

"Huh? What?" Amir suddenly became aware of the TV.

"Weren't you paying attention? Someone shot a school principal, out in Lynchburg. An elementary school principal. I cannot believe it. Why him of all people?"

"I'm sorry," Amir said. "I was thinking about something else. You know something? I've been wondering if I wouldn't be happier not watching the news. Maybe I should focus on what I'm doing and not worry about what everyone else is doing."

"Sometimes I think we should move to Canada," Serena said.

Amir heard the Beast chuckling. *But we have unfinished business right here in Virginia. Hey ... if the NRA were in Wyoming, would we be trying to shoot its executives?*

Amir winced, then glanced at Serena. Wyoming? I'd need to move there and learn to wear a funny hat. I'd look ridiculous. No. No way. Serena would go crazy, and I would stick out like a painted rooster.

"I'll think about it," Amir said. "I hear it's cold ... but maybe Panama. I hear Panama's nice." Amir thought, this is off point. After all, gun people are everywhere.

"Somewhere that crazy people aren't running around, shooting people because 'God told me to'," Serena said.

*I'm sure she wasn't referring to you, Amir.*

No, I doubt she was. She knows my beliefs, or lack of them.

The bass voice chuckled.

"That's outrageous. Did they catch the shooter?" Amir said.

Serena shook her head. "Not yet."

"They've got to do something."

"I'm sure they will," Serena said.

Maybe the police will get busy with the Lynchburg shooter, Amir thought.

*So, our next target is ...?*

In Lynchburg maybe.

*The local gun shop?*

It can't hurt to look. Not Bob's. Somewhere else.

*Kick 'em while they're down.*

From behind.

The bass voice laughed.


Heywood Miles sat at the video workstation. Roundtree sat next to him. Both of them were staring at a black and white image, taken from a security camera at 4:01 p.m. on Shooting Day.

"This guy, right?" Heywood's finger touched a fuzzy image of Conduit Man within a larger image showing the parking lot in the back of the building. "Conduit Man," Heywood said. "A catchy name."

"Yep. That's the guy," Roundtree said.

"So what's so interesting about him?"

"We haven't found anyone in the building doing mainline plumbing work on shooting day. They did have a plumbing crew in, working on something, toilets, I think. Not a mainline repair. So why is he carrying conduit? The overalls could be a disguise. And that conduit could hold a rifle."

"Not much of one," Heywood said. "It looks about six inches in diameter, maybe eight. Most rifles wouldn't fit. I mean, forget a semi-automatic, or anything with a scope or a sizable magazine."

"True," Roundtree said.

Heywood's fingers flew over the keyboard, and the image suddenly expanded, with Conduit Man filling the screen. "He looks short, just a bit," Heywood said. "Wearing a baseball cap and overalls, carrying a piece of conduit and a plastic bucket. What else can we see?"

"I can't tell race," Roundtree said.

"Me neither, but maybe that'll come out of the other images." Heywood leaned back. "Anyway, I think we have enough. Let's run the software over these. When you return from lunch, we should have all the images with Conduit Man in them."

Roundtree grinned. "Excellent. Thanks, Heywood."

"Hey, we always get our man," Heywood said.

"We do?" Roundtree said.

"I just say that sometimes to make myself feel better."

Returning from lunch, Roundtree had just walked into the video center when his cellphone rang. He pulled his phone out of his pocket.

He had a text from Max Pressler to the task force: *I'd like to close the crime scene, take down the tape at the close of business tomorrow. Can we do that?*

Roundtree sat down at the video workstation thinking about forensics. Had he missed anything? Oh yeah, where's the damn bullet? Trouble with rifle shots, they punch right through a guy. Hell, the bullet could be out in Loudoun County.

He sent Elaine a text: *Have you found anyone who heard a gunshot on Shooting Day?*

The forensics guys had found gunshot residue inside the maintenance room. Roundtree had their report. The shooter shot from inside the room, two hundred and sixteen yards to where Marcus Long went down.

A rifle shot? How could no one have heard that? The guy shot a rifle from inside a room on the first floor of a busy, crowded office building. No one heard that? No way. No effin' way.

He got a text from Elaine: *Interviewed eighty people at the building. So far, zippo. Nobody heard a shot, not even a truck backfire.*

Roundtree decided to go to the crime scene the next morning. He turned back to the camera stills. There was an open window in the middle of the screen, a file manager with fifty-seven files listed.

"Hot damn," Roundtree muttered. He put them into a grid view, each image minimized. Then he started moving from one to another, looking at them carefully.

The software had done its job. Most of the images gave a distant, grainy rendition of Conduit Man. Several showed him in the lobby, with two dozen other people. Most showed him in the same pose, walking along, the conduit on his shoulder, the bucket in his other hand.

Three images were close-ups. One was a view from behind. The other two were more useful.

Roundtree stared at the images. He was disappointed; he could not see the man's eyes. He could see the hands - the guy wore what might have been a cheap wedding band on the right hand.

He had a medium complexion. Roundtree shook his head - that was irrelevant. The complexions of most people showed up as 'medium' on a black and white photograph.

Roundtree squinted, the guy was wearing work boots covered in paint.

"Geez, this guy could be anyone." A medium complexion, married, wedding band on the right hand. He's not from here. Americans wear wedding bands on their left hands. This guy's an immigrant or a naturalized citizen. Looks like he stands about five nine or five ten.

Roundtree stared at the screen and thought, I know you're the shooter, my man, if only because it can be no one else. If it's not Conduit Man, it's got to be the Invisible Man. But who the hell are you? What's your name? If I don't have that, then I don't have you, I don't have anything.

The truth is, I got nothing. Zippo.


Amir and Serena sat in the living room, Amir in an easy chair, Serena on the couch. They were watching the evening news, the usual litany of shootings - most in other places, thankfully - house fires, and bad weather.

Serena had her cellphone out and glanced at it occasionally. Amir was looking at a laptop, at a listing of search returns for 'NRA politician ratings endorsements'.

Amir looked up at the TV. A male announcer was talking in front of police tape, over the caption 'Lynchburg, Virginia'.

In his head, the bass spoke. *They're not talking about the NRA anymore. Is that a sign?*

Maybe. Amir glanced at the TV, then returned to the laptop.

Serena shook her head sadly and said, "Why would someone shoot a school principal?"

Amir looked up. "Maybe he pissed off a Tiger Mom?"

"Oh, good heavens."

Amir looked at her and shrugged. Then he looked down at the search returns and thought, wow, these guys have been busy.

*Yeah, look at all those scrubbed, God-fearing, heavily armed Republicans.*

Welcome to the white boys' gun club, Amir thought.

*We live in a target rich environment.*

Yep, headquarters of the free world. If we nail one of these guys, you think someone will spot a pattern? You think they'll tie the shootings to guns?

*It's more of a stretch than you think.*

Maybe so, but the paranoid will spot a pattern first, Amir thought. We'll get conspiracy theories on GunCraziesRUs.net. *Maybe they'll start shooting each other for a change.*

I doubt it. Safer to shoot the unarmed. Little kids are perfect. They're easy to kill, and they can't testify.

*I was just hoping.*

Amir thought, nothing to be done about that. We need a pol with an NRA endorsement.

*No shortage there. We want a white male.*

That's redundant.

*Someone who would be an easy hit. On the other hand, we already got the NRA President. How hard can one of these other guys be?*

Don't get cocky. It depends on where they are, where we have to shoot. Outside the White House? Or the Pentagon? Not good.

*Fair point. Okay. What have we ... let's see. Here we go, Mr. Richard Gilbertson, Republican Senator from Georgia. He is up for election next year, and the NRA is endorsing him.*

Where's he live?

*Georgia.*

No, idiot. Locally, I mean.

*Ah, sorry, Capitol Hill.*

Save him for later, after we've shot the easiest guy in the Senate.

*You don't want to take a shot on Capitol Hill?*

I don't want to get captured. Or mugged. Or shot. So let's stay away from DC.

*But you'll be armed.*

They'll be armed too. They might have machine guns. Let's just avoid DC, Amir thought.

*You're such a Candy Ass.*

Why are we still discussing this?

*Okay. Fine. We'll avoid DC.*

Thank you.

*You know, as murderers go, you're a bit of a pussy.*

And you are a whiner. When do you ever do anything? At that moment, Amir's right hand burst into flames. Amir reared back in terror, his eyes wide open. Then he realized that the fire was not real. He felt no pain, there was no smoke, no injury, and the easy chair did not catch fire. Holding his breath, he watched his hand burn, then he looked sideways at Serena. She was peering at a stitch and had not noticed his fear.

The bass voice laughed. *You don't want to know what I can do, Amir. That was just a taste. All it takes is a bit of imagination.*

Roundtree ducked under the police tape and slowly walked around the building. It was nine a.m. and latecomers were still trickling into the office, entering the building on the other side. By now the workers barely noticed the police.

Roundtree went to the corner of the building, approached the maintenance room, and put on latex gloves. He tried the doorknob. It was unlocked, so he opened the door and entered the room. He turned on the lights and closed the door.

Then he stood there and smelled the air - it still smelled like cordite. He felt the floor through the soles of his shoes and listened. He could hear a delivery truck motoring past the building. He could hear one end of a telephone conversation. He could hear a copier, running off copies, fast, one after another - kathock, kathock, kathock, kathock.

No way these people don't hear a rifle shot, Roundtree thought. No way.

So what's going on? He looked around the room. Mowers and seed dispensers filled the middle of the room. Elsewhere, there was junk. Tools littered a work table. Paint cans and chemicals occupied one corner. A stack of cardboard boxes, all folded up, occupied another. Much of the maintenance room looked like a fire hazard.

Roundtree walked over to the stack of folded cardboard boxes. He picked one up, looked at it, then flipped up another, then another, and another.

He froze. That last one had been cut. Roundtree went back and looked at the previous box. On one side, there was a portion cut out, about an inch by six inches, aligned with the lines of the box. He picked up the piece of cardboard and assembled it. Now he had a box with a top and a bottom, marked 12" x 12" x 12".

He held up the box. On a side opposite the cut, there was another cut, a parallel cut, of the same size. Roundtree peered through the cuts.

"Un-fucking real." Roundtree stood there, his mouth open. The sneaky son of a bitch made a silencer out of a goddamn cardboard box. That's why no one heard the shot.

The shooter cut the box just enough to admit the muzzle and allow a sight line. The box would confine the gun blast. It would sound muffled, maybe like a bursting balloon, not like a gun at all. In addition, the box had enough volume not to spoil the shot. When he finished, the shooter folded the box and left it behind.

Because who would notice a cardboard box?

Jesus, who is this guy?

Roundtree put down the box and sent a text to the forensic supervisor: *Get a guy to the NRA shooting site ASAP. I want prints and full chemical analysis of a cardboard box. Look for gunshot residue.*

The reply came within a minute, *On our way.*

Roundtree stood there and looked around the room. He wondered, is there anything else I need to know?

Twenty minutes later, one Garrett McCain arrived, wearing a windbreaker marked FORENSICS. "Hi there, Inspector. Whatcha got?"

"Two items, both high priority," Roundtree said. He pointed, "Test this box for prints and gunshot residue, on the inside and outside, mind you. Full chemical analysis."

McCain looked at the box. "Uh, you sure about that?"

"It was used, I think, to silence a rifle shot," Roundtree said.

"To silence … wow." McCain looked at Roundtree. "That's slick."

"While you're at it, dust those other boxes for prints, and run a black light over the entire room."

McCain said, "You mean we didn't do that already? My apologies, Inspector."

"It's okay, better late than never."

"OK. Anything else?"

"When you know something, contact me," Roundtree said.

"You got it."

## *Dreams of Mayhem*

Amir stepped out of the shower and grabbed a towel. It felt good to wash off the sweat and the dirt. It would feel good to sit down.

"You're home late," Serena said. She was sitting up in bed, reading a book.

"I went for a walk. I'm not exactly sure where," he said. "I started out in Timberlake. At least I think that was the name. I saw a sign."

"Timberlake? Where's that?"

"Up near Lorton. I know that because I was wandering around farmland and townhouse developments for a couple of hours."

*That's a good story, Amir. Keep it roughly accurate. Be a little vague on exactly what the truth looks like.*

I think she'd react badly if I said, well if you must know, I spent the evening scoping out a man, a complete stranger, whom I wish to kill.

*Yeah, you probably should keep that to yourself.*

"Doesn't your phone have a map?" she said.

"I don't always use a map. That's part of the charm. When was the last time you did not know exactly where you were? That makes the walk interesting. It's interesting not knowing where you are, so you have to navigate with your eyes."

"I thought the point was exercise," she said.

"That's a means to an end, not the end itself," he said.

"So what is the point, anyway?"

"Calm. That is the point," he said. "I'm in search of calm."

Serena nodded. "I think you've been calmer lately. You seem to be doing better."

A bass laugh was sly. *She's perceptive. Murder can be so ... renewing.*

You just made that up? Amir thought.

*Yeah.*

I forgive you.

*Yeah, and calm is good. Stay calm. It will improve your aim.*

You're all work, no play, you know that?

"I think I'm better too," Amir said.

*Really? At the moment, you're just a one hit wonder.*

Amir frowned. I'm working on that.


Amir quickly fell asleep. He briefly thought about making love to Serena, but she was tired. Reading the signals, he let her slip off and soon he fell asleep.

In the early morning hours, when the dying give up the ghost, he was dreaming he was out with Serena and Lelah, at a shopping mall. Lelah was between two and three feet tall, a beautiful child, with large, luminous hazel eyes. She got so many compliments that she would tell people - usually the granny brigade at the shopping mall - "I'm Lelah, I'm two years old, and I have really big eyes."

They were in a women's clothing store, just off a corridor lined with other stores. There were racks of colorful blouses, scarves, and purses. The store had many excellent hiding places.

At one point, Amir looked around, did not see Lelah, and said to Serena, "Hey, have you seen Lelah? I don't see her." Serena's eyes got wide in fear, then panic replaced the fear, and she began running around the store, looking for her little girl. She soon had all the sales girls looking too.

Amir thought, let's make sure she doesn't leave the store, so he went out into the corridor and kept an eye on the entrance. Sure enough, in short order, here came Lelah, running up to Amir, laughing, playing hide and seek with Mommy. When Serena finally found them, relief overcame anger, and she walked up to Lelah, picked her up and hugged her.

Later, they were in a wide open space on the lowest level of the shopping mall, the food court. It was a colorful, kaleidoscopic place, with an active and busy crowd. There were a number of kiosks, purveyors of salt, fat, and calories. There was even a display showing a luxury automobile, with a helpful salesman hovering nearby.

One moment, they were together, Serena smiling, Lelah laughing and cavorting, and the next, Lelah was not there. Without saying a word, Serena headed off in a direction, and Amir looked in that direction. He stood there and turned a full circle, staring intently into the crowd, but he could not see Lelah. Amir began to run about the shopping mall, calling for Lelah, but he did not see her, and she did not answer his call.

No one would help him. He kept wondering, why won't anyone help me?

Amir returned home late in the evening, exhausted, drained with worry, depressed. He came into the house. Serena was in the kitchen. When Amir entered the kitchen, Serena looked up, tearful, and said, "She's gone."

"Nnnnoooo!" Amir shouted and sat up fast in bed. His eyes opened. Serena was lying next to him.

She rolled over and said in a blurry voice, "You okay?"

Amir took a deep breath and tried to wake up. "Oh, God, I think I pulled a muscle. But yeah, I'm okay. It was just a nightmare. Sorry to wake you. Go back to sleep."

"Poor baby," she said. She rolled away from him.

He sat there for a moment, then he thought, screw this. He got out of bed. He went downstairs to the living room and sat in the easy chair. He could not sleep. He felt as if he had awoken from one nightmare into another.

Amir walked down a quiet street, lined with dirty businesses of the industrial sort, dealing with dirt, concrete, metal, and oil, their employees used to dirt, oil, sweat, and body odor. In the failing light, the businesses were closed, their parking lots empty, the employees gone home.

He was exploring the neighborhood. Most people who saw him would think, out for a walk, how healthy, how civilized.

It only looked civilized. He was looking for a shooting spot, a spot with a rifle at one end, a target at the other, and opposite the target a secluded exit route, hidden from questing eyes.

The prospective target was Route One Guns of Lorton, the largest of several hunting and fishing stores in Lorton, VA.

He walked past the store, a couple of blocks off U.S. 1. He thought about going in, but decided not to. He did not want to show himself to the security cameras. As he passed the store, he noted two larger industrial buildings across the street, an alley separating them. He could see from one end of the alley to the other.

Amir walked around the block and looked at the alley from the other end. He walked halfway down the alley. On both sides were high walls in brick and concrete, without windows.

If I shoot a rifle in there, the alley will amplify it. They'll hear it in DC. So, either extend the muzzle outside the alley or silence it. Or shoot somewhere else.

He walked back out of the alley, crossed the street, and found a walking path between two buildings. The path ran for three blocks into a residential neighborhood.

Amir hurried along the walking path. It was dim, with only the occasional light. A dog ran up to a backyard fence and barked at him.

Amir stopped. "Hey, fella. Good job. Are you on guard duty tonight? Yeah? Well, keep up the good work."

Amir let the dog smell his hand. He scratched its throat. The dog wagged its tail. Amir continued his walk.

He decided. He returned to his car. Night fell.

In the car, the Beast broke the silence, *Well, what do you think? Do we have a target?*

Yes, we have a target.

The weekend came and went. A high time for business. The gun shop rang up sales at a brisk rate. Monday was quieter. There were a few shooters who showed up to touch the new guns. They shot pistols a bit, but they did not buy anything. At least, not much.

The owner spent most of the day updating his books, running his forecasts and thinking about new orders. At the end of the day, he looked at the revenue total. He reminded himself again, I should retire. It is past due. I can afford to retire. Why keep working?

As always, he answered himself. Why? Because making a pile of money is fun. The kind of fun that eating chocolate cake used to be, back when my doctor let me do that.

At nine p.m., he put up a sign - *CLOSED*. He began locking up the place, starting with the back door and the front windows. Some folks would break open a shop to steal guns, then resell them. That was bad for business.

As a last step before leaving, the owner armed the alarm system. Its alarm would go directly to the distributor, the insurance company, and the Lorton police department.

He pushed the outside door open, then turned and closed the inside door. He slid his key into the deadbolt lock.

That was the last thing he would ever do. From behind, a bullet smashed through his upper chest and blasted a hole in his left ventricle. The bullet shattered, the fragments continuing their journey, smashing through a rib and finally embedding themselves inside the gun shop. The hydrostatic shock knocked him out. His heart fluttered and stopped. He was dead by the time he hit the concrete on his front steps.

Inside the shop, the alarm shrieked, with no one there to hear it.

Seven minutes later, a police cruiser came screeching to a halt in front of the gun shop. Two officers saw the owner, flat on his back before his door. They looked around and called for backup. Then they emerged with flashlights and weapons drawn.

There was nothing to defend against. The shooter was gone, damage done.

Roundtree showed up at the Fairfax PD Tuesday morning. He had relaxed over the weekend, for the first time in a long time. He felt good.

Just as he sat down at his desk, his phone beeped; there was a text from Max Pressler: *I need to go to Lorton. Join me, if you can.*

Roundtree replied, *What time?*

*Now. Come to my office pls. Visit a crime scene. Bring what you need.*

Roundtree checked the charge on his phone, then walked to Pressler's office. The door was opened, so Roundtree knocked twice and entered.

"Hey there, Dan," Pressler said. "We had a shooting yesterday evening in Lorton. Lorton PD will take the lead, but our forensics is better, so we'll help them with that."

"Okay."

Pressler looked at him. "You don't carry a sidearm?"

"Oh, do I need to shoot someone?" Roundtree said. Pressler stared at him, so Roundtree said, "I usually don't carry a gun. If I need protection, I'll sometimes pack a tactical flash and a Taser."

"Interesting," Pressler said.

"I disarm with charm," Roundtree said.

"Charm."

"Yes, sir."

Pressler pursed his lips. "If you say so."

They walked to Pressler's car, a dark Chevrolet sedan, and left the parking lot. Soon they were cruising along, passing traffic on the Fairfax County Parkway.

At one point, Pressler asked, "Anything happening with the NRA shooting?"

Roundtree shook his head. "Not much. I think this guy was a pro. He left no tracks. We have some grainy photos. That's it."

"Oh, Jesus," Pressler muttered. "That's all we need."

Roundtree began gesturing as he talked, "He's all over the security cameras, dressed as a contractor, white overalls, baseball cap, but we see no identifying marks, not even his face. After about three p.m., he stops showing up on camera, even though the shooting didn't occur until five ten. We think he walked in and walked out. So no car, no tire tracks, no plates," Roundtree said.

"So what are you doing?"

"The team is branching out, conducting interviews over a wider group of people, mostly shop employees and residents in nearby neighborhoods. And we're looking for anyone running private security cameras."

"Sounds like the ground campaign has run into mud," Pressler said.

Roundtree nodded. "So what's in Lorton?"

"The owner of Route One Guns was closing up Monday evening. He goes outside a bit after nine p.m., turns to lock his door, and someone shoots him in the back. We have it on the security tapes. The Lorton guys think it was a rifle."

"A rifle?"

"Maybe. Probably. It's a question."

"Any leads?" Roundtree asked.

"Not yet. Remind you of anything?"

"I hope not."

They drove in silence the rest of the way. Fifteen minutes later, Pressler slowed and parked down the street from Route One Guns. Several police cruisers were parked on the block. Yellow tape encircled the gun shop and a commercial building directly across the street.

Pressler and Roundtree got out of the car and walked towards the gun shop. Roundtree said, "Looks like the NRA scene. Buildings across the street from each other, the shooter fires from one building to another, after business hours."

"Coincidence?"

Roundtree shrugged.

They ducked under the police tape, walked up several steps and entered the gun shop. Pressler approached a detective. "Hey Mick. This is Dan Roundtree. He's working the NRA shooting."

The detective nodded at Roundtree.

"What do you have here?" Pressler said.

Mick said, "The owner was shot in the back as he was locking up, dead when found. The bullet hit him, and the fragments blew through the door. We've been searching for them all morning. We found a couple."

"What kind of gun?"

"A rifle, 25 caliber," Mick said.

"That might have been used in the NRA shooting," Roundtree said.

"You don't know yet?" Mick said.

Roundtree shook his head. "Last I checked, we hadn't found the bullet."

"You think they're connected?"

Pressler shrugged. "Two victims, both male, both involved with the gun trade. Maybe."

"How many times was he shot?" Roundtree said.

"Once," Mick said.

Roundtree nodded. "Uh huh. Have you found the shooting site?"

"That alley across the street."

Roundtree turned and looked through the front window at the alley. It was dark all the way down, then light at the far end. He needed to come back in the evening, to see what it looked like in low light.

Roundtree left the gun shop and crossed the street to look at the alley. You are so slick, aren't you, my man? I'll bet you quieted the shot.

If you fired a rifle from within that alley, with concrete walls on both sides, it'd be incredibly loud. Everybody within a mile would hear it. 911 would light up. Yet if you silenced it and shot from the near end of the alley, nobody would hear anything.

That's what you did; you took your shot, your absurdly close shot, collected yourself, and walked out the other end of the alley.

Except that a blind man could have made this shot. Do you have a confidence problem, my man? Or was this one just for convenience?

Or is this something else entirely? That thought stopped Roundtree for a moment, then he thought, two rifle shooters, same town, same time?

No way.


Amir sat in the easy chair in the living room. His laptop was open and he was reading headlines, every so often stopping to read an entire news story. In front of him, the TV was on, tuned to the local news, the sound off. Amir could see the headlines scrolling across the bottom of the screen. Since the headlines repeated, he quickly learned what the station had to say without the screech of advertisements.

In the prior quarter, GDP increased by point three percent. Another savings and loan emerged from bankruptcy. Someone crashed a self-driving automobile. An actress Amir admired - or, to be honest, lusted after - had finished rehab. For the fourth time.

He wondered yet again, would she stop having sex if she quit drinking, or would she adapt?

An academic question.

Amir looked up and there, in the middle of the screen, was the NRA headquarters building. He quickly grabbed the remote and turned the sound on.

The scene switched to a man at a lectern facing a room full of reporters. The caption at the bottom of the screen read:

**NRA Board Selects New President.**

The man at the lectern was speaking, "... and with that said, allow me to introduce Jeffrey Winton the Third, the new President of the National Rifle Association."

The Beast spoke up, *Jeffrey Winton the Third? Where do they get these guys? Do they have a secret fop training camp?*

Be quiet for a moment, I want to hear this, Amir thought.

Jeffrey Winton the Third began to speak, and the Beast chimed in, *college in Switzerland? This guy went to college in Switzerland? And brags about it? What kind of guy goes to college in Switzerland and talks about it in public? Cunt.*

Shut up.

The man spoke for another minute, and Amir listened.

*I have a question. When are we going to shoot Little Lord Fauntleroy the Third?*

I'm working on it, okay? Now be quiet.

*Okay. Do good work. I want this guy's blood on my gun.*

Eventually, the news show ended and Amir turned off the TV.

*We need to scope this guy out. Find out everything about him, where he lives, his country club, servants, guards, public events, everything. So why don't you just fire up that little laptop and let's get going on that?*

I cannot think of a better way to have a swat team busting down the front door.

*Ah. You might be right.*

We need to visit our local public library, Amir thought.

*Hey, I got it. Let's visit the public library and use one of their computers.*

Yeah, okay. Good idea.

*That's me, always helpful.*

## *This Animal Schemes*

Approaching the front doors of the NRA building, Skip Taylor was angry. The new president had offered to meet him at the headquarters but declined to come to his office in Richmond. Some blather about high crime rates in Richmond.

High crime rates? The AG could not resist. In front of the NRA building, he stopped and carefully examined the spot on the sidewalk where the previous NRA president bled out after being shot. The concrete was still stained. Taylor snorted, apparently removing blood from concrete was a bitch. He took his time and looked down from several angles. He resisted the urge to photograph the spot. Barely.

High crime rates, my fat white ass.

Nevertheless, he could not help but think, here I am, coming to him and not vice versa. That says it all - I need him more than he needs me. So let's try for as much dignity as possible, and leave it at that.

He entered the building and signed in as a visitor. He passed through an elaborate detection system rivaling those in big city airports.

The AG wondered, does the alarm go off if I'm not armed? He looked at a directory on the wall; the president and the executive dining room were on the top floor; the staff cafeteria, in the basement. The AG grunted, that figures. He took the elevator to the top of the building, found the door to the president's office, and walked in.

A young blond woman, professional eye candy, sat behind a large desk.

Taylor approached her and smiled. "Hi. I'm Skip Taylor. I have a ten o'clock appointment with Jeffrey Winton."

"President Winton is running a bit late this morning. If you will please have a seat?"

President Winton? Skip Taylor swallowed the undiplomatic joke that came to mind. He sat down, reminding himself to be polite.

The blond spoke into an intercom.

Five minutes later, the intercom buzzed, and the blond called out, "President Winton will see you now, Mr. Taylor."

Taylor stood up. Did they rehearse this? He mumbled, "So soon?" He entered the office of President Winton and saw a short, thin, pale man sitting behind a large desk. The man looked young, reminding Taylor of the Boss's Wayward Nephew, sitting in the Big Chair and pretending, as children will, that he belonged there.

"Mr. Taylor, thank you for stopping by. I'm pleased to meet you," Jeffrey Winton said. He stood up and reached out and let Taylor shake a limp hand. Both men sat down.

"I understand that you had conversations with our previous president, regarding our joint efforts to defend the second amendment," Winton said.

Taylor thought, not exactly. You help me get into the Senate, and I'll help you arm the public. Instead of saying that, he said, "That is correct.

I sought, and the NRA offered, support for a Senate run next year. In that regard, we discussed concealed carry, which I offered to support."

"Ah yes, I remember seeing that in the notes," Winton said. "Well, I cannot, of course, promise anything. The Board has asked me to evaluate the NRA's business model. For that reason, I need to hedge a bit on the promises made by my predecessor. Nothing personal, you understand. I am asking the Association's partners and political sponsors to be patient while I finish my evaluation."

"What changes are you looking at?" Taylor said.

"Oh, the answer to that is a long one. The short answer? In recent years the Association has focused on state and local politics. That's worked well. But adapt and survive, they say, so I'll be looking at realigning our lobbying more towards national politics. You would welcome that change, I would think. But it would be a big change, and I need to look at it without making promises."

"I understand," Taylor said. "And you're right, that does suit me."

"Yes, I thought it might." Winton paused, then said, "There is another matter. One that might be more important to me, though perhaps less important to you."

"Oh? Tell me, please. Perhaps I can help," Taylor said.

Jeff Winton hesitated and looked down. Then he looked at Taylor as if thinking. After a moment, he said, "Well, as you know, the previous association president was shot and killed not far from here, right out on that sidewalk. Killed, mind you, right out there." Winton waved a hand at the window.

Taylor stared at Jeffrey Winton and suddenly noticed a sheen on his forehead and his upper lip. He said, "Mr. Winton, forgive me for asking, but don't you have executive security? The NRA is an important organization, right up there with major corporations. I would think your executives don't go to the bathroom without security. Isn't that so?"

"Yes, of course we have all that. If I go for a walk or a latte or whatever, two armed men accompany me. Of what use is that, if someone can just buy a rifle and shoot me from hundreds of yards away? It's terrible. Please tell me that you can offer me some protection. The prospect of following my predecessor's example weighs heavily on my mind," Winton said.

Skip Taylor sat there, stunned. Wow, if I were to tell this story, no one would believe me. The president of the NRA, the biggest cathedral in the Church of Guns, is shitting his silk underwear at the prospect of being shot. And I thought I'd seen everything.

"Mr. Winton," Taylor said. "America is a violent nation, in part because we arm our citizens. You know that. I know you know that. So, living here involves some risk."

"Guns don't kill. People kill," Winton said.

Taylor laughed. Yes, they do. A rifle helps. "Sure. And people with guns kill more people faster. We have data on that."

Winton looked disgruntled. "Is there nothing you can do to protect me?"

Taylor said, "Let me ask you a question. Do you remember the DC sniper?"

*207*

"John Muhammed? Yes, of course. It was in the papers."

"Where were you living at the time, if I may ask?" Taylor said.

"Southern France," Winton said.

"Lucky you. You missed all the fun. Muhammed and a sidekick killed seventeen people in three weeks. DC was in terror. You ever hear of the DC Shuffle? You know what that is?" Winton shook his head. The AG continued, "Somebody standing at a bus stop shuffles, side to side, hoping to make themselves a more difficult target. Some of the gas stations covered their pumps with tarps after a guy was shot pumping gas."

"Really?"

Taylor nodded. "Really. I was there. Of course, a tarp wouldn't stop a sniper, but it helped folks feel better. The victims were random. CEOs were scared. Normal people were scared, but they continued to trust their luck and go about their business. The city did not shut down. Most people came through okay. After all, it's a big city."

"That's easy to say when no one's hunting you," Winton said.

"Do you remember how Muhammed was caught?"

"No," Winton said.

"He taunted the police and the city. His remarks led them to him. Back then, I talked with a young patrolman who served on an anti-sniper team. I told him that if Muhammed had not contacted the police and the media, he would never have been caught. The patrolman agreed with that. Back then I was surprised that some enemy nation - Iran or North

Korea, for instance - had not dispatched a sniper team to DC, with orders to kill randomly, disrupt the city. If they were professionals, they would stop only when they ran out of ammo or money."

Taylor gave Jeffrey Winton a sad smile. "All you can do, Mr. Winton, is trust your luck and go about your business. There is no defense against a sniper who is shooting randomly and who deep down inside does not want to be caught."

"Well, now I'm more frightened than I was, and I was frightened already."

"Sounds like you need better security," Taylor said.

"But you said that's no guarantee," Winton said.

"It's not, but it might make you feel better."


Serena left the living room and climbed the stairs. She had been putting this off long enough. Try as she might not to think about it …

… Lelah was gone, never to return.

She trudged up the stairs, one step at a time. Everyone says, you need to accept your loss and move on. Well, nowhere in my body or soul do I want to accept that I have lost Lelah, entirely and forever. I hate the idea of living in a world without her. I know I have no choice.

But I do not like it. I hate this feeling. Grief clamped down, a heavy yoke, the gravity of sadness. She was walking around with a dead, dull feeling inside. It felt like trying to swim with a bowling ball tied to your ankle. As soon as you got in the water, you went down. Give up any hope of breathing.

It felt like that. She was suffocating, yet taking deep breaths did not help.

She stopped at the head of the stairs and took a deep breath, then another. She frowned, took two steps, then opened the door to Lelah's bedroom. She moved inside for the first time since the shooting. Serena stood in the middle of the room, closed her eyes, and listened carefully, her mind and spirit open to any sign, any signal from the afterlife.

She was hoping for a sign, a whisper, from Lelah's ghost. She sensed nothing.

She opened her eyes and thought, okay, let's turn this into the guest bedroom. Maybe we can have guests someday. We have no other children, but the families have brothers, sisters, cousins. Someone someday might wish to visit Richmond without staying in a hotel.

Serena's mouth twisted sideways. If this were Washington or San Francisco, I'd be confident. But Richmond? Most of our relatives could not find it on a map. And let's face it - it is not as if America falls all over herself welcoming people from the Middle East.

Serena sighed and thought, they've got their reasons. Nine One One is an occasion here, a sad holiday.

She suppressed her doubts and her grief and looked around the room. Most of the furniture can stay. I will keep the large furry tiger in the house, though not in the room. The rugs will stay.

I will keep the decorative items - posters, art, and the knick knacks that Lelah accumulated. Links to my daughter - maybe they will ease the passing of the years. At least, I hope so.

She looked into Lelah's closet, came across a box, and opened it. It was filled with documents – photographs, letters, notes from teachers, school reports, old homework assignments, scrawled pictures, cartoons, notes in Lelah's handwriting. When she saw all that, Serena closed the box, pulled her hands away from it, and took a step back.

No, I cannot look at that. Not yet. I am not ready. Just the clothes this time. There will be plenty of time for the rest. Not soon.

With few exceptions, the clothes could go into the trash, or to Goodwill. She pulled out the underwear and socks and threw them into a pile on the bed. Next followed the slacks, pants, jeans, and shorts. Soon the clothes covered the bed. Serena moved the piles to make more room.

She started flipping through t-shirts, a large category since Lelah was so active. Some were generic t-shirts, quickly sent to the rag pile. Others were older. Lelah kept a few favorites long after they no longer fit.

Serena's memory replayed the scenes associated with each of the t-shirts. There was the rebellious ten-year-old Lelah, in a t-shirt that read: *Strangers have the best candy*.

There was the third grader who loved chocolate and laughed at any sentence containing the word 'toilet'. Later, there was the slender, near-woman who attracted boys and then delayed all that by criticizing them for being dolts. She wore t-shirts with captions such as, *I'm with that >>>*.

Serena had to stop every so often and cry for a while. Then she would go back to packing the clothes. She lifted the last t-shirt, a pink one that read, *Have a Pheasant Plucking Day*. She tossed it onto a donation pile.

Serena paused for a moment, in the grip of a memory. She stood there and stared down at the bed. A few months ago, she had stood in that same spot, but it was a sleeping Lelah in the bed instead of piles of old clothes.

It had been late in the morning on a Saturday. Serena stood there without Lelah's noticing or moving. Finally Serena said, "Are you getting up today?"

Lelah did not move.

She repeated it louder. Still no response.

She reached over and put a hand on Lelah's shoulder, gave it a squeeze. Lelah woke up a bit, eyes swollen with sleep, hair a tangled mass, swirling around her head, falling in front of her eyes. She turned her head and looked at Serena through her hair. Finally she spoke, "Oh God." She opened her eyes narrowly, briefly, squinting at Serena. "What time is it?"

"Ten thirty-three."

Lelah nodded. "No wonder I feel so good." She closed her eyes and settled back onto the pillow.

"What time did you finally get in?"

Lelah's head turned, but her eyes remained closed. "I don't know. After six, I think."

"This morning?"

"Yeah."

"If it wouldn't be too much trouble, I would like an explanation," Serena said.

"Explanation? About?"

"What you were doing, and who you were with, that you couldn't make it home before six o'clock this morning."

Lelah's eyes opened. She lay there for a moment, then she sat up. She squinted at Serena. "If you must know, Mother, I was having sex. With the football team. One at a time, of course. It's a long story. Let's just say I lost a bet. We'll leave it at that. I tried to hurry them along, but you just try hurrying a guy once he's ... uh, never mind. Anyway, that took all night.

"You know, there are forty-five guys on the football team. I thought they'd never finish. Anyway, if I'm not perky this morning, there's a reason. I'll be better, with more sleep." Lelah raised her head and looked at Serena. "That, by the way, was a hint."

Serena stood there getting angrier, a pot boiling over. She yelled, "Lelah, dammit, this is no laughing matter. I want to know exactly what you were doing and with whom. And I want to know right now. Right now, Lelah."

"Okay, then. Okay," Lelah pushed the mass of dark hair behind her head and looked at Serena. She straightened up and held up both hands. "We can do that. Let's clear the air, since you didn't think the football joke was funny."

"Yes, let's do that, and no, it wasn't."

"I was with Riley. You've met Riley," Lelah said.

"Of course I've met Riley. And?"

"We were in fact talking about sex," Lelah said.

Serena looked towards the ceiling, "Oh God. You're not kidding, are you? Oh God." Serena put a hand to her head.

"Relax, Mom. Take a breath. It's not what you think. Riley thinks he's gay. That's what we were talking about. He's been having a rough time, so it took a while. He had a lot to say," Lelah said. "He's my friend, maybe my best friend, so I listened. But you've got nothing to worry about."

"Nothing to worry about?"

"Being gay is not contagious," Lelah said. "And just so you know, I haven't dropped my undies for Riley."

Serena stood for a moment, thinking, trying to absorb this latest news. "Riley. Gay."

Lelah nodded. "So he says. Welcome to my world. Most of the girls in the theater think most of the guys in the theater are gay. Riley's been catching some of that." Lelah turned her head for a moment. "I wonder if they're just looking for someone to have sex with." She shook her head. "That's speculative."

Serena thought back to the dozen high school musicals in which Lelah had danced or sung. Amir and Serena attended every one. Of course they had. Some of them, many of them, were wonderful, even to an unbiased observer. At least, Serena thought so.

Serena stared at Lelah. "They're gay? Which ones?"

"John is, definitely," Lelah said.

"John? You mean, Nathan Detroit? Mercutio? Scrooge? He's gay? But he's a handsome boy. Doesn't he play football too? How can he be gay?" Serena said.

Lelah yawned and spoke through the yawn, "And a couple of the others."

Serena said, "Are any of your friends gay?"

Lelah nodded. "Michael is. Bradley is gay as hell. But I don't think Riley is."

Serena was stunned. "I can't believe it. And these are your friends?"

"Why not? What do I care if they're gay?" Lelah said.

"Because it's …"

Lelah's eyebrows rose. "Yucky? It's yucky? Do you think they're yucky, Mother?"

"Well, I don't know, it's just that …"

"I'm not sleeping with any of them, so I don't have a dog in this fight," Lelah said.

"A dog in ... what?" Serena said.

"Gay vs. not," Lelah said.

"You lost me."

"Don't worry about it." She looked at Serena for a moment. "It's okay, Mom, I get it. You probably haven't run into a lot of gays. You don't even like to talk about them. I understand. After all, if they were back in the old country, people would be throwing rocks at them, wouldn't they?"

Serena nodded vigorously. "You better believe they would."

"Uh huh. Well. Since we're clearing the air, I have a question for you, Mother. And I want an answer. Which is worse, in your opinion? Fucking the football team, or throwing rocks at a gay guy until he's dead? If you had to pick one, if you had to make a choice, which would you prefer to do?"

Serena thought about it and frowned. She said nothing. There were two answers. Serena could not bring herself to say either.

Lelah stared at Serena. "Uh huh. Well. It's okay. No kidding, it is okay. I think there's hope for you, Mom. If you wouldn't throw rocks at a gay guy, then there's hope."

Serena shook her head. "No, I wouldn't do that."

Serena caught Lelah looking at her, a sly look, from the side, through a curtain of hair. "So … it's the football team, then?" Lelah, her eyes dancing, stared straight into Serena's eyes. She started laughing loudly.

After a few seconds, Serena chuckled in spite of herself. "I don't know, but I wouldn't throw rocks."

"You know, I think you made the right choice. But people might not understand, so let's keep that to ourselves. Okay, Mom? We'll let that be our little secret," Lelah said. She laughed, tilted her head, and looked up at Serena. "The football team." She laughed again. "That'll be in my head for a while."

Lelah suddenly opened her eyes wide. "Oh man, I cannot believe it. I am awake."

Serena again saw the bed and the piles of old clothes. She thought, Lelah is gone. I would do anything to get my angel back. Serena smiled. Even the football team. But that choice is not available.

For a moment, she felt lousy again. She took a breath and turned to the dresses, a small category. There were several dresses for little girls, stored for reasons unknown. Serena put those in a donation pile.

She came to an evening dress and two gowns. The peach gown had a high neck, no collar, and a drape beyond mid-calf. On a hanger it looked chaste. It was anything but. Lelah had worn it her junior year, to her first formal dance with one of the most popular boys in the school. It covered everything and concealed nothing. Lelah used that dress to enhance her sexuality, with stupendous results. Her date stopped by to pick her up and on seeing her acquired a dazed, bovine expression that he still wore when he dropped her off six hours later.

Lelah wore another evening dress to a wedding, ill-conceived and best forgotten, as it turned out. Serena decided to donate that dress.

The last gown, in midnight blue, Lelah wore to her senior prom. She used it to bedazzle another young man. They were out with friends all night. When Lelah returned home in the morning, her makeup was awry but she was disappointed not to have lost her virginity. Her date had commanded himself, too intimidated to deflower the most beautiful woman he would ever hold in his arms.

Lelah had complained before realizing that Serena was too embarrassed to discuss it. Serena remembered the crestfallen look on Lelah's face, then teared up so badly she could not see.

Serena decided to keep that gown. She held it up and looked at it and thought, someone should have sex in this gown. Maybe a cousin. I think Lelah would approve. I am certain of it.

In the late afternoon, Amir sat at a small table in the Red Boar Inn, a roadhouse in Potomac, Maryland. His laptop was open in front of him. He was looking at the webpage of Senator Joe Hollins, an Independent, age 79, the junior Senator from Tennessee. Senator Hollins was independent because he was too conservative to be a Republican. He was incapable of civil conversation with a Democrat.

The Senator opposed food stamps, health care for low income children, subsidies for primary and secondary schools, rural subsidies for electricity and the internet, and publicly funded inoculation against infectious diseases.

He vigorously supported TVA and the University of Tennessee football team.

Amir did not care about any of that. The NRA was endorsing Senator Hollins for the upcoming fall election. In Amir's eyes, that made the Senator special.

He was sitting right in front of Amir, no more than a dozen feet away, talking with three other people at a small, square table. As he talked, he gestured, an impromptu performer. Amir sat there, staring at his laptop, listening to the Senator without looking at him. The man was jovial and confident. He was a man who caused considerable damage yet slept well at night. A man who lived in a world of My People and Other People. He got a kick out of sticking it to Other People.

*Can you hear it, Amir? Can you hear it?*

Amir thought, Hear what? What are you talking about?

*Your rifle, begging for his blood.*

You're imagining things, Amir thought.

*Is that a joke?*

We need less patter, more planning.

*I like people who profit from the pain and misfortune of others.*

Oh do you?

*Yes. I especially like to see them hit the pavement.*

I'm impressed. You're just too too terrible for words. Now be quiet. There remains the large matter of how it can be done.

*You'll figure out something, Amir. I have faith in you.*

The Red Boar Inn was a medium size restaurant, with several dozen tables on the inside, and a dozen tables outside on a patio. At the moment, the Senator and his party sat inside.

Amir looked outside. Beyond the patio was a two-lane road connecting Montgomery County's most prosperous neighborhoods with the Beltway. A steady stream of cars and trucks passed the restaurant. Amir thought, that is why the good Senator and his friends are indoors. No one is sitting out on the patio. Too much noise from the road. So, either I shoot him through a window here, or I find a different location or a different target.

*You're not going after him here?*

Not yet. There's no hurry. Shooting here would be difficult. Not impossible, but difficult. We need to stick to the basics.

*Which are?*

We are not shooting for enjoyment, or pride, or for the challenge of a difficult shot. We are not shooting to make a statement. We are shooting to kill, at minimal risk to ourselves.

*You know what you are, Amir?*

What am I?

*A buzzkill. A homicidal refugee from the accounting department.*

Yeah? You know what I think I am?

*What's that?*

Pissed off, lethal, and alive, all at the same time. I intend to stay that way.

# *A Near Miss*

Back at the Fairfax police station, Roundtree was sitting at a video workstation, shouting at a computer monitor, "Are you kidding me? Where is he? Are you trying to tell me he evaporated into thin air? That he hung out for two hours but never appeared, not once, in front of a damn camera?"

A police technician, a young woman, approached him. "You okay, Inspector? You need help?"

"Sorry. I was just venting. My bad guy is not cooperating," Roundtree said.

"What did he do?"

"Okay, first, let me ask you a question," Roundtree said. He turned towards her and wound up for his story, like a pitcher winding up for a pitch. "You ever have a case where nothing works, the bad guy is always one step ahead?"

She shook her head.

"Lucky you. Well, several weeks ago, my bad guy showed up at NRA headquarters, a few miles from here."

"Oh, that one," she said.

"Yeah, that one. Early in the afternoon, he appears in more than twenty frames from various cameras. The NRA is across the street, and the buildings on that block are lousy with cameras. We've got their feeds. Nonetheless, no one remembers the guy, no one spoke with him. Or so they say. That is hard to believe, but that is what everyone says.

"So, after about four p.m., he doesn't show up any more. Not once. Shortly after five, he shoots the NRA president. He then vanishes without a trace."

"He sounds good at what he does," she said.

"Oh, he's good, alright," Roundtree said. "But I don't get it. How do you make yourself disappear?"

"Simple. Park yourself off camera. Take a nap."

Roundtree nodded. Right. People notice movement. So don't move. Hey, maybe the guy's a ninja. Roundtree shook his head and swore.

"I'm sure you'll get him," she said. "People tell stories about you."

"Don't be too sure. We usually don't catch the pros. That's what makes them pros," Roundtree said.

"Well, hang in there. You're a pro too."


After lunch, Heywood Miles stopped by and found Roundtree in the video room.

"Heywood, give me some good news," Roundtree said.

"I put together a database of all the vehicles picked up on camera from five o'clock to seven o'clock, within an hour and two miles of the NRA shooting," he said.

"That's thousands of cars," Roundtree said.

"Rush hour? 157,841. Those are the cars whose plates the cameras could pick up. Naturally, many of them are double counted. With the toll collections going electronic, the sampling is good. Even on secondary roads, metro Washington is lousy with cameras."

"So, how do we use it?" Roundtree said.

"If this guy hits again, we'll do the same drill in the neighborhoods near the new crime scene. Most cars won't be near both crime scenes. People follow patterns, right? If anyone shows up in both datasets, we should talk to them. And bug their phone and their car."

"Interesting," Roundtree said. He shook his head. "Policing has changed since I was a rookie."

"Also, just so you know, we have a 'bot' running around the internet, looking at references to the NRA shooting." Heywood waggled his fingers to indicate quotes.

"We find anything?"

"Thousands of hits," Heywood said. "Nothing of any value to us. No surprise, NRA members are pissed off that somebody would shoot their president."

Roundtree laughed.

"You think that's funny?" Heywood said.

"I think it's ironic," Roundtree said. "NRA guys upset because someone got shot? When has that ever happened?"

"Yeah, they don't object when someone gets hit in the 'hood'."

"Most people don't. I'm surprised the news shows still report shootings," Roundtree said.

"Most of them don't get reported. Mostly, just the mass shootings," Heywood said. "The news shows don't have enough airtime to report all the shootings."

Roundtree frowned and shook his head. He sighed, the news shows are just trying to sell advertising. So which do you suppose folks would rather see, the policeman who rescues a kitten, or another shooting over a parking space?

Two weeks later, the barrel of Amir's rifle was resting on a tree branch, his crosshairs on the throat of Senator Hollins. The Senator sat in a folding chair next to a folding table which held a basket of orange slices, a pitcher of lemonade, and a bowl of pretzels. Children were playing soccer in front of the Senator. Amir could see him applaud from time to time.

The children were playing the game on the athletic fields of an elementary school. Opposite the school, looming over the playing fields, was a wooded ridgeline. Amir was up there among the trees. The wind was blowing, not hard but noticeable. The sight picture in the scope was moving around. Amir spread his feet and tried to stop breathing. That helped some.

Patience, Amir thought. I am a stone, with no eyes, no mind, no pulse. Stay … still.

He closed his eyes and tried to be quiet. Then he took a deep breath, exhaled half of it through his nose, and opened his eyes a bit. The scope was steadier. He saw the Senator clearly in his crosshairs. He gently put pressure on the trigger. He waited through a long moment before the rifle bucked against his shoulder.

Amir immediately went to his knees, put his rifle back into a 48" telescope case, and looked around for anything he might have left on the ground. He slung the case over one shoulder and began walking, with speed but without hurry, through the woods.

Two minutes later, he could hear the distant sound of sirens behind him. Every so often he would stop and listen carefully for sirens in front of him or approaching him. The sirens stayed behind and far away.

Amir could not avoid everyone. Walking along a footpath, he passed a row of new houses with tiny backyards. A man was watering a flower bed. He looked up, spotted Amir. Amir grinned, gave the man a thumbs-up - watering flowers, yes, that is good. The man waved the hose at Amir.

The Beast rumbled, *He saw us. That's unfortunate. If we show up on his security system, we are screwed.*

Golly, you think this is risky?

Later, Amir was about to emerge from the woods onto a two-lane road. There were no houses nearby. Suddenly, a police car came around a curve and went flying by without a siren, its lights flashing.

It happened so fast, Amir barely had time to freeze. He watched the car zoom past and disappear around a curve.

"Good God," he said. His pulse was suddenly racing.

He backed up, further into the woods.

*If he saw us, he'll come back and check. He'll radio in too.*

Amir quickly crossed the road and went deep into the woods. He knelt down and did not move for ten minutes, senses on high alert. Mother of All Gods, that was close.

Then he stood up and scanned the area with his eyes. After a minute, he kept walking. Thirty minutes after pulling the trigger, Amir came to a secluded, dead-end street where he had parked his car next to the woods. He put the telescope case in the trunk, closed the trunk, got into the car, and drove away.

Amir stayed on the back roads in Maryland, avoiding Washington, moving north and then east. Eventually, he found himself in the tail end of rush hour traffic, heading east towards Annapolis on Rt. 50. He exited to Rt. 301 south, away from DC and towards Richmond.

*Well? Do you think you got him?*

I don't know, Amir thought. He turned on the radio and tuned into a news station. The announcer was talking about "… a close call today for Senator Joseph Hollins, hit by a stray bullet while attending a youth soccer game in Potomac, Maryland. According to family members, a bullet struck the Senator in the upper body. He went by air to Bethesda Naval Hospital. The hospital says the Senator's condition is critical, but they expect him to recover. He will need extensive rehabilitation."

The audio track switched to the statement by a hospital spokesman.

*Shit! We missed him. Damn, damn, damn.*

No. We hit him. He survived, that's all. It happens.

*We should have stayed and finished him off.*

Yeah, okay Rambo, thanks for your input.

*That was a long shot, in the wind. Ambitious.*

Too ambitious?

*Maybe.*

How far do you suppose we can shoot accurately?

*Three hundred yards. That shot was longer, three fifty or so.*

I am surprised I can hit a target at three hundred yards, Amir thought.

*You're getting good. You would've been a kick ass soldier.*

No thanks. Been there, done that, got the t-shirt.


At the end of a long day, Skip Taylor sat in his office and watched the national news on TV. He was too tired to pay close attention. The public did not pay attention, thus newsmakers did not make major news on a Friday.

Instead, the media released items that were minor or embarrassing - increases in the foreign aid budget, military sales to friendly dictators, that sort of thing. News that should be marked, IGNORE THIS.

The announcer turned to a local story, a US Senator shot while watching a soccer game in Montgomery County in Maryland.

Taylor sat up. "What?" He grabbed the remote and turned up the volume. The announcer said the Senator might have been targeted. Local police thought it could be an accident by a hunter. They were looking into that.

The news item closed by saying the condition of Senator Hollins was unknown.

Taylor thought, that's brilliant, what a cover for a sniper. *Uh, I was hunting, had a ten point buck in the crosshairs. I missed him. Sorry. My bad.*

Any red-blooded outdoorsman can understand that mistakes happen occasionally.

Then Taylor remembered the NRA investigation right here in Virginia. That reminded him, it had been two weeks since he checked into that matter. He punched a button on the intercom. "Abigail, place a call to Max Pressler, the police chief up in Fairfax. Ask them to page him, if need be. I need to talk to him, ASAP."

"Yes sir."

Taylor sat back in his chair, thinking. The AG bore no ill will to a stranger, and he hoped Senator Hollins would recover. Nonetheless, the Senator was neither a friend nor a political ally, so his recovery was irrelevant. Taylor shrugged, a waste of time to worry about that.

Fortunately, the shooting took place in Maryland and not Virginia.

He thought, I have enough problems already. We're investigating our own shooting. God, I still can't believe it. What timing! Just when I need help from the NRA, someone slips through all that corporate security, kills the NRA president, and disappears.

I wonder if the NRA's new leadership will hold me responsible. It's not hard to imagine that.

If they blame me, I can kiss a Senate run goodbye. I could go back to being a prosecutor. Ugh. That'll be like eating cold French fries the rest of my life.

Unless I can turn the situation into a prosecution. Catch this shooter, prosecute his ass, and with any luck at all, have the state put him to sleep. That's workable. Virginia can be vindictive; it makes everyone feel better.

That would be heavenly. If I can do that, the NRA will be happy. In that case I might not need their help. Instead of making speeches, I could let my record speak for itself.

In life as in baseball, it ain't over til it's over.

The intercom came to life, "Mr. Attorney General, I have Chief Pressler."

Skip Taylor picked up the phone. "Max? It's Skip Taylor. Do you have a couple minutes?"

"Yes sir, of course."

"I just wanted a status report on the NRA investigation. I assume you've heard of the shooting up in Maryland? Is that connected?"

"Yes sir, we've had a few developments in the investigation. First off, we have ourselves a serial sniper. I just received the lab reports. A couple of weeks ago there was a shooting in Lorton, a gun shop owner. Then yesterday, a US Senator was shot up in Maryland.

"Sir, you're not going to like this. We did chemical testing of the fragments recovered at the NRA, and at Lorton, and up in Maryland. Chemical residues from the bullet fragments match."

"Okay, Chief, I need that in dumb lawyer talk," Taylor said.

"Sir, we think the bullets used at the NRA, at Lorton, and up in Maryland came from the same box of ammunition."

"You guys can figure all that out?"

"Yes sir. Competition shooters are picky about their loads and ammo. So some manufacturers make each box of match ammo as uniform as possible. Shooters pay extra for that. Every bullet from a box appears identical to a chemical analysis. That ensures consistent performance. Shooters like consistency."

"So we have ourselves a sniper who might be a competition shooter," Taylor said.

"At least he acts like one, sir," Pressler said. "And there's more. A half dozen of the best investigators in the business are working this case. They think the shooter might be a pro."

Taylor's mouth dropped open. "Oh great. What makes them think that?"

"He shoots and doesn't leave a trace. He's a ghost. Most guys who shoot are angry. Deep down inside, they're looking for a fight, and they'll stick around to shoot it out with police. Not this cat. He shoots once, then …" the sound of fingers snapping came over the intercom, "… he vanishes."

"You sure he's not ex-military?" The AG thought, we'd have data on those guys, wouldn't we?

"Sir, we're not sure of much at this point."

Taylor sat for a long minute. He turned and stared out the window, wondering how to maneuver around the shootings. "So what do we do next?"

"Let me get back to you on that. We're still digesting the information ourselves."

Taylor bit back a snarky comment about 'doing your job.' Instead, he exhaled heavily and said, "Okay, thanks Chief. If you need anything from this end, or from the governor, let me know. Let me know about any news, good or bad. Okay?"

"Will do, Mr. Attorney General."

"Have a good weekend." Taylor punched a button, ending the call.

He sat there staring at the phone and thought, damn, damn, damn. The AG did not move.

Shit.

If I start campaigning - hell, forget that, if I just continue to hold this job - I'm going to look like a pathetic idiot if we get a rash of sniper shootings.

I need to get on top of this, and fast.

Amir and Serena sat in the living room. They had just watched the evening news. Two days ago, the news program ran a story about the shooting of a US Senator in Maryland. Yesterday, they said the Senator would survive but would need rehabilitation.

This evening, they did not mention him at all.

"That's odd, don't you think?" Serena said.

Amir was staring at his laptop. "I'm sorry, what?"

"They didn't mention that Senator who was shot. I mean, he's a Senator, but he seems to be old news. I'd expect a little more attention."

Amir shrugged without looking up. "I don't know. I heard a blurb on the radio. The police are looking into it, but they don't know what to make of it. It might be someone with a grudge. It might be a drunk hunter. So what can the news guys talk about? Rehab?" Amir sat up, a plastic smile pasted across his face. "Senator blah blah did twenty pushups today. We are all very happy."

She laughed. "You have a gift for cynicism."

Amir looked at her. "Yes. Yet you love me. Have you had that looked at?"

She grinned. "Uh no. And I won't, either. I like my sick self." She stood up, turned off the TV. "Well, I've had a long day. I think I'll hit the shower and turn in early."

"Okay."

"Care to join me?"

"I'm sweaty and stinky," he said.

"In the shower, then," she said.

"Oh ... yeah, sure," Amir said.

Half an hour later Serena was spread-eagled on the bed. Amir was on top of her. Warm gushing delight cascaded and spread throughout her body, a lovely liquid feeling that slowly grew more urgent. She convulsed and by gritting her teeth managed not to scream. The sex became vigorous, then it became rough. Serena turned her head sideways and opened her mouth, gasping for breath.

When Amir finished, Serena lay on the bed, spent, used up, flaccid. She soon fell asleep.

The next morning she awoke late. Amir was gone. It was a Saturday, she could afford to lie in bed for a while. She opened one eye. Yellow sunshine was entering the room. She closed the eye.

She thought, Amir is finally getting past Lelah's death. He used to sit around for hours, quiet, hurting, miserable. Now look at him, he's getting out more, he's exercising, he's in shape. Boy is he ever in shape! He is bouncing from one hobby to another. Sometimes he seems desperate for entertainment.

Something's changed. Something happened with Lelah's death. Maybe it's a coincidence, but something's going on. He has always been reserved, but now there's a core, something down deep, that I can't reach at all. He'll talk to me; it's not as if he's blocking me out. But he'll go only so far when I ask him what's on his mind.

The sex has changed. He used to be subtle, delicate, leisurely. He used to make jokes in bed, make fun of me, of himself, make me laugh. We used to talk during sex. Now every so often - often enough to notice - he turns into a hammer, rougher, more explosive, more spectacular. More of an angry lover.

I guess that's no surprise. We all need to work our way past Lelah. God, that sounds cold. I hope I can help him. And if roughing me up helps, then let's ride.

Serena laughed. Yeah, cowboy, let's ride. She shook her head.

I am so funny. I need to be funny.

If I mention this to Dr. Templeton, she will want to write an academic paper about it.

I can imagine what Amir would say to that.

Amir slowed the car, pulled to the curb, and killed the engine. He briefly looked around the block. It was a prosperous, well-kept neighborhood. The houses were large, each with its own style and landscaping, with multiple bedrooms, bathrooms, carports. The lawns were large, most often cut by a riding mower. Many of the houses sat behind perimeter walls or gates.

*They call this place Arcturus. So very Roman.*

Amir thought, Uh huh.

He grabbed his music player and a baseball cap, stepped out of the car, and locked its doors. He put on sunglasses, the cap, and headphones, and turned the music player to some jazz. There. Now, he looked like an old guy, out for a healthy walk through a pleasant, quiet neighborhood. He would fit right in.

A cane would complete the image. That would be perfect, but he did not have one. Maybe next time.

Amir walked down the road, his eyes scanning from side to side. He studied the details, looking into shadows for places to be quiet and unseen, dark places to walk, lines of sight. On his left was a row of old houses. Beyond, the Potomac River rolled past. To his right, upslope from the river, the land rose to offer good views - and sight lines - to homeowners further up the rise.

Amir had studied the neighborhood. Two hundred years ago, George Washington owned property here; his Mt. Vernon estate was downriver. Soon after, the Winton family acquired a plot of land overlooking the river. Now, centuries later, Jeffrey, freshly minted president of the NRA, heads the Wintons. He lives in the same house as his ancestors. Right there, next one on the left.

A beautiful house. The Wintons had a good eye for waterfront property.

Amir glanced at the house, careful not to stare. The front wall was the original gray stone, shielding a shallow front yard. The backyard was long and deep and descended all the way to the river. The house had two stories with windows every six feet, a wide, solid front door, a semi-circular driveway under a porch that shielded visitors as they once emerged from carriages, then Duesenbergs and Bentleys, and now Cadillac SUVs. A black SUV and a black sedan sat in the driveway.

Judging from the twinkling of interior lights, the window panes were crystal.

Amir slowed down and scanned the house as he passed. He thought, how delightful, how quaint. His bedroom is on the other side, facing the river.

At that moment, Jeffrey Winton emerged from the house. Two doors opened in the sedan, the driver's door and the back door nearer the house. Two young men emerged, but instead of looking at Jeffrey, they turned and scanned the neighborhood, their gaze resting briefly on Amir before moving on. Winton hurried to the car and climbed into the back seat.

Well, well, Mr. Winton got himself some rent-a-guards. I guess that rules out the baseball bat strategy. Amir snorted.

The bass voice chuckled. *I hear the new aluminum bats are durable. I wonder - when you hit someone in the head, does the bat go 'ping'?*

Who knows? Or cares? Amir thought.

*You don't think that's funny?*

Amir ignored the remark. He walked down the road for another half mile, then he turned around and walked back. He again passed the house. This time he saw no one. The car was gone. He continued to walk until he came to an intersection, where he turned and walked up the rise to the next street. He turned to walk down that. Halfway down the block, he passed a white van parked on the street. The van was shiny. A pigtail antenna emerged from the roof.

He thought, well, hello there. Peek-a-boo to you too.

He repeated the exercise, moving to the next street higher up the hill. There were only a few houses. A wooded area was uphill. Ah so.

## *Circling the Wagons*

Roundtree sat in a conference room at Fairfax police headquarters. Max Pressler was there. Task force members were still arriving. It was a few minutes before the scheduled start time.

He looked at Pressler; the Chief looked frustrated, as if he'd been trying to crack a problem that would not crack.

The other members of the task force entered the room and sat down. Most were in good moods. Roundtree wondered how long that would last.

"Okay," Pressler said. "Thanks for coming. Let me start by saying that I think we're stuck. We need to find a way to resolve this matter. This is an open meeting. I'd like to hear ideas for getting us unstuck.

"Let me update everyone. We have a serial shooter, a sniper. The lab guys gave us that. Bullet fragments recovered from the NRA building, from the gun shop in Lorton, and from the Senator in Potomac were chemical matches."

Roundtree nodded. So, we finally have the bullet at the NRA. That's a relief.

"So the guy is shooting match grade ammo," Ed Shapiro said.

"That's right," Pressler said. "He's picky about his ammo. He picks a target, comes in, shoots once, and disappears. He is a decent shot. We think he shot from a wooded area near the school in Potomac, over three hundred yards. In Lorton, he shot from less than a hundred yards."

Shapiro said, "He's not military. We're taught that distance is safety."

Not in a city, Roundtree thought. Concealment is what counts.

"A talented amateur," Pressler said.

"Unpredictable," Roundtree said. "But better that than a pro."

"Have we given any thought to how he is picking his targets?" Kelly Nelson said.

"I've given that some thought," Roundtree said. "The three victims had nothing in common. They did not know each other, and I suspect the shooter did not know them. Except for guns, that is. The president of the NRA, a gun shop owner in Lorton, a US Senator endorsed by the NRA. Either the guy is a nut with a beef against the NRA, or there is some organization out there using a sniper to put pressure on the NRA."

"For what reason?" Kelly Nelson said.

"Many organizations don't like the NRA," Roundtree said.

"AMA," someone said.

"Urban League."

"Foreign Service Officers," Shapiro said.

Pressler laughed. "Seriously?"

Roundtree propped his head on a hand and rolled his eyes. "Yeah, right. Those outfits might apply pressure for a political end. But using murder to exert pressure? That's a stretch. A national spy agency, maybe. Organized crime? Sure. An American corporation, or a non-profit? I don't believe it, not for a second."

"Okay so ... it's a psycho?" Pressler said.

Several people nodded.

Pressler looked at Dr. Nelson, "Kelly? You got something?"

"Or a victim," she said.

"A victim? Aren't most of them either screwed up or dead?" Rick Summers said.

"A victim, friend of a victim, family member, anyone suffering extreme loss and emotional pain after a shooting," she said.

Summers said, "Okay, but that would be, what? ... Thousands of people, right?" He laughed out loud. "Hell, tens of thousands of people. Maybe a million."

Roundtree nodded. "Maybe he's both. In any event, it's a long list."

"Where does he live?" Pressler said.

Roundtree said, "My guess is not too far from the shootings. Virginia or Maryland. Maybe DC."

"So only thousands of suspects," Summers said.

Heywood Miles looked at Summers and said, "C'mon, man, stop being a killjoy. We're making progress."

"Yeah, right," Summers said. "This guy will die of old age before we ID him."

"Alright," Pressler said. "This is good. Let's assume we're looking at a nutcase who can shoot. How do we stop him?"

"Summers has it right, Chief," Roundtree said. "We ID him, we can stop him. The problem is ID'ing him."

"Okay," Pressler said. He sat silent for a moment. "Alright. I think I have enough to get through my press conference without looking too stupid."

Ed Shapiro said, "Will there be reporters?"

"You know, Ed, I can delegate press conferences, so watch yourself," Pressler said.

"Yes sir," Shapiro said.

The meeting began to break up. Pressler left the room, and several others stood up to leave. Roundtree caught the eye of Heywood Miles, tapped the table, and mouthed, *stay here*. Miles sat back in his chair.

When they were alone, Roundtree said, "So, any news on license plates?"

"It's delayed. The records are there, I just need to get computer time. It's just a law enforcement investigation, a local matter. So I'm delayed, not done."

"Okay, I have another request, slightly different," Roundtree said. "Maybe you can run it concurrently with your other stuff. Make a list of the family members of victims in the Whitetop shooting. Include any friends we know about. Limit it to people who live in Virginia or Maryland. Look for their license plates on highway cams and tell me as much as you can about where they've driven since the shooting."

"Jesus, Dan, that's a big one. I don't know if I can run both concurrently. I'm already fighting to get computer time."

"Okay, in that case, drop the other one and focus on this one," Roundtree said.

"You sure?"

"No. I'm playing a hunch," Roundtree said. "I ask myself, why now? I can see someone going a bit crazy because they lost a loved one. But you get over it. You bury the dead, pick up the pieces, and move on. I know, I've done it. Any urban black has done it. So we should focus on the recent local shootings. Whitetop is by far the biggest of those. I'm just playing percentages."

"Okay," Miles said. "I'll get going on that."

"Maybe we'll get lucky."

Heywood sat there, blew out a long breath, and nodded.

Roundtree left the conference room and hurried off to Pressler's press conference. Roundtree stood in the back of the room. Klieg lights and cameras and a forest of toxic microphones and handheld recorders all aimed at Pressler.

He began by summarizing the high points of the investigation, much of which he had just discussed with the task force. Then the chief made an appeal to the public, "We think we have a dangerous, troubled individual among us. If you know anything about this, if you know who might be committing these crimes, please contact the Fairfax county police. Our number is at the bottom of your screen."

Pressler looked directly into a news camera. "And to the shooter, if you are watching, please, I beg you, please stop the senseless violence. Contact us. We can help you, we can put you in touch with people who can address your pain.

"I will now take your questions."

A dozen reporters tried to shout out questions, all at the same time.

Roundtree was thinking and not listening. Nothing spoke louder than the chief's appeal to the public. This is what we do when we have no clue, no leverage, he thought.

This is what starting from scratch looks like.


Amir was sitting in the living room, his laptop open. Serena was out with friends.

He was reading an internet news story, *Police Chief Appeals to Public to Help Catch Sniper*. One item at the end of the story caught his eye:

*The Chief's appeal told us what many of us already knew - we are close to helpless against a determined sniper. In combat, snipers hunt snipers, but that is impractical in a peacetime urban area.*

*The police cannot protect everyone. They will probably protect the rich and the powerful. The rest of us have to trust to luck.*

*So stiff upper lip. Let us all keep our eyes open and our cellphones charged. Any of one of us, in the right place at the right time, could provide that critical push to help catch this guy.*

The bass voice spoke. *Well, you want to quit? Let these guys off the hook?*

Which upsets them more, Amir thought, the NRA guy, the gun shop owner, or the Senator?

*Not the gun shop owner. He was probably just another schlub trying to make a living.*

Amir sat there thinking. I think their fair share of the blood is more than three guys. Sorry. Color me vindictive.

*How about three of their executives?*

Not bad. That might be worth discussing.

In Amir's head, the Beast laughed long and loud.

What?

*They are asking us to stop. When have the police ever asked for anything?*

We're making them eat crow.

*So this isn't murder exactly. It's remedial mayhem. A teachable moment.*

It is getting riskier. And it will get riskier.

The bass voice was droll. *Are you kidding? Riskier? They're going to have the police running all over the place, following misguided tips about normal people. This story is a gift. We should send money to their widows and orphans association.*

Perhaps. If we get the new NRA president, though, the risk will go sky-high. Then they'll know that we're going after gun people.

*Are you afraid? You have enough money. You could move. You could quit. Quit while you're ahead.*

Amir thought about it. They will learn over time. People always do. It will happen through tips, patterns, data, and whatever else they can use. They will assign more people, spend more on surveillance. They will deploy drones and more cameras. They will start arresting people on a hunch. It will get more difficult.

I am scared, Amir thought. Let's face it, I am scared. A SWAT team could come busting in here at three a.m. My life would be over.

Am I scared enough to quit?

Amir sat there thinking, then he decided ...

... No. These people need to bleed. They need to see a shooting that happens to them instead of 'other people'. Maybe then they would develop a little empathy. Maybe then they wouldn't be so quick to accept the blood spilled by others. By the children of others.

*That's the spirit.*

We need to be careful. We need better disguise.

*Disguise?*

Maybe a handicap. Sunglasses and a cane. A wheelchair. A gray wig. Or birdwatching equipment, binoculars and a book. That sort of thing.

The bass voice rumbled, *I love this stuff. Any pathetic little psycho-turd can murder school children. They're easy. But going after hard targets, going after the guys pulling the strings, the guys pushing the buttons ... that takes nerve.*

And planning, Amir thought. And luck.

*Someone should write a song.*

Springsteen, maybe. Or the Rolling Stones.

*Who?*


Amir stood on the street, two blocks above the Winton family home, his binoculars pointed skyward. He was out for a walk in the neighborhood, just another birdwatcher enjoying a diverting and healthful hobby.

*Either that or a Peeping Tom.*

Shut up, asshole.

A bass laugh burst forth from inside Amir's head.

Amir was not looking at birds. He was looking at trees. In particular, he was looking for places where the foliage was so dense that he could not see. If he could not see, with binoculars, then others also could not see.

Amir walked into the wooded area and stopped. He could see the Winton house through the foliage.

He saw several of the windows. Through a second story window, there was an easy chair next to a lamp in what looked like a library. In the background, books lined bookshelves.

No Kindle for this guy. Now that's interesting, he thought.

The bass voice spoke. *Does he smoke a pipe while reading one of his rare editions?*

Who knows? Amir thought. He scanned the property. The driveway was empty. There was no one outside.

After looking for several minutes, Amir took a photograph. A birdwatcher might do that. Then he continued his walk.

Shoot from up in a tree? Could that work? After a 911 call, the police would try to shut down this neighborhood quickly. I would have to stay put and hide rather than move. If they brought dogs or infrared, they would find me … unless they were even dumber than I think they are.

*That does not sound promising.*

Amir thought, No, it does not. We need to figure out something else.

It was dusk; the evening light failing. Soon, the residents would begin to turn out their lights and go to bed. Amir parked his car on the street, two blocks above the Winton house.

He sat in his front seat. He could afford to wait. The NRA president often came to work at ten a.m., sometimes later. So Amir wondered, is the man a night owl? What does he do in the evenings?

Dusk turned to darkness. Amir got out of the car, opened the trunk, and pulled out a golf bag holding several woods and a few irons. He had bought them second hand, four dollars a club. He shouldered the bag and slowly walked down the street, a middle-aged golfer, stiff and sore, returning home after a long day on the links.

He was looking for a specific house. He soon found it. It had an old-fashioned mailbox next to the curb. Amir walked up, opened the mailbox, looked inside. Junk mail was stuffed inside.

He closed the mailbox and moved into a shadow between that house and the one next door. He placed the golf bag, a standup bag, so it would be upright and stable on the slope. Then he pushed a wood to the side and pulled a rifle from the bag. He unzipped a side pocket and pulled out a roll of masking tape and a pre-measured strip of plastic foam. He rolled up the foam, taped it, and slid it around the muzzle. Then he hoisted the rifle and peered through the scope to make sure the foam did not block the view. It did not.

Suddenly, Amir heard a sound behind him. A mailman had walked up to the mailbox and opened it. "Oh good grief," the man said.

Amir froze. His eyes slid to the left. He slowly lowered the rifle and moved against an evergreen. He thought, Jesus Christ, that guy is working late. For a while, he dared not breathe.

The mailman took a bundle of mail from his shoulder bag and rolled it into a cylinder. Then he jammed it into the mailbox.

Amir watched him.

After seconds that felt like minutes, the mailman turned, closed the cover on the mailbox, and continued his rounds.

Amir took a breath, then slowly exhaled.

He turned back to the rifle. He wondered if the foam would mess up the shot. No way to know. He could not test it at *Bob's*. Gun people would be curious. Worse, they would remember him.

*So? Take the shot, see if it works.*

Right. Amir knelt down, put the rifle to his shoulder, and laid the muzzle across a convenient spot on the golf bag. He looked downslope at the Winton house.

The lights were on and the windows stood out like yellow beacons. Through the scope, Amir could see inside clearly. He could see the library and its chair. The chair was empty. He could see no one in the yard.

He took his eye away from the scope and looked at the Winton house with the naked eye. From where he was, the wooded area partially blocked his view. The scope could see through the foliage far better than the naked eye.

For the next half hour, Amir occasionally took quick looks through the scope, but the chair in the library stayed empty. Then, sitting there quietly, he thought he noticed a change in the light through the second story window. Curious, he put his eye to the scope, and there, right in the crosshairs, was Jeffrey Winton.

*Ha. The little shit is smoking a pipe. You're kidding me, he's wearing a smoking jacket. Do you believe this guy?*

Be quiet please, Amir thought.

The view through the scope settled down as Amir locked himself into position. He slowed his breathing, waited for his heart rate to slow. A downhill shot, no elevation necessary. No wind to speak of.

Amir turned all of his senses to his heartbeat. Between beats the rifle bucked against his shoulder, making an odd sound that was sharp but muffled - *crick*.

*That went well. It was quiet. It did not sound like a rifle.*

He lowered the rifle, removed the foam, slid the rifle and the foam into the golf bag, shouldered the bag, and walked back to the car. Minutes later, Amir was driving through an intersection, crossing Route 1, heading west. He listened for sirens but heard nothing.

*You think we got him?*

Shit, Amir thought. I don't know. Maybe. I haven't heard any sirens. He turned on the radio in the car, and soon found a news station. It was conducting a call-in program on local politics. No mention of a shooting.

The bass voice rumbled, *We will have to figure out something else.*

Amir thought, not any time soon. If we missed, they will have this guy surrounded with guards, cameras, dogs, everything.

*Maybe they'll ship him back to Switzerland.*

Or an island somewhere.

Damn.

Amir winced. Damn, damn, damn.


Amir got home late in the evening. Serena was waiting for him in the living room.

He walked in and stopped on his way to the kitchen. "Hi there. How was your day?"

"I'm fine," she said. "Where have you been?"

"Oh … I'm sorry, did you stay up? I got waylaid. I was out walking, and I passed a sports bar. I looked in and they had a soccer game on TV. Now, I don't care much about soccer anymore. But there was a crowd, and everybody was cheering and having a good time, so I went in. It was a good game, and I forgot about the time." Amir went into the kitchen.

"I thought something might have happened," she said.

He called out from the kitchen, "Well, it did, I guess, but nothing out of the ordinary. Look, I'm sorry." He opened the fridge and looked inside. Then he returned to the living room. "You know, you could've called. I always have my cell. I don't always answer, but if I see the message light, I'll return the call, even if it means pulling over."

"I didn't want to interrupt."

"Uh huh. Look, don't worry about interrupting. If I can't talk, I'll text you," he said.

Amir sat down on the couch and opened a soda. "How was your day?"

"It was okay," she said. "Not much happened. I'm thinking of cutting back on the therapy sessions."

Amir looked at her. "I see. Well that's good, isn't it? That means you think you're doing better?"

She nodded. "That, or the therapy is not doing much good."

"Those sound the same to me."

Serena nodded. "Maybe they are." She looked at Amir. "Tell me something. How are you doing? How do you feel about Lelah? You don't say much about it. Do you mind talking about it?"

*Careful, Amir. Be careful. She doesn't need to know this.*

Amir shrugged. "I don't mind. I don't say much because what is there to say? I don't want to be consoled. I don't want to be treated and cured of anything. I don't want someone to tell me that it's God's will, or that these things happen. I don't want to be told that I have to move on."

He looked at her. "I want one thing - Lelah. I want Lelah back." With every word, Amir slapped his hand on his thigh. He winced. "Ow."

He looked at Serena, who was staring at him, eyes wide open. He continued, "That's one thing I can't ever have. Weeping and wishing and talking are not going to get it done. So what's the point? Forget about it."

Serena nodded. "Yes, I noticed. Your hobbies. Walking. That's good. You haven't been shooting in a while, have you?"

Amir shook his head. "Not as much. Learning to shoot is fun. Knowing how to shoot is less interesting."

*Unless there's a warm body at the other end of the rifle, especially if it's the warm body of an asshole.*

"So what's the latest hobby?" she said.

"I'm not sure. I'm thinking about birdwatching," Amir said.

"Birdwatching." Her tone was neutral, controlled.

Amir's eyebrows went up; he looked at her. "You don't like birds?"

"I like them fine. They never struck me as a hobby," she said.

"It is a bit dull," he said. "I mean, birds are cool, but … it is a bit dull." Talking about Lelah was interesting, talking about bird watching was not. He waited to see if Serena would drop the subject.

She did.

"Well," she said. "I'm glad you're doing better. I'm going to bed."

"Okay."

She leaned over, gave him a light kiss, then left the living room.

*I keep waiting for her to realize that when someone gets shot, you're always gone.*

Relax, Amir thought. You worry only because you know which people I've shot. But around Washington and Richmond, strangers get shot every day. For most of those, I'm home. Mr. Nice Guy. Mr. Innocent. Mr. Normal. I don't think she suspects anything.

*Good. Let's keep it that way.*

Amir thought, yeah, agreed, let's keep it that way.


Amir awoke the next morning. He explored the bed with his hand - no Serena. He briefly considered staying right where he was. Though he was tired from the previous day, he got up, put on a pair of pajama bottoms, and went downstairs. He found Serena in the kitchen.

She said, "Hello there, sleepy head."

Amir dropped into a chair. "Ugh. I can't do these late nights. Good morning, I think. Is there coffee?"

She got up, poured a cup of coffee, laced it with sugar, stirred, and put it on the kitchen table in front of him.

"You're an angel, angel." He took a sip. "What time is it?"

"Nine twenty-three."

"Well …," he took another sip. "It could be worse." He moved a bit in the chair, got more comfortable. "So, what are you doing today?"

"I don't know," she said. "No plans."

"Want to go for a walk later?"

"Your walks make me sweat," she said.

"Yeah, but then I get to shower you off, just like a champion racehorse."

Serena chuckled, a sound deep in her throat. "Yeah, and then you get to breed me."

The bass voice spoke. *Just like a champion racehorse.*

"Not exactly, but I like your thinking," Amir said.

She smiled.

Amir nodded. "Okay, no problem. Maybe later."

"Later," she said. They sat for a moment. "There was another shooting last night."

Amir shrugged. "There's always another shooting somewhere."

"This one's different. Someone shot the president of the National Rifle Association. In his home. They found his body this morning."

"You're kidding," Amir said. "Didn't somebody shoot the last one? Isn't that two in a row?"

"Yeah. What a world," she said. She took a sip of coffee and looked out the window.

The bass voice was gleeful. *Yeah, yeah, yeah, yeah, yeah. Fuckin' A, baby. We got him. Yeah!*

Try to restrain your grief, Amir thought.

*Two in a row. Great shot, Amir. Yeah. I wonder who number three will be. This is getting to be like the Kennedys.*

I liked the Kennedys. He paused for a moment. "Well I don't care much, frankly. I think the NRA is a bunch of jerks."

Serena nodded. "I don't like them either. Still, I don't want to see anyone murdered."

*What? What the hell is she talking about? We just nailed the president of Murder dot Org. How can anyone with a family or friends object to that?*

She's opposed to murder, no exceptions.

*Oh fine. A theoretician.*

"Remind you of the old country?" he said.

She nodded. "Yeah, a bit."

"There's always Canada."

"Ugh. Cold."

"They rarely shoot each other."

"And everyone says they're funny. I could use a little funny right now."

## *Fire Drill*

Skip Taylor hit the button killing the conference call and leaned back in his leather chair. He looked up at the ceiling. Sitting in his chair and listening for the last hour, he was exhausted. The recent sniper attacks had thrown the governor into a near panic. He wanted action, action on every front, and now, now, now. He wanted the sniper caught, so the state of Virginia could chop the guy into little tiny pieces. In public. Then they'd roast the pieces and feed them to pigeons, turn the guy into pigeon shit. Then they'd rinse the runny remains down a sewer.

The AG nodded. Yeah, that'll show him who's boss, alright.

Thus the conference call. The governor did most of the talking. Everyone else no doubt sat there imitating bobblehead dolls. Thank God, the call was not on video.

Taylor hit the intercom button. "Abigail, cancel my appointments for the rest of the morning."

"Yes sir. Your first meeting will be at two."

"Perfect."

The governor reacted to the murder of a second NRA president. There was a new, larger collective effort to stop the sniper. The FBI, with its databases and other resources, was now a full partner. The U.S. Marshalls would help. Virginia National Guard units would deploy in a limited role; that probably meant counter-sniper teams. Airborne assets would assist - helicopters, sensor drones, and ultralights.

Somebody had mentioned getting time on Washington's dedicated surveillance satellite.

Skip Taylor thought, Washington has its own satellite? So what does that make Richmond, chopped liver? We want one too. Could the governor arrange it? He grinned. This may not be the best time to ask.

Coordinating these assets was the AG's job. At the moment, he was somewhat paralyzed. The Governor had the ability to induce paralysis.

So Skip Taylor sat there thinking, what the hell am I supposed to do with ultralights, drones, and helicopters? Are we planning an air war? Do I get nukes? That would be effective - the Attorney General laughed out loud - we get a call, the sniper's been spotted in Hopewell. Three minutes later, KABOOM, bye bye sniper, bye bye Hopewell.

No one lives there but little people. They're renewable. Hopefully no one lives downwind of Hopewell. But you know that somebody does.

It is always something.

Then he thought, Skip, get a grip.

It's politics, the power of politics. Democratically elected governments dance only to politics or money. The NRA's value to the governor dwarfs their value to me.

That's why he's in the Big Chair. That's why his career path ends at the White House, while mine ends at the Senate. In either event, this sniper is killing the Golden Goose.

The governor and I have that in common. If it's the NRA that makes all political prizes possible, then we cannot tolerate someone nailing their presidents, even if they are a collection of silly fops.

This has gotten ridiculous.

If we don't stop whoever is killing their executives, the NRA will stop supporting our elections.

The AG frowned. Of course, I must admit, we have been pathetic. Our efforts following the first NRA shooting were perhaps … routine, to put it kindly, maybe even half-hearted.

When that gun shop owner got nailed, nobody said much. But a Senator and a second NRA exec? Now you're messing with the establishment, with the pillars of the establishment. Can't have that.

Skip Taylor thought, on the other hand, bugger it all. Maybe I should plan for a change of careers. Something easier. I could teach in a law school. Maybe not any law school; I doubt the Ivy League would come calling. But surely a school somewhere in Virginia. Somewhere warm. Maybe near the ocean. The pay would be okay and I could chase co-eds until my lower body gave out.

Would that be okay?

Then he straightened up in his chair. No way, that's the weakling's way out. I'm stronger than that. So how would a strong man, a real alpha dog, solve this problem?

I can see two choices. One, I can hit the books, study up on all the law enforcement and military assets they're about to hand me. I can learn to use those assets. Or two ... I can find someone who already has the military knowledge. Let them do it.

That's what a strong man would do. Therefore, that's what I am going to do. If you can't be strong, fake it, then delegate. You don't need to convince everybody. You delegate the problem, take the credit if your people succeed, and blame them if they fail. Never admit to an error. Win, win, and win.

He hit the intercom button. "Abigail. Get me a line to Max Pressler, up in Fairfax."

Amir was in bed next to Serena. She was on her back, eyes closed, mouth open, after a session that Amir thought he would remember for a long time.

He lay there thinking, she likes sex. Before, I thought she offered it just to please me. Doing her duty. Good girl, and the right girl. I married the right girl. Now she is doing it because it is fun. All I had to do was get myself in shape.

Not that shooting people has anything to do with this.

*You don't think murder can be ... renewing?*

Don't bother me, Amir thought, not until tomorrow.

He drifted into sleep and began to dream. He was walking downtown, in a neighborhood rich with entertainment and restaurants, their menus on display outside their front doors. Some even had an attractive young girl outside, describing the evening specials. He passed clubs with gaily decorated posters promising musical and theatrical performances.

Amir walked around, looking at everything, enjoying the crowd, the buzz, the pageantry. It was fun, he felt happy for a change. It comes from the crowd, he thought. Happiness is contagious if you let it be.

If only I were a football fan. Or maybe basketball.

I wish I were a happier person. I should try to be happier. How do you do that, exactly?

Walking past a theater, he looked in and there was a poster with the smiling face of the late Marcus Long holding a rifle under the caption, *The NRA Wants You.* Mr. Long looked happy.

Amir stared, then looked away. When he looked back at the poster, a skull wearing a bony grin had replaced Mr. Long's head. Amir walked past the theater. In the next block he passed a club. A poster proclaimed dance music and showed a four-piece band. One member of the band held an assault rifle instead of a guitar.

He kept walking. He passed another poster, this one showing the late Jeffrey Winton, advertising *Trick Shots to Amaze You.* Winton, in life an effeminate little man, looked absurd in cowboy regalia with wide-brimmed hat, boots, and two six shooters. Fur lined his leather vest. His clothes looked two sizes too big.

Amir stared at the poster and laughed.

He kept walking and found himself standing next to a pot-bellied man. The man turned and smiled at Amir.

"Do I know you?" Amir said.

"I used to own a shop in Lorton," the man said.

"Ah, yes. I have seen you. I never learned your name."

The man shrugged. "I no longer need one." Then he walked away.

Amir continued to the next block. He passed a man in a wheelchair, holding a metal coffee cup. The man was panhandling.

Amir stopped and looked down at the man. "You were a Senator, and a nasty one. Now look at you."

"Yeah? Well, fuck you and the horse you rode in on." The man rolled away.

Amir watched the man leave. You finally understand, don't you, Senator? Life looks different from the muzzle end of the rifle, doesn't it?

Amir walked another block and came to a theater, its ad on an automated billboard that flipped between three images. The first said, *Come and Be Amazed*. The second said, *Watch the Lady Vanish before Your Very Eyes*. The third was a massive black and white photograph of Lelah.

"Son of a bitch!" Amir shouted and sprang upwards into a sitting position. He was breathing heavily, his heart hammering. He was in bed. It had been a dream.

Serena rolled towards him, reached out, touched him, and murmured, "Poor baby." Her eyes did not open. Then she was quiet.

Amir looked at her and thought, hell with this. He got up, went downstairs, and poured a glass of milk. He sat in the living room, sipping milk and trying to think about something other than that black and white photograph.

Amir sat on a bench outside of Old City Hall in Richmond. The bench was ten yards from a bus stop sign. A middle-aged woman sat several feet away. He looked around, identifying landmarks, trying to register the neighborhood in his mind. He needed to remember everything later.

It was a complicated neighborhood, containing the major agencies of the state government. Down the block was the new General Assembly building, where the Attorney General had offices. Past that was the state Supreme Court. In the opposite direction, the governor's mansion.

If I were one of these office holders, I would be a little bit nervous, Amir thought. Moreover, if I had public ties to the NRA, like donations or endorsements, I might be butt-pucker nervous.

He had seen the Attorney General on TV, announcing that Max Pressler, the Chief of Police of Fairfax County, would be managing the expanded effort to catch the sniper.

So Amir thought, where better to see the extra resources than downtown Richmond, in the middle of all those government office buildings? If the government would want anything protected, surely it would start with itself.

Amir sat idly on a bench, not doing anything, hoping to see those extra resources in action. He did not have long to wait. One moment, it was quiet; the next, a flying drone, about two feet across, buzzed over the roadway, its camera pointed directly at Amir. He held up his hands and extended both middle fingers at the drone.

The woman next to him on the bench laughed.

Amir turned to her and said, "I'm sorry. I didn't mean to implicate you in my conspiracy to commit profanity in public."

"That's alright," she said. "Virginia could use a little free and candid expression."

The bass voice was lively. *How true. You know what they call idiots in Virginia?*

No, what? Amir thought.

*Thomas Jefferson scholars.*

Oh, good one. "Let's wave," he said. He and the woman waved at the drone. It flew away.

"Oh well," she said. "Show's over."

Minutes later, a bus came and stopped. "My ride," she said. She stood up and moved to board the bus.

"Have a nice day," Amir called after her. She waved without looking back.

Amir sat there by himself. Soon, a second drone came buzzing along. As it crossed in front of him, it suddenly stopped, hovered, and its camera slewed towards Amir.

He was tempted to expose himself to it. But it might be illegal, and who needed that hassle?

The bass voice was sly. *What is the penalty for wagging your wienie at a camera? Does a camera have rights?*

Do we? Amir thought.

After hovering for a dozen seconds, the drone turned and flew away.

Amir looked up at the tops of buildings. He was hoping to see an ultralight aircraft, but none appeared. Nor did he see any drones up high. They were all at low altitude.

He thought, how many drones would I see near the NRA headquarters?

*Probably many. Politics and money, baby.*

You think they actually have a satellite to use?

*Possibly, but how could a satellite distinguish your gun from all the others going off around here? After all, you are not the only one shooting at people. I believe they can detect a gunshot. They can see the heat signature, but it does not do them any good. Not in this environment.*

It's a puzzle, Amir thought.

*Of course, your targets have been from the upper classes. So the police might gang tackle, at least in the richer zip codes.*

I don't know what that means.

*It means, a wise man does not laugh at a live dragon.*

Max Pressler sat in his office in the late afternoon, exhausted and numb. The Governor got into the act with the death of the second NRA president. He dumped the matter on the Attorney General, who then dumped it on Max.

Politicians. Pressler thought, I don't like politicians. I thought I didn't like them, and now I'm certain of it.

I have to deal with it. Virginia has a sniper. Virginia's finest have been looking for the guy for a few months, with no results at all. That second NRA assassination clarified matters. No one knew why he was shooting people. Roundtree thought the guy was a pro. Someone else said, he might be a nutcase.

Hell, he could be both, probably is both.

Well, now we know, Max thought. This guy has a serious beef against guns. He's got a hard-on for the NRA. First, he shoots one executive, the president no less, at NRA national headquarters in broad daylight. Then, when the NRA selects a new president, our shooter sails right up to a couple layers of professional security, shoots the new president, at night and at home. Then he vanishes. The security team did not even know the executive was dead until the next morning.

His security was crap.

No one heard a gunshot at the NRA headquarters. No one heard a gunshot at the second NRA shooting. That is creepy.

Pressler was talking to himself. Everyone says, we cannot stop a sniper in a peacetime environment without knowing his motives. Too large an area, too many targets. The book says, well, ask the guy - what is it you want, can we negotiate, can we help you with anything? That lets you narrow the targets and track the guy down. We tried that. It went nowhere. Dead silence. Some people even thought, maybe the sniper just went away.

Then BOOM.

So no, he has not gone away.

Pressler's phone beeped at him, a new text message. He checked it. It was from Roundtree.

*You busy? Can I stop by?*

Pressler grunted and texted a reply. *If you have good news, then yes. Otherwise, no. It's already been a long day.*

Roundtree answered, *I'll stop by.*

Two minutes later, there was a knock on his door. Pressler looked up to see Roundtree entering his office. Heywood Miles was following him.

Pressler waved them into chairs. "Welcome. What's up?"

Miles looked at Roundtree. "You want to tell him?"

Roundtree shook his head. "It was your data."

"Your idea," Miles said.

"Okay," Roundtree said. "We may have a lead on the shooter."

Pressler sat up straight, his eyes wide open. "If this is a joke, you're a cruel bastard."

"No joke," Roundtree said. "Heywood and I have been working on datasets, mainly collections of license plates pulled from traffic cameras in various locations around Maryland and Virginia."

"Okay," Pressler said.

"You will recall, we mentioned the shooter might be a pissed off family member or friend of a shooting victim," Roundtree said. "Remember?"

"Sure," Pressler nodded. "Thousands of victims. Tens of thousands."

"Okay," Roundtree said. "Well, I asked Heywood to put together a database tracking the automobiles owned by friends and family members of the victims at Whitetop Mountain College. Remember that case?"

"Hell yeah. It seems long ago. A bad shooting," Pressler said. "Multiple fatalities, including the shooter. That case closed."

"That's right. The shooter's dead, so there's nothing to be done. Even so, it was the biggest shooting incident in recent months. Heywood's database tracked the family members and friends for that incident and came up with several hits on one Amir Hawari. He's fifty-three, born in Lebanon, immigrated thirty-five years ago. He became a citizen sixteen years ago. His only daughter was killed at Whitetop Mountain College."

"You got hits on this guy? What does that mean?" Pressler asked.

"Okay. The first NRA shooting happened in late September. On that day, traffic cameras detected Hawari's car at two intersections in Fairfax county, one on route 123, the other on route 236. Both of those are within two miles and forty-five minutes of the shooting," Roundtree said.

"That does not prove anything," Pressler said.

"That's right," Roundtree said. "It doesn't."

Pressler leaned back and exhaled heavily. He looked disappointed.

"There's more," Roundtree said. "A month later, in October, the day of the Lorton shooting, Hawari's car was photographed on Pohick Road, less than a mile from the gun shop, forty minutes after that shooting was reported."

"Okay."

"Three weeks after that, in November, Hawari's car is at four different intersections on Bradley Blvd., within two miles and forty-five minutes of that shooting."

"Impressive set of coincidences, you have there," Pressler said.

"And a couple weeks ago, on December 8, the day of the shooting in Arcturus …" Roundtree said.

"Don't tell me, let me guess," Pressler said.

"A camera at an intersection on route 1, Jeff Davis Highway, less than a mile from the home of the late NRA president," Roundtree said. "That makes four for four."

Roundtree looked at Pressler. "Chief, either it's a staggering coincidence, like a billion-to-one, or Hawari is the shooter. He lives a hundred miles away in Richmond, yet he was near every shooting, up around metro Washington. It is almost a certainty that he's the shooter."

"Any other plates satisfy this test?" Pressler said.

"No," Heywood said. "Just Hawari. A number of plates show up near two of the shootings. None at three or more. Except Hawari."

Pressler leaned back, stared at Roundtree and Miles, then grinned widely. "This may be a break. We need a break, bad."

He looked out the window, then back at the two men, "Four for four, eh?" Pressler looked down and shook his head. "Traffic cameras. Unbelievable." He looked up smiling. "Gentlemen, the state of Virginia does not pay you enough. Not even close."

Amir parked his car at the Virginia Lakes golf course, a public course in Fairfax County. He got out, popped the trunk, and pulled out a putter and three golf balls. Then he closed the trunk and walked from the parking lot past the clubhouse and out to the practice green. He dropped the balls on the green, lined up a putt, and tapped the ball.

The ball did not go into any hole. It did not even stop near any hole. Amir did not play golf. He had bought the putter the previous day from a used club barrel in the clubhouse for three dollars and twelve cents, counting tax.

He continued to putt, with little success. Every so often, he would glance over at a corner of the parking lot. There were several police vehicles there, three trucks and a car, and a dozen uniformed men carrying rifles and wearing windbreakers with 'SWAT' on the backs.

The rifles had long scopes. Amir thought, those guys are looking to reach out - way out - and touch someone. A counter-sniper team.

A TV reporter had dropped a comment about the state's expanded effort to capture or kill the sniper. Policemen at a golf course? Amir was there to check it out. He glanced in their direction. What can they be doing? Maybe they think they know where the sniper will strike next. Even I do not know that, so how can they?

Amir stood there thinking. Those guys are a threat only if I have a gun in my hands.

The bass voice echoed in his head. *You think it might be time to retire Amir, the Anti-Gun Gunner?*

Perhaps for a while, Amir thought. We know they are using a counter-sniper team. We know they have drones. We know a large team is working this matter. The real problem is, we do not know what else they have.

*You nailed two NRA presidents, back to back. They've got their reasons.*

I think we need to ditch the rifle and get another.

*Drop it in the river?*

No, I have something else in mind, Amir thought. Something better.

On a Saturday afternoon, after a shower, Amir and Serena were lying in bed, bathed in sweat. Their breathing had finally returned to normal.

Amir thought, we are clean, yet sweaty. Delightful.

Serena turned to face Amir. "Let me ask you something."

"Sure."

"Are you happy?"

"Are you kidding? You mean, lately?" He chuckled. "We've been through some rough times. I still think of Lelah every day. I think I'm getting through it. I think you're getting through it. What choice is there? But happy?" His voice rose to a peak. Serena laughed. He shook his head. "No. I'm just trying to adjust to what they call a new normal. I wouldn't call it happy. At least, I hope this isn't happy."

"I just wondered if I was being a good wife," she said.

Amir nodded. "You are an excellent wife. No complaints. It doesn't hurt that I'm nuts about you. Of course, I should point out, men are simple. If you take care of yourself, so you look okay, bang us regularly, don't spend too much money, and don't snore too loud, then we're happy. Most of us, anyway." He looked at her and smiled. "I know I am, or would be."

"Women are from Venus; men, from Mars," she said.

"I don't know about that," he said. "I think it's more that ... women are cats, men are dogs."

"Dogs?"

"Yeah, you know," he said. "We waltz right up to you, sniff your crotch, then say 'hi, I'm Ralph. Want to have sex?'. That's a dog."

He looked at her again, hoping for a laugh. She was not smiling, she looked pensive.

Uh oh, something's percolating, Amir thought.

"I was just thinking back over the last couple months," she said. "You're gone a lot, and I was wondering if you were avoiding me, or if there was something that you felt you had to seek elsewhere."

The bass voice rumbled, a harsh tone. *Amir, you need to fix this. Now. We do not need her misbehaving right now.*

Fine, as long as you understand, she is off limits.

*Maybe they'll put that on your tombstone.*

Amir sat there thinking, then said, "I've been trying to stay busy. I did some shooting for a while. I messed around with golf for a while. I ramped up my exercise. I toyed with birdwatching. I don't like to sit around and think. When I do that, I start feeling sorry for myself. I hate that. And you stay busy with your friends, so I didn't want to interrupt that." He looked at her. "I'd like to spend more time with you."

"I was thinking of going back to church."

Amir was deadpan. "Anything else you'd like to do together?"

Serena chuckled. "That bad?"

"Church? Please."

"You don't even know which church."

"It doesn't matter," Amir said, shaking his head. "Blah, blah, blah, blah, blah. There, you'll live forever. Eternal bliss. It'll be great. Now give us your money."

Serena shook her head.

"I'd rather get mugged. It's more honest," he said.

"You're terrible."

The bass voice was sarcastic. *Someone choke me, lest I speak.*

You be quiet, Amir thought. I have enough to deal with.

Amir looked at Serena. "When I was a kid, my family worshiped at a mosque. My mother's idea. My father was indifferent. Still, it was good for a while. The imam was a smart man, an educated man. An articulate man. I enjoyed listening to him. He talked about life's little lessons. The stuff that happens every day. Then he was promoted, replaced by this idiot who would stand up there and read from the Koran, as if none of us could read.

"At one point, the idiot said that good Muslims would all go to heaven. Everyone else would fall into torment. I looked around, thought it over, and made my choice. I did not want to be in the same long line as that asshole. That was the end of religion for me."

"Maybe church is a bad idea," she said.

"I'd rather go to a shopping mall," Amir said.

"Jesus."

"Not him either."

Serena said, "I am wondering if you are beyond repair."

"Definitely. I have earned that much."

## *Fall Back and Reload*

Amir walked into the gun shop, approached the counter. "Hey Chas."

Chas turned towards Amir, but his eyes stayed behind, on a sheet of paper, columns of numbers. He looked up and smiled. "Amir. How you doing? What you been up to?"

"Trying to stay busy," Amir said. "Exercising a lot."

"You trying to self-improve?"

"Truth is, I lost a family member recently," Amir said. "So I've been trying to muddle through that."

Chas stared at him. "Oh, I'm sorry. Well then, what can I do to help you muddle?"

"I was thinking of getting another rifle," Amir said. "I like the bolt action. But I was thinking another type might be fun, just for variety."

"You picky about caliber?"

"A little. I like the twenty-five ought six," Amir said.

Chas turned and touched rifles on the wall rack behind him, one at a time. He muttered, "No … no … nope. Ah, I've got it." He turned to face Amir. "I've got one sitting around you might like. Twenty-five oh six, hammer action, long barrel. A good plinker."

"How much?"

"A hundred and eighty bucks. For you? Let's say … one fifty."

"Wow. Does it shoot straight?" Amir said.

"Oh, you'd be surprised. It breaks down, too, so it's portable. And it comes with a little 4x scope."

"I'm interested," Amir said.

"Come back tomorrow, and you can shoot it," Chas said.

On the way home from the range, Amir was on a multi-lane road in light traffic. He was cruising along at the speed limit, checking his mirrors, keeping track of other cars. He noticed a dark, late model Ford in his rearview mirror. The car was odd - it stayed behind him when everyone else was passing him.

*That might be a tail, Amir. Some asshole might be tailing us.*

I didn't know they still did that, Amir thought. That is so … 1974. Maybe I should pull the leisure suit out of my closet, have a little fun.

He took an exit, drove for a couple of miles, then re-entered the road. The Ford was no longer behind him.

*Look for someone further back. We might have switched tails.*

If we have a tail, then we're being watched in other ways too.

*Definitely.*

What should we do?

*Go about your business. Detecting the tail is 90 percent of defeating it.*

What do the police know, do you suppose?

*Not enough to arrest you, that's for certain.*

Yeah. Once they get enough, we'll be the first to know.

The next day Amir got out of bed early, had breakfast, and went for a brief walk around the neighborhood. Few people were out in the neighborhood, so it was easy to spot a tail. He saw no one following him.

The thought of being spied upon was creepy. On his way home, the hair on the back of his neck stood up. He could feel unfriendly eyes burrowing into his skull.

There was a car rental business in a nearby shopping mall. Amir stopped there and rented one of their cars for a day, the tiniest Chevrolet he had ever seen. He took it and headed west, running at 65 mph. That seemed to be its top speed, so he had to stay in the right lane while other drivers whizzed past him.

Back at the gun shop, Chas showed him a simple little rifle, a used single shot twenty-five oh six with hammer action and a removable heavy barrel. Amir took it out to the range, centered it for two hundred and fifty yards, shot several dozen rounds through it, then returned to the shop.

Chas was waiting. "It's a sweetheart, isn't it?"

"Yeah, it's accurate. Also simple, which I like."

"Vintage technology, with a lot of blood on it."

Amir looked at him, puzzled.

"Mostly deer," Chas said.

Amir nodded. He paid for the rifle, then returned to the mall, dropped off the rental, transferred the gun to his car, and drove home.

---

The morning sun lit the alley where Mike Stanton slept. The yellow light gradually intruded through his eyelids and into his brain, the growing traffic noise added its voice, and after a few minutes, sleep lifted and he opened his eyes.

Getting up was hard these days. The summer was easy; you could sleep in your underwear and be just fine. Now it was late December. The nights were cold. He weathered it. He could weather just about anything. Nonetheless, it was harder to leave the warmth of the sleeping bag and accept the sharp slap of cold air.

I have to get up, he thought. In several quick motions, Stanton unzipped the sleeping bag, stood up, and put on pants and a jacket over his long johns. He slipped his feet, already in heavy socks, into a worn pair of hiking boots. Now he was ready to face the day.

Today would be easy. A day for errands, not a day for work or money. He had plenty of money, a hundred dollars at least. He would stop at the Methodist church, have breakfast, and use their kitchen to wash his clothes. He kept his clothes in a duffle bag. As they got dirty, they moved into a black plastic trash bag. When his clothes filled the trash bag, and the trash bag filled the duffle, he would do laundry.

At the church he saw all the usual guys, first at breakfast, then doing the laundry. No women, just men. He said hello to the minister and a few other people. Then he stripped to his underwear, put his clothes into a plastic laundry basket, took them to the kitchen, and dumped them all into a tub of hot soapy water. Several such tubs were heating on top of the stove. A ten-minute soak, then ten minutes in clean water, then he removed his clothes and squeezed the water out of them.

Then off to an overheated room with drying lines stretching across the room. He took line number three, hung his wet clothes, and took a quick shower. An hour and a half later, he was clean and his clothes were dry, so he packed up and went back out into the wide world, feeling wonderful.

It was early afternoon. Rather than waste the upcoming rush hour, Stanton walked a block to a stone wall a hundred yards from city hall. Any closer to city hall, the police would hassle you for panhandling. He sat down and pulled out a porcelain coffee cup with a colorful Apple Computer logo on it. It was a beautiful cup; he had paid money for it at Goodwill. When someone walked by, he would hold out the cup, thank them if they contributed, be silent if not.

In the afternoon, a slender, middle-aged man walked past Stanton, then stopped and turned. "How you doing, buddy? You okay, what with the winter here?"

Stanton looked at the man and smiled. "Oh, that's no problem. It doesn't get all that cold here. Thanks for asking."

"Do you have a place to stay inside?"

"Nah, I'm usually right over there, next to the FedEx. It's warmer than you'd think."

The man held out a twenty. "Well, you take care."

"Hey, thanks, brother. Happy Holidays to you."

The man walked away. He was a little bit out of the ordinary, dark skin, dark eyes, black hair, a bit shorter than average. Prosperous, athletic, nice shoes, brown leather. He looked middle eastern, or Indian, acted like he knew what it felt like to be poor.

Maybe from a previous life, Stanton thought.

Stanton shrugged, people came to Fairfax from all over the place. He had seen plenty of people from south Asia and the Middle East.

The next morning, Stanton woke up in the same sleeping bag, now clean, in the same alley. As before, he took his time waking up, the sleeping bag so warm, the outside air so cold. A weak sun cast yellow morning light. Birds flew through the sky. The day seemed promising, so Mike Stanton did his usual maneuver, jumping into warm clothes and rising to face the day.

He saw something further up the alley. He moved towards it and found a little bolt action rifle leaning against the wall. It was a single shot job, like he had as a kid. He picked it up and for a moment remembered hunting squirrel and deer with his uncle in the woods in western Kentucky before TVA ran a lake over his uncle's land.

He hoisted the rifle to his shoulder and lined up his eye to look through the scope. The sight picture was jumping around, as it began to do after he was wounded. The weight was all wrong, the center of gravity out towards the barrel. He adjusted his left hand and thought, you could get used to it, maybe. He looked through the sight again. The tremor was there. It would always be there.

He sighed. I was good at this, a long time ago.

Suddenly, he heard a loud male voice, "You! Stop right there. Put the weapon down." Stanton looked down to the end of the alley and saw a young patrolman, his weapon drawn and pointed at Stanton.

"Yes sir," Stanton said. "Anything you say, sir." With two fingers, he held the rifle by the muzzle, bent over and laid it on the ground, then moved away from it, his hands held high.

A second patrolman appeared at the end of the alley.

"I'm not armed," Stanton called out.

The first patrolman pointed his pistol at the ground, then holstered the weapon. The two men approached Stanton. The shorter of them bent over and picked up the rifle. He opened the breech and a cartridge popped out. He caught it as it fell.

The taller patrolman, whose name tag read MECKS, said, "You can drop your hands. Could we see some ID?"

"I lost it."

"Where do you live?"

Stanton gave him his name and waved at the alley. "This is where I spend my free time."

Then Mecks asked, "Can you tell me what you are doing with a loaded rifle in the middle of Fairfax City?"

"I don't normally have one," Stanton answered. "I just found that one leaning against the wall, right there, just this morning." He pointed.

"Uh huh," Mecks said. "Okay, Stanton, we would like you to come with us. I think my captain may have a few questions for you."

"Sure, officer," Stanton answered. "Can we get a ride?"

"Yeah, okay," Mecks said.

"Should I bring my stuff?"

"Yeah, I think so. Someone might take it," Mecks said.

"Better safe than sorry," Stanton said.

The other officer chuckled.

Skip Taylor was in his office, trying to manage the affairs of the office while keeping a corner of his brain tuned to the sniper investigation.

Lately, he was coming home every evening exhausted. He would miss dinner, say hello to his wife and his two kids, collapse into an easy chair, and spend the evening in semi-consciousness.

Near the end of one day, he got good news. Abigail's voice came through the intercom, "Mr. Attorney General, I have John Hunt of the National Rifle Association on one."

"Put him through, Abigail, thank you," Skip Taylor said.

"Hello," Taylor said. Not the president? he wondered.

"Mr. Taylor, this is John Hunt of the NRA. Normally, the president would make this call, but we have not filled that position. We're leaving it open until the sniper is caught."

"I see. Who is running the place, if I may ask?" Taylor said.

"It's rule by committee, by several of the senior vice presidents. They've asked me to work with you on your campaign, on endorsements, fundraising, and advertising."

"That's a big relief," Taylor said. "I was working with Jeff Winton, but that stopped when he was shot."

"Yes, well, let's get that moving again. No one is irreplaceable. Here at the NRA, it's full speed ahead. We want good outcomes in the elections. It's my job to make it happen."

"As I said, that's a big relief."

"Later this week or next, let's meet for a couple hours. Can we do that?"

"Let me see." Taylor looked at the computer monitor on his desk. "I think Thursday would work."

"Thursday at 3?"

"Yes. Three would be fine. I look forward to meeting you, Mr. Hunt."

"As do I. I'll pick you up Thursday at three. Have a good day."

The line went dead. Taylor thought, he's picking me up at three; that's a nice touch. It was all he could do to keep from jumping out of his chair and shouting in glee. He stood up and began pacing around his office. He almost danced - I'm still in the game, not dead yet. We'll get it moving. Everything will work out.

It ain't over til it's over.

Yeah, yeah, yeah.

He smiled.

Yeah.


Roundtree and Miles came into Pressler's office, sat down, and waited for Pressler.

Pressler spoke into the phone, "Yes sir, we'll get right on that. Thank you, sir."

He replaced the handset and looked up at the two men. "Well, guys, that was the AG. The judge rejected our request for surveillance. No active surveillance, no phone tap." Pressler rubbed his hands across his face.

He continued, "He agreed the evidence is suspicious. But he thinks it would not withstand a challenge."

"It's a billion to one coincidence, then," Roundtree said.

Pressler leaned back and looked up at Roundtree. "I'm trying to remember the last time I convinced a lawyer with a math argument."

Roundtree's mouth went crooked and he looked sideways at Miles.

Pressler continued, "If he's right, he did us a favor. Our investigation is still alive. We will just forget that little incident of your tracking this suspect. No harm no foul, since he shook off your man so fast that we could not in all honesty call it surveillance."

Roundtree sat there and thought, it could have been worse. The FBI had lent them a field agent. So they said. In fact, the guy was less of a field agent, more of a glorified lab technician. His first try at surveillance did not go well.

Pressler continued, "I agree with you, this guy is the only promising suspect we have. Okay, we can do normal information collection, so let's do that. I want to know every fact about Amir Hawari contained in any public or law enforcement database. Ask the FBI to help. Maybe they can do something right. Come back when you've got it all, and we'll take it from there. Meanwhile, do not approach Hawari."

"Understood," Roundtree said. He wondered, does that let me put an RFID tag on his car? Better not to ask. If they catch me, I'll plead ignorance.

"Yes sir," Miles said.

Roundtree and Miles stood up and left Pressler's office, closing the door behind them.

Out in the hallway, Roundtree put his hand on Miles's shoulder. "Listen, give this to the FBI. They know they screwed up, so give them a chance to make it right. Max is disappointed, so back them up, okay?"

"Don't worry," Miles said. "I'll get what can be got. Legally."

"Good. Legal would be good," Roundtree said. Miles turned away and Roundtree said, "Uh, Heywood, run another search of the traffic tapes, Hawari's car only. No one else."

"Okay."

Ed Shapiro knocked on Pressler's open door and poked his head into the office. Pressler was at his desk, staring at a computer monitor.

He looked up and said, "Ed, come in. What's up?"

"You got five minutes?"

"Sure."

"Okay, I have news. I know you've been working with Roundtree and Miles on traffic camera data. I hear that you have a suspect for the sniper," Shapiro said.

"Correct," Pressler said. "There's a guy who lost a daughter at Whitetop. Traffic cameras spotted him near all four of the sniper shootings. We're checking him out. We asked a judge for a surveillance order, but he turned us down."

"Well, your bad guy's got competition," Shapiro said. "Two days ago, a couple of Fairfax City patrolmen picked up a homeless man with a rifle. The man's name is Mike Stanton."

"So?"

"Turns out, he's from Arkansas, an ex-army sniper, combat vet, two tours, seventeen kills. He's been sleeping in an alley in Fairfax City, not far from city hall. Two years ago, he got a medical discharge for nerve damage."

"He doesn't sound like a candidate for sniper school," Pressler said.

"He's not. They picked him up because he was holding and pointing a rifle. A single shot, twenty-five ought six, with a heavy barrel. Loaded," Shapiro said.

Pressler looked up at Shapiro, his mouth open, his eyes burrowing into Shapiro's. "Don't tell me. Don't you dare."

"Yep." Shapiro nodded. "It's the murder rifle, alright. The ballistics match, and we fired the cartridge and ran an NMR and a chemical analysis. That cartridge came from the same box of match ammo used in the killings."

"Sorry, remind me, an NMR is …?" Pressler said.

"Nuclear magnetic resonance."

"Ah, of course. That. But none of that means Stanton is the sniper. The bad guy could have dropped the rifle in the alley, and Stanton picked it up," Pressler said.

"I agree," Shapiro said. "Stanton is clearly not sniper material. He has nerve damage and a tremor in his left hand. He's homeless, broke, and does not own a car. He's got a disability pension he doesn't even collect. The guy's a bit of a mess. Even if he could shoot, how would he get around to targets in Fairfax, Lorton, Alexandria, and the Maryland suburbs? I doubt he's taking a taxi.

"The bitch is, we have to tell the AG that we picked up a guy whose rifle is a match in a murder investigation," Shapiro said.

"You think the AG will listen to reason?"

Shapiro rolled his eyes at the ceiling, then returned to look at Pressler. "No."

"No? I gather you don't trust lawyers."

"I know too much," Shapiro said. "Ever watch a lawyer try to do mathematics? The first time I saw it, I thought the man was kidding. It was surreal."

Pressler said, "I see. Okay. Thanks, Ed." He took a deep breath and exhaled slowly.

Shapiro turned and left the office.

Pressler pushed himself up and out of his chair, walked over to the window, and stared out into the evening. Several people were searching public and law enforcement databases for information on one Amir Hawari. He was a naturalized citizen from Lebanon, father of one, a daughter, Lelah, killed at Whitetop Mountain College.

A Richmond resident, Hawari had no criminal record. He retired two years ago from running a small export-import business. He was successful and well off, with a home in a prosperous neighborhood with safe streets and good schools. Married for thirty-four years, he had an old car and a plus-800 credit rating.

Pressler thought, this is a stretch. No matter. Let's assume that Hawari is the sniper. Let's say he goes crazy after his daughter is murdered. He gets a gun, starts shooting people in the gun business. Let's suppose he's good at it. He gets away with it. How is any of that possible? Pressler sat there for a long moment. Maybe he was in combat before, in Lebanon. That's been a war zone for ... forever.

But forget all that ... thanks to our ham-handed FBI agent, Hawari discovers he's being tailed, therefore must be under suspicion. He decides to cool it. He leaves the rifle in an alley where a homeless guy sleeps. The homeless guy picks it up, then the police catch him with it and arrest him. Maybe the homeless guy even gets indicted.

The homeless guy might get screwed. What's worse, Hawari just divorced himself from the single best piece of evidence. Naturally, he wiped it clean. Now how do we indict Hawari? Catch him in the act?

Good luck with that.

In addition, it's an old hunting rifle. A modern assault rifle, we could trace, probably. But an aged, single shot hunting gun? It might have been bought or sold or gifted a dozen times with no records. Untraceable.

Pressler frowned. Untraceable and lethal.

Our evidence consists of a collection of improbable coincidences. We could convince a statistician. An MBA would get it. However, I can imagine what even an average defense attorney would do with our traffic camera evidence. It'd be catnip.

Now we get to start over.

"This thing is a pig's favorite mudhole," Pressler muttered.


Roundtree was so tired he fell asleep at his desk. The other guys in the department were so tired, they let him.

The chime on his cellphone went off, waking him up. He picked it up, looked at it, and found a text message from Pressler - *Come here, I need you.*

If I go back to sleep, what will he do? Roundtree wondered. Probably come looking for me, and when he finds me, shove me out of my chair onto the floor. I am tired, but he will not sympathize. There's a level of exhaustion that comes with being a cop.

Jesus.

Roundtree stood up, wavered, and thought, come on Dan, you got this. He turned and went to Pressler's office. The door was open, so Roundtree knocked twice and went in. Pressler was listening to the phone pressed against his ear. He pointed to the small table. Roundtree moved to the table and sat down. A minute later, Pressler hung up the phone and joined him.

"I have another assignment for you," Pressler said. Pressler waited, expecting a complaint followed by an argument.

Roundtree pointed a tired, sagging expression at Pressler. Then he put on a jaunty grin and, without focusing both eyes, said, "Sure, Max. What is it?"

Pressler grinned. "You have an odd sense of humor, but it's better than nothing."

"So I'm told."

"You've probably heard this story - a few days ago Fairfax City cops pulled in a homeless guy who was playing around with a rifle in an alley near City Hall," Pressler said.

Roundtree focused on Pressler. "Yeah?"

"Yeah. The rifle was a single shot, twenty-five oh six, with a 26 inch, heavy barrel and a dinky little scope."

"You're shitting me."

Pressler shook his head. "Nope. It's the murder weapon. The chemical residues match those of bullet fragments found near or in our sniper victims."

"Can we pull the serial number?"

Pressler nodded. "Sure. It was first sold in 1971. The original buyer is dead. No other paperwork."

Roundtree chuckled. "Of course." He sat there thinking. "Max, this could be a ploy. The shooter leaves the rifle in the alley, the homeless guy picks it up, takes the blame. Now we can't catch the shooter with the murder weapon. Even if they don't charge the homeless guy, the shooter is off the hook."

Roundtree looked out the window and murmured, "Slick, my man. That's slick." He looked at Pressler. "I know the answer already, but … no prints?"

"Sure. The homeless guy's, from one end to the other."

Roundtree nodded. "Well, now what?"

"You don't think the homeless guy is the shooter," Pressler said.

"Hawari is the shooter."

"Okay. I want you to interview the homeless guy. His name's Mike Stanton. Find out as much as you can, and think about convincing the AG not to indict him," Pressler said.

"You think he would?"

"For political advantage, yeah, I think he would."

"Where is Stanton now?"

"Fairfax City jail," Pressler said. "They're detaining him. He's not under arrest."

"He's not? Sounds like he needs a lawyer."

"Feel free to mention that to him."


Roundtree walked through the door of the Fairfax City jail. He looked around. This is the nicest, cleanest jail I have ever seen. Most jails stink. This one smells better than a hospital, without the disinfectant tang.

There was a single counter facing the door, manned by a patrolman. Instead of bars, the jail spouted RFID receivers, security cameras, and motion detectors. Roundtree moved to the counter and showed his badge. "I'm Dan Roundtree, attached to Fairfax County police. I have an appointment to speak with Michael Stanton."

The patrolman hit a button on an intercom. After half a minute, a second patrolman came to the front desk. He looked at a computer screen, looked at Roundtree, and said, "Stanton?"

"Please," Roundtree said.

"Follow me."

Roundtree followed him to a small conference room with a table, a pair of chairs, and no windows. Roundtree sat down. The patrolman left and a minute later returned with Mike Stanton. Stanton had showered. They had given him a shave and a haircut. He was wearing a standard orange jailhouse jumpsuit.

Stanton sat down and Roundtree held out his hand. Stanton shook it.

"I'm Dan Roundtree. I'm working with the Fairfax County police. I'd like to ask you some questions, if that's okay."

Stanton looked puzzled, then said, "I have a question of my own."

Roundtree looked up at him. "Okay, shoot."

"Am I under arrest?"

Roundtree held up his hands. "I don't know, are you under arrest? Did somebody say you're under arrest?"

"No. I thought they had to do that, read me my rights."

"They do have to do that. So if no one read you your rights, then you're not under arrest."

"I can leave if I want to?" Stanton said.

"I think so, yeah. Did they ask you to stay?"

"Not exactly. They said I could. They offered. They were polite about it."

Yeah, that's Fairfax City alright, Roundtree thought. Everybody here is polite.

"Has anyone explained to you what's going on?"

"No. We talk about stuff, but no one's explained," Stanton said.

"Okay. In Virginia and Maryland, a sniper has been shooting people. So far, he's shot four people, killed three."

"I read about that in a newspaper."

"Okay. The rifle you picked up? That's the murder weapon," Roundtree said. "We tested it. The residues match material recovered from the victims."

Stanton shrugged. "You can have the rifle, no problem. Easy come, easy go."

"Yeah, well, that's generous of you, but here's the problem," Roundtree said. "Some people might think that you were the one who did the shooting and the killing."

"But I didn't," Stanton said, with some heat. "I haven't shot a rifle since my discharge. Not once."

Roundtree paused, then nodded. "I believe you. I'd like to talk about that, if that's okay."

"Yeah, sure," Stanton said.

Roundtree smiled. "Okay. I went over some information about you. You were in the army, weren't you?"

Stanton nodded. "Five years, two tours."

"A scout sniper?" Roundtree said.

"Yes. Other jobs too. I was just a grunt at first, til they found out I could shoot," Stanton said.

"How did you learn to shoot?"

"Hunting back home in Arkansas as a kid," Stanton said.

"What did you hunt?"

"Anything I could eat," Stanton said.

"And you had seventeen kills in a combat zone," Roundtree said.

"I don't know about that," Stanton said. "I don't like to talk about that, or think about it. It was … unpleasant."

"We don't have to talk about it," Roundtree said.

Stanton nodded. "Thanks, cause I don't want to."

They talked for an hour about anything that Stanton seemed willing to talk about. Rifles, hunting, baseball, politics (a minor subject), camping, churches (another minor subject), job hunting. They talked about Stanton's medical discharge, which followed being hit in the left forearm by a Taliban bullet.

Near the end of the hour, Roundtree reached into his pocket and pulled out a 4" x 6" black and white photograph, "I have a photo here. I'd like to know if you know this man, or have seen him."

He handed Stanton a DMV photo of Hawari. Stanton looked at it casually, and said, "Yeah. I've seen this man. He gave me money for the holidays. He was friendly."

"He gave you money? How much money?"

"Twenty dollars," Stanton said. "I hang out on sidewalks, ask for money. He gave me some."

"Did you have to do anything for the money?"

Stanton shook his head. "I don't think so. Not that I recall."

"Did you talk about the rifle?" Roundtree said.

"No."

"You sure?"

"Yes. I would remember. I didn't see the rifle until a few days ago," Stanton said.

Roundtree leaned back in his chair and looked at Stanton. "I believe you."

"Good. I'm telling the truth," Stanton said.

Roundtree nodded. "Listen, thanks for talking to me. So, how do you like this place?"

"I like it." Stanton shrugged.

"They treat you well here?"

"Yeah, not bad."

"Okay," Roundtree said. "One last request - if anyone here tells you that you're under arrest, I want you to give me a call. I can help you. Will you do that?" He held out a business card.

Stanton took the card and said, "Why would you help me?"

"Because it's my job to find the sniper, and I don't think you're him," Roundtree said.

"Okay. I'll do that. Thanks," Stanton said. He pocketed the card and looked at Roundtree, then he nodded towards the photo. "You're after that guy, aren't you?"

"Yes, I am. How can you tell?"

"You've got the look," Stanton said. "A hunter, or a predator. I saw that look a lot in Afghanistan. Some guys have it, some don't." He shrugged. "Most don't."

"Huh. How about that," Roundtree said.

"Uh … the guy in the photo?"

"Yeah?"

"He's got that look too," Stanton said.

# *Metamorphoses*

The intercom came alive, scratchily, "Mr. Attorney General, I have John Hunt of the NRA."

"Show him in, Abigail," Skip Taylor said. Ten seconds later his office door opened and a balding, middle-aged man in a gray tailored suit entered the office.

"Mr. Taylor!" John Hunt approached him, his hand held out.

"Mr. Hunt!"

"Please, call me John."

"Skip."

They shook hands.

Hunt said, "It's good to meet you. I have a question, do you have dinner plans? I know a good roadhouse out on 295, serves a fine burger. Pretty good beer, too."

Taylor's face brightened. "Yeah? Lead on."

"We'll take my car," John Hunt said. They took an elevator down to the street level, where Taylor learned that Hunt's car came with a driver who looked like he turned down the Captain America role for a better gig with the NRA.

"The NRA now protects its executives when they're out and about. Sign of the times, I'm afraid," Hunt said.

Have Americans ever been better armed and less secure? Skip Taylor looked at the driver - how many weapons is he carrying? "Better safe than sorry."

"Yeah, don't we know it," Hunt said.

The car escaped the downtown traffic and briefly drove on the interstate. It dropped them off outside the front door of the Gray Fox Inn, located in a remote wooded area just off an enormous cloverleaf.

Inside, the restaurant was dark and quiet with tarnished brass and varnished wood in the walls, floors, long bar, and furniture. Hunt walked to a corner booth, away from other patrons, and sat down. Taylor slid onto the bench across from him.

"Is this okay?" Hunt said.

"Yeah. Never been here. It's nice, kind of dusky."

"It feels to me like a men's club," Hunt said.

Taylor nodded.

Hunt looked around the restaurant. A waitress noticed them, came over, and took their orders for beer and two burger platters. A minute later, two large steins of amber beer thumped onto the table.

Hunt turned his beer mug, grabbed the handle, and picked it up in a toast. "Your health."

"Long life," Taylor said, raising his mug.

Hunt chatted for a couple of minutes - a local basketball team was in a college tournament. Just as Taylor's mind began to wander, the food arrived. The men began to eat.

"I understand that Marcus Long originally approached you," Hunt said. "And that you spoke with Jeff Winton as well." He took a large bite out of his burger and turned sideways to look at Taylor around a mouth stuffed with food.

"That's right. It was a political deal," Taylor said. "I would support the NRA on concealed carry and they would support my candidacy for the U.S. Senate." He took a sip of beer.

"Mumph," Hunt said. Then he swallowed mightily. For a moment, Taylor wondered if he could remember how to do the Heimlich maneuver.

Hunt chased the burger with beer. "Look. I'd like to be honest with you, and I hope you'll be honest with me. Here's a question - what do you think of concealed carry, just between you and me and the four walls?"

"Honestly? It's a sideshow. I think it's a bad idea in urban environments. That's what the police tell me."

Hunt stopped chewing and stared at him.

Taylor continued, "The real problem is bigger than that. Politics at the national level. The Constitution guarantees gun rights. Since it's the Constitution, no matter how you craft it, the rule is one-size-fits-all. But one-size-fits-all makes no sense for guns.

"Take concealed carry. It makes sense in Wyoming. I've never heard that questioned - sparse population, police scattered all over a big state. Numerous four-footed critters around, some of them dangerous. A gun comes in handy in that environment."

Taylor took a drink. "But the same rule is a recipe for disaster in downtown Richmond, or Chicago, or New York City. Completely different environment – ample law enforcement, no critters, high population density. In New York City, you carry a pistol to shoot people, not critters. That's why the public is divided along rural-urban lines on gun control."

Hall nodded. "Not to mention the casualties."

Taylor nodded. "Black urban males are butchering each other. There's a nasty racial side to gun regulations. White folks in the suburbs scared of black burglars from the ghetto."

"So why did you offer your support?" Hunt said.

"Politics," Taylor said. "The art of standing in line. I want to get into the U.S. Senate. I can't do that without making a deal. I'll do a deal with the NRA, even if I don't agree with them." Taylor paused and looked at Hunt. "But I think it's a pity we can't have a relaxed, candid conversation about gun control. Maybe that's the reward for decades of lying to each other."

Hunt had a sheepish expression on his face. He looked around the restaurant and said, "Keep this under your hat, but we've been having similar conversations within the Association."

"Seriously?" Taylor said. "In the NRA?" He stared at Hunt for a moment and wondered, is this a test? "Wow. Mr. Hunt, you display unsuspected depth."

Hunt laughed.

Taylor said, "Don't worry. Mum's the word."

Hunt nodded. "Yeah, many of our members would happily string us up if they knew that. Nonetheless, it's true. The shootings shook people up. Someone killed two of our presidents and got away with it." He held up a hand and looked at Taylor. "No offense."

Taylor grimaced. "What can I say? It speaks for itself."

"Anyway, it makes us wonder, are we sure we want everybody wearing a gun on their hip?"

"Well, like I said. Okay for Wyoming, not okay for New York City," Taylor said. "There are advantages to letting the states and the cities handle this one."

Hunt emptied his beer, then looked around as if hoping for a quick refill. "I'm shocked. You don't think the right to bear arms deters tyranny by the state?"

Taylor paused, then said, "Okay, you want to play, let's do that. Here's the problem: let's say I'm a patriot, and I'm worried about my government turning to tyranny." He put a French fry into his mouth.

"Okay."

Taylor chewed for a moment, then said, "Now ... the second amendment doesn't refer to guns. It refers to arms. Okay. Well, my eyes work just fine. What I see is, the government is well armed. Therefore, if I want to deter tyranny, I need what the government has. Otherwise, I'm outgunned and deterring tyranny is a suicide mission."

Hunt nodded.

"Do you disagree with any of that?" Taylor said.

"No."

"Okay. So ... modern times being what they are, I want more than pistols and rifles," Taylor said. "I want tanks, RPGs, wire-guided missiles, land mines, germ warfare. I want machine guns, cannon."

Taylor took a long swig of beer, looked at Hunt, and swallowed. "Jet aircraft, smart bombs ... hell, I want nukes." Taylor shook his head. "But let's face it - that would be insane. Everyone understands that, right? Even crazy people understand that, don't they?" He stared at Hunt.

Hunt laughed.

Taylor continued, "Okay. Bottom line – the deterrence argument makes no sense."

"I think it made sense in 1781."

Taylor nodded. "Sure, until rifled weapons and Gatling guns hit the stage. After that it kept getting worse."

"Yeah."

"Bio-weapons." Taylor took a bite of cheeseburger. "I can hardly wait for beam weapons to hit the market. Predatory drones. Miniaturized explosives. Venomous mini-bots."

"Okay. Point well taken." Hunt stared at Taylor, a hard executive stare, weighing likelihoods. "It sounds to me as if we can work together. I don't think either of us is much of a virgin, and we're not looking for an ideal world. But we can work together."

Hunt picked up a napkin and wiped his mouth. "So let's make some plans. You need to kick off your candidacy. There's a social club in downtown Richmond that we often use for major announcements. We need to throw a party of sorts. You'll make a speech. I think you should discuss policy positions that are a bit weaker than those of the past. You should promote a softening of the debate, with more tolerance, more willingness to compromise."

Taylor thought for a moment, then said, "I could talk about whether law and order is compatible with a world in which folks are willing to take the law into their own hands," Taylor said. "I could talk about America's exceptional homicide rate. What do you think about that?"

"Write up something and let's get going on it," Hunt said. "We'll plan on announcing three or four weeks after your speech."

Taylor held out his hand. "Deal."

They shook hands, then Hunt looked around. "I wonder what happened to the waitress, and could I trouble her for another beer?"

Their business settled, Skip Taylor and John Hunt stayed at the restaurant for another twenty minutes, relaxing and drinking beer. Then they left, and Hunt dropped Taylor back at his office.

Everyone had gone home. Skip Taylor entered his office, microwaved a cup of old coffee, and sat there trying to slow himself down, to think. Hunt's views came as a happy surprise. Taylor could see new possibilities in law and politics.

A more flexible NRA and a better world, Taylor thought. I could make a name for myself. I could be the guy who solves the gun control impasse, who brings together two enemies who have not had a civil conversation in decades. I could lead them to a workable agreement.

I could be the guy who walks down the street and people would point and say, that man saved twenty thousand lives a year. Or maybe only ten … still, ten thousand people … every year. That would add up.

I could be an ancestor. A hero. A name.

I could be Forever.

The next day, the intercom came to life, "I have Chief Pressler on the line."

"Thanks, Abigail," Skip Taylor said. He hit a button on the intercom. "Max. How are you? Tell me some good news."

"Good afternoon, Mr. Attorney General. Yes, I have news. It's going to sound like good news at first, but we're skeptical."

"Let me guess. Allie McKenzie is dying to have lunch with me," Taylor said.

"Uh ... I don't know who that is."

Taylor's mouth dropped open and he hurriedly closed it around the wisecrack on his lips. Allie McKenzie was a rock and roll singer, a songbird with looks as rare and wonderful as her voice. "Chief, you need to get out more. So what's your news?"

"We recovered the rifle used in the sniper murders."

"What? Why, that's great, Max. Congratulations. How did you manage that?" Taylor said.

"Ah, there lies the problem. We didn't. Fairfax City police picked up a homeless man living in an alley. He had the rifle."

Taylor wondered briefly, how many times was the homeless man shot? His voice dropped an octave. "Uh oh. Tell me everything."

"No, no, it's not like that. The homeless man did not resist. He gave up the rifle. The officers detained him for questioning."

"Oh. Well, great." Taylor exhaled. For once, nobody got shot. "So what's the problem?"

"Sir, we tested the rifle and it matched evidence collected from the four shooting sites. It's the murder rifle. But we think the sniper planted the rifle to mislead us."

"Ah so. The homeless man is not the sniper, then?" Taylor said.

"We don't think so, sir."

"That's too bad. Explain."

"He's ex-army, a combat vet, a former sniper with seventeen kills in Afghanistan," Pressler said.

Taylor laughed. "Chief, I could make a case out of that right there."

"Yes sir, but his discharge two years ago was medical. He was hit in the left forearm in combat and suffered irreparable nerve damage. He has a pronounced tremor as a result. The guy literally cannot hold a rifle still, not even close. He could hit a barn from a hundred yards ... maybe."

"I see. That's a problem." Taylor wondered, could I suppress the medical records? As a matter of ... what? National security?

Oooohhh, of course. Privacy. Yeah, privacy ... nah, that's stupid. I'd be using a man's right to privacy to convict him of a capital crime. Surely, no judge is that stupid.

Are they?

Pressler continued, "Sir, our sniper - the actual sniper, the guy we should be looking for - shot a president of the NRA, in the dark, past a team of security professionals, from over two hundred yards away. I don't think this homeless guy could do that."

"So you don't want to arrest him?" Taylor said.

"No sir. I'm inclined to let him go. He's not the sniper."

"Uh, I'd like you to hang onto him for questioning, as a person of interest. If you let him go, do you think he's a flight risk?"

"I think he would go back to the alley where he sleeps at night," Pressler said.

"Tell you what. Ask him to wear a security band. Tell him it lets us get in touch with him if we need to," Taylor said. "That way we can scoop him up any time we want."

"Sir, I will need a court order."

"No problem, Chief. I'll arrange it," Taylor said. "Anything else?"

"No sir."

"Okay. Enjoy your evening, Max. I'll be in touch."

Taylor killed the call and sat back, a grin on his face. What a week I'm having, he thought. The NRA is supporting me and agreeing to be less bloodthirsty than expected. Who was it said, the prospect of being hung at dawn focuses the mind wonderfully? Was it Twain?

Apparently, losing your executives to gunfire has the same effect.

A homeless man, a combat vet. An ex-sniper, no less. It feels like Christmas, except Santa Claus could never offer gifts like these.

If I prosecute the homeless man, Taylor thought, Virginia will cheer, loudly. Snipers scare the shit out of people. Our sniper has killed. How many dead? Is it three or four? Whatever. Anyway, let's focus ... it is less than a year to the election. That's enough time for a criminal prosecution, especially considering the homeless man is broke. His counsel will be a public defender.

*312*

Who would his counsel use for witnesses? The only people who know much about the evidence are the police, and they cannot testify opposite the state. I guess he could hire a couple of experts. Good luck with that.

I need to delay a few months. The initial ruling needs to come out after the election. Ha. I'm a pro. If I can't stall that long, I'll eat my underwear on the way to the laundry.

Of course, we'll lose. If I were the guy's counsel, I'd take him to a range, have him shoot, and see if he could hit anything smaller than a barn. As to the army's medical documents, I cannot keep those out of the court record. In fact, I don't want to.

This guy is not our sniper, but if our legal system is awake, he'll be acquitted. No harm done. It is not as if he is busy. Also, they will feed him better in jail than he can get on the street. Isn't that right?

The AG leaned back and looked up at the ceiling. Okay, admittedly being prosecuted for multiple murder will cause the man some stress. In Virginia we execute, at least in theory. That is unfortunate, but he will get off. I want to prosecute him, not convict him.

That is an important difference.

Taylor thought it over. Before I move to the Senate, I need to appoint one of our dimmer attorneys to lead the case. Better safe than sorry. I do not need a murder-by-judge on my conscience.

Skip Taylor took a government car with a driver to a VFW center just outside downtown Richmond. That allowed him to roll the car right up to the front door and get out in front of the cameras. Everyone knew, important people sat in the back of big black automobiles. It was important to look important, so voters understood they were voting for someone already proven to be important.

It made them feel better, Taylor thought. It let them vote for you. Little people often admire important people, even when they hate them.

Sure enough, when the back door opened and the AG got out of the car, two news cameras were filming less than ten feet away. Before he had taken two steps several reporters shoved recorders in his face and started asking questions.

Taylor held up his hands in defense. "Take it easy, guys. I'll be here awhile, so you'll each have a chance to get all the material you need. I promise."

He had given plenty of speeches. This would be a straight shot, number six in the corner pocket. He would lay out a well-rehearsed theme in broad strokes: the Constitution is the law of the land. Unfortunately, it is one-size-fits-all, which can create pointless and unproductive conflict.

We're not all the same, we're all different. Maybe you've heard the joke - everybody's beautiful in their own silly way. That's actually true, you know. What is right for Wyoming is not necessarily right for New York City. In this era of the browning and yellowing of America, we need to work around our differences rather than swing the law as a great hammer to flatten them out.

Skip Taylor, the Great Unifier. The thought almost made him dizzy.

Now then, you might ask, don't guns give a person the means to defend themselves and protect their families?

Ah, my friends, the Attorney General would say. What is good for the individual is bad for the public. Among developed nations, we have the most guns, the highest homicide rate, and the highest rate of gun deaths. By far. Is that really your idea of law and order?

Peacetime in America has become an oxymoron. We have two speeds - war and more war.

Maybe Americans are more cantankerous than other people, but we lose thirty to forty thousand people every year to guns. That hurts us all. Our lives would be better, our nation stronger, if we could save ten or twenty thousand Americans every year. Do you doubt it?

The central question involves ways and means. Here is something to think about - suppose we took the second amendment out of the U.S. Constitution and replaced it with ... nothing. Just pretend for a moment. What would happen? Well, states and cities would be able to write their own gun laws, customized to fit their own environments. For example, New York City wants carrying a gun to be a criminal offense? Well that's fine, in New York City. By contrast, Waco, Texas allows a person to carry an assault rifle into schools, churches, and campuses? Equally fine. In Waco.

Different strokes. If you found a place whose gun regulations look good to you, you could move there. Or if not, you could leave and move to some other place more to your liking. You would not be trapped into one-size-fits-all.

Would you favor that arrangement? Or would you rather Washington wrote the gun regulations for your city and your neighborhood? Those are the choices.

Losing the second amendment would mean one thing: we have chosen to tolerate each other. The problem is not moral, nor is it personal. It is political.

That is the issue. I have an opinion. But what is yours? This is important. If we're kissing off thirty thousand Americans every year - ten times the number killed on 9/11 - we must have a good reason for doing that. What is that reason? If we are tolerating the murder of our children, we must have a very good reason for doing that. Again, what is that reason?

Skip Taylor's head swam in argument and counter-argument. He moved through the crowd and encountered acquaintances and a few friends. He was talking, smiling, and shaking hands all the way through the hall. Several prominent state politicians were there, surrounded by news cameras and reporters.

He reminded himself to aim the speech properly, to position the discussion squarely in the middle of the political spectrum, a relaxation of the NRA's long-held advocacy. Without the Constitution hammering down our differences, each of us would have to tolerate better other

Americans who look funny, talk funny, think funny, eat funny, and smell funny. As would Other People, who think we look and talk and smell equally funny.

A victory for tolerance. Let cowboys be cowboys. Let poets be poets.

Unification, tolerance, compromise. Better life for everyone.

Taylor thought, this will piss off many people. He continued smiling and nodding.

They'll come on board, and if they don't, well, that's too bad. In a few weeks, I'll announce our sniper prosecution. After that, no one can question my law and order credentials. A few weeks after that, the NRA will endorse me for the Senate.

It'll be like being blessed by the Pope, but more valuable.

Moderate folks will think that I've managed to convince the NRA to be more accommodative. That is how it will look.

And that, my friends, will be the end of my practicing law. It will mark the beginning of an honest attempt to solve our most tangled problems. Made possible, in part, by a homeless man living with nerve damage in an alley in Fairfax City.

That was the speech Skip Taylor gave to the VFW.

John Hunt stayed away from the Attorney General to study him. Afterward, he approached Taylor and shook his hand. "Nice speech. If you're right, the Association might have to redefine itself."

"You think so? Guns aren't going away," Taylor said. "The NRA will still have plenty to do." He grinned at Hunt. "Anyway, thanks. Thanks a million for the opportunity. I owe you."

"That you do." Hunt smiled back. This guy's good. He could go far.

Roundtree put down the phone, stood up out of his chair, and walked slowly to Pressler's office. The door was open, so Roundtree knocked twice and stuck his head into the office.

Pressler was sitting at his desk, looking tired at the end of a long day, a day filled with phone conversations with policemen, politicians, even a few reporters. Roundtree thought, he always looks tired. So what? We have a shooter out there. We're all tired. It comes from running around in circles.

Running around in circles is tiring.

Pressler looked up, saw Roundtree, and waved him into a chair on the other side of his desk. "I don't usually entertain during office hours, but in your case I'll make an exception. So, Inspector, what can I do for you?"

"I just heard - the AG had Stanton arrested."

"Swell," Pressler said. "That's just great." He put his head in his hands and rubbed his eyes. Then he looked blearily at Roundtree.

"Can you tell me what he could possibly be thinking?" Roundtree said.

"What do you mean?"

"I mean, I realize he has not met the man. But does he actually think Stanton could have shot anyone, intentionally, from a distance?"

"Oh that. I think I can help you there," Pressler said. "The AG's not thinking of innocence or guilt. His perspective is different. He's thinking of how it will look if he runs for office. He'll get the prosecution going. He'll get a lot of media coverage. Then he'll quit to campaign for a better job. I hear he's running for the Senate."

"The U.S. Senate? I wish he would give more thought to doing his current job," Roundtree said.

"You understand how naive that sounds, right?"

"I know. I'm an idealist. Or maybe I'm just stupid. If you tell anyone, I'll sue you. Then I'll apply for unemployment," Roundtree said.

Pressler sat back in his chair and looked up towards the ceiling. "How many AG's have I worked for? Six? Seven?"

He looked at Roundtree. "Memory fails. But I've learned. The people who apply for the AG spot are not satisfied with doing a job well. No. They want a better job. Define better any way you like - more money, bigger car, bigger budget, corner office, whatever. When they get it, they want an even better job. Their eyes are always to the future. They always look up, never down."

"That explains a few things. I've known people like that. Most of their work was shit," Roundtree said.

"That's why they delegate."

"And we have elections coming up," Roundtree said.

Pressler nodded. "Stuff that normal people don't think about, our AG is watching like a hawk."

The two men sat there for a long minute, neither speaking.

"Well ..." Roundtree stood up. "Thanks, Chief. I don't know how, but I'm going to figure out a way to help Stanton. He went to war for us and left a piece of himself in a combat zone. He deserves better."

"You can't testify, Dan," Pressler said. "You can be an expert witness, but only for the AG, not against him."

"And if I were to retire?"

"Oh well. Then you could tee off on his ass," Pressler said. "With my blessing."

Roundtree shook his head. "Yeah, that's probably not realistic. Okay. Thanks, Chief." He turned away and left the office.

Pressler sat in his chair and stared out into the hall for a long time.

# *Head Fake*

"Whoa. What's this?" Amir said. He stared at his laptop, his mouth open in surprise. He and Serena were sitting in their living room. She had just turned off the evening news.

Serena looked up from her knitting at Amir. "You just see a ghost?"

Amir sat there reading for a moment. "No. No, it's an article, a news article, says here they arrested a guy for the sniper killings." He continued reading.

"Oh," she said. "Well, good. Crime doesn't pay. Yes, that's good news." She returned to her knitting.

The Beast chimed in, *So, they went for it, did they? Well now, that is good news. Excellent news. While they're screwing around with that guy, we can get back to it.*

Amir thought, they arrested a homeless guy.

*Of course. You gave him money. Remember?*

Yes, I remember.

*Ah. It bothers you.*

Yes.

*If he's innocent, then he's got nothing to worry about.*

Oh very funny, Amir thought.

*Thank you.*

Remember when we started, we agreed, we were going after gun people. Only gun people.

*And we have done that. We didn't shoot the guy.*

We set him up. We planted the rifle.

*He set himself up. He didn't need to pick up the rifle and wave it around.*

Don't be a moron. It was predictable he would pick up the rifle. We parked it right under his nose.

*True. And you knew that. But now you've changed your mind?*

Now he's been arrested. They execute in Virginia.

*Bad luck for him, good luck for us.*

It wasn't bad luck, it was bad conduct, our bad conduct.

*Bad law enforcement too.*

Yes. The police have been ... disappointing.

*Pathetic. And now you are thinking of doing something about this.*

Yes.

*That's unusually stupid, even for you.*

So we should let them execute this guy?

*That would be best. That's the smart move.*

That's the weak move, Amir thought.

*Promise me we won't do anything astronomically stupid.*

Nothing stupider than normal, I promise.

*So now you're making plans?*

I am thinking. If we shoot someone else, someone deserving, the authorities will realize they arrested the wrong guy.

*Or ... they will choose to believe that they already have the right guy. Lawyers do not like to admit error. They believe in trial by jury, preferably a jury of idiots. If there's another shooting, they will claim it's a copycat. They will investigate the copycat and continue to prosecute the homeless guy. By the time they realize they prosecuted the wrong man, he might be dead.*

Yeah, but the copycat creates doubt. It raises another defense, Amir thought. Maybe it would be enough to get the homeless guy off.

*Dicey.*

I cannot stand by and do nothing while they execute this guy.

*Fine. But if we get caught, don't say you weren't warned.*

But you're right. We need to convince them the next shooting is not a copycat.

*Yes, we do.*

I have it.

*Yeah?*

It smells like a plan. Maybe it is. Amir thought about it at length and concluded, yes, it's obvious. And simple. It requires no more effort on our part. I know what to do. Yes.

*I like it already, sight unseen. So, what is the plan?*

Roundtree sat at his desk, staring at a computer monitor. The AG had requested that a transponder be placed on Hawari's vehicle. The judge granted the request.

The transponder built a record showing Hawari's movement. Since they had good data on his location, Roundtree also ordered up a running video log of the car as it passed traffic cameras.

They also tapped into Hawari's personal and financial records including bank, credit card, and brokerage accounts. Heywood Miles did the work and came back with nothing useful.

"Sorry, Dan, but this guy is a prosperous, penny pinching, conservative businessman. Doesn't drink, doesn't smoke, doesn't kick the dog or beat his wife. In Loudoun county, they breed these guys. Hell, I'll bet he cuts his own hair - no barber bills in the data," Miles said.

"He pays cash," Roundtree said.

"Yeah. Judging from the transponder data, he walks to the barber," Miles said.

So Hawari was a tightwad. Though prosperous, he relied on cash for daily transactions.

For weeks Roundtree tracked Hawari from a distance. Pressler kept pressing him for news, but he had none to offer. One day, Pressler asked him, "Are you sure Hawari is the shooter?"

"No," Roundtree admitted. "If I were sure, I could prove it."

"Are you certain this homeless guy is not the shooter?"

"Chief, the only way Stanton is the shooter is that he's insane. Remember, I've spoken with him; he's not insane. He's just your typical, troubled vet, dealing with trauma and combat wounds. His primary emotion is relief at surviving Afghanistan. He's been living on the street for two years, taking decent care of himself under the circumstances, causing no trouble. No. Stanton is not the shooter. No way."

"Alright, just checking," Pressler said. "Has surveillance told you anything you didn't already know?"

"We know exactly where Hawari has driven. At no time has he returned to any of the shooting sites. His being nearby when the shootings occurred was an anomaly. Either he's the shooter, or his presence near each shooting site was a staggering, unlikely coincidence. A billion to one, against."

"Well, coincidence or not, since the AG publicly claims to have arrested the shooter, and lacking evidence to the contrary, we need to show results to continue working the Hawari angle."

"I understand," Roundtree said.

The next day, Roundtree decided to tail Hawari even though the court's order specifically forbade that. After all, he had nothing to lose. Without results, Pressler would close the investigation. Dr. Nelson, Rick Summers, and Ed Shapiro had already returned to their home police departments.

Roundtree decided, if Hawari can randomly show up at the shooting sites, then I can randomly show up where ever he happens to be. Even if our paths cross, I can fade into the background.

Roundtree decided to tail Amir throughout the day. He would not be missed at the office. The few times that someone asked him how he was doing, what he was doing, Roundtree replied that his work had slowed down, so he was taking a bit of a break.

"Enjoy it while it lasts," was a common reply.

He had to be careful, though. The undercover guys had taught him a few things. First, don't look like a policeman. Most people, from Roundtree's bearing and rumpled suits, would take him for an Inspector. They might also take him for a recent divorcee, or maybe a homeless man who bought suits at Goodwill because he could not afford Walmart.

Roundtree put together outfits that were, to put it politely, different. One was a denim overall over a t-shirt. Another was a golf shirt with madras shorts and black socks. In either ensemble, he looked more like a bumpkin or a tourist than a police inspector.

Changing his bearing was more difficult. Over decades as an inspector, he had learned to exercise rights that most people did not possess. That resulted in a quiet but noticeable confidence. He would ask questions without hesitation. That was his job. Roundtree tried to suppress that by interacting with people as little as possible. He was striving for quiet and dim-witted.

It occurred to him, the police department might monitor the movements of its officers and other employees. Before he left for work every day, he checked underneath his car, looking for a bug. He did not find one.

The active surveillance began. Roundtree quickly ran into trouble. Hawari did not go through a normal day as most other people did. He was a walker. On most days he would drive somewhere, then take a walk lasting two to three hours. Roundtree could not keep up with him. The man walked fast.

If Roundtree did manage to keep up while tailing Hawari on foot, he would stick out like a guy in a clown suit. Roundtree laughed - in fact, a guy in a clown suit might make a better tail.

Tailing someone on foot needed a crowded environment. That was sometimes not available, so Roundtree tailed Hawari from a car, moving from one vantage point to another, watching Hawari at times, losing him at others. The transponder helped. Nonetheless, the surveillance was incomplete.

This continued for a week, with Roundtree following Hawari from a distance, until Roundtree got lucky. Hawari drove to *Bob's Guns*, near Lynchburg. He pulled into their parking lot, got out, and went inside. Behind him, Roundtree passed *Bob's Guns* and pulled off across the highway, near an ice cream parlor opposite the gun shop.

Roundtree thought, so, my slick friend, you have just made your first mistake. You are interested in weapons but have never registered one. Ah, but wait a moment Mr. Inspector, he told himself, you have not seen Hawari with a weapon. You don't know that he owns one.

Roundtree got out of his car, went to the window and ordered an ice cream cone. Two adults were treating a youth basketball team to ice cream. Roundtree sat down so they were between him and the gun shop. He ate the ice cream and listened to the occasional boom and crack of shotguns, rifles, and pistols.

He got back in his car, typed a command into a laptop mounted on his dashboard, and waited. The internet had much information about *Bob's Guns*. Roundtree scrolled down through the entries. *Bob's* was a stable business, last sold and renamed more than twenty years ago. It was a reputable gun shop, with sales and repair. It had a full rifle range, 275 yards deep.

"Two seventy-five? Now that is interesting," Roundtree murmured. He stared at that entry and thought, there are many gun shops in Virginia. Most have pistol ranges. This close to DC, rifle ranges are rare. Deep ranges are almost non-existent. And yet, here I am and here he is.

Why am I not surprised?


Roundtree put on his 'sporting' clothes - tan slacks, lime golf shirt, argyle socks, brown leather shoes. Then he left for *Bob's Guns*.

The transponder placed Hawari at home in Richmond. Roundtree did not want to meet the man at the gun shop.

He made the drive to Lynchburg humming a tune in his head and looking at dark green forests in rolling terrain. He arrived at the gun shop, pulled into the parking lot, and killed the engine. He got out of his car and winced. Though the range was behind the building, the booming sound of gunfire was just short of deafening.

Roundtree walked into the shop and looked around. The shop was cool and quiet, a genuine hunting and fishing emporium, selling to the serious and prosperous outdoorsman.

He walked up to the counter. A lean man in a frayed cotton dress shirt greeted him from behind the counter. "Good morning. Something I can help you with?"

"Yes, there is," Roundtree said. "I thought I'd do a little plinking. I was hoping to borrow a rifle."

"Sure. My name's Chas, by the way."

"Dan." Roundtree shook the man's hand.

"So, what would you like to shoot?"

"I'm thinking, maybe a varmint gun. A twenty-two two-fifty, or maybe a twenty-five oh six. Something like that."

The man turned around, scanned the rifles sitting in the wall gun rack. He pulled down three, one after another. "Okay, here's a twenty-two …" he laid a rifle on the counter. Then he turned and reached for another. "And this one's a twenty-five …" then he laid down the last of the three, "… and this one's a twenty-five with a twenty-six inch barrel."

"How deep's your range?" Roundtree asked.

"Two seventy-five. Three hundred at a stretch."

"Okay, I'll try the twenty-two."

"Ah, looking for a challenge, huh? It's breezy out there today," Chas said.

"Just lowering expectations," Roundtree said.

Chas chuckled.

Roundtree picked up the twenty-two dash two-fifty, opened the breech and removed the bolt and laid it on the counter. "You got any cleaning supplies lying around?"

"Sure." Chas reached down and laid a cleaning rod, a cotton rag and some cleaning patches on the counter. He offered a can of cleaning fluid and a small squirt can of oil.

Roundtree methodically cleaned the barrel and the breach, then said, "Can I take the rod and the cleaning fluid to the range? I'll return them when I'm done."

"Okay," Chas said. "If you clean it, I don't have to."

"And a box of ammo and a target sheet, please."

"You got a favorite brand?"

Roundtree pursed his lips and shook his head. "Whatever's cheap."

"Czech it is." Chas handed over a rectangular black target sheet with several concentric circles in the middle. Then he offered a box of copper-colored cartridges.

Roundtree inserted plastic ear protectors and put on a pair of yellow tinted goggles. He picked up the rifle in his left hand, the muzzle pointing skyward, grabbed the other items, and walked out the back door onto the range.

Two men were off to the far left shooting skeet. A woman, firing what Roundtree first took to be a small cannon, was at the pistol range. On the right two men were firing semi-automatic rifles.

He moved to the right, nodded at the range master as he passed him, then stopped. After several minutes, the red lights came on. Roundtree walked to a station on the far right and laid his items on what looked like a redesigned picnic table.

"Four minutes," the range master called out.

Roundtree took the target sheet and positioned it a hundred yards downrange. Soon after he returned to his station, the green lights came on, and the guns began booming again.

Roundtree adjusted the iron sights for a hundred yards and fired six shots. Then he lowered the rifle, removed the bolt and began to clean the barrel. While he was moving the rod up and down in the barrel, he caught the eye of the range master, who nodded in approval. Roundtree nodded back, then finished his cleaning, laid the rifle on the table, and sat there. Several minutes later, the range lights turned red, and he walked out and inspected the target sheet. The sheet had six holes scattered within two inches of each other, left of the bullseye.

He walked the target sheet out to the two hundred and seventy-five yard line, positioned it, and returned to his station. The lights turned green, but Roundtree did not resume shooting. Instead, he took a small screwdriver and worked with the rear sight.

Several minutes later, the lights turned red again. Roundtree went to the back wall of the range and bought a can of soda from a machine. When the lights turned green, he was back at his station. He took ten shots at the distant target.

Twenty minutes later, Roundtree pulled off his goggles, collected his target sheet and the rest of his paraphernalia and went back inside the shop.

Chas was waiting. Roundtree put the gear on the counter and laid down the rifle. Then he held up the target sheet. The original group was left of the bullseye. Another group was within three inches of the bullseye.

Roundtree removed the ear protectors and motioned with his hand. "These are from a hundred. And all these ... are from two seventy-five." He looked at the sheet, then at Chas. "By my standards, this is good shooting."

Chas nodded. "By anyone's." He stood there, politely admiring the sheet. "Where'd you learn to shoot?"

"The army."

"Middle east?"

"I'm flattered, but no. Asia."

"Ah," Chas said, understanding. "I think shooting paper is preferable. It doesn't shoot back."

Roundtree said, "Yep. That's a plus." He grinned. "Well, thanks for lending me the gun." He settled his bill and returned to his car. He would return to the range in a few days. He and Chas could then talk about used rifles.

After Roundtree left, the range master came into the shop. "That black guy? He can shoot a bit," the range master said. "You know him?"

Chas shook his head. "Nope. I think he's a cop, masquerading as a colorblind eighteen handicap."

The rangemaster rubbed a hand across his whiskers. "Well I'll be dogged."

Roundtree sat in the front seat, left hand on the steering wheel at twelve o'clock, eyes on the highway. A corner of his mind was driving, staying between the lines, ignoring the crazies who hurled their European sports sedans and Asian coupes past him at eighty-five or more. He was too preoccupied to try to save a mamma's boy using daddy's credit card to pursue a death wish.

He thought about 'plinking' at *Bob's Guns*. It was a haven for good ol' boys, a men's club, with anonymity and without the heavy ad budget and the protesters. The club hid itself in a modest little gun shop. Men could gather, do manly things like shoot holy hell out of paper targets. They could tell stories to each other, inflating their manliness and joking about the less manly, present company excepted, of course.

Was Hawari in the club? Did he shoot there? Roundtree remembered watching him walk into the shop. If he was the shooter, then he would not want to attract attention. Yet the little man went through that front door as if he owned the place. You'd think in those surroundings, a man of color might be shy. Not Hawari.

"Huh." Maybe serial killers are not easily impressed.

I would love to know exactly what that Chas character knows. Bitch is, I'm a black man and those are southern boys. My chance of gaining their confidence is exactly zero.

What is Hawari's connection to that shop? I need to find that out.

Amir and Serena were watching the evening news in their living room. Serena was knitting. Amir was staring down at a laptop, scanning the headlines.

Europe was staggering into another financial crisis and issuing alarmed commentary on near-border movements by Russian military forces. Amir read that and paused. The EU is several times the size of Russia. More, in terms of money. So what's with that?

He smiled. The Russians are more cantankerous, that's what. They remember being a world power. Unlike the Brits, they miss it.

U.S. housing starts were up. Another Hollywood grand dame died well into her nineties, a shattered, decaying memory of the beauty who captivated millions decades ago. Minnesota's cleanup of a toxic battery recycling factory was hundreds of millions over budget. Congress was heading into another still-born vote on the federal budget. A married

Congressman was on a video feed being antisocially horny with a sales girl.

Amir shrugged, so what?

The announcer turned to a political story, "The National Rifle Association announced it will endorse Virginia Attorney General Skip Taylor for this fall's open seat in the U.S. Senate. This makes Taylor the favorite to win that seat, given the NRA's position and record in political lobbying."

Serena looked up and glanced at the TV. Amir stared at it, then sat silent, thinking.

"Amir?"

"Hmmm?"

"The NRA ... they're the ones who think everyone should have a gun," she said.

"More or less, yeah."

"Do you think we should get a gun?"

"You mean a pistol?" he said.

"Yes. Something to defend the house."

"Have you ever shot a pistol?" Amir said.

"No."

"Would you like to?"

"Not much," she said. "They do it on TV. How hard can it be?"

Amir chuckled, "Well, you can get a gun if you want one. You will need to take a firearms course."

"I was thinking, if I were alone at home, I might feel better if I had a pistol."

"You think you could shoot someone?" Amir said.

Serena thought for a moment. "Maybe not. I'd probably try to scare them."

"That's a really bad idea."

"Really?"

Amir looked at her. "Yeah. You're inviting them to take your gun and use it on you. Listen, you ever see me pull out a gun, you should plug your ears, because what you're about to hear is BOOM, BOOM, BOOM. You pull out a gun to shoot someone." Amir shook his head. "Not otherwise."

"I see. Are you still shooting?"

"It's been a while," he said.

"Well, but … what do you think?"

Amir shrugged. "I think a gun makes you a target. Also, accidents happen around guns, more than you think."

"What would you do if someone attacked us?"

"Run away, if I could. Otherwise, give them the car keys, the credit cards, and ten bucks for gas."

She sat there thinking. "I know that's sensible. But what if you had to fight?"

"I'm a lover, not a fighter," he said.

"Come on," she said, with some heat.

He looked at her; she was staring at him, her executive stare. He said, "If I had to fight, I would want a tactical flashlight. They're portable, easily concealed, and blinding. Hit them in the eyes; they'll be blind for a minute. That's when you run away and call the police. In addition, no one ever killed a neighbor or a relative with a flashlight." He paused for a moment. "I guess you could bash 'em over the head with it."

"Where can I get one?" she said.

"Try the internet."

"Okay. Thanks," she said. After a pause, she said, "Do you have one?"

"No, but if I did, I would give it to you, 'cause I love you so much," he said.

"That's nice, dear. You're not worried about being attacked, are you?"

"I'm more worried about getting hacked by Russians, or Chinese, or Ukrainians. Or a dozen other flavors of ex-communists." He glanced at the TV. "Why is it that when their system collapsed, the communists all turned into crooks - capitalism at its purest."

"They're pragmatic?"

Amir laughed. "Yeah, right. Anyway, it's a jungle out there. Keep your eyes open, but don't worry about it. Nobody lives forever."

"That'd make a good James Bond title," she said.

"Yep." Amir turned back to his laptop.

*Well, it's good to see you're having a little fun, but what's the answer, Amir?*

What's the question? Amir thought.

*Are we going to dust the AG, or not? He's going to be pushing guns to the violent and the insane. If that were not enough, he's also prosecuting that homeless vet. Remember that guy? Your buddy?*

Your lawyering is improving.

*So what's the answer?*

I'll think about it.

*You know I'm right.*

Yes, you're right. So I'll think about it.

## *Cul de Sac*

It was a Saturday. Amir had invited Serena to go walking. She finally agreed to do that, in the form of a shopping trip to Aveda, a local shopping mall.

Amir thought about it - Aveda is vast. You could do a brisk walk around it. Two or three laps would give you a couple of miles. It is air conditioned, with no pollution, traffic noise, or bugs. It would be educational. You could look at all that flashy merchandise. Somebody actually buys that junk. Otherwise, it would not be there. That makes a shopping mall a bit of a freak show. Cheap entertainment.

So Amir agreed to go shopping. He knew that people gravitate to pleasant places. In fact, they gravitate to pleasant places until those places are no longer pleasant.

Amir and Serena arrived at the mall. Amir spent twenty minutes driving in circles, looking for a place to park. He finally found one, under a tree holding more birds than leaves.

He looked at that, shrugged. I'll need soap and water in a couple of hours. A lot of soap and water.

They made the long walk across the parking lot. When they got inside, Amir was sweating.

That was the end of the walk and the recreation. The mall was jammed with families herding young children. Half of them were asleep;

the other half were crying or screaming in an effort to get their parents to buy candy, or a rubber duck, or a new blankie. There was little open space for brisk walking. Amir and Serena settled into an irregular zigzag at half a mile an hour. That allowed maneuver around the unpredictable motions of several thousand other people who were all trying to buy the same stuff in the same place at the same time.

They stopped at a shoe store, where Serena tried on several pairs, buying none. They went to a department store, where she bought a towel. They went to a jewelry shop, where she admired the glittering rings and bracelets. They stopped at a cellphone kiosk, where she looked at the latest phones, shook her head in dismay over the prices, and left complaining. They went to the food court - spring rolls for Amir, a salad for Serena. After they ate, she approached a brand new electric car, admiring its style and shine.

Amir was staring at the car when the bass voice spoke quietly in his head. *Amir ... Amir.*

Amir thought, Eh? What? What is it?

*Don't turn around, but there's a man watching us.*

We're in a crowd. He's probably one of several, Amir thought.

*I have seen him before.*

Describe him.

*Black guy, middle-aged, big shoulders, might have been an athlete. Bit of a paunch, blue shirt, tan slacks. If the fancy car is at noon, he's at four o'clock, thirty yards away.*

As I said, we're in a crowd. Serena looks good. He's probably checking her out.

*I've seen him before, I tell you, and not here at the mall. The cocksucker might be tailing us.*

Is he armed?

*No, I don't think so.*

Then relax, Amir thought. He looked to the right but did not look directly at the man. Okay, I see him. He does look familiar.

*I've seen him before. I'm certain of it.*

You know, that does happen. You meet someone in one place, then you see them in a different place. It's normal. Amir turned his head, stole a quick glance at the man. Yes, I've seen him before, at the police department in Abingdon. He investigated the shooting at the college.

*Not just there. Somewhere else.*

As I said, these things happen.

*I know. I have it. I saw him at Bob's Guns. And not inside either. Outside.*

Well, I haven't seen him there. Look, it's probably nothing.

*Amir, we shot four people, killed three. He's a policeman, and he showed up at the place you learned to shoot, where you bought a rifle, now a murder rifle. And you think he's not tailing us?*

341

Amir stared at the beautiful black car for a while but did not see it. He was thinking about the man. Roundtree. That was the name, Roundtree. Well shit. No, you're right. We have to assume he's after us.

*We cannot ignore it.*

We won't.

*We don't have a gun.*

No matter. We're not going to shoot our way out of this.

*We ought to shoot him.*

Stop being stupid. Be quiet and let me think.


They returned home. Serena held a single shopping bag in her lap. Amir drove and did not say much.

When the car stopped in the driveway, Amir did not turn off the engine. He turned to Serena and said, "Listen, the car is running a little rough. I'd like to have it checked out."

"Sure," Serena said. "What do you want to do for dinner?"

"I don't know. You want to go out? Indian food, maybe? That new place, what's it called?"

"I forget, but I know the place." She leaned over to kiss him, "Okay, see you later." She got out of the car, closed the door.

Before she entered the house, Amir called out, "I'll call if I'm held up." He backed out of his driveway and drove for ten minutes to an auto mechanic he had used for years. Harv's Auto Repair was in the back corner of a warehouse, near a shopping center. Amir found the man's small corner of the parking lot and maneuvered through the half dozen cars waiting to be serviced.

Inside the door there was a counter which held an indestructible layer of decades-old grease and dirt. Harv washed it every so often, with no apparent effect. The air smelled of grease. On the counter was a bowl filled with bent, twisted, or distorted engine parts that Harv had pulled out of blown engines.

Harv stood there looking down at an invoice. Without looking up, he said, "Hey, Amir. How you doing? You still driving that heap?"

Amir nodded. "I'm a one car, one woman kind of guy."

"I see. Well, your taste in women is excellent. So … what do you need?"

"I need you to look her over, bumper to bumper. Check the hoses, belts, fluids. Tell me if there's anything out of the ordinary," Amir said.

"Just a check? Okay. Can you leave the car? Pick it up Monday?"

"Sure," Amir said.

Amir called Serena and asked her to pick him up. They continued to an Indian restaurant. An hour later, he felt like his head was on fire, a spice glow on his tongue and in his nose. His eyes, ears, neck, and lips were sweating.

He loved Indian food.

The next day Amir and Serena drove out to the cemetery and placed two large bouquets on Lelah's grave, red roses from Amir, white roses from Serena. Four months had passed since Lelah's death.

They stood at the foot of the grave. They stared at the headstone for a long time.

"This is a beautiful spot," Serena said. "See? The mound has receded, and the grass has covered it. As time goes by, these trees will grow and provide shade."

As time goes by? Amir thought. That should have been her time.

While Serena stood there, taking in the grave, Amir looked to the side and saw a three-year-old Lelah running and skipping and cavorting among the headstones. Amir wondered, if I know what I am seeing is not real, is it still a hallucination?

The Beast spoke up, *You tell me, Amir. Do you think I'm real?*

Amir stood there, thinking about Lelah. He could not stop his thoughts; he became unhappy and miserable. Tears began to flow down his cheeks. He made no effort to stop them or wipe them away.

In his head, the Beast roared, *Fuck them, fuck them, fuck them. A curse on the bastards and all their spawn. A curse forever. On them and their seed, all of them, forever.*

Serena stood there staring at the headstone. "You know, I often wonder what Lelah would have turned into. We talked about it. She could have been a model, at least I think so, but modeling never appealed to her. She talked about going to graduate school in international relations. A freshman, already talking about graduate school. Can you believe that?"

Amir stood there and did not reply.

The bass voice rumbled in his head. *Let's kill them. Kill them all. Let's stick them with pins, peel their skins off and pour alcohol on their flesh. Tear off their fingernails. When they lose consciousness, we can take a break, start again when they awaken. Then before we slit their throats, we'll do a number on their children, their lovers, their friends.*

*Or we could set them on fire, watch them burn and scream. Give them all a proper introduction to the Hell they so richly deserve.*

Amir raised his hands to his face and stood there for a long moment.

"I think she would have had fun in college," Serena said. "With her studies and her art. And dance, and parties, and movies. We talked about her studying overseas. She even talked about spending a semester in the Middle East."

The Beast again roared, louder this time, and Amir felt a stabbing pain in his head. "Over my dead body."

Serena looked at him, then turned back to the headstone. "I didn't try to talk her out of it. I just talked about Greece."

Amir nodded, yes, shrewd. Greece is beautiful. Mankind's good news began in Greece, a long time ago. It's still beautiful, though not as clever as it once was. He glanced at the headstone and thought, two steps forward, one step back.

"I'll bet she would have married. She was a lovely girl - beautiful, smart, funny, charming." Serena linked her arm with Amir's. "We made a good kid, you and me, Amir."

The Beast's roar rose to a crescendo. Amir had a stabbing headache that almost brought him to his knees.

The fantasy in her head made Serena smile. "I wonder who she would have married. Maybe an actor. Better yet, a banker. Ooooohhhh, a Swiss banker. She could live in Zurich." She stared at the headstone.

Anyone but an Arab, Amir thought.

"She would have raised beautiful kids, our grandchildren, Amir."

Perfect, Amir thought, the Swiss banker could provide the money. She would provide the beauty, brains, and talent.

A sharp pain made Amir inhale suddenly.

Serena turned to him. "Are you alright? Is something wrong?"

"I have a headache."

Serena looked into her purse. "I'm sorry. I don't think I have anything for that."

The Beast continued to roar, then stopped suddenly.

Thank you. You are hurting me.

*I want to hurt them, Amir. I curse them. You know what else?*

No, what else?

*You are the curse. You will provide the revenge. You will do the hurting.*

Amir thought, great, that's great. That makes me a slave assassin, under contract to a psychotic hallucination.

*It could be worse.*

How could it be worse?

*You could turn yourself in and confess.*

Amir nodded. That would be worse.


On Monday at noon, Amir returned to the repair shop and found Harv behind the counter.

"Hey, Harv," Amir said. "I have a question - do you ever do any real work?"

Harv smiled. "Only when no one's watching. All is well. Your junker runs flawlessly. It must be stubborn. It refuses to break."

"Great. Ugly but true."

"Except for one item. I put it on the lift and found this." He reached over to the side and picked up a small device. It was shaped like a box, in black plastic, two by two by one-half inch, one side made of stainless steel. A red indicator light was blinking.

"What is it?" Amir said.

"I don't know," Harv said. "I don't recognize this, it's some kind of electronic gismo. It's not an auto part. If you take a magnifying glass, you can read the brand name right here," his finger touched a corner of the device.

"What's it say?"

"TellieTrack," Harv said. "I found the company on the internet." He pushed his hat back and rubbed a grimy hand across his face, "These guys make products for surveillance. According to their webpage, they sell to insurance companies, police departments, and divorce lawyers."

Amir held the device and inspected it. He moved it to a piece of metal; it stuck to the metal. "It's magnetic," he said. "Interesting."

"You want me to crush it?" Harv said.

"No. No, that's okay. I'll keep it in the car."

"This is weird," Harv said. "Are you a spy, Amir?"

"Yeah, I'm a spy, Harv. Some countries will pay good money for the insights of retired shopkeepers."

"So I'm being stupid," Harv said.

"And I'm flattered. But you're right, this is weird," Amir said. "I wonder who put it there."

Harv looked at it, touched it. "If it were anyone else, I'd say your wife was getting ready to divorce you."

"Serena? Nah. She still likes me. I hide my dark side," Amir said. He stood there, looking at the device.

*That guy is a serious threat, Amir.*

Who, Harv? Amir thought.

*No, the black guy. The guy who's tailing us.*

Knowing about the trap is the first step to avoiding it, Amir thought. You told me that, remember?

*So you still don't want to shoot him?*

Why shoot him? I know something he doesn't. I have him right where I want him.

*Just gun people then?*

Correct. Just gun people. That actually makes sense. I will go that far. You have been persuasive.

Amir looked up. "Thanks, Harv. I'll let you know if I learn anything about this."

The bass voice rumbled, *Yeah, right. That'll never happen.*


Roundtree sat at his desk and stared at his computer monitor. He had turned on the mapping software that packaged and formatted data from the transponder attached to Hawari's car. There lay the problem. He sat there looking morosely at a map showing the jagged, meandering lines - Hawari's movements over the past five days, ten days, and month.

A month ago, the man ran all over the place, traveling a hundred or two hundred miles from Richmond. Roundtree suspected what was obvious, that Hawari was scoping out prospective victims. Heywood Miles ran a counter check to find if anyone near Hawari's route had any connection to guns. That uncovered several prospects, but no shootings occurred.

Two weeks ago the man's habits changed. He became less active. He stayed within metro Richmond. Most of the time, he stayed close to his neighborhood.

If this keeps up, Roundtree thought, I cannot arrest him. I won't have the evidence. Since I don't have the gun, I don't have any forensic evidence. This guy has left no prints, no photos other than a pathetic few from the first shooting. No internet posts, nothing. The transponder has given us nothing useful. He does not follow a pattern.

It is as if he changed his spots, Roundtree thought. Most people cannot do that, even if they try.

Roundtree shook his head. Pressler wants results. But without a murder weapon, I am stuck.

He paused. Is it possible that Hawari is not the shooter? Yes it is. However, if he is not the shooter, then this is all an astounding, amazing coincidence.

Roundtree knew enough, had lived enough, to know what it felt like to spin his wheels. This was one such time.

"Hell with it," he muttered. "I need to get back out to *Bob's Guns*."

Amir drove up to Lynchburg. As always, he enjoyed the scenery. He drove through town, past the police department and library. He passed a couple of banks and a Safeway. Then he headed south on a highway for two miles and made the sudden stop and turn into *Bob's Guns*.

He killed the engine and leaned back, listening to the booming. It was time to try out his new rifle. He got out of the car, opened the trunk and pulled out a satchel and a canvas bag holding his shooting gear. He closed the trunk and hurried into the shop. Chas was behind the counter.

"Hey Chas, how you doing?"

Chas looked at Amir and at first did not say anything, then he smiled. "Hey, Amir. How's the new toy? Done any shooting?"

"I've been busy. No, I haven't shot, but that's why I'm here today."

"You need anything?"

"Box of twenty-five oh sixes ..." Amir said.

Chas reached down for a box of ammo.

"... and a couple target sheets."

Chas handed him the sheets.

"Okay," Amir said. "Hide the women and children, I'm going to do some shooting."

Chas nodded. He was looking down at a sheet of paper, columns of numbers. "Go get 'em, tiger. Nothing but strikes."

As Amir entered the range and nodded to the range master, Roundtree parked in back of the ice cream shop across the highway. He killed the engine and looked at the laptop mounted on the dash. The transponder data said that Hawari was across the street, at the gun shop. He had been there ten minutes.

Roundtree walked around to the front of the ice cream shop and ordered a vanilla soft serve. He sat down, a group of people between him and the gun shop. Then he pulled his cellphone and began checking email and other information. Every so often, his eyes, behind dark sunglasses, would scan the gun shop.

Amir sat down at his station and waited for the range lights to turn red. When they did, he walked out to the hundred yard line and stapled a target sheet there.

He returned to his station and sat down, but when the lights turned green, he made no effort to shoot. The new rifle broke down into components. Amir sat there, screwing the threaded barrel into the receiver and adjusting a modest 4x scope.

It was slow work; the barrel and other parts were finely machined. Finally, he finished assembling the rifle. It was ready to shoot. Then the range lights turned red again. Amir slid a cartridge-shaped laser into the breech.

The lights turned green. He raised the rifle. The laser lit up a straight line from the barrel, putting a bright red dot on the target sheet. Amir adjusted the scope slightly to put the crosshairs over the red dot. Then he removed the laser and took six shots. When the firing stopped, he walked out and inspected the tight grouping around the bullseye. He moved the target sheet further out to the two seventy-five line.

He returned to his station and bore sighted the rifle for the greater distance. He adjusted the sight again and fired another six shots. Back at his station, as everyone else continued to fire, Amir sat still, looking through the scope at the now-tattered target sheet. He smiled ... excellent. Even at two seventy five, he had not missed the bullseye by more than two or three inches.

The Beast spoke, *Looks like you've still got the touch.*

Amir thought, that's a gorgeous little rifle. He unscrewed the barrel and cleaned it. Then he stood up, collected his rifle and his gear, and went back inside the shop.

"So?" Chas said. "How was it?"

"Shoots like a dream," Amir said.

"Good."

"Thanks for putting me in touch with this one, Chas," Amir said.

"If you want to shoot, we're here for you," Chas said.

The Beast chimed in, *Sure, they're supportive as long as you're shooting paper. Just don't get too friendly.*

You think I'm stupid?

*Sometimes I wonder.*

## *Cat and Mouse*

Roundtree watched Amir return to his car, load a couple of bags into the trunk, and drive away. Oddly, he was not carrying anything that looked like a rifle. Okay, Roundtree thought, so he did not bring a rifle. Maybe he has not replaced it.

Then why stop by the gun shop? Is he shopping?

He may not have a rifle. So much the worse. In any event, he has stopped shooting people. I guess that's good, but this case is slipping away. If I arrest him and he turns out to be clean, I'll look like an idiot. After that, I won't be able to arrest him again, even if he shoots someone else.

Roundtree fumed, I am at ground zero, back at the beginning. Unless he makes a mistake, I can only wait until he starts shooting again.

How much time, and how many bodies, will it take to get this guy?

Back in the bullpen, Roundtree opened the mapping software and looked at the zig-zag line describing Hawari's route. After visiting the gun shop, the man had gone home to Richmond.

Roundtree's cellphone buzzed. He opened the phone. A text from Pressler said, *Come see me.*

Roundtree got out of his chair and made the slow walk to Pressler's office. He found the door open, so he knocked twice and poked his head inside. Pressler, on the phone, saw him and pointed at the chair on the other side of his desk.

Roundtree entered the office and sat down.

Pressler finished his phone call and hung up the receiver. "That was the AG. It's official, he's prosecuting Stanton. They will file papers in a few days."

He paused and looked at Roundtree. "You look tired, Dan. You okay?"

Roundtree nodded.

"Hmmmm, well … you don't seem okay. Do you need some time off?"

Roundtree thought about that. "You know … now I think on it, yeah, I guess I could use a little time off."

"Okay. Good news and bad. In a couple of days, you can take time off." Roundtree rolled his eyes and smiled. Pressler continued, "Right now, I have a job for you."

"Okay."

"First, anything new in the sniper investigation?"

Roundtree thought, be careful here, pal. "No, sir. Nothing new. Hawari has stopped shooting. We have the rifle, so at the moment we are stuck. We will stay stuck until he shoots again."

"Okay," Pressler said. "I was afraid of that. Okay …" He sat there for a long moment. "I think we'll back burner that case. Meantime, the AG is giving a press conference in three days next to the assembly building in Richmond. I would like you there, to provide another set of experienced eyes."

"Yes, sir. I would imagine security will be high for that."

"Snipers on the rooftops, and a few other precautions too," Pressler said.

"Who's handling it?"

"Richmond PD. Highway patrol has a small piece of it."

"Sounds like easy work."

Pressler nodded. "I'd like to keep it that way. Your job, since you're familiar with the matter, will be to check out the site, alert Richmond PD to any obvious vulnerabilities. At that point, it will be their problem. After the press conference, you can go home to Abingdon."

"Yes sir."

"Thanks for helping out, Dan," Pressler said. "Maybe we got the right guy. It's possible, isn't it?"

Roundtree's lips twisted. He said, "Yes sir." He thought, no way. No effin' way did we get the right guy.


Amir and Serena were watching the evening news, which relayed the usual collection of mayhem, house fires, car crashes, death, and scandal. The candidates for the fall elections were beginning to campaign. The reporter took great delight in noting where the candidates contradicted the station's version of the truth.

Amir thought, this feels like the blind leading the blind.

The bass voice rumbled, *Are you thinking of getting into the political discussion? What's next, a blog?*

Amir thought, you just be quiet.

For the hundredth time, he thought, thank God for the internet, and for Reuters, and Bloomberg, and CNBC, and BBC, and CNN, and all the other genuine news organizations.

With that, he fired up his laptop, logged onto the internet, and started looking for news. Several dozen headlines later, one caught his eye, reprinted from a reputable Richmond newspaper:

**AG to Brief Lawmakers on Sniper Case**.

Amir read the article, smirked when he got to the end, then re-read it.

He thought about the AG. The man would not brief lawmakers unless he was planning to prosecute. That's what the briefing is about. And a short news conference on the steps of the Assembly building? That's the baby briefing, for the public. Sniper bad, me good, let's fry him.

The Beast chimed in, *See? I told you so. This guy is a dickhead. So, are we going to pop him or not?*

Ways and means.

*Huh?*

We need to examine ways and means, Amir thought.

*Yeah, yeah, yeah. Good. Now you're talking. I want this guy. Let's not quit until the NRA is having a collective shit attack.*


Roundtree drove down to Richmond, cruising on the interstate, listening to the tires run rhythmically over seams in the concrete - kathump, kathump, kathump. Eventually the sounds faded from repetition.

He exited near Capitol Plaza, a large rectangular park occupying several city blocks, ringed by government buildings and a couple of churches. The neighborhood was gray and tan, the office buildings dating from the Great Depression.

The AG would hold a press conference just off the south entrance of the assembly building, facing the park. Roundtree parked his car and walked to that spot. He stood there, scanning the plaza. To the south, old trees blocked the view. Massive government buildings stood to the east and west. The general assembly building was immediately to the north.

Roundtree thought, the park is the big open space. Richmond PD will place several sniper teams at the highest points, atop these buildings, adjacent to the park. Trees will block much of the park. That is okay. Hawari will be in a building. He will not be in the park. He will not be out in the open.

His eyes swept the Plaza. This is a hard target, isn't it, my man? I would not want to shoot here. You'd be a fish in a barrel. No easy shot from anywhere. These buildings are all government buildings, with good security at the entrances. Armed guards and sensors. Dozens of cameras. How can you get inside? No, if it were me, I would not want to shoot here.

This would be a Canyon of Death.

Besides, you don't have to shoot here. You must know, I know you know, the AG is a public figure. His public appearances are on the AG's website. He will be out in the open, unprotected. There will be other places, other times offering a far easier shot. Are you going to pry into the security net and put yourself under the scopes of the sniper teams? Or are you going to chicken out? Psycho shooters usually pick soft targets. What do you think, my man? Will you skip this one for something softer and easier?

Then a memory tugged on Roundtree's mind. On the other hand, you surprised the security team guarding the NRA president, the second one. They thought they had the neighborhood covered. Maybe they thought you would not shoot through a glass window at night. Maybe they figured that would be a difficult shot.

They were wrong. You made that shot. Then you disappeared.

That was a hard target, not the move of a psychotic. Not at all.

No one found the executive, and the hole in his chest, until the next morning. His wife thought he had stayed up late. He sometimes did that. She woke up to a nasty surprise.

Roundtree stood there with his mouth open, consumed by his thoughts. So ... you have to get inside one of those government buildings, past the guards with the guns, past the metal detectors. Nothing else will work here.

Can that be right?

Roundtree walked around the edge of the park. He walked down a sidewalk, then turned left and went down another sidewalk. He passed the Virginia Supreme Court, which had a visible guard out front and probably another dozen hidden from view. He walked past an old church - two stories, heavy stained glass windows which would not open, a view blocked by trees. He looked up at a hotel and thought, there you go, my man, you could rent a room and shoot from that hotel. Of course, those windows do not open. If you cut through one, it would stand out like a beacon and attract every rifle in the plaza.

That is the path to a closed casket funeral.

He continued his walk. He passed the Department of Justice and the Governor's Mansion, both of which, though tempting, had cameras, sensors, and armed guards.

As he walked down the sidewalk, he passed a police dog on a leash, leading an unsmiling handler who looked at him briefly and then moved on without saying anything.

Roundtree passed the old City Hall. It was set back from the park. Its view of the press conference would be blocked by the general assembly building.

He pulled his cellphone out of his pocket and sent Pressler a text: *I surveyed site for news conference. Armed camp. Hard target. RPD knows to post sniper teams at the highest points in the park. All the buildings are closed up, guarded, cameras, sensors, dogs. A difficult shot. A more difficult retreat. R.*

Thirty seconds later, Pressler replied: *Do you think he will shoot?*

Roundtree replied: *I don't know. There are no good shooting sites.*

*OK, thanks.*

At that moment, Roundtree glanced towards the interior of the park. On a park bench, a hundred yards away, reading a newspaper, was Hawari. Roundtree stared, then almost tripped on the sidewalk but managed not to fall on his face. He kept moving as if nothing had happened.

Roundtree stared at the man and then quickly looked away. Hawari did not seem to notice him. He seemed unconcerned, a man enjoying a leisurely newspaper in the middle of a park on a sunny day. He was facing away from the location of the press conference. As Roundtree was digesting this latest surprise, Hawari stood up and walked away from him.

Roundtree stopped for a moment. Then he turned and hurried after Hawari.

Roundtree thought, this cannot be a coincidence. I may not be able to prove it, but this guy is the sniper. He just happens to show up in a public park in advance of a press conference there? That's another coincidence?

Bullshit.

Let's keep our eyes on him. Then Roundtree hesitated, hang on ... if I arrest him on a hunch, I won't be able to detain him. People will say, oh, Roundtree's on a witch hunt. The best I can do is delay him for a couple of days. Bring him in for questioning. Tie up his time. That will prevent him from shooting anyone ... for a few days.

Then they'll release him.

Roundtree kept walking. Hawari took no steps to hide or evade him. The man just continued down the sidewalk at a leisurely pace.

If I cannot stop him, if he is going to shoot at all, where better than right here, in Capitol Plaza, surrounded by government buildings and sniper teams? This is a lousy place to try to shoot someone ... and the best place to catch or kill the shooter. If I can't prevent him, at least I can pick the ground.

Roundtree slowed and then stopped walking. No, let's chance it. Let him shoot right here. Good luck with that, pal. I hope one of our guys blows your head clean off.

He stood there on the sidewalk and watched Hawari walk away.

He turned and headed for the garage where he had parked his car. When he got there, he climbed in and turned on his laptop. The transponder data appeared on the screen. Hawari's car was several blocks away.

And who knows? Maybe this is a coincidence.

Another coincidence.

Another staggering, incredible coincidence.

Roundtree laughed.

Two days later, on the morning of the press conference, Amir woke up and kissed his wife goodbye. She was planning to spend the day shopping with friends. He got into his car and drove to the large supermarket that he and Serena had used for the last twenty years. The supermarket was busy. The parking lot in front was almost full.

Amir drove around to the back of the supermarket. There were several delivery trucks parked there. Some were waiting, a couple were backed against loading bays, unloading their bread, canned goods, fresh produce, and kitchenware for the store to sell.

Amir sat in his car, the motor running, and stared at the trucks for several minutes. He spotted one and thought, that one will do nicely. Yeah, that one is perfect. He turned off his engine, picked up the transponder, got out of his car, walked over and knelt down next to the truck. He reached down low. There was a small sound - *chink* - as the transponder stuck to the frame.

Grinning, Amir stood up, walked back to his car, and drove away.

The AG's legislative briefing would be at nine a.m. The press conference would follow at ten. Roundtree got out of bed, showered, and drank some coffee.

He was in his car by seven o'clock. He turned on the laptop and activated the transponder software. The screen showed a map of Richmond. An icon showed Hawari's car, sitting in his neighborhood. He was not at home. Roundtree started his car and headed for the interstate.

It was an hour and a half to Richmond. Traffic was heavy in places. The big Ford cruised along, ten mph over the limit, a quiet car. Babysitting this press conference would be Roundtree's last job on detachment. After that, he would return to Abingdon. His life and daily routine would return to normal. The quiet life.

Today, they would get Hawari, or not.

Thirty miles outside Richmond, short of the Richmond beltway, Roundtree glanced at the laptop. "Son of a bitch, what's this?" He pulled the big car off the road and gave the screen his full attention.

Hawari was moving. He had left Richmond and was driving north, on a secondary highway heading towards Manassas. Roundtree thought, what can he be doing?

That chance encounter at Capitol Plaza was just a coincidence? What's with this move? What's in Manassas? Roundtree began typing commands into the laptop. He scanned news items, looking for something in Manassas that might attract a shooter with a grudge against guns.

Suddenly, there it was - a gun convention in a concert hall near Dulles Airport, open to the public. A gravel parking lot and a buyer's market. Kiosks. Barbeque. No questions asked. Pudgy, heavily armed suburbanistas.

Son of a bitch. Roundtree stared at the screen. You're not as ballsy as I thought, are you, my man? Rather than take on a hard target and put yourself in front of counter-sniper teams, you're diverting to Manassas.

Good move. It gets no softer than that. Just think of all those defenseless targets, all those fat, paranoid, prosperous, gun-loving suburbanites. Heavily armed white men. You've always taken one shot, just one, before leaving. But this time, how can you turn down all those soft, immobile targets?

Go to Manassas, then. You could retire the title. The Champ. Undefeated.

Otherwise, you'd have to stick around and shoot in Capitol Plaza. That will take courage and no small amount of stupidity. Do you have it?

I don't think you're that stupid. But if you go to Manassas, I will respect you a bit less.

"Hell with this," Roundtree muttered. He started up the engine again, put on the siren, and quickly had the big Ford well over the speed limit, heading for the nearest exit. He needed to get north and west as fast as possible.

He got on the radio and asked Manassas PD to dispatch a squad car to the gun convention. He would contact them when he arrived.

Amir hobbled along a Richmond sidewalk, in the government district near Capitol Plaza. A knotted kerchief covered his hair. A half inch riser in his right shoe induced a limp. He was wearing a thin painter's smock and carrying a backpack. To accompany the limp, he was using a metal cane fashioned from the heavy twenty-six inch barrel of a breakdown rifle. The cane, capped with a plastic handle and a rubber cap, tapped a quiet rhythm as he moved along the sidewalk.

Amir was looking for a church. He rounded a corner and there it was - an old, two-story building in stained red brick, under a brick steeple. Its age and years adorned a neighborhood of larger, boxy government buildings. They were built to please utility.

The church was built to please a God.

It was one of those old, established denominations. Founded long before the Civil War, many Honored Dead had walked its halls and sat in its pews. The original parishioners, all ten of them, lay buried in a little courtyard opposite the plaza. The original church faced the plaza. The church also operated a school, daycare, and other facilities. Those were further back off the plaza.

Amir wanted the old church. He started up a shallow set of front steps, over which millions of worshipers had passed before him. He approached the door and read the sign in front - Episcopal. These people were Episcopal, whatever that was. Islam held that everyone worshiped the same God, whom they called by different names. Amir had stopped believing that long ago.

After all, the rules of the major religions were different. How could even a God, a single God, navigate the conflicts?

As he climbed the steps, he wondered, did their God exist? Was he real? Was he indeed the same as Allah? Did He take sides in conflicts such as this? And if He did, which side would He favor in Amir's little war against the gun people who had murdered Lelah?

He thought it over. Well, there are the Ten Commandants. Killing is prohibited. On the other hand, the gun people have blood on their hands, as I have blood on mine. So God could perhaps go either way.

Amir smiled. It will soon be clear. If I succeed, then He must be on my side. If not, then the answer is 'no' – either he is not there, or he does not favor me. He paused and felt a surge of fear wash over him. Am I walking into a trap? Will I survive this day?

I am afraid.

But I am also right. I am trying to do what is right. I just need the courage to do it.

He opened the heavy front door and entered the church. There was a foyer just inside the door, a coat room on one side, the chapel through wooden doors in front of him.

Amir entered the chapel. He walked halfway to the front, closer to the lectern used by the minister. A young man in a black robe and white collar spotted Amir and nodded at him. Amir smiled at the man and nodded back. Then he moved into one of the pews, laid down the cane and the backpack, dropped to his knees, and bowed his head.

The minister had turned to face Amir. He was about to say something when Amir knelt to pray. The man stopped, hesitated, then went about his business. Five minutes later, convinced he was alone, Amir walked to the front of the chapel, past the lectern, past the candles, and into the bell tower. He climbed three flights of stairs, looking for an open room. He found one used for maintenance. It was unheated and had an opening to the outside. Louvers and a wire screen covered the opening to keep out bugs and bats.

Amir looked around the room. This will do nicely. Now ... we've come this far. Am I doing this or not? He paused, then lowered the backpack to the floor. He knelt and took the receiver out of the backpack. In three minutes he had the barrel threaded into the receiver. He took a cartridge from his pocket, opened the breech, inserted the cartridge, and closed the breech. He snicked the scope into place.

He did not cock the rifle. Not yet.

He reached up, pried loose a corner of the screen, and tore it away. Then he reached up and grabbed a louver, broke it, and moved it aside. He now had a space several inches wide.

Amir glanced at his watch: 9:43 a.m. He sat in a chair, lifted the rifle to his shoulder, and sighted through the scope. Leaves partially blocked his view, but he found the lectern through the leaves. He adjusted the focus to bring the lectern into sharp relief.

The lectern was more than two hundred yards away.

He adjusted the scope to focus on the leaves. There were no thick branches in his scope. Satisfied, he readjusted the sight to focus on the lectern, then he lowered the rifle.

He settled back to wait.

Roundtree was on an uncrowded four-lane highway. The big Ford was made for this. Relieved of curves and turns, relieved of traffic, blue lights flashing, it flew.

He got a radio call: "This is Manassas PD. Repeat your request, please."

"This is Dan Roundtree, detached to Fairfax County PD. I have received a tip that a sniper might be approaching the gun show at the convention center. I am headed there now. Please take all precautions. This man is extremely dangerous."

"Understand and thank you, Roundtree. We will send three units. They will be on channel fifty-six. Manassas out."

As he drove, Roundtree glanced at the laptop screen every so often. As he approached the convention center, the transponder data took an unexpected turn. Hawari was near Manassas but nowhere near the convention center. In fact, he had stopped; the transponder icon was no longer moving.

Roundtree stared at the screen. What is this? Is this another wild goose chase?

He double checked his own location - he was less than four miles from the transponder. He turned onto a slower, two-lane road and soon came to a strip mall with a small supermarket at one end.

Roundtree killed his lights and maneuvered through the parking lot until the laptop showed his car less than twenty feet from the transponder. At that point he looked up …

… and found himself looking at a delivery truck. What the hell? He looked back at the computer. The icon was directly in front of his car. The transponder had to be on that truck.

He read the markings in bold red letters:

**Dave's Donut Delights**.

"Oh, no." He stood there staring. "No, no, no." Then he laughed. Donuts. Our shooter is a funny guy. Hilarious. Goddamn donuts.

Ha, ha, ha. Shit, shit, shit.

Roundtree reached for the radio and contacted Manassas PD, "Cancel that request, Manassas. The tip was false."

They came back: "Understood, Roundtree. Cancel request."


Roundtree tuned his radio to the common channel used by the police teams covering Capitol Plaza. The radio suddenly produced a rush of noise. It sounded as if all hell was breaking loose. Several voices were yelling at the same time:

"… man down, man down. We have a man down.

"… shots fired. Multiple shots fired on the plaza.

"… eyes on the shooter. Does anyone see the shooter?

"… unit one, negative eyes.

"… unit three, negative eyes.

"… okay, okay. Did anyone hear the shot?

"… it came from the hotel.

"… no, no, belay that, it came from the Supreme Court building.

"… roger hotel, roger Supreme Court. This is leader. I am calling for backup and a cordon around the Plaza.

"… what are your orders, sir?

"… continue scanning. Let's find this guy. Find the shooter."

Roundtree was holding the steering wheel in one hand. He closed his eyes and lowered his head to rest it on his hand.

# *The Cobra Strikes*

Skip Taylor was sitting halfway down a long polished table, a dozen other men and women sitting on the other side of the table. He had just delivered his briefing on the sniper prosecution, describing the shootings, the now indicted suspect, and the primary evidence.

The chairwoman of the judiciary committee, a tall blond wearing heavy makeup, looked at him and smiled. "Thank you, Mr. Attorney General. I have just one question. If you convict, will you seek the death penalty?"

Taylor thought, No, mam, I will not seek the death penalty, because by then I will be in the Senate, worrying about other matters. Bigger matters.

"Good question, Madam Chairwoman. This matter is just beginning. If we win, if the defendant is rational, and if the murders were premeditated, then I might seek the death penalty."

"That's a lot of provisos, Mr. Attorney General."

He nodded and thought, very perceptive of you. "Yes, Mam. I think the death penalty deserves a lot of provisos." He asked himself for the thousandth time, why do people trust attorneys to make life and death decisions? What entitles us to do that?

Law school? Seriously?

"If you win election to the Senate, what then?"

Taylor reached for his tie, tightened it, straightened it. "We have excellent attorneys in the office of the Attorney General. They will continue the prosecution, of course." He did not add, surely you don't think I will conduct the prosecution. My people will do that.

She looked disappointed. Taylor wondered, is that real?

Then she nodded. "Alright. Then ... I believe I speak for everyone here in wishing you success."

Taylor stood up. "Thank you, Madam Chairwoman, and thank you, everyone. Now, if you will please excuse me, I need to run out and make a speech."

A couple of people laughed. Even the chairwoman gave him a thin smile.

He left the conference room in a hurry, walked downstairs, through a hallway, and out the back door onto Capitol Plaza. It was a sunny morning. A crowd had gathered in a semi-circle in front of the lectern. There were a dozen reporters, numerous policemen, and several dozen office workers. He would have preferred a larger crowd.

When I become a Senator, the crowds will be a lot larger.

Skip Taylor walked up to the cluster of microphones and looked around. "Hi everyone. Good to see you." He took a breath and reminded himself, you are not speaking as the AG, you are speaking as the next Senator from Virginia. So ... big picture.

"Yes. Good morning. I just briefed the Judiciary Committee on an important prosecution, that of one Mike Stanton, for murder and attempted murder. The evidence will prove that ..."

More than the victims, society itself is harmed. Say that.

"Our society bears the weight of far too much violence. Murder is a despicable crime, seldom warranted by circumstances or just cause ..." I wish I could say murder is never justified, but people would laugh. I'd look like an idiot.

Stop that. You're drifting. Focus.

Even permissive gun laws would not have prevented the harm. Say that.

"These murders, done coldly and unashamedly from a distance, were premeditated. The victims were not armed. Had they been, they could not have defended themselves. They were murdered. No, worse than that, they were executed. The state must step in forcefully to deter deviant individuals from violence against the defenseless ..."

Taylor's mind began to wander as he listened to and became mildly mesmerized by the sound of his own voice. Then he felt a hard punch go through his body. It was odd, not painful, but most definitely a sharp impact.

It shook him. What just happened?

He stopped speaking and then realized that he could not speak, he could not form a word and force it through his lips. Suddenly it was hard to draw a breath.

He glanced down and saw a widening red stain on the front of his chest. He watched with fascination as blood spurted out from his chest, as if pumped. He felt his throat clog up. He coughed, and blood sprayed over the front of his shirt and onto the lectern. Taylor looked at the crowd. Everyone was staring at him and several people were yelling. Taylor could not hear them. What's with that? He glanced at a policeman standing nearby. The man's mouth was open in shock, then he was looking away and reaching for his sidearm.

Taylor felt his legs go numb. Mother of God, I think I've been shot. I can't believe it; this feels awful. He tried to take a step but his body would not obey his commands. His legs would not move. Slowly, easing into it, he began to fall backward, like a tall tree taken down by an ax. As he drifted towards the pavement, his eyes caught a flicker, a piece of lint floating in the air. Then he hit the pavement. Oddly, it did not hurt. He felt hands on him. Someone was at his side. Taylor looked up at them, tried to see who it was. Then his eyes focused and he recognized them. He knew them, but he could not remember their name.

Now, wasn't that odd? He could remember many things, but not that. The seconds since the last breath stretched out. They ticked by, one by one. The AG thought, I'm hurt, but still here. Now if I could just manage the next breath. It ain't over til it's …

Amir felt the rifle kick against his shoulder. He immediately lowered it, pulled out a handi-wipe and wiped the rifle with disinfectant. Then he grabbed the barrel, avoiding the hot end. He began to unscrew it from the receiver. He detached the barrel and shoved two plastic pieces, a rubber stopper and a handle, onto the ends. Now the barrel was a cane.

He wiped down the receiver and put it into his backpack. Then he pulled off his latex gloves and put the gloves and the wipes into his backpack. He shouldered the backpack, picked up his 'cane', and left the room.

Amir walked through the church, heading away from Capitol Plaza. As he was limping along, he met a woman.

She walked up to him. "Excuse me, can I help you? This part of the church is not open to the public."

Amir looked at her for a moment. "I'm sorry. I believe you, but I'm lost. I came to pray. I was leaving when there was some kind of commotion over in the Plaza, so I tried to go see it. That's when I got lost. If you'll point the way …"

"Oh …" she looked at him. "What kind of commotion?"

"I don't know. It sounded serious. There were sirens going off. You didn't hear?" Amir said.

"No. Some parts of the church are quiet."

He nodded. "Oh … that's good, I guess."

She turned and pointed down the corridor. "Go down to the end. There's a stairway on the left that goes to the first floor."

"No elevator?"

"No, I'm sorry."

He winced and nodded. "It's okay. I can manage. On the left, you say." He nodded again. "Thank you, you're very kind."

When Amir emerged from the church, he could hear a dozen sirens screaming. Several were police sirens. Two others were the yodeling sirens of ambulances. He hobbled down the sidewalk and turned towards Capitol Plaza. A crowd was on the Plaza. They made considerable noise, voices of fear and dismay.

He walked in that direction, but a patrolman approached him with his hands out and told him to stop.

Amir stopped and stood there, suddenly paralyzed with fear. It was difficult to breathe. He was not sure he could speak.

He thought, shit, shit, and shit. I am so screwed.

The bass voice rumbled. *Don't panic. Do ... not ... panic. Keep control. You have rights. You don't have to answer questions. They can't arrest you without cause. So keep your mouth shut and do what the nice policeman asks, but don't give away anything.*

If they smell cordite, I am genuinely and heroically screwed.

*If they smell cordite, someone else did the shooting. If they find the rifle, you picked it up somewhere.*

Yeah, Amir thought, you can ask that homeless guy how well that works.

The situation clarified a second later - the policeman was only closing off the block. As Amir watched, two other policemen ran yellow tape in front of him, reaching all the way across the street. The tape read: POLICE LINE, DO NOT CROSS. When they finished with their tape, one stood there and watched the tape. The others turned and hurried towards the Plaza. Amir turned in the opposite direction and walked away.

Christ on a crutch, that was close! Amir reached out to steady himself against a wall. He took a deep breath. Allah is on my side. He must be. Thank you, kind Sir, for helping the faithless. I will try to be a better man from now on. I promise.

*A better man? In whose opinion, yours or His?*

We can discuss the details later, Amir thought. He turned away from the Plaza and walked to a street corner. He hailed a cab which took him ten blocks. He got out and walked two blocks to the garage where his car was parked. He climbed into the car and took the lift out of his shoe. He sat there for several minutes, waiting for his pulse to return to normal.

*How's your underwear?*

Shut up, asshole. Amir tuned the radio to a news station. The announcer was loud and excited, almost hysterical, talking about today's shooting of the Attorney General in Richmond's Capitol Plaza. Everyone had something to say about it.

Amir left the parking garage. Instead of going home, he drove east out of the city to a barber shop and had a hot towel, shave, and haircut. When the barber finished he handed Amir a circular mirror.

Amir looked into the mirror.

"There you go, bud. You look like a new man."

"I feel like one too," Amir said, admiring the new haircut. "Excellent. Thank you."

Amir drove to an old mansion and plantation, a Civil War historical site, overlooking the James River. He paid the entrance fee with a twenty dollar bill and entered the grounds. He took his cane and backpack with him. He saw a few tourists and several groundskeepers as he walked through the main residence, across the back lawn, and through a garden.

A wooden bench offered a view of the river. The bench was in the shade of two large trees. Amir sat down and watched the water drift past. He looked around him. The location was peaceful and quiet, the river flowing slowly in front of him, right to left, under a canopy of cawing and crying birds. The occasional fish jumped up to snare a bug.

They are going to be looking for me, Amir thought. It would not surprise me to find the police waiting at home.

The bass voice rumbled, *You think so? But you got him. You got the AG. Well done.*

Yes, I got him. The crowd on the Plaza was stirred up.

*I don't think we were seen.*

Of course we were seen. That lady at the church. And out on the sidewalk there were cameras. Whether the police will figure it out, who knows?

*The disguise might trip them up.*

Maybe. But we just shot the Attorney General. And two NRA presidents before that. And a Senator. Blue chip people. At some point, they will throw out the rule book. They'll start jailing people on suspicion. They'll hire witnesses. They might even use torture. It happens now and then.

*So much for the Golden Mountain.*

Yeah, Amir thought, not as Golden as everyone thinks.

*Overrated, I would say.*

Amir thought, it's going to get more dangerous. Maybe we should quit. Quit while we're ahead.

*We've only shot a few people.*

Yeah, but honestly, you think it matters? You think we've accomplished anything?

*Difficult to say. We got that homeless guy off the hook.*

That we did. Amir hesitated. Yeah, we did that. It just took the right bullet. Okay, granted, we got him off the hook, but we also put him on that hook. So that was a wash.

The bass voice rumbled, *therapeutic violence.*

Perhaps. We could shoot a dozen more people. So what? It wouldn't make any difference. The NRA will pick another president. The same guys who picked the last two will pick the next one - another rich, remote, greedy, gun-happy Nazi. They will continue to buy politicians. They will continue to push guns on the dim, the desperate, and the insane. In a few weeks, some lunatic will shoot up a college ... or an elementary school ... or a library.

*You are depressing me. But I am confused; are you arguing for us to quit shooting, or keep shooting?*

Amir rolled his eyes. His hands began to move as if punctuating words. Ha ha ha. Very funny. I am asking you to stop and think. Don't be a zealot; think. Revenge makes sense to me. Therapeutic violence, as you put it. But it is contagious. It rebounds. You hit somebody, then they or their friend soon show up at your door wanting to hit you. It's a cycle. Forgive or die. Those are the only choices.

Lately, my life has been lousy, but I do not want to die. I have lost Lelah. I do not want to lose Serena and everything else.

*You think your revenge would satisfy Lelah?*

Amir sat there thinking for a long minute. I hope she would be better than that. I hope she would not wish for revenge. I hope she would be smart about it.

The bass voice laughed. *You ask a lot.*

We just sent four people into the Abyss. If Lelah wanted revenge, I hope that would be enough. I would be sad if it were not.

*You regret what we've done?*

Amir snorted. No, he thought. Those guys had blood on their hands. They were fair game. A man with a gun is a threat and a fair target. Any soldier knows that. The police certainly know that.

*Many people have blood on their hands.*

True. Americans are heavily armed. That is no accident. Nonetheless, I cannot kill them all. It is beyond me. I can take my revenge, I can offer my kills to Lelah if I see her again. But I cannot change the world.

*If you wait long enough, maybe they will kill each other.*

Now it is you who are depressing me.

*Alright. Enough philosophy. Let's figure it out later. Let's get back to business. That rifle needs to go bye bye.*

Yes. Amir picked up his cane. He stood up, pulled off the handle and the rubber stopper. He looked at the barrel for a moment. It was a finely machined piece of stainless steel, with its own hard beauty. Amir wondered, how did they make it black? It is not painted.

He shrugged, who knows? Then he looked around but saw no one else near. He stood up, grabbed the barrel at one end, spun, and hurled it out into the James River. The barrel helicoptered through the air for thirty yards, produced a small splash, and disappeared into the muddy, turbulent water. He took the receiver apart and threw the pieces into the river, one by one.

Finished, Amir stood there looking at the river.

*So, time to go and face the music?*

Yes, Amir thought. Time to go home.

Serena was at home, in the backyard doing yard work. The police were not there. Amir tapped on a window and waved at her. She looked up and smiled at him. He went upstairs and took a shower.

That evening they were in their living room, she on the couch, he in the easy chair, watching the evening news. Every channel covered the heinous murder of Virginia Attorney General Skip Taylor, a handsome, able, and upcoming politician with a bright and - some said - unlimited future. He was shot to death while giving a press conference - ironically, about prosecuting a murder case - in Capitol Plaza in Richmond. The shooter was still at large.

Police were asking anyone with information to call the Tip Line. Anonymous donors offered $100,000 for information leading to an arrest.

The Beast spoke, *A hundred grand for a tip. They'll be looking at this for a long time. They will not quit. If they catch us, that will be the end of us, no kidding around. They'll stir fry us and feed us to homosexual child molesters. Then we'll take the Chocolate Speedway into the sewers.*

Amir pursed his lips. I think so too.

*So. You and I are finished here?*

Amir glanced over at Serena. Yes, I think so.

She sat there, shocked, her hand covering her mouth. "My God, Amir, every time I think I've seen everything, this place comes up with something even more horrible. You know, I wonder if we wouldn't be better off back in Beirut."

"I doubt it." Silly idea, Amir thought. I'd rather move to Alabama. Or the moon.

*You know, Amir, if she ever discovers that you were behind these murders, you can kiss her love and fond regard goodbye. No matter what your vows might have said about richer or poorer, better or worse, or any of that stuff, they were not written with homicide in mind.*

I know. She would not be wrong, but I had my reasons.

*Had?*

I think so. Yes. You need to know when to cash in and walk away.

Roundtree made it back to the Fairfax County police station at the end of a long day. He had not witnessed the Keystone Cops routine at Capitol Plaza. He shook his head, the AG shot and killed, in broad daylight, in front of much of Richmond PD. Unbelievable.

The transponder lead was a fiasco. Fucking donuts. I'd like to grab him and stuff a dozen donuts down his goddamn throat.

Roundtree winced. Hawari is a cocky son of a bitch, with good reason. My God, what a day.

He looked around; the night shift was taking over. He turned on his computer. The screen popped into view. Suddenly, there it was: a message from Pressler - *Come to my office.*

Roundtree blew air through his mouth. Oh, this will be fun. Well, no point in delaying bad news. He pushed himself out of his chair, walked across the staff room and a couple of corridors later showed up at Pressler's door.

He knocked and walked in. Pressler was at his desk, talking on the phone. He waved Roundtree into a chair and kept talking, "Yes, Madam Chairwoman, we will get right on that." He sat for a moment, listening to the receiver. "Uh ... I will have to get back to you on that, Mam, but we'll do our best ... yes, Mam, thank you. We will talk soon."

Pressler hung up the phone, leaned back in his chair. "Well, that was fun. That was the chairwoman of the assembly judiciary committee, demanding instant and magical action to catch this sniper." Pressler looked at Roundtree. "I've grown tired of hearing that."

Roundtree nodded.

Pressler looked Roundtree in the eyes. "So, honey, how was your day?"

"Better than the AG's, though not by much."

Pressler sat up in his chair. "What happened in Richmond? I got reports, but I want to hear it from you."

"I got a tip that Hawari might be heading for a gun convention in Manassas, so I contacted Manassas PD and diverted to that location.

Well … the tip turned out to be false. Hawari was not there. I heard about the shooting over the Richmond PD frequency."

"A tip, you say. That tip wouldn't happen to be from the department's transponder software, would it?"

"Yes, it was." Roundtree decided to say as little as possible.

"I see. So, you went to the transponder signal. Did you find it?"

Roundtree nodded. "Yes."

"But no Hawari."

"No." If he asks about the donut truck, I will lie.

"I see. Well, isn't he the clever one," Pressler's eyes were lidded.

Roundtree thought, it is hard to lie to this man. He sees a lot. He's smart enough not to bash me over the head, even though I richly deserve it. "Yes, he is clever. He has evaded us. He has certainly evaded me." Pressler nodded. Roundtree hesitated, then said, "May I ask, what happened at the plaza? I listened on the radio. It sounded like all hell breaking loose."

"Sure." Before speaking, Pressler extended his hands. He closed them into fists, then dropped them, as if he was about to say something, then changed his mind. "Most but not all agree, there was a single shot. The plaza is lined in stone from all those buildings, which messes up the acoustics. Everyone agrees on one thing, though - the AG was dead shortly after he hit the pavement."

Pressler's expression was troubled. "No one knows where the shot came from. The sniper teams saw nothing, so Richmond PD is going over the entire place, inch by bloody inch.

"They put a cordon around the Plaza and detained a thousand people while they looked for the shooter. Naturally, that pissed everyone off."

"And no shooter?"

Pressler shook his head. "No shooter."

"Sounds like a Chinese rat fuck," Roundtree said.

Pressler laughed loudly. "Jesus, Dan, don't say that in polite company." Then he laughed again.

"I didn't … sir."

After a moment Pressler continued, "Meanwhile, the chairwoman of the judiciary committee is yelling for results. I was on her call list. Personally, I find that reaction useless, but I can understand it. She spoke with Taylor just before his press conference, the last person to speak with him. So she's feeling quite creeped out at the moment."

Roundtree thought, I seem not to be in trouble. I am not the only Virginia cop having a bad day.

Pressler's face brightened. "There's some good news. Though I promised Madam Chairwoman the sun and the moon, we do not have to deliver, since this shooting was on someone else's turf. That means I can deliver on my previous promise. I can detach you back to Abingdon, with my thanks. It's been a pleasure working with you, Dan."

Pressler held out his hand. Roundtree leaned forward and shook it. "Thanks. I'm sorry we weren't able to nail that guy."

Pressler shrugged. "Win some, lose some. Listen, if you'd like to help us a bit more, I'd be grateful. I made the same offer to everyone. Heywood Miles is staying. The others are going home."

"Let me think about that, Chief. The problem is ... well, remember Mike Stanton? What's he doing?"

"The homeless vet? They're still prosecuting. One of Taylor's deputies will supervise. I suspect the competition to fill the AG spot is already underway." Pressler looked at Roundtree. "You still thinking of rescuing Stanton?"

Roundtree nodded. "He could not have shot the AG. The state has to let him go. If they don't, I might retire and testify on his behalf."

Pressler stretched, then looked at Roundtree. "Tell you what. Hang around a while, work on this case. Maybe you and Miles can do some more magic. Talk to me before you retire."

Roundtree stood up. "Thanks, Max. I'll think about it."

He left the office.

Just as Pressler leaned back in his chair, thinking that he might leave the office early, his phone rang. He neither looked at it nor answered it.


Roundtree decided to stay in Fairfax a bit longer. The first order of business - since Pressler did not object - was to put better transponders on Hawari's cars. The FBI gave Roundtree transponders that looked like auto repair stickers. They were piezoelectrics. They generated electricity from vibration. The transponder would broadcast any time the car moved.

Fairfax PD lent him a surveillance drone, with endurance, a camera, and an internet connection. The drone stationed itself high over Hawari's neighborhood.

Roundtree did not have to wait long. On a Saturday, Hawari and his wife went to dinner at a restaurant. Roundtree followed them at a distance. Just after they went inside, he placed one transponder on Amir's car and then went to their home and placed another on his wife's car.

With the transponders in place, Roundtree and Miles got real-time data on the locations of Hawari and his wife. Serena's daily routine was predictable and stable. She had several hobbies, a set list of errands, and a few friends. These occupied her time in a recurring pattern.

Amir's daily movements were less predictable. He had errands of his own and only one friend, whom he saw seldom. His hobby was exercise, mostly long walks. His routes changed daily.

The surveillance naturally focused on Amir. Roundtree spent many days and hours in his car, tailing Hawari from a distance. It was tiresome duty. It was also risky since police cars and other official vehicles were easy to identify.

Roundtree got the department to rent a boxy little compact car for surveillance. It was yellow.

Eventually, the surveillance became more difficult. One day, Roundtree followed Hawari into a modest residential neighborhood. There were no NRA employees or politicians living nearby. So why here? Roundtree wondered.

He pulled over to watch Hawari, who had parked his car next to the curb. Hawari emerged from the car, opened his trunk, and pulled out a bicycle. He clipped on the front wheel, climbed aboard, and rode away.

"No!" Roundtree pounded on the steering wheel.

The bicycle made surveillance far more difficult. Hawari could go where an automobile or motorcycle could not follow. Roundtree solved the problem by tailing Hawari on a moped, using a helmet to conceal his identity, and placing a transponder under the seat of Hawari's bicycle.

Roundtree swore to himself, if I break my neck doing this job, I'm going to shoot that man.

In both knees.


Roundtree conducted surveillance for several weeks. Eventually, he and Miles were satisfied that they were getting as much information as possible about Hawari's daily movements.

However, a different problem arose. Hawari was not doing anything objectionable, suspicious, illegal, or even interesting.

At no time did Hawari go anywhere connected with guns. He did not visit fishing or hunting stores. He did not go hunting. He did not carry a rifle in public. He did not go to *Bob's Guns*. He did not go to any rifle or pistol range.

Roundtree continued to keep Hawari under surveillance. He thought, that man might be a gifted amateur, but I am a professional. Professionals - certainly homicide inspectors - do not quit. Someday he will slip and I will nail him.

As the days passed, Roundtree realized he could not continue the surveillance. People began to ask, are you available? Are you busy? It was a matter of needs versus resources. Homicide inspectors were in high demand. While Hawari kept a low profile, other Americans stayed busy murdering each other. Other matters cried out for resolution.

That is why, one day, Roundtree walked into Pressler's office and recommended that Pressler close the sniper investigation.

Pressler slept on it. Then, the next day, he released Roundtree to return to the Abingdon police department.

## *Settling an Account*

Roundtree reopened his modest two-bedroom condo. It took a day to change the sheets, do the laundry, and re-stock the kitchen. The next day, he returned to a smaller and quieter police department.

The department had changed in his absence. There was a new Chief, a late-twenties woman from Yale. She had replaced the former Chief when his doctor detected a heart murmur. Roundtree had dinner with his old Chief, who had retired on a standard pension plus a disability pension. He looked terrific, twenty pounds lighter and deeply tanned, reminding Roundtree of an ad for a luxury spa.

The Chief said, "There's a trick to retiring, Dan. You need a medical problem that could kill you but probably won't. That's what makes the money flow."

"I'm not that subtle. Or that lucky."

The new chief's name was Anna. Tall, polite, and reserved, she was thirty years younger than Roundtree. She believed in big data and predictive policing. She believed that crime was a sociological event caused by poverty, diversity, the phase of the moon, high fructose corn syrup, and other factors.

She had data on all that.

Abingdon, close to the Blue Ridge and to Virginia's tallest mountains, had a large tourist population. Roundtree worked the evenings since tourists attracted the occasional criminal. The routine involved being in the right place at the right time, rather than running around the county, chasing down phone calls and complaints.

Roundtree thought the new methods were nonsense until a drunk tried to rape a small woman right in front of him. It happened one evening; the woman was splayed out on the hood of the man's Chevy in a dance hall parking lot. Roundtree walked up behind the man, who was on top of her. She saw him and mouthed, *Help me.*

Penetration had not yet occurred.

Roundtree predicted that it soon would occur. So he tased both of them, which ended their immediate prospects for sex, consensual or not. Since the man was standing on the ground, he got the worse of it.

Both of them recovered soon enough. The woman withdrew the rape charge - apparently she was warming to the idea just as Roundtree intervened. Roundtree nonetheless filed an indecent exposure charge. He had a photograph of the man's exposed rear end, framed on the hood of the Chevy between the woman's spread legs. As a result, the man spent a few days sweeping sidewalks in Abingdon and swabbing the toilet in the police station. And the woman? No one could see anything of her.

She declined to file a complaint, and there the matter ended.

Roundtree was satisfied with that. Don't have sex in public places, including parking lots. It disturbs those who are not getting any. So have a heart, eh? We have hotels for that. Or you can buy a tent and go camping.

Or hell ... rent a van and buy an air mattress. Eight bucks at Walmart. They're bouncy. Then get nuts ... in the privacy of your van.

Roundtree kept up with the news of the sniper prosecution. Mike Stanton was in jail in Richmond, awaiting trial. A young attorney from the AG's office, Milton Lord III, now led the prosecution. Roundtree read that news and snorted - another country club twit from U Va.

Stanton's public defender was a thin black woman named Gillian Thomson, a graduate of Emory Law. One day Roundtree dialed her number in Richmond.

She answered and he said, "Ms. Thomson, this is Dan Roundtree, of the Abingdon police department. Could I have a couple minutes of your time?"

"Yes, Inspector Roundtree. Of course. We have not met, but I read the transcript of your interview with Mike Stanton."

"Yes. Well, I am calling to find out if you could use an expert witness on this matter. I believe I know as much about the sniper investigation as anyone, and I even know a bit about Mike Stanton."

"Yes, yes ... believe me, Inspector, I need all the help I can get. But I don't think you can serve as an expert. Virginia rules do not allow you to testify opposite the state."

Roundtree nodded and said, "Right ... that's right, which brings us to the point. Coincidently, I have been considering retirement. I believe - correct me if I am wrong - that once I retire, I can serve."

"You know, I think you might be right. I have to ask, why would you do that?"

"I don't believe for two seconds that Mike Stanton would be able to do what the sniper has done," Roundtree said. "The state is prosecuting the wrong man."

"You would be willing to say that in court?"

"Of course," Roundtree replied. What kind of question is that?

"In that case, Inspector, let me get back to you. I would welcome your help."

"Excellent." Roundtree gave her his cellphone number. She thanked him and hung up.

Gillian Thomson dialed the number. The speakerphone came alive, "Office of the Attorney General."

"This is Gillian Thomson, calling for Milton Lord, please."

*"Hold please."* A stream of nondescript instrumental music came from the speakerphone. After a brief pause, the music stopped.

A male voice came over the line, "Ms. Thomson. How are you this fine morning?"

"I am well, Milton, how are you?"

"Good, good. I am well, as always. What can I do for you?"

"This is a courtesy call. You'll get a backup letter later today, but I wanted to notify you of a witness I might be calling. His name is Dan Roundtree. He is presently ..."

"Let me interrupt you right there, Ms. Thomson. You mean Inspector Roundtree? He cannot offer testimony."

"I was about to get to that. Hypothetically, if he were to retire, he could offer testimony. Even expert testimony, I might add."

"Ms. Thomson, do you know that Mr. Roundtree is going to retire?"

Gillian sat there grinning, thankful that she was not on a video call. *God, I love baiting rich white boys. Especially this one.*

"No, I do not know that," she said.

"Then why do you bring this up?"

"Because I know he is thinking about it. It is possible. So I'm calling you to give you notice."

"Maybe I will call Mr. Roundtree to testify for the government."

"Given his views on the case, that would be an odd tactic," she said. "Of course, I cannot advise you on tactics."

"You object to my talking to him?"

"Not at all."

She thought, *you'll talk to him, one way or the other. Whose witness he is, and who pays his bill, are irrelevant. What's important is that Roundtree cannot be excluded. Good old Milton cannot know whether I* will call Mr. Roundtree, until we are in the courtroom. I have no further duty to disclose.

Suppose Roundtree testifies as I think he might. Then Milton Lord III will get to be the nasty, privileged white boy who tried to get a handicapped combat vet executed for a crime he could not possibly have committed. *After all, that is why the Army gave him a medical discharge. If he could still kill people, they would have kept him. They would have encouraged him to keep doing that.*

In that world, little Milton, you can kiss that cozy country club law partnership goodbye. We could all then wonder if we will ever see a Milton IV.

"Ms. Thomson, try as I might, I cannot help but think that you are trying to manipulate me."

"Your suspicions are your own business, of course."

"Alright, thank you for the notice."

"You are more than welcome, Milton. Have a good day." Gillian broke the connection. With a wide grin on her face, she leaned forward and laughed out loud.

Gillian sat there, relishing a good feeling. Then she opened her email and scanned the latest messages. One came from Max Pressler, forwarded from Richmond PD, marked 'URGENT'. She opened it and began reading, then burst out laughing.

The message contained a lab report from Richmond PD, reporting that bullet fragments recovered from the AG's body were a chemical match with fragments recovered from the other sniper victims. So … either Mike Stanton tip-toed out of jail, got a gun, made his way to Richmond, and committed murder without anyone noticing, including a hundred policemen and counter-snipers, or

… the state is prosecuting the wrong man.

Gillian leaned back in her chair and placed her hands behind her head. She smiled at the ceiling.

"This case is so over."

A week later, Gillian walked into the Richmond jail where the state of Virginia was holding one Michael Stanton, U.S. Army, ret'd. She showed the custodial officer a piece of paper.

He leaned an ample frame back in his chair, read the piece of paper, looked up at Gillian, then read it again.

"According to this, I have to release Stanton. Right?" he said.

"You can make a phone call if you wish, but yes, this orders you to release him."

"I don't need a phone call," the officer said. "I've played cards with the judge; I know his signature." He grinned. "Seen it plenty of times."

The officer walked to a barred frame over a doorway, placed his thumb on an electronic device, which beeped as the door swung open. As he passed through he ducked his head to avoid the bars that ran across the top of the doorway.

Two minutes later, he returned to the desk, walking behind Mike Stanton, who smiled when he saw Gillian Thomson. "Hi there, Ms. Thomson. You're looking fit."

"Hey, Mike. You too."

"Harold here tells me I'm free to go."

She nodded, "That's right, you are."

It took several minutes for Mike to sign out and receive his belongings. The officer let him keep the orange suit as a memento. Stanton finished, then looked up and said, "Well ... thanks, Officer Miller. Thanks for letting me stay in your place. I enjoyed it."

Miller reached out and squeezed Stanton's shoulder. "This is a jail, Mike. I don't want to see you back here."

Stanton tapped himself on the head. "Knock on wood, you won't."

He and Gillian left the jail and walked out into a sunny afternoon.

Stanton said, "Thanks, Ms. Thomson. I'd rather be out here than in there."

"Mike, would you like to live in an apartment instead of the street?"

"With a shower?"

"They all have showers."

He nodded and smiled widely. "Sure, that would be great, but I think it costs more than I've got."

"Well, as to that, I want you to meet someone." They approached Gillian's car and a woman got out of it to meet them. Gillian said, "Mike, this is Susan, a friend of mine. She works for Social Services. She and I have been talking about you. She thinks you might have enough money for an apartment."

"How could she possibly figure that?" Stanton said.

"Hi Mike," Susan said. "Let's go somewhere and chat."

He looked at Gillian.

Gillian said, "Well, off you go. Good luck, Mike. Susan, give me a call when things settle."

Susan nodded.

Gillian walked around her car to the driver's door and opened it.

Stanton said, "Hey, Ms. Gillian. Before you go, how did you spring me out of jail?"

Gillian stopped and turned towards him for a moment. "Remember Inspector Roundtree?"

Stanton thought for a moment. "Uh … yeah. Black guy. A cop."

"Yes. Everyone knows him. He didn't think you shot anybody."

Stanton nodded. "I see. Okay, thanks."

"So the state decided to let you go … and now, you need to talk to Susan and maybe get yourself off the street," Gillian said.

"Uh huh ... we'll see," he said. "The street's not bad. I'm used to it. I've got friends there."

"Okay," she said. "Well, suit yourself. You do what you want."

"Thanks, Ms. Thomson."

Gillian nodded, got into her car, started the engine and, with a last wave, drove away.

Susan looked at Stanton and said, "Okay, Mike, let's look at your situation. I don't understand why you're living on the street. You could collect a pension. Disability payments too."

Stanton winced, "Yeah, but then I got to keep track of the paperwork."

"So?"

He shrugged. "I'm bad at it."

# *Resolution*

Amir got out of his car and closed the door. The solid metallic sound broke the silence. It was a peaceful, quiet place, a green place. Birds, trees, dirt, flowers. Gravestones. Amir enjoyed looking at the trees and flowers, the landscaping. He moved away from the car, walking slowly, lingering over the occasional tombstone. Sometimes he stopped and learned a bit about the story buried beneath each stone.

He passed many old gravestones, heavily stained, stones lying flat on the ground and marked with the single inscription, 'Child'. No date, no name. A long time ago, everyone had to earn their name by surviving for a while. Some did not make it. That brought them here, no name, little to remember.

Amir stopped and read several grave markers, a look of sadness on his face. He thought, it is official, then. Children are a privilege, not a right.

Maybe it's easier if they die before you get to know them. Can that be right? He shook his head.

Eventually, he stood before Lelah's tombstone and looked down at the inscription.

*Lelah Hawari*

*b. October 11, 1997*

*d. September 12, 2015*

*A life*

*bright beauty*

*remembered forever*

Amir looked at the tombstone and at the grass covering her grave. She was almost eighteen years old. At least she had that.

We are not guaranteed tomorrow.

He raised his head and looked around the cemetery. He half expected to see a vision of Lelah playing among the tombstones. It would be just like her to ignore the sanctity of a cemetery. But he saw no such vision.

Finally, Amir spoke, "Hey, Scooter, it's Dad. I just thought I'd stop by, pay a visit, maybe talk a bit." He paused for a long minute, thinking. "I guess I need to apologize. Or at least explain myself."

He put a hand to his mouth and thought about his next words. "I've been doing some bad things lately. I can't tell anyone else about that. Maybe I can talk to you. I need to talk to somebody."

Amir opened his mouth as if to speak, then closed it. He took several deep breaths. "When you were killed, I sought revenge. I got it too. If you want to know the score … I shot five people, killed four. High and low, I killed them."

A half smile crossed his face. "Gun people. The Beast and I killed gun people. The Beast is what I call that little voice I've been carrying around in my head. He's angry beyond belief. His voice was constantly in my head. After a while, I was hoping to hear your voice, but I never did."

He looked around the cemetery. "I wonder if a couple of our gun people might be buried here. I haven't looked. It doesn't really matter."

He put his hands in his pockets, then took them out. "I don't regret the killing. A better person might. I don't. Those men lived on blood money. So I picked up a gun. I made them earn their money with their own blood for a change.

"I think that was fair. I hope you agree."

Amir looked away. He turned and looked at the gravestone and knelt down. "I made a few discoveries. Grief, and anger, and pain, they're contagious. I'll bet you didn't know that. Well, they are. I shared mine with a few others."

Amir reached for the bouquet of flowers at the base of Lelah's tombstone. The flowers were old and dry, well past their peak. "Damn, I should have brought fresh flowers. I'm sorry. I've had a … difficult day." He picked up the flowers and put them down next to him.

"I learned something else ... it's easy to seek revenge, but you need to know when to stop. It's a cycle. It won't stop on its own. If you want to keep living, you need to see that."

Amir chuckled. "And yes, I know what you would say - what idiot wouldn't already know this? And sure, it is obvious. Except that when you live in pain, it is sometimes hard to think. You can stumble over the obvious. People do it all the time. I certainly have."

He picked up a small stone and bounced it off the gravestone.

"Anyway, the bottom line is, I have to stop or die. I don't want to die.

"So I came to tell you, I'm stopping now. I threw the rifle into the river. I will return to my life if I can, try to make something of it. I will cherish my memories. I will try not to lose your mother. And I will remember you every day."

Amir reached up and wiped a tear away. "If there's a God, then someday I'll see you, Lelah. On that day, you can tell me what a shit I am.

"And if there's not, then I am wasting a little time talking to a block of stone. Not the dumbest thing I've ever done."

He picked up the dried flowers, walked to a trash can, tossed the flowers into it.

"Okay, that's it. I'm done."

The bass voice rumbled in Amir's head, *So, Amir ... you're done? You're letting the rest of them off the hook?*

Amir thought, Yes, I'm done.

*That does not make you a coward?*

Amir thought, I don't think so. I don't think you do, either. I proved it. We proved it together. We did enough. Now, I want to return to a life with Serena. I choose life.

*Then I don't see how I can be of further use.*

Maybe not.

He turned and walked to a stone bench twenty yards from Lelah's tombstone. He sat down, leaned forward, his elbows on his knees, and looked down at the grass in front of him.

He thought about Lelah, about life and death. Years ago, he would occasionally think about his descendants. He would think about his daughter, and her children, and theirs, and theirs, and theirs. No longer. That fantasy was gone, dead to a bullet.

Allah, if He is there, gives. Or he does not.

Amir lost track of time. He sat there looking at the scenery, the gravestones, the crosses, the green trees, the sun yellow in a blue sky. Suddenly, he noticed a black man in a rumpled sport coat walking towards him. Ah, what is this? Here comes my shadow. Most people have a shadow that stays with them, but mine wanders a bit. I see him now and then. Suddenly, here he is, in the flesh.

The bass voice rumbled, *this looks like trouble.*

Yes, here is our shadow, on this of all days.

The black man approached. He came close and stopped in front of Amir. "Hello there."

"Good afternoon," Amir said.

One of the man's hands gestured, "Mind if I share the bench with you?"

"Not at all."

Roundtree sat down. "You know who I am?"

Amir nodded. "Inspector Roundtree. You were working with the victims of the Whitetop shooting."

"That's right, Mr. Hawari," Roundtree said. "I did that. And I've been investigating the recent sniper shootings in Virginia and Maryland."

"Ah, yes," Amir said. "I may have seen you on TV."

"I'll get to the point, Mr. Hawari, I think you committed those killings. I think you are the sniper."

Amir sat there and nodded. "I see." He leaned back against the bench. "So, are you going to arrest me?"

"Would you like me to do that?"

Amir chuckled. "What I would like has nothing to do with it."

"You want to talk about it? Tell me how you did it?"

Amir smiled, did not even look at Roundtree.

"No ... I guess not," Roundtree said. "Okay. Here's why I walked over here. I think you're the shooter. We don't need to argue about it.

We won't prove it here. It doesn't matter. I cannot arrest you, Mr. Hawari. I think you know that. You have been skilled."

Amir turned to look at Roundtree.

Roundtree reached up and rubbed a hand across day-old whiskers. "However, whether I can arrest you or not, I cannot allow you to keep shooting people. You need to understand - we all have guns. You are not the only person who knows how to use one."

Amir looked into Roundtree's eyes. "I'm surprised. I thought a policeman would have more respect for due process."

Roundtree looked away. "Maybe in an ideal world. But in this one, it's more of a muddle. In any event, you of all people are in no position to complain."

Amir thought for a moment, then nodded. "I believe I see your point."

"So ... I don't want to hear about any more sniper shootings, Mr. Hawari. If I do, I will come looking for you. I will find you. You understand me?"

"I believe I do."

"Good." Roundtree stood up. "Enjoy the afternoon." He stood up and walked away.

The bass voice rumbled in Amir's head, *Golden Mountain, my skinny brown ass. What a crock of horseshit.* The laughter echoed in Amir's head.

Amir thought, you don't need to climb up on your high horse. Let's be honest, you and I have done some questionable things.

*I will climb up in spite of all that. And ride off into the sunset.*

Amir replayed the conversation with the policeman. Unbelievable. Should I keep shooting? Just to show him who's the boss? Then Amir shook his head. That's stupid. I decided to stop. That's the sound thing and the right thing.

I will not kill again. That will please the policeman, for what that is worth.

It will please me too. I can live for Serena. I will not need to be looking over my shoulder. I can be normal. I can be a citizen, taking my chances, along with everyone else, every time I walk out the door.

Amir felt a weight lift from his spirit, a cloud rise from his mind. He turned his head and spotted Roundtree, still moving away.

Suddenly, the day offered promise. He could do something today. But what?

Something useful. Or maybe something fun?

Did the Beast just say goodbye? Was that real?

Beast?

Beast, are you there?

Amir sat for a minute, for longer, waiting for the bass voice to answer, but it was silent inside his head. For the first time in a long time, sitting on the park bench, Amir was alone.

# *Epilogue*

Sam approached the red light on Market Street, moved to the right lane and came to a full stop. He would normally have rolled through while turning right, a near-legal move that on most days would have been ignored. However, a police car sat in the middle of the intersection, its blue lights flashing. Sam did not want to attract attention. He braked.

Jesus, is this the new normal?

Policemen and guardsmen were patrolling the city, especially the intersections. In some, there was a single patrolman. Others had a car in the intersection and a second car nearby, its engine running. The larger intersections were occupied by tactical vehicles and SWAT teams.

Sam blew out a breath and checked the light. C'mon, turn green. He glanced at the police car. Guys, I know the AG was popular, but I am not a terrorist or a sniper. I am just a guy, trying to get to *Angelo's* for some beer and pizza.

Richmond felt like an occupied city. The governor had called out the National Guard. Sam passed a camouflaged Humvee with a 20 mm gun on top, an incredibly nasty weapon. He had seen one in action.

Is all this necessary? To most people, these guys are your tax dollars at work. To a sniper, they're just targets, easy ones at that. What happens if our sniper nails a soldier?

How close are we to a curfew?

After making his turn and taking two detours, Sam finally came to *Angelo's*. He parked his car, made his way to the usual table, and sat down. While he waited, Sam thought about Amir. God, that guy has been through some shitty times, losing his daughter like that. I cannot imagine. He is not handling it well, nor is he getting much help with it.

I think he has a bad case of PTSD, combat fatigue, the thousand yard stare. Call it what you will. Many soldiers don't survive that. A combat zone is no place to develop a psychiatric condition.

He smiled to himself, nor is peacetime America.

I need to pick him up and get him to talk to somebody. Maybe he needs a prescription - anti-depressants - anything to get out of this nasty hole he's in.

He drinks beer now. Maybe I can get him to smoke pot. That might help.

God … it's been ages since I was stoned. I'd like to smoke pot again. Something light, to help me stay calm while the world goes down the tubes. Settle back and enjoy the ride while everyone else is freaking out.

There was movement outside the restaurant. Sam looked to it and saw Amir coming through the door. Amir stopped for a minute and talked to the owner, a tone of disbelief, probably talking about the police and military presence. He seemed relaxed, his face just a fraction away from a smile or a laugh. That was hopeful. Then Amir spotted Sam and nodded to him. A few seconds later, he detached himself from the conversation and approached the table, a smile on his face.

"Hey, Sam. Do you believe this shit?"

"You mean the police and the guns? Interesting times, no? They're everywhere, a big show of force. I had to take several detours to get over here. Police and soldiers are jamming the intersections."

Amir shook his head. "Unbelievable. Reminds me of Beirut in the bad old days. So … putting aside the war, or terrorists, or whatever these guys are fighting, how are you?"

Sam said, "I'm okay, though I wish the police and the soldiers would get out of the way. It's the AG, right? I mean, that's got to be it. Is anything else going on?"

Amir shook his head. "It's got to be the AG. You know, I'll be the first to admit, I'm no military expert. But draw a line for me from our sniper to the show of force." He looked outside, then he turned back and looked at Sam. "Can you do that?"

"Beats the hell out of me."

Amir laughed and shook his head. "What a world. I'm having a strange day. This morning I went to the cemetery to say hi to Lelah and drop off some flowers. I kept forgetting to do that, and it was driving me nuts.

"Anyway, I'm out there sitting on a bench, and it's calm, peaceful … quiet, you know, like cemeteries usually are. After a while I make my little speech to Lelah's tombstone, then I leave for Angelo's. On the way, I pass a couple police cars and a military truck, and I don't think much about it."

A waitress stopped by their table. Sam ordered a beer. Amir ordered a soft drink at first, then he said, "No, heck with it, I feel like misbehaving. Make it a beer. Maybe a couple." Amir grinned at the waitress.

The waitress left and Amir continued his story. "Anyway, on the way I'm sitting in a line of traffic at a red light. There's a military truck parked in the curb lane. People have to maneuver to get around it, and they're doing that. Suddenly, this sergeant type shows up, a real hard ass, a white guy built like a grain silo. He walks up to the driver's door of the truck and starts yelling at a soldier sitting behind the wheel. It seems the sergeant wants the truck moved.

"So the soldier starts it up, and he's flustered. He manages to back the truck into this crappy old Plymouth with this fat old black woman wedged behind the wheel."

Amir looked up as the waitress returned and thumped two beer steins on the table. "There you go, guys," she said. She left.

Amir looked back at Sam. "Well, the old lady gets all pissed off. She hauls her three hundred pounds out of the car and stomps over to the sergeant. She starts giving him a ton of shit about his manners, his dress, his voice, his ancestry, his shoes, and every other thing she can think of. He says, hold on, lady, I'm not the one who bumped into your car. But she doesn't care, since he's in charge. So after a minute, I catch the eye of the soldier in the truck. He's sitting there enjoying himself, and I start to get into it. For a while we just sat there, the two of us enjoying the fireworks and watching that fat old woman cut Sergeant Silo a new asshole."

Sam laughed. Amir looked at him and shook his head. "Everyone is so tense." Amir took a swig of beer. He lowered the mug and smacked his lips. "So … Sam … how is your day going?"

Sam looked back at Amir and for the first time noticed Amir's eyes. They reflected relaxed humor, even merriment. Sam had missed that look, missed it for a long time. Now it was back. He noticed something else, Amir's eyes were a rich, deep brown, shot through with the occasional hint, the rare spot, of yellow.

Sam said, "I haven't had the excitement that you've had, but yeah, this has been a good day. I'm doing okay."

"Well good," Amir said. "Glad to hear it."

Sam held up his beer. "Cheers. Now, where's the food?"

"And more beer."

*The End*

## *Acknowledgments*

More than words can say, I am grateful to Michael Klein and the other members of the Arlington Writers Group, of Arlington Virginia, for their friendship, kindness, genius, and support. A great place to learn about writing fiction.

My thanks to Robin Lawrence, Chris Becker, and the Durham Writers Group for comments and critique. Thanks also to Bonnie Cole for advice on prospective cover art.

## *About Roger Alan Bonner*

Roger Alan Bonner is a retired economist and ersatz mathematician, now busy creating works of fiction. His stories can cover just about anything, though he tries to stick to science fiction because science is exploding these days. There is a lot of material to work with, a lot to think about. His number one goal is to give the reader a good experience and a good story.

He recently escaped from an increasingly waterlogged Florida and now resides in the purple part of North Carolina.

Readers with comments and/or questions can send them to rogeralanbonner.com.

Made in the USA
Columbia, SC
15 May 2019